MW00398934

Tiger

a novel

Ashley Mayne

Tiger

DR. CICERO BOOKS

New York Rio de Janeiro Paris
First Edition
Manufactured in the United States of América

www.drcicerobooks.com

Dr. Cicero Books

ISBN: 06923449588
ISBN-13: 978-0692349588

"Signs are taken for wonders. 'We would see a sign':
The word within a word, unable to speak a word,
Swaddled with darkness. In the juvescence of the year
Came Christ the tiger."

Gerontion, T.S. Eliot

PART I

THE BIRD CATCHER

ONE

A young man offered his hand to me in the middle of a crowd in Cyprus. I was fifty, head-over-heels, as Americans say. It was summer. For the last twenty years I've known I did my lover wrong. I can call him that now, can I not, though I know that it may not be strictly true? Always uneven, these favors. There is always a lover and a loved. He was young, as I said, outstripped in age twice over, and so the burden of worship fell on me; it would make me his lover, I suppose, more than the other way. When you are old, no one cares if you are a saint or just another old wolf. You will be a saint if they expect it of you. And that is good enough.

There were lemons in crates, girls in cotton dresses walking by. There was a scattering of red-wrapped candy in the gutter. He smoked Sweet Aftons, like a Rive Gauche Parisian. And who, now, can I tell? Who will hear me?

I wish, as I have many times, that I might call a woman named Savage who lived and perhaps still lives in Birnam, Connecticut. I would like to sit with her the way we used to do, our hands around warm cups, chin-wagging, as she called it. But Savage told me I was never to speak to her again, and so the knowledge of my wrongness is now my closest friend. A young man who had done me no harm offered a hand. He offered me time, and I did not take it. Such a small thing, and it drives me frantic. Why did I refuse what he gave me? And who, who can I tell?

There is a memory that comes to me now. I have tried to forget it so of course there it is, the day my father taught me what happened – how hard it is to say it – to little boys like me. It was, in many ways, the first revelation of my life. There was a name he called me. I was no higher than my father's breastbone at the time, so perhaps ten or eleven years old, and I did not understand how he knew the tender secret I had never revealed to another soul. And though he always said the worst was done for my own benefit, his pleading, watery eye led me to understand he did it all for pleasure. There was a purgative effect to knowing his joy was more wrong than anything I had done to offend him. At the time, like any good Catholic boy, I believed unearned suffering to be redemptive.

Or is it even stranger than this? Did I actually pity him?

My father named me. This is what happens, he said, and I suppose he meant this is what happened in the army, though who knows, who knows. The heart may desire, he seemed to say, but the offending hand is always punished. And he was right, I suppose. He took me through our house to the front door. There were no other people to witness it, one of those moments when my father and I had the house to ourselves. There were rubber work boots standing in a row, an overcoat and wire basket hanging, filled with the leather cups of work gloves. My father used his weight to pin me against the door frame. Then he held my hand in the door to slam it four times, once for each finger; not so strange, I suppose, that this is a memory I keep when others dim to nothing. It lives in my bones. A summer day, rich with the taste of grass, the drunk wisteria, the dark odor of my father's sweat. His grey cheek burned my forehead at some point in the struggle; I couldn't help but struggle just a little.

Before he did it he explained it to me, like a surgeon, so I was under no illusions when I let him take my hand and set it on the frame. That was Santos' way, deliberate, explaining the physical mechanics of a thing. I remember the sound of it, the door jumping back from each interrupted swing. His tongue protruded from the corner of his mouth. But I was giving nothing away. With my father's arms around me, his weight holding me steady on the door frame, an embrace holding me up, I could smell his sweat and cigarettes, the nutritious, dark smell of him, as close to me as he would ever be, and my love for him in that moment was without end. He swung the door. I pitied him. When it was over I leaned on my father, hand clutched against my chest, feeling the bite of a hard button into my cheekbone where I lay, at his shirt collar, newborn. I longed, I long still, for the affection he will never give.

Father of mine, every day of my life I have honored you, by one name or another. There are rooms in my life that God has never entered, but you have been there. Your footsteps move away from me. You are the shape of love, the man who punishes and turns his back. Blood marked the doorway of our house. You left by that same door, and went to get the mail.

It was hot, flies buzzing around the kitchen. Through the open door, still drifting on its hinges, I saw the sheets my mother had hung out in the wind, a yard where chickens scratched, and beyond that the dirt road of our little town, our little nineteen-fifties, our Iberian family of men, proud boat builders with a hatred of Franco and no kind words for what I was. I looked at my fingers, each one broken between the joint and the palm, four straight lines of blood. My teeth chattered, but no sound came. There were no tears. The old town doctor had poor eyesight. He made splints with tongue depressors, wound my hand into a soft mitten of gauze. A polite man, asking no questions, God rest his incurious soul.

Could my lover have suspected any of this, and the full meaning of his hand on a table between two cups of wine, extended to me? Could he ever know why I did not take what was so freely given? Perhaps I myself do not. I am old. I have shied my way through so many painful rituals, trying to avoid these things, made offering of myself in tortured gestures. But I, too, have been called Father. In the nameless fear of reaching, I find all the fathers, sons and lovers I have ever known.

I awake to find myself on a bus bound for Scranton, Pennsylvania. I feel tired and lean my forehead against a warm, bright sheet of glass, and the shadows of trees streak by behind my red lids, and I am saying, No, no, that's impossible, I've never heard of Scranton. A voice near me presses closer, a hand slipped into mine. "Are you lost, Father?" Yes, I want to say, yes, I am. But I say nothing, wondering who it is who has claimed me this time, turning to see a young woman with earnest eyes and freckles on her nose, a gingham dress like a faded blue iris buttoned up high to her throat, a little golden cross dangling there, and I wonder if she is my child because she has called me father and I can almost recognize her, and so I pat her hand. All is well, I say, with authority. And then I think that she has called me Father not because she is my own but because of the starched collar showing from under my raincoat. Bless you for your kindness, I add, and she sits back, satisfied. People call me Father. These days, I call myself Lopez, though my name has been Ochoa. Both good names for a wolf; what does it matter? Father Wolf.

Drops of water streak the glass, and I am curious to see where we are going. Beyond the window trees flash past, trees and bright white sun. If I look directly at the sun between the trees my whole mind will be suffused with light, fierce enough to scrub the grit from behind my eyes, and I might remember then where I am going, and know it when we get there. The trees flash away to an empty field, and horses stand in it like grass huts, their heads down and tails sweeping, black and green. "Aren't they beautiful?" I lean to the girl sitting at my side, pointing them out to her, and she can see them as well; she smiles at me again. We watch the animals and the rolls of hay, the plowed black furrows of a newly turned field. There is water standing in the low places, and it gives back the blue of the sky, blue and black lines flashing past, a giant animal's slender, running legs stretching away from us, bounding and galloping. And then it is trees and sun, trees and sun again, and all the leaves have gone but the window is warm against my face and I sleep.

When I awake again the seat next to mine is empty. There is no water on the window, and the glass is still warm with day, so I think I might as well get out and walk for a while. I make my way up the aisle of the bus, holding myself steady on the backs of seats. People look up at me as I walk past and then away again. The only thing that distresses us more than the dying is the living lost. And I can understand that, being as I am these days, two people in one body. The clear self looks on the demented self in horror. More and more, I live in the past, because it is clearer to me, and somehow more real, than where I have only just been.

But here I am, here we all are, on an American Greyhound bus, a day of sunlight and rain. I tell the driver that I have arrived, and would he please be so kind as to stop, and he says that he can't because there is no stop here. He will have to let me off at the next stop. I say this will be fine, and stand by the doors holding a warm pole. The floor of the bus is also warm; I can feel it through the bottoms of my shoes, and the breathing of it, the quivering running up my legs and settling in my knees. A pair of Japanese students sit three rows down from me, clutching their backpacks; they are watching a red pastille rolling in the aisle, forward and back with the motion of the bus, wobbling as it rolls. When the bus stops and the doors fold open, I thank the driver and climb down the stairs. The bus rumbles and coughs and flies away with a damp wall of wind, and I am alone beside an empty road.

I sit for a while on a bench, thinking I once had a cane, and must have left it on the bus. My pockets are empty, except for a leather wallet and a few stray licorice seeds. I once had a rosary. Where has it gone? On the far side of the road I can see an opening in the trees, the mouth of a path, inviting me. The forest is a good place.

Things become unclear again. I tire so easily these days, I who once ran solo races to calm myself, mile on mile, breathing through my nose, measuring my breaths against the pace of my little worries. Face relaxed and raised to the wind, tongue pressed up behind my teeth, giving in to each sprung footfall, running to maintain a state of perfect emptiness. So many tricks of the trade.

The footpath is short, and ends in a clearing where a large, flat rock serves as a resting place, gouged with names and dates, decades of clumsily monogrammed hearts. No races left in me; I sit in the sun on this rock, folded over knees, exhausted. I have lost my quiet, in these days.

Pleasant to lie back, looking at the ceiling of the trees. Blue, trees curved in around the borders of it, a large and soft eye above. Blue, the last color humanity learned to see, so I am told. Cars whisper on the road, somewhere beyond the trees. After a while, the eye becomes a pinnacle of darkness, and I can feel the ache of cold settling in my lungs, but all is well.

I am not a fearful man, whatever else can be said. Used to solitude, used to the night and all that lives in it; there is nothing to fear in this place. This is the architecture of the beautiful deep. In the darkness, a soft, heavy creature shifts itself, and a twig breaks under the weight.

The stars shine down on a field in Araba. Araba, in the country where I was born. There is a single tree, an oak, sheltering a black horse with a white star that is sleeping.

Soul of Christ, sanctify me. From the wicked foe, defend me. Permit me not to be separated from Thee.

Dear X,

Was it you, on the train from Tel Aviv to Netanya? Three years ago it was; I thought it was you, hands folded over a crossed knee, sitting next to some schoolgirl you didn't know, stealing glances at the contents of her newspaper. But you never looked like yourself from the side.

I don't know if any of this is true. I have come to hold all memories as suspect, like any person who forgets, fabricating what I no longer know. If there is one lesson you taught me, it's that faulty memory is the greatest magus, having not only the ability to invent but to render truth where truth doesn't belong. I am one gifted with a faulty memory. In that regard, I've always been an artist.

There's a memory I've been saving; the two of us together in the Slaughterhouse door, green, aqueous light and the sky above us, and we both seem to be smiling, which is how I know I'm once again inventing everything. The only indisputable truths are that I am fifteen and you are forty-six, and that I am in love with you.

Here we are, in the forest where the wolves are also, and the cry of the black witch birds, at least in my imperfect memory. There are warm bricks behind me, a polyester tie around my neck, a *bruja's* charm in my back pocket, and the forest is a confusion of seasons, dry leaves sharing boughs with flowers, a bed of snow beckoning at the corner of my vision, hidden eyes, appalled, in every tree. My belt buckle swings in such a way that it chimes against my knee, that half-muted ring of a weary horse in harness, zipper lolling its tongue. You have brought me out. And I draw your head down to my shoulder. I am nothing; the need to comfort you is all. Nourished by our presence, withes of thorns come nipping at our ankles, in this animistic story of mine. They go about their secret business in the dirt, oblivious to what we do, each root a finger and an eye, gripping small hard stones for their water, discovering the bones, you say, of Indians.

Yours is the power of sign and wonder, and these weapons, these holy mysteries, will never be known to me. I am your boy, not your initiate. I am your fifteen-year-old lover, and we cower together, hiding from the watchers of the sky. What is there for me to do but hold you, in the way all secrets must be held?

I know this can't have occurred, but I see myself leaning back on that crumbling, defaced wall, witch talisman digging into my buttock, and, because I fear you in the way we are all taught to fear God, do you the courtesy of looking the other way. There is a taste of kerosene and cigarettes. Even now, I feel the weight of your forehead pressing down on my collarbone, that stunned hesitation, one hand at the fork of my legs and the other hanging empty. Because this is my vision, I know without seeing that the knuckles of the empty left hand are raw and bruised, that they are the partners of my aching jaw and the zinc residue across my tongue. Of course, you are formidable from the right as well, not a mere southpaw, but ambidextrous.

Or have I invented this? I'm forever guessing.

Your hair tickles my neck, with its brown smell of fox. Your caress is patient, almost absent-minded. In the leaves, I shift my sneakers to accommodate you, rightness forgotten, offering more of myself. And somehow I am staring at blue and white glass growing out of a tree, a tree bearing glass fruit; can this be possible? I am staring at white death. "It's alright," I say, "It's alright." Always, the urge to comfort you. But I am leaning on you, I realize, more than the other way around, and the death's head, the *calavera*, looks over your shoulder. My muscles are slipping into that slow, cold seize. You tip your face back to study my expression, as I remember it, and I try to feign detachment but my breathing has gotten away from me. My knees are the next to rebel. "Hush," you say. "Stop it." And as if my tolerance is a vessel that has brimmed full at your will, a sound spills over my lips, a moan or a whimper, stifled in time by the bad left hand. At your word, I fall. I always do.

Afterward, you tell me you are sorry. Sometimes I remember it this way.

You will grow tired of me, of course you will. The bells of St. Ignatius ring the vespers, and we are both expected somewhere.

In the house where I grew up, every glass object will be shattered when you are gone, and I will turn my fury on the horses, reveling in the sadism I never would have dared with an equal. I do it because I am a prince, a tyrant in my own home, fifteen and loved too much and no one but you has ever told me "no". I will throw the doors open and watch the horses gallop across green, clipped hacienda lawns, turf birds thrown skyward. All set free, except that Tereus I've always hated, the one cherished by my mother. As a young child, I saw no distinction between human and animal, and saw no reason why my mother would not leave us all and mate with the horse she clearly loved. She did leave all of us in the end, including Tereus, who is older now, retiring as I come into my strength, his muzzle going grey. And I can't resist swaggering back and forth in front of him with a dressage whip of my mother's, striking it down on the top of a gate, whipping the air and clattering the bars; no warden is crueler than a jilted boy. I will be driven on by the animal's large innocence and the grinding of his teeth, old Tereus moored on a hook, a shadow all ribs and hair and shrunken balls, plunging left and right, saved only by the appearance of a frightened stable boy and a scandal that will lead to my banishment again. Horses have something of you about them, your helplessness and charm, overexposed, your lashes fine as the points of a sable brush, your quiet dignity of being. Do you see how this is all your fault?

At my count, you are sixty-two now, which seems impossible to me, though I am now thirty, which seems equally impossible. How afraid you must have been back then. While I am telling stories, I may as well give myself the power of speech and action, able to drive you away with stones, to curse your name, or at least to say at the right moment the word that might have relieved you. "Never cry in front of a man," was your parting lesson. You said, "Weakness makes men cruel." If I had only been less weak. What then? Would you have found it in your heart to spare me this?

There are fire stories I've been collecting. Dr. Orpel (she would rather I call her Anna, but how can I resist that surname?) would make much of the fact that I am now telling you one of the five or six stories I tell when I want to make a woman fall in love with me. As you know, fire stalks my life; no doubt I will eventually burn this letter. In the fall of 2001 I was walking after the yellow arrows of the Camino de Santiago. When I arrived at the Compostela Cathedral, the town was buzzing with the news, jets full of passengers used as weapons; you know the rest. I was too much of a coward to go back to New York, so I went to Asia, Laos and Thailand, lingering in Japan. I put on my hiking boots again, walked stretches of the famous trail of Basho from the Sendai to Ogaki, those that were passable in the winter, and I did take some pictures but I couldn't carry much equipment and the real goal was just to be alone. You would have liked it there. I almost froze to death on my twenty-seventh birthday, alone with an orange sunset, walking the final miles to Naruko. And I saw those birds crashing earthward through the sky towers, portents foretelling the dawn of an age of fire. In Ogaki I added a stone to the little mountain marking the journey's end, one more pilgrim looking for solace, following the cold trail of the poet. You are nowhere, and in being nowhere, are now everywhere.

By the time I went home to Brooklyn it was early summer. Or was it? In my memory, it is always winter in New York, the cold, hurrying persuasion of this place. I was drunk on tiny, duty-free bottles of Grey Goose as the plane tipped its wing over the city; yes, I know. After months abroad I wanted to stand in front of the massive carnage of girders and stone I had seen on the news, with the arc of fire hoses. I went to the site, but I'd waited too long. After so many months no trace of it was left, nothing I could grieve or touch. What remained was a hole in the city, gouged, packed dirt and construction vehicles, photographs stuck to a giant board bleaching in the rain. I swear the wind still carried a scorched smell.

Someone walked off with my backpack at Ground Zero. It seemed fitting that I should have nothing but my camera and the keys in my pocket by the time I got home. You would say this is the way I am, running from bereavement, fighting against the moment of farewell; you would say, "Can you not see, dear boy, how you set up these situations for yourself?" I returned home, lost no friends and nothing that belonged to me, but another corner of my life had been carried away on thin air.

Dr. Orpel says I should write these letters to you; humiliating to be bossed by a shrink, but she is right. Because you too are disappearing, at least the version of you that I once loved. It is not that you are gone, no, that could never be. But you are warping as my life brings me closer to you, bending into something else. I have heard that the most well-handled memories are the most inaccurate, that because each one is a work of art, hammered by our own desires, the only safe memory is one locked in the mind of an amnesiac. Perhaps I'll get there, in time.

Dear X, I call you X in these letters not just because it suits you, but because I'm afraid to write your name in case these go astray. There are stories I tell myself, ghosts that now follow me across oceans and continents; wherever I can dream to go, they follow. They gather close, and say to me: will we ever be redeemed, you and I?

Yours,
Tony

TWO

To Tony Luna's eye, the feral girl's hair was black as a gun. She stood with her back to the wall, naked except for a pair of graying panties and one shoe. Light and shadow striped the girl's face and upper torso, half-illuminated by the window opposite. There were scratches on her abdomen, just above the shadow of her pubic hair where the lifeless, grey elastic gapped away. As if she had been clawed, he thought. As if she had walked the city bearing a coyote. It made sense to him, as an image; she was a wild girl. She turned for him again, face in shadow, showing off her back and pale, flat buttocks, hair cut high on her neck to reveal the fearsome spur between her shoulders. There was a dark birthmark on her ribcage. It spread slightly with her breath. The girl coughed huskily, cursed, set her palm against the wall, and crossed her ankles. Around the bare left ankle, she had tied a red string.

The feral girl had been wandering the streets of East Williamsburg. Tony found her by the mouth of Grand Station, by the all-night grocery, where the subway steps went down. He took her for a vagrant at first because she was dirty and neither coming nor going, just standing on the pavement, watching the street, a girl with mussed black hair and an oversized coat, all bones, biting a fingernail, frowning. Tony passed her going down the stairs, then retraced his steps, said, "Excuse me," and handed her his card. He had a speech he used for these situations, and it began with, "This may sound strange, but..." Tony believed that this introduction gave him the upper hand, stepping into the moment of discovery that every aspiring siren covets, the dream of that special breed of New Yorker. He said she had an amorphous danger. He was a vetted professional, and would pay well. His studio was on the corner of Grand and Bogart Street, should she be interested in making some extra cash.

The feral girl tilted her head back, looking at him down her sharp cheekbones, his card between her fingers. She wrinkled her lip. "Pervert," she said. "I'll kill you." She ducked into the station, ran down the stairs, the duffel bag she carried bouncing off the backs of her legs. He wondered what she had been waiting for, standing there alone. He walked off into the street, feeling all the hair on his arms raise and the groaning of the train below his feet, too afraid to follow the girl down the stairs and forgetting why he had come there anyway. On the sidewalk he saw a man's briefcase fall open and scatter its contents, some large unbound document, the evening suddenly alive with the sharp edges of paper carried high on the wind, rolling and whisking down the street. The owner of the briefcase watched the paper fly with a grey fallen-in face, not bothering to chase it down, a man in a shabby, tired suit stooping for his keys and pens.

For two years, Tony had lived on Bogart Street. He could fling out expressions like, "Money's no object," in certain company, and did when required. But he chose Bushwick over Manhattan. He loved this place, its low-slung buildings and corrugated metal, industrial silos looming up against the orange fires of the city. From the Morgan stop, he walked home along Grattan Street, past junk lots and snarling pit-bulls, a riot of graffiti ranging from artful mural, skeleton beasts and distorted, ravenous portraits of men with pompadours and gleaming teeth, to the spray-painted catch-phrases, "working class hero," "*puta madre*," "justice". His building was a tan brick affair. Until recently it had been a warehouse, and still had that feeling of hellish industry, high ceilings, huge, rusty window frames opening from within, levered on a complex system of cogs and winches, a lackluster stairwell smelling of cat urine and a freight elevator wide enough to accommodate a piano. The halls and stairwell were painted mint, the color of a sanatorium. The window looked out over Bogart Street. In the lot behind the building, heaps of tormented metal rusted away, the grass grew high, and the cats were random. As far as he knew, the property was owned by a cement plant, but was used as a scrapyard. A metal fence surrounded the place, and it would have been easy to ignore, if he wasn't looking for it. Like every disused space in the city, it had become a haven for the transitory. On cold nights, vagrants lit fires to warm themselves; on his way home Tony would walk past them, hurrying in the brisk wind, dark shapes in a metal graveyard glimpsed through a gap between chain and sheet-tin. To him they looked otherworldly, denizens of a crack in the other Brooklyn, a place of artists and the people who pursued them, of streetlights and girls with cropped hair and low-heeled boots smoking cigarettes, of scrawny hustlers, come-on smile and goods in the top of their sock, of perishable beauty, of old couples dancing on illuminated basketball courts. He slummed along the edges of that other place, never finding it, never quite managing to catch its eye. It smelled fear, that place. It kept him reaching.

When the feral girl pressed the buzzer at his apartment two days later, Tony was surprised. "Hey, it's the girl who called you a perv," she said.

"Oh," he said. He imagined her standing down in the street, bouncing with the cold and her own wiry energy, cursing him quietly, leaning the weight of her whole thin frame on the buzzer. "Sorry," he said.

"Here's the thing," she said, her voice crackling with flat, nasal complaint through the intercom by his door, "I'll do it, but you have to pay me first. In cash. And no funny business. I have a friend, Saskia. She knows where I am, and if I don't come back, she'll call the police and haul your ass to Immigration."

Tony stared at the metal speaker. "What do you imagine would happen to you?"

"So are you still interested?"

"I'm busy right now. You should call the number on my card, and we can arrange something. There's papers I need you to sign. I don't like to be surprised."

There was a pause. "Hello?" he said.

"Tony, is it? Look, Tony, I don't have a phone, and I don't want to come all the way over here again."

"I'll be right down." The girl waited for him on the street, and he could tell from the look she gave him that she knew he had run down the stairs, and was amused. "Hi, Tony Luna, photographer," she said. "Catch your breath."

She was smaller than he had realized and looked like a young punk, hair a black, tangled mane cut higher on one side than the other to fall across her face, defying the delicacy of the bones beneath. There were dark smudges around her eyes. Perhaps eighteen, perhaps not; her condensed, aggressive front made her seem older. He stood on his own doorstep and marveled, arms crossed against the cold, wearing what must have been a foolish expression.

"Did you say you don't have a phone?" Tony said. "Who doesn't have a phone?"

It was the way she yielded, the feral girl. She yielded, though she didn't have to, retreating into the darkness of herself, drawing the eye in after her. Her body was bewildering, somehow unformed, unlived in, as if the essence of her turned inward from the extremities, leaving them clumsy and translucent. It was an undiscovered body. In his apartment, she shucked off her coat without ceremony, signed the papers marking her a consenting adult, took his money and said, "Where do you want me?" At that point, how could he resist? Beyond any artistic interest, he was curious about the girl herself. He led her to the studio, which, at that moment, held lights, a desk and typewriter in one corner, and the denuded engine of a motorcycle. Instead of drawing the blinds aside he flipped them, letting in soft stripes of light. He handed her a robe.

She said, "This had better not come back to haunt me. Where's your bathroom?"

He led her there, and then retreated. When she came back, the girl was lost in the large darkness of the robe, carrying her clothing in her arms. She stood before him, one foot on top of the other. "So, I just…?"

"If you would." She turned away from him to shed the robe, dropping it in a pile on the floor with the rest of her things, kicking it away, the belt wrapped briefly round her ankle. "Here," he said, cradling the camera to his chest. "Just be yourself. Let me do the work."

She told him her name was Schwartz, and that she was starving. When he failed to respond adequately, she said,

"Literally starving. You should know that I haven't eaten in two days." At the diner around the corner the girl ate like a hyena. He watched her devour a ham sandwich, a small mountain of French fries, cups of black coffee thick with sugar, and a chocolate malt. While she ate, she clutched at the damp army duffel, chewing and swallowing rapidly, scanning the room with her eyes. She told Tony that she was from Valencia, PA, and that she had no parents. She said it just that way, no parents, as if they had never existed at all, as if she had fallen, fully fledged, out of a novel. When she told him again that she was eighteen – in such a way that he now suspected it was not true, but giving him some license to believe – her chin pushed forward and she stared him down, daring him, and her fingers, stub nails shrink-wrapped in battered, black enamel, curled and uncurled on the shoulder strap of her bag where it pressed down the folds of her shirt between her boyish breasts. It was inspiring, thrilling, the way the girl could lie. Tony had heard once that a good liar is one who could convince themselves of everything they say. Listening to her speak, Tony felt like he was conversing with another foreigner, recently arrived. Her use of the English language suggested foreignness, as if she had studied the casual speech of the American teen from some great distance, and come away with a dialect that was too deliberate to be credible. Her slang, for instance, was slightly out-dated. She peppered her otherwise well-formed speech with "hella" and "mad" and "tough shit." The romantic in him would have liked to pity her, though in truth there was something off-putting about Schwartz; he had a distinct feeling that the girl would do, or say, anything. It left him with an uncomfortable notion that he might actually be physically endangered by her presence. It was a feeling not unlike placing one's head in the mouth of a lion, he thought.

He said. "I've never heard of Valencia, PA."

"That's not surprising," she said, looking at him quickly and then staring at the ketchup bottle, and he discerned from her tone that the town, like her parents, did not actually exist. "I mean, why would you? It's a hellhole." She leaned forward into the bottom of her chocolate malt, her lips pulling at the straw, and Tony watched the impression of her back in the scarlet vinyl of the booth as it slowly disappeared.

His fingers were itching with the sudden heedless desire for a cigarette, though this was one of the things he did not allow himself. His eyes traveled to the next table, to the balding man with a birthmark like spilled wine on his forehead who was hidden up to the eyes behind a tabloid that said something about a tiger. The man's cunning, watery eyes flitted across the girl and lingered there for a moment, then sidled hurriedly away.

"Schwartz," Tony said. "Doesn't that mean black, or something?"

"Swart," she said, "swarthy. Sable."

"Shisou," Tony added, showing off an ingot of sophistication to see what would happen. "Shadow of death, in Japanese."

The girl shrugged, unimpressed. "Sure."

The waitress came by, administering to Schwartz's empty coffee. The girl warmed her hands around the cup. She said, "Have you photographed runway models and actresses and things?"

"Not often, thankfully."

"I researched you, before I came. It was just a bunch of boring, artsy shit."

"Oh?"

"Lived in Brooklyn ten years. Before that, Boston. Went somewhere expensive and majored in studio art. Mexican father, French mother. You were born in 1973. Five foot nine."

"How could you have found out my height?"

"The interwebs, son. You'd be shocked."

"My height is on the internet?"

"Just kidding," she said. "I guessed."

"What's your first name, Schwartz?"

She frowned at him. "J."

"Just J?"

"To you."

"Do you have any place to go, J Schwartz?" he asked, knowing the answer.

"Not a domicile."

"Relatives in the city?"

"No."

"And you're a minor."

"Oops." She smiled pityingly. "Not like it makes a difference."

"Yes, it does."

"Money seems to be easy for you. I'm guessing family money, not to knock your art or anything. The rest of us have to do what we can. And it is high art, right, not pornography. It's like the Maja."

"The Maja." Schwartz was brimming with surprises. "I'm not sure your parents are going to share that view."

"My parents are dead."

"You expect me to believe that you're actually an orphan living on the streets?"

"Believe whatever you want."

"And you're planning on...what, blackmail?"

"In this town, you could have a person killed for fifty dollars."

"I wouldn't know anything about that."

"You're awfully passive, aren't you? Submissive, I'd say."

She was drooping, drowsy, under the influence of heavy food and the heat of the diner. The man at the next table flicked his pouched eyes again, this time at Tony, who glared at him. The man gave an almost imperceptible nod, then got up and ambled out of the room, leaving his tabloid behind.

"Are you going to call the police?" The girl was looking sidelong at him. She was scratching at a red spot on her neck, and he wondered if it was infected.

"Why would I do that?"

"It's just a thought I had. You're dressed very carefully. You could be one of those well-meaning people."

"Disabuse yourself of that idea."

"I don't buy, use or sell drugs, in case you're wondering." She looked away from him, out the window. "Why are you being so nice to me?"

"You know why."

"I'd like to hear you say it."

"You're really something."

She turned her head to the side. "Oh?"

"You've stirred my curiosity."

"Stirred, huh? I'll bet you use that line on lots and lots of girls. You come on all depressed and sophisticated. I'm the Tormented Artist. Deny me nothing. Right?"

"It almost never works."

The girl leaned toward the window, scrubbing a circle of light into the condensation and resting her forehead against it. "Right," she said softly.

"J," he said, "can I call you J?"

"I don't care."

"Is that a piece of plastic stuck through your ear?"

She fingered her earlobe, which was pierced in several places by studs, safety pins, and what looked like a black sawtooth nail. The girl shrugged her shoulders in a tired way and rubbed her left eye, glaring at him from under the black makeup. "So?"

"Did it hurt?"

"Yes," the girl said. "It hurt."

He knew that she could, as indicated, be explored for the asking. He was bored. He had spent the last two weeks working for a design firm, shooting metal joints. And he liked the feral girl. There was an indifferent, preternatural sexuality about her, somehow striking him as slightly masculine, odd in such a girlish body. It might have explained her clothes, he thought, how she seemed to go the extra mile to defy her looks. Even without clothes she had come across as a contradiction, sullen but prurient, a precocious female boy. While it was fashionable nowadays to defy one's gender, to uglify beauty, it seemed to him that Schwartz would never have been any other way. He smiled across at her, snapping his fingers quietly to Werewolves of London. And with the beginnings of that odd chill he knew as desire's warning shot, he tried to remember how it went, that thing people said about mystery. That was what it was, he thought, about this genderless, adult child, this ugly-beautiful person sitting across from him. He liked to think he could charm almost anyone, but had been unable to say anything to soften the feral girl. She had turned her face to him unwillingly, wearing a flat, lazy expression that seemed to him false, hiding inside her stillness, waiting; even her naked back had that waiting quality. The images would only promise at the life below, not reveal it, an effect that was discordant rather than pleasing. But that was everything, that discord, the enigma of her.

Under the table the girl shifted her foot, grazing his ankle without seeming to notice, though he wondered if she had done it deliberately, suggesting a game of co-ed footsie. If it was deliberate, she also wanted him to know that she wasn't even trying, that she could take it or leave it, and it was up to him. She focused on her straw, prodding the dregs of her glass. If he took his eyes off her, even for a moment, he knew that she would disappear again.

"You hate being seen," he said. "Even just having a body makes you uncomfortable, not just your own body. Why is that? It's very captivating."

She laughed.

"I'd like the opportunity to do this again. If I could prepare a bit more."

"In the morning, say? After you make me breakfast."

"You're flirting with me. Am I that intimidating? Why don't you just ask?"

"It seems like a shame to walk around all night in the cold. And seeing as you just want me to come back again..."

"Say it. Say, 'Dear Perv, may I...'"

"Crash at your place?" She cocked her head to the music, mouthing along, eyeing Tony with her smiling confrontation. "Don't mess with him. He'll rip your lungs out, Jim."

"Come on," he said. He tucked a couple of twenties under a sugar caddie, a pleasant warmth working its way downward from his scalp. Schwartz licked her finger and dragged it through the rime of salt left on her plate, grabbed her bag and climbed out of the booth. Tony stared at her shoes, worn, black boots covered with buckles and straps, steel worker's boots, sentimental articles, he imagined, stolen from a slight-footed brother. The Schwartzes; horrifying. The boots were too big for her, and she had to hook her fingers into the dark mouth of the boots where her ankle disappeared, pulling up her socks before standing. As they were heading for the door, Tony picked up the tabloid that the man had left behind, folded it, and, feeling like a murderer, tucked it under his arm.

Schwartz had been sleeping in Grand Central Station. "Some kids sleep under it," she said, "not me. I'm not a mole." She had worked out an unspecified arrangement with the night watchmen, who allowed her to sleep in an alcove by the door, in the big granite atrium, frigidly cold but with a view of the constellations. "There's this lady who stands there all day with a milk crate and a cup," she told Tony. "She has someplace to go home to; I never saw her there past nine o'clock on a weeknight. Sometimes, she brings me a thermos of coffee."

"Maybe it's performance art," he said. "One of those bag lady acts."

She told Tony that she couldn't have stood it there much longer anyway because the cold was going to give her a kidney infection. But there were things she liked about the place: sometimes, in the middle of the night long after the Bangladeshi janitors had waxed the granite and the last trains come and gone, an old man would change the light bulbs in the stars.

"Come on," said Tony, "that's ridiculous."

But it was true, Schwartz assured him, he had a long, long ladder, one that stretched all the way up to the ceiling of Grand Central. And Tony knew the girl was lying, but it didn't matter, because the image was beautiful; an old man with an over-large coat and hair like candy-floss, perched on an endless ladder, polishing Orion. J Schwartz's lies were not really lies, he thought, but a heroic effort on behalf of an ugly world.

It was with only mild pangs of guilt that he went through Schwartz's bag while she was in the restroom. It was a reeking army duffel printed with the name Dubois. She was, after all, accepting his money, which gave him a certain entitlement (a slippery slope, he knew). He found such things as might be expected to be in the possession of an urchin; underwear, a box cutter, feminine necessities, a half-empty can of black spray paint, seven dollars, a jar of Peter Pan peanut butter, rolling papers and a sock-full of Tylenol and acid. A testament to the modern age, he thought, that even street children go medicated. The paperback dictionary in her bag did surprise him, but it made sense, he thought, for a girl who loved words to carry a dictionary on her person, like a bible. Months after she was gone, when he thought he had destroyed all evidence of J Schwartz in the apartment, he would find a wad of chewing gum stuck beneath the lip of a bathroom cabinet, and a long hair pressed between the pages of *Portnoy's Complaint*.

In a court of law, Tony would have said that he did not recall having made any actual propositions to J Schwartz. But the wild girl followed him home, quiet as the shadow of himself, past evening crowds and snatches of music, past steaming street grates and the headlights on Bogart, crystalline and shivering. They walked slowly. Schwartz followed him all the way to his building, and up the stairs. And when he reached his own door, he fumbled the keys and then held it open, letting her enter first.

In his poorly stocked but well-lighted kitchen, it was suddenly clear just how alien she was, how aberrant, how dirty, black hair matted, wet coat steaming in the heat, neck gray around the collar. When he applied a bandage to her scraped wrist (cuffed with ringworm and black rubber bands), holding her arm steady as he did so, he noticed how small her hand was, how pale against his own, how she had chewed her black lacquered fingernails as if in hunger, leaving oily darkness only on her nails' inner moons, revealing the true color of her blood. The near-flesh there looked sore, raw and pink, rimmed with soot and unimaginable city filth. She was painfully young. She shamed him. A foreigner, some bizarre visitor from another world, a world of orphans sheltering in subway tunnels; she had that distinctive, underground scent.

The girl rubbed her wrist and scanned the white surfaces of the kitchen with her eyes. "Clean in here," she said. "I didn't notice before. And you've got high enough ceilings for two more apartments in here. You could have a trapeze, if you wanted."

"That's what it's missing. A trapeze."

A long pause, the girl glancing sideways at him, waiting for him to do whatever it was he would do.

"You know," he said, and trailed off. Schwartz looked at him suspiciously, letting another awkward silence drag between them.

She said, "After all that? You're kicking me out?"

"To tell you the truth, I'm uncomfortable with this," he said.

"You mean you've changed your mind. 'Cause I certainly didn't force you into anything."

"This isn't a good idea. And come on, 'my parents are dead'? Why don't you go home to them? They can't be that bad."

"Wow," she said, "great. Now I'm a kiddie hooker, I suppose."

"Why lie about your age? It's not even funny. You're barking up the wrong tree."

"That's what it looks like, from here," she said. "You know, you wouldn't do well in prison."

"You lied to me. How was I to know?"

"That'll go over well."

"Get out," he said.

The girl said, "Go fuck yourself." She grabbed her bag, struggled with the doorknob, leaving the door swinging behind her. He watched her make her way down Bogart street, from one light to the next, hoisting the heavy duffel on her shoulder, not looking back.

The images would be searing and beautiful, shocking even, with her wary eyes and gaunt cheekbones, an angry female animal. Her unwillingness to reveal, to be known, was a confrontation with the viewer. He had come in close enough to see the smooth grade of her skin and its shading of dirt. But he sensed somehow that the ship had sailed; the girl had lost something with her close proximity to him, moving from artistic concept to frightening reality as her foot passed over his doorstep for the second time. Why had he let her follow him home? On edge, he went through the motions of preparing for sleep, brushing teeth, straightening a pile of magazines leaning by the bathtub. He went to the front door, checking the lock. He unlocked it and locked it again. Then he unlocked it. Then he locked it.

In the safety of his own bedroom, he dropped his clothes in a heap and looked out the window at the passing headlights on Bogart, at the various backlit kitchen and bedroom scenes, people crossing and re-crossing through the squares of gold in the windows across from him. It was pleasant to watch the lives of other people, to feel that shiver of inspiration that came with an image, pleasant not to think. In the middle of that cold firmament of windows, his whole skin sang. Bushwick was blue, and smelled of snow. He spent ten minutes listening to phone messages. The first was from his agent, suggesting a meeting to reassess the situation with Aperture (what she meant was "damage control"), and the second was from Lena, a philosophy major he had met behind the counter of the

Bobst Library, intermittently crying and shouting into the phone as she called Tony a pervert and a liar and a two-faced cock who had broken her heart. All true, thought Tony, except that he had never been able to lie. And what kind of girl studied philosophy, a doomed major, besides a girl who was crazy and heartbroken to begin with? On the other hand, maybe Lena was being too gentle with him; he wondered what kind of things she would scream into his answering machine if she knew about the feral girl, and fought the urge to laugh, imagining a situation in which Lena and Schwartz could somehow be introduced, and if Lena's jealous hysteria would somehow complement J's scrappy rage. He held Schwartz's brief presence in his home as being symptomatic of his inability to say no. Some kind of warped fantasy, a perverse coupling of Nabokov and J.M. Barry, something Freudian and far too close for comfort; Orpel would have had a field day with this one. He could remember J with fondness later, a wandering sojourner who had come in from the night, rude, hungry, scratched by wild dogs, tubercular strawberry on her breath. He missed the first few seconds of the next message because he had to hold the phone away from his ear to soften Lena's voice. The message was from Matt Kelly, an old schoolmate of Tony's who he hadn't spoken to in twenty years at least. Matt was sorry to bother him, but wanted him to know that Ochoa had died. He left a number. Tony had to listen to the message three more times to get it down. When he put down the phone, there was a tiny roaring in his ears. He had not smoked in months, but tonight, before he went to bed, he smoked three cigarettes by the open window, foot on the sill and forehead resting on the molding to stare out into the night, stood there long enough to watch the couple in the window across the street fight without sound and then finally kiss against the refrigerator, the cold wind lifting his hair, lighting one cigarette from the tip of the other.

On the front page of the tabloid, there was a stock photograph of a tiger, stagey, garish, obviously touched up, staring into the camera with blood staining its lips. But even with the indignities visited upon it by the Daily Paparazzi, the power and sadness of the animal, the carnal wisdom of its eyes, like those of a betrayed king, could not be mistaken.

The tiger had been kept on a chain on an empty lot in Hoboken, in an underground space below a motocross track. He had been there for years, fed on tripe and butcher's bones, walking in circles around a metal stake; a spokesman for SPCA said he had worn a furrow into the ground with all his pacing. Raj — that was his name—had a lame leg, an old break not properly healed, and walked with a limp. They had tried to remove him, but the tiger had somehow escaped. "Disappeared" was the word they used. The last sighting had been along the marshes, just beyond the Lincoln tunnel, Raj the Bengal tiger looking back once before sliding without a sound into the birches. They had seen no evidence of him since, just traces now and then, a track, a marking, kills of deer, a mouthed child's shoe. On the trunks of strange, Western trees, he left his musky notices for other tigers. It was the assumption that Raj was only biding his time in the woods, waiting for his moment of glory, when he would avenge himself forever on mankind, mistaking a child playing in a sandbox for some kind of slow, wounded animal on the banks of the Hudson River. Keep track of your children, the paper advised. Be vigilant. Keep your pets indoors.

There were stories about a Mexican rail yard decapitation, and a mysterious circle burned into a little league field. Tony read without comprehension, because he was listening for some sign of the feral girl sneaking back into the house, her quiet breathing, her moving through the dark rooms on stealthy feet, striped with light and shadow, looking for drugs or money or God knew what. If there were sounds, Tony did not hear them. But the fear remained, along with that sense of physical invasion, that newly skinned feeling, that shock, making all colors brighter, all sensation like a knife; from that place of heightened living, he remembered the first insomniac he had ever known, the man who never slept. He lay as still as possible, trying to minimize the sound of his own breathing, as if, by remaining still enough, he could fall through the bedclothes, through the coldness of the city, could fall into a land of tawny, swaying grass. He thought of Raj the tiger, freed at last from his chain, imagining him as an elderly tiger now, one eye clouded, soft paws quiet as a ghost, how he would sit on a hill somewhere between the trees, watching the lights of the city move below. Or maybe he would turn his back on the light, slide forever into the deep woods, held at last by their charitable shadows, if there were any deep woods left for him to wander. Tony lay in the dark, wondering if his own sleeplessness would be a fitting tribute to Ochoa, wondering how long this lack of feeling would persist.

Who had chained the tiger? He wasn't born on a chain, and he wasn't ever meant to be a pet. Had he once been wild, haunting a grassland somewhere, hunting and killing and sleeping in the sun, doing whatever it was that would indulge his tigerness? Or maybe he was a circus castoff, born into a cage, beaten with whip and chair until he cowered in the corner, beautiful fur gone dull and lank with urine, a broken tiger no one wanted to see, sold to some eccentric for four hundred dollars or traded for a used car.

Tony liked to think the tiger had been loved once. Someone had held him when he was small as a lapdog, adored him, given him a name and fed him from a bottle, someone had gazed lovingly into his milky, kitten's eyes, once. And then he grew too large to fit in anyone's arms. He grew sleek and powerful, reeking of *amrit*, hungry for meat. He destroyed things, shattering the crockery, painting the walls with urine, leaping up on furniture. So they chained him to a stake and left him there for years, and he walked around in a circle, always pulling slightly on the chain, clockwise and then counter-clockwise. His paws wore a furrow into the ground, and the heavy collar wore a furrow into his neck, and this was how he had lived, if one could call it life. What did he think about, alone in the darkness beneath the Hoboken motocross? Did he feel angry, if that was all he had ever known? Could he even remember that someone had adored him once? It might be that he hated that one above all others, the one who had given him up. He must have had thoughts, and time to think them. It might have occurred to him, somewhere in his red, tiger brain, a basic animal sense that there was no place for him left in the world, that he would neither be a tame pet nor a wild animal, there being no grassland that could hold him, no chain long enough for him to run. When he knew this, did he long, above all things, to disappear? He would walk, head bobbing, through dark days and nights, gnawing on that sense of wrongness he would worry like a bone, listening to the distant laughter of playing children, soft paws dragging the floor. And when the chance came to disappear, he would go without looking back.

When Tony finally slept, it was in the grip of the white pills. But he still dreamed. He dreamed of Ochoa's warm breath on the back of his neck, of the scent of myrrh and

funeral spices and the clatter of many birds, startled up
from a cobblestone square in the old town, a morning
glimpsed through a hotel window, a day hot and the color
of honey. He dreamed of Lena, her copper red hair and
arms around herself, sitting with her back to him in a room
full of the illuminated pictures of shattered scapulae. He
dreamed of Jude, the patron saint of desperate causes. He
dreamed that Alvara was in his arms, and that they lay
together, children once again, in the sacristy of Wolf
Chapel. In that space, which was quiet all through the night
and dark as the belly of an animal, Alvara said they would
be safe. Alvara said this was the safest place, because no
one could see them but God. There was no safer place
anywhere.

In a tattered bathrobe, Tony barricaded himself inside his
studio. The large white space, once a second bedroom,
contained the instruments of his art, as well as a desk, a
chair, and a tall, Baroque radiator. On the desk was a
typewriter, a manual Smith Corona, heavy and the color of
steel. Tony did all his writing on this loud contraption,
perversely refusing to use a computer. The truth was that
he enjoyed the tactility of the thing, the way the keys
resisted him, the way it turned the act of writing into a tiny,
physical triumph. With this in mind, he was fiercely
devoted to the fussy, manual machine, the kind that you
had to swing back with your whole body every time it
reached the end of a line. He typed slowly with firm,
punchy movements, never retracing his steps (that
clattering beast of a machine lacked correction tape as well),
occasionally stopping to sit on the wide windowsill and
look down at the street. There were ginkgos on his street,
now leafless November, and mothers walking their children
to various places, and many people who walked alone,

heads down and breath rising from the folds of their hoods and scarves. The windowsill, which was almost like a park bench in its generous proportions, was one of the reasons for which Tony had chosen the apartment.

The office was cold in the morning. In the pocket of the bathrobe he found a piece of string and a half-smoked cigarette stubbed into a gum wrapper, which he unwrapped, held briefly and then returned to his pocket. He sat at his desk. His hands on the grey typewriter keys had a pinched, contracted look, and he felt in them that stiffness that came with cold lately, what he supposed to be the beginnings of arthritis. Of course. A thirty-six-year-old vegetarian. And he thought of Matt Kelly, and his pinched voice, and wondered why he himself, who had so much more right to it, had never been able to grieve. What reason had Matt to grieve at all, he wondered. What right? From what he remembered of Matt, it seemed likely that he had been unwilling to pass up any opportunity for drama, but if so, he didn't know Tony well. There would be no dramatic outpouring, at least not to Matt Kelly.

Tony thought of himself as an image artist, a silence artist. Ochoa must have been about sixty-eight or seventy, he thought, and it troubled him that he could not picture him a day older than he had been the last time they were together. Late forties, he thought Ochoa had been, perhaps fifty, but strangely ageless, as if time had startled him. A trim, deliberate man with brown dog's eyes and a tan-colored raincoat over one arm, picking his way around a street grate, sliding into a crowd. Tony had been young enough at the time to not wonder over any of it, but at thirty-six, the beginnings of grey in his own hair, he thought it odd that Ochoa had seemed so un-ravished. Did it denote a lack of remorse? Ghosts did not age. It haunted Tony, not knowing how the man had died.

A decade ago, fire swept through a gallery in Chicago, taking with it the original one-off prints of five years of Tony's work. It wasn't really a catastrophe for him, not like the painter he had shared the space with ("It's like losing my children," she had wailed to Tony over the phone, to which he had replied, "You obviously don't have any children, Imogen"). But the event shook him. He took it as a portent. He swore off photography and started traveling again, eventually settling in Barcelona to spend a year crowd watching, cultivating a romantic haircut and tossing small change into fountains, going home at night to write. He purchased a black coat with large pockets and a typewriter, his first, a 1953 Corona which would have been pristine if not for a malfunctioning question mark key, searched the entire city for oxblood-red typewriter ribbon, and sat down to write a series of static and vivid stories which he came to realize were actually photographs. The experiment produced nothing but self-loathing and a fresh determination to move back to New York and continue making visual art. But the typewriter stayed with him.

For most of his life, people had written letters to one another. He had never understood the appeal of an instantly delivered message. For Tony, waiting was the point, waiting and risking that the message would never arrive at all. He enjoyed the idea of a letter traversing space, held and passed along by many hands, so that when it got to its destination it contained something of that distance, purpose and experience. He liked the ink's glister, and the smell of paper. A letter was a thing you could keep, it existed in the real world and would not change. Letters were his cathartic obsession; when he had briefly seen a shrink in his late twenties, a woman named Dr. Orpel, she had suggested he write letters to Ochoa, among other figures of his past, never to travel further than his own hands. Tony had eventually dropped the shrink but kept up the letter writing. In his heart, there was always the fear that he, like a failing machine, would one day find himself bereft of stories.

Tony reflected that in the twenty-odd years since Ochoa had disappeared from his life he had not grieved, really, for anything. He stood by the window at 9:15, the time the man he called The Prodigy always passed by on his bicycle. Tony stood by the glass and peered down at that patch of sidewalk where he knew he would appear. He did not wait long, The Prodigy was punctual; yes, there he was, bundled against the cold, mounted on a graceful, bottle-green ten-speed, a Cannondale, carroty hair in the wind (Lena, too, had red hair and pale lashes, electrifying details Tony would miss about her). His hands were covered today by red mitts from which his fingertips peeked; Tony did not remember seeing those before. Strapped to his back was a violin in a black case. His face was tilted upwards as he passed beneath the window, so that Tony could almost see his white lashes and the freckles that bridged his nose, and The Prodigy could have seen him, just for an instant, looking down and framed by the reflection of barren trees. But he was looking at something else (a plane? The sky?). His lips moved; was he singing? Tony liked to imagine the young man conducting symphonies in his imagination as he rode through Bushwick in the morning. And then he sailed past the frame of the window on the sleek Cannondale, and was gone. Tony turned his eyes to the opposite side of the street, because the passing of The Prodigy meant that it was almost time for the old couple to walk by on their slow way to wherever it was they went every morning. But Tony did not see them; on the other side of the wall, his neighbor was playing Season of the Witch. It was not loud, but it was unmistakable.

His typing must have been quite loud, Tony thought. Loud enough to disturb his neighbor, the old stoner. And he wondered not for the first time if it was, as Mrs. Kaufmann, the retired concert pianist downstairs, maintained, also loud enough to wake the dead. He counted silently to five, then dug in his pocket for the stub of cigarette, finding in the other pocket a cardboard book of matches from an East Village bar. The first tarry lungful tasted like the breath of life. By the third drag, the shaking in his hands subsided. On the other side of the wall, he could just make out the dull blows of soft, pacing feet.

THREE

My name was Lopez when I was a boy, before I became Ochoa. I shed the name of my father when I left for seminary school, having no wish to take with me anything that had belonged to him. I named myself after my mother, Ochanda. How an Ochanda should come to marry a Lopez, one wolf drawn to another, is a mystery that has always seemed holy to me, despite the fact that Santos Lopez should never have been any child's father. After all these years, it has become a mark of pride with me; whelped by two wolves, I could only have been a Jesuit.

It seems appropriate to be looking back on the beginning from where I am now, surely nearer to the end. I want the world so fiercely. I hunger for it all the more when every breath is painful. And I see a backward tendency to my life, a way in which dying resembles nothing so much as young love. Or so I think; what would I know about that second adventure? Of that visitor I knew little at the time I should, having only experienced it through others. Like a clever sociopath, I could recognize it and could describe it for you in much the same way I would now be able to describe God, in practiced words, a beautiful abstraction to be wished for but never owned entirely. But any abstraction embraced often enough can become truth. So it is with God, I think, for some of us. So it is with love also. In the end, what is the difference between those who come to grace by trickery, and those who come by any other means? We cannot help but fall for our own charade.

There was a sign I used to pass outside the Baptist church on the outskirts of Birnam: "God's arms are always open!" Its occupants frightened me, evidently expecting more of their shepherds than the lofty, cool serenity I can usually manage in public. The minister, a Mr. Bronson perennially stained with sweat, was civil to me from a distance, though I did not have the impression that his arms were as free and welcoming as those of his God. I wonder if he is still there.

I have told stories about a God I have only sensed on occasion, grasping, describing broken images in water. Small wonder; illusion has been my dearest art. But I will speak little of God, now. I have given Him my life and made my peace with Him. And He, I think, has made his peace with me. We are both of us too old for petty jealousies. So understand me when I say, this confession does not belong to Him. This will not be the story of a priest.

Back to the beginning.

The songs my father sang were those of revolutionaries. He sang them, and he cried. I loved him most at those times, strange and unattainable in his war memories. When he sang the songs, I knew he was a man of flesh still raging at the cogs of Fascism's engine, and I saw my father in his younger shape, the lean Maqui, crouching with his rifle in the grass.

"The black rooster is big, but the red one is fierce. The red rooster is brave, but the black one is treacherous. Wind, what shall we do?"

When Santos beat my mother, I would throw myself around the room, upsetting things and scratching at the walls. I looked for something I could use as a weapon. What had I, but my own body?

"Hit me," I told him. "Do it."

The wind will carry my song away, if I have said what none should hear.

"Come on," I snarled, lip raised at him. "What kind of man are you?" He would hit me until I fell; then, if I could, I would get up again. Those marked by God must be marked from childhood, surely, before they even know themselves. What did old De Rosa say to me? A priest is not meant to be happy?

Santos struck with a closed fist. When he was near me, I would smell old blood in the creases of my father's hands, and would not understand until much later in my life how deeply we can love the instruments of our ruin.

Two generations of my father's line had lived, died and eaten by the slaughter of horses, but in his youth Santos had escaped this fate; in the war of which we must not speak, he had briefly been a butcher of men, the scourge, as he used to say, of the Great Butcher, Franco. He called himself a decorated rebel, though I didn't know, and still don't know, what this meant. For if he was a *Maqui*, as I suspect, I cannot guess who would have done the decorating, in medals of sand and blood. The words once put me in mind of an Easter Tree; I would see my father standing at the crossroads, his arms hung with delicate, hollow eggs. I did not know what side Santos fought for, or how it was he had come to live an anonymous existence in a Basque town. I do not see Santos in the history of my country. To me, *maquis* is a French word to describe a small mountain clothed in briars, *macchia* a Corsican forest. My father called himself a soldier.

I remember the pop of his loose, flat knuckles, the muscle that jumped out in his cheek, belying gritted teeth. I remember him coming home with his arm laid open by the teeth of a horse, how he took thread and needle from my mother's sewing basket and sat at the kitchen table with a bottle of vinegar, calmly stitching it up. I remember the sound of his boots on the stair at three in the morning. Martyrdom was always in my nature.

"He was glamorous, like you," my mother told me, smoothing my hair, as if this explained it all, my father's dark glamour, his undeniable charm. It was the fifties, and you didn't leave your husband because he beat you; when that happened you went to a priest. But the truth was, my mother was in love with him. In time, I would come to understand this.

My mother and I had a mania for walking together out beyond the town, over fields and goat tracks, to pace along the chalk cliffs in the hills. Some Republicans had been shot there, she told me, but I was an infant then; we could walk to the foot of the cliff, putting our fingers into the broken places, finding the impression of machinegun fire in the white chalk. On these walks, my mother seemed to me less a mother of children than a child herself, a girl skipping stones in stout leather shoes. This was where she had been walking when my father saw her for the first time, robbing bird's nests in the chalk cliffs, wind in the grass and the sound of goat bells, a fifteen-year-old girl in a rust-colored dress who watched my father with suspicious, gypsy eyes, Santos the dashing guerilla fighter, a man of the South in Araba, offering rationed sugar. Or so I imagine the scene of their meeting, that first gaze. I was born a year later, son to a soldier and his forlorn, half-tamed bride. Ochanda would cherish me more than all the siblings who would come later, I being the product of love, an ally in the empty house of her husband. I was a child of the war years.

At the age of twelve, I decided I was strong enough and made the mistake of fighting back. I had hoped to placate my father with a show of brutality because my gentleness was so displeasing to him, knocking my childish fist against his hard blue jaw. "I'll kill you," I said. He looked startled, his lip bleeding, and then a light went out inside him and he caught me like a rooster by the neck. That night, he beat me past forgetting, like a soldier, as a man would beat a man, the ghost of the war years described in every bone of his hand. I stumbled from the house and fled into the night, determined to never go back.

I walked for miles along the paved road leading out beyond the lights of town, listening to the bark of dogs and manly laughter, late-night revenants spilling from closing bars, staggering their way home. A voice called out to me, a woman leaning in a doorway. "Xavier Lopez? Out so late?" I came toward the woman and recognized her as Aldonica, a friend of my mother's who, since I could remember, had pinched my cheek and smiled at me. But at this hour she looked wild, flushed and painted around the eyes, all round hips, leaning crookedly in the doorway with a halo of light around her. I turned my face away, sliding into the deeper shadows across the street.

When the lights faded and I left the town behind, there was only hot wind and the groan of insects, a summer night in Araba. The road became packed dirt beneath my feet. In the hills beyond the town the stars grew bright and multiplied in the darkness of the night, and I allowed myself to wonder where under them I was going. I feared for my mother and younger siblings, left alone with a drunk

Santos in the house, with nothing left to draw him now. But the anger I felt then was great enough to eclipse these fears in me; it was as much for the mother and siblings who hid behind me as it was for Santos himself. Pride kept me walking the dirt road, dazed with pain and only half lucid, though the next town was over ten miles away. I had run before. All children run away. But this time I truly meant never to return. I walked on, feet dragging, and in the hours before morning, with the road rocky and stars dim in the sky, there came behind me the sound of my salvation, the whisper of an approaching truck. I stepped into the middle of the road as the truck drew near, waving my good arm, cradling the other to my chest.

"Xavier?" A man leaned out the window of the idling truck, Schaefer, on his way to work in the early hours of morning at his pastry shop in the neighboring town. I was flooded with relief to see a familiar face. Schaefer, like Santos, was a tall man with thick forearms and coarsened hands. But Schaefer had always seemed benign, even drab, for all that he was referred to as "arrotz" by the boys in town and whispered about incessantly ("arrotz-herri, otso-herri"), deemed a suspicious character, a blond immigrant bachelor who stumbled with our local tongue and gave white sugar pastries to the younger children. I was never to know his given name. All any of us knew was that had come to Araba in '46 or thereabouts, speaking the single Spanish phrase, "Soy extranjero. Ayudame."

His oddness made him more appealing to me in that moment than someone more familiar and personable. It was not Schaefer who turned a blind eye. It was not Schaefer who hailed Santos on the daylight street, and spoke to me as if nothing was wrong; Santos spat into the dirt whenever the baker passed. "Arrotz," the other boys whispered. But that night, I hated the entire town. This man was not of the town.

Schaefer opened the passenger door for me, and in the lights of the front panel I could see his square, colorless face, creasing around the eyes when he saw me better. "Xavier," he said, "the blood." I raised my fingers to my face, finding it thick and sticky below my cut scalp, lying open like two lips at the hairline. I had pushed my hair into the cut to clot it as I walked, and now it only wept slightly, but the dried blood streaked my neck and forehead, coagulating in my eyebrow. Exhaustion had made me numb. I felt, if anything, like laughing. Schaefer said, "Sorry, Xavier." And he shook his head, hauled in silence on the steering wheel.

Schaefer asked me no questions as the truck bounced slowly down the road. We sat together in silence, him clearing his throat with a growling sound from time to time, and I felt grateful to him for leaving me to myself and not asking what had happened or what I would do now. The radio played softly. I sat hunched on the wool blanket stretched across the truck's seat, which was like one long bench between Schaefer and myself, itchy to the touch and smelling vaguely of dog and powdered sugar, guarding my hurt wrist in the circle of my body. But then I felt a desire to cry, and knew I would if I didn't start talking, so I said, "I'm not coming back." Schaefer said nothing, only glanced sideways at me, blond-scrubbed face half lit by the instrument panel. "I hate him, and I can't ever go back."

"I ran away once, when I was a boy. There was a storm. I hid under a rowboat." He had a plain, wistful voice. The Basque tongue, paired with the coarser bones of his own accent, produced a strangely harmonious clangor. "I was gone three hours. You should go home. You will make your mother cry."

I said, "I'll kill him."

"Your arm," he said. "Can you move it?" There was no pity, only clinical enquiry, which was a relief. I dared for the first time since the fight to swivel my wrist, finding it locked, as if the bones no longer passed smoothly over one another.

"A little."

"May I?"

At first I didn't know what he was asking for, and then I realized he wanted to examine my wrist, and gamely held it out. Schaefer had strong, square paws like my father, but much more deft. With one hand still on the wheel, he felt down the bones with an index finger, palpating them gently. Tipped toward me, his head smelled cleanly of sugar and what I thought were Carreras cigarettes. The breath whistled through his nostrils. I remember feeling ashamed of the thinness of my forearm in his large, solid hand.

"Does it hurt?"

"I don't know. Not much."

"Shock," he said, giving me back my arm. "You will feel no pain for a while, hoffentlich. But you are lucky. You could have wandered off into the fields, and collapsed. Your father…" he stopped, uttering a deep, long-suffering breath, and rubbed at the corners of his eyes with thumb and forefinger, pinching the bridge of his nose where the glasses would have cut, if he had worn them. "He is not a good man, you know this?" I watched him fiddle with the buttons of his coat, still shaking his head on my behalf, the only display of human passion I was ever to see from him. Beneath the coat, he wore a rumpled shirt of blue cotton, its collar buttoned to the chin. He said, "Your arm is not broken. Sprained. You will be alright."

I had a wild notion to ask him if he had been a doctor before the war, in some other life. I never did. For some reason, the idea frightened me.

Dawn was coming, and I thought we must be nearing the town, but Schaefer pulled off onto a small side road, white dust bouncing in the headlights. "One minute," he said, shifting his hands on the steering wheel, and I said nothing, not wanting to seem ungrateful. After a mile or so he stopped the truck, drawing up alongside a barbed-wire fence, and climbed out, leaving the engine idling. I could see him in the rearview mirror, fussing with the tarp at the back of the truck, then walking around the hood and standing for a while, the fallen carriage of his shoulders, eyes illuminated briefly by the headlights like those of some night animal, looking east into the field beyond the wire, kicking at a stone in the road. I thought he must be waiting for someone. I slumped against the door, surrendering to the growing agony of my headache, waiting for Schaefer to finish what he was doing and take me into town. But the pain was returning, riding in waves on the truck's rough idling, making my eyes slide in and out of focus. There was fresh blood on my neck, a ringing in my left ear where Santos' fist had caught me; I noticed it now in the stillness, dizzy and nauseated. I was losing my anger to a dull sense of worry.

Usually, once Santos' rage was spent, he would leave the house or go to sleep. But what if tonight should be different? Doubled over on the long seat of Schaefer's truck, sticky with sugar matted deep in the wool blanket, I could almost hear the chain of my mother's Saint Christopher medallion dragging between her teeth, that worried habit of hers. My eyes rested on the gearshift, tall and industrial as with most automobiles of the day, wooden knob polished by long use, its leather pocket a resting place

ASHLEY MAYNE

for dust, crumbs and tiny metal elements. There were gears, springs, silvery washers, important-looking things Schaefer needed, I supposed, for the repair of mixers and the tools of his trade. It occurred to me that I had no money, and nowhere to go once we got to town. Maybe Schaefer would give me work for the day, a few reales for a meal and bus fare. I had cousins in St-Jean-de-Luz. I feared I might be sick before we reached the town, and wondered what sign or visitation Schaefer was waiting for.

I sat up when he opened the door of the truck and climbed in again. He leaned across my knees to rummage in the glove compartment and handed me a pistol, a cold, square, heavy thing. I held it in my good hand, not knowing what to do, while he appraised me with a blue, bloodshot eye. "No bullets," he said. "Just for show." I nodded, intrigued in spite of myself. "Pull the trigger," he said, and I didn't want to, it was counter to my nature to do it. "Go on," he said. I pointed the gun out the truck's open window into the roadside scrub, set my teeth and squeezed the trigger, which gave slowly and then suddenly engaged, producing a loud click that made the hair on my neck stand up. "See?" said Schaefer. "More difficult than you thought. How will you kill your father, if you are not man enough to touch a gun?" The mournful, blue eyes searched me, and I looked at the dashboard, both confused and cowed by this little speech. I supposed Schaefer was trying to teach me a lesson, but what was it? He took the thing from me and lay it on the dashboard. He leaned across me again to the glove compartment and this time handed me a flask, a terrible rotgut liquor I drank at first out of politeness and then at his insistence. "It will help," he said. I continued to drink the burning stuff, becoming aware of his humid breathing which was, I thought, strange. He handed me a cloth.

"Clean your face." I did, as best I could, smearing at the sticky mess of my forehead and ear. Schaefer said, "You look like your mother, Xavier. Do you know? Very much." I nodded, though unsure of what he meant by it, weighted down by a foggy intensity. I can be forgiven my innocence, can I not? "Ochanda Lopez," he said. "Mothers are sacred, Xavier. Do you know that? You should never leave your mother." I dabbed at my face again, forehead mostly clean, neck and eyebrow still sticky. In the light from the instrument panel, the cloth he had given me was stained black now, as with oil. "Spit," he said, and I obeyed, damped the cloth with my mouth, and scrubbed again. He took the flask from me and drank, then handed it back. "What will your poor mother do, when you have gone? Who will take care of her?"

I said nothing.

"You know I'm going to take you home," said Schaefer. "I have to. I'm doing you a favor. Ochanda would be sad, if you went away. You would never forgive yourself for breaking your mother's heart. I'm sorry about this, Xavier."

"Please don't," I said. "I won't tell anyone."

And he said, "Don't argue." The flask slipped from my hand and spilled over my leg, running down into the grooves on the truck's seat. And suddenly Schaefer's hand was on the back of my neck, forcing my head down into his lap. The radio played on in the darkness, the great Amalia Rodriguez pining for her lost love, Gaivota, "if a seagull could come bring me the sky of Lisbon," and the hand on my neck tightened, coaxing but determined and too heavy for me to shift, and I was choking on the half-swallowed liquor in my throat, confronted by the warm lap, unzipped and presented, and I was wondering what to call this thing that was happening because I with my Catholic upbringing believed that rape was a war atrocity, or a thing at least ensconced exclusively in the domain of women. It was not something that happened to boys, and certainly not in our town. I tried to raise myself but could not manage it, and crumpled in pain. "Hush," said Schaefer, his fingers in my hair, and I knew I must have been whimpering. "You know I don't want to hurt you."

"What a perfect heart would beat in my chest," sang Amália, "my love, in your hand, that hand which would fit my heart perfectly."

I broke for him. It had no name, this live, hot mouthful there even as I tried to resist it, teeth coaxed open, nose grinding mercilessly against a heavy brass belt buckle, ear knocking the steering wheel. I was suddenly lost in an unknown jungle without language, stalked by shadow animals. The pressure of his fingers on the nerves and tendons of my neck made me feel faint. He pushed my head down harder as if trying to stop my meek, frightened sounds, and I thought, in a remarkable moment of adult clarity, somehow hovering above my own body and small number of years, that I was being asked to make a choice between collusion and victimhood. With that, the world went black.

Take me away from here.

In the field beyond the headlights and barbed-wire a single tree stood, and under it, in the summer dust and cool before the dawn, there was a black horse with a white star. The boy, Xavier Lopez, had seen him from the truck's window while Schaefer paced the road, nerving himself; the headlights threw their beams across a black flank. The horse raised his head and turned to look at the boy, ears pricked and white between his eyes, a crooked cross glowing out of the night.

I have often wondered how it would be if I could remember just the horse with his crooked star, just Xavier the boy, bewildered and concussed, held by the night. Just this, and not the rest. There have been times when the horse is the clearest memory I have of that night. There have been times when I thought him a messenger, angelic in the way of all horses. Large and innocent.

I could not escape completely. There are other memories: how I slipped lower into Schaefer's lap, recoiling from myself in a stupefied ecstasy. How I cowered under the weight of his heavy paw, feeling him go rigid when I accidentally scraped him with my teeth, knowing all the while that in his other hand he was holding the pistol. How I gagged for breath, a hot, unspeakable ache in my groin, and wondered, listening to the sound of no bullet in the gun's chamber, its cold muzzle drawn along my backbone, why God chose not to strike me dead. But it was God who made me a survivor. Like some tough bacterium, I was born to it.

Later, I would wrestle with the meaning behind the act.

To my child's eyes it was not Schaefer who attacked me, but my own pleasure, all cold sweat and nerves, this tortured thing that labored on the seat of an idling truck, one hand holding it down. For how could I have been crossed by such dark gifts, if they were not, by some quality of mine, elicited? And if they were provoked, were they not desired? Would Schaefer, friend and neighbor, take something that was not offered? The breath of his coarse, hot fur burned my nostrils, baker's yeast and confectioner's sugar, cigarettes, laundry soap. His thumb pressed into the soft of my neck, fingers gone tense as iron. But despite the obvious and brutal physical invasion, I felt that I was alone in the idling truck. As if it was only I, at that moment, struggling against myself. The fear of my revelation flooded through me with an almost physical sensation of tearing.

Then I let go, and the blackness returned, and it was tolerable again.

In my ear, Amália sounded as if her heart was breaking, a Portuguese sailor wandering the seven seas, crying the words more than singing. And I, who had spent my life acting as a pliant receptacle of Santos' rages, had learned that violence was a kind of love, and submission would carry me through it, boneless and inscrutable as the calm, flat sea.

Schaefer, as I recall, shifted with a rusty groan of springs, offering more of himself, his hand finally lifting from the scruff of my neck. I did not pull away. To pull back would have been to fight him. To be unwilling would have made me a victim. Do you understand?

These days, I find it both ironic and horribly appropriate that the boy in the truck, the one who decided he could purge himself of victimhood by a supreme act of will, would later choose a vocation that involved the comforting of all manner of survivors. And I know the preferred term is survivor now, not victim. I understand why this is so, that it brings comfort to redefine one's own mythology; we are to say survivor, as if the dark subject is a bridge we fell from, a horse that threw us, as if we have left in our wake some terrible accident, smoking on the road. I know that it is often the illusion of choice that haunts us most, as if it was our choice to cross that bridge, to ride that horse. Yet, we choose agency; the pain of having made poor choices is more tolerable than the act of seeing ourselves helpless, bereft of choice. We cling to our notions of control, do we not? We would not believe in such a random, brutal world. We would rather take on the sins of those who do us harm than see ourselves as sheep without a shepherd. At least, that is how it seems to me. By insisting on our own agency, we defend both ourselves and God from the threatening void.

I was a boy practiced in survival, not only sturdy, but marvelously pliant. In the truck with Schaefer, I committed a disappearing act. I found it familiar, at least as natural as holding back my bile and salty tears. Schaefer did not hurt me; it may be that he truly did not want to. After the initial show of force, there was an awkward gentleness about him. He was surprisingly clean. I remember noticing that. I held myself steady against his knee, and the heavy pistol tumbled from his fingers and lay staring, empty, somewhere in the darkness at my feet. His fingers circled the little raised bones between my shoulders. "You will be alright," he said. I could not see him, not any part of him, other than what was immediately in front of me. Why do I imagine his face covered, in those last seconds, by his pale, ursine hands, stained green by the lights of the instrument panel? But I do. I see him clearly, sprawled low on the seat, the predator slain in the act. As if I were a ghost, torn from myself to stand above us both, I see him. He covers his face. In the moment of truth, he cannot look at me. Or perhaps it is that he cannot risk being seen.

Was there ever a boy so hell-bent on survival? I would come through it all, even that awful tearing. As if my soul had slipped its moorings to my body.

Amália sang, "If, when I die, the birds of the sky would bring to me one last look of you, that look that was yours alone, that look when first I saw you..."

He tasted of iron at the end, his fingers counting the vertebrae of my neck, a hot blood pulse I drowned on and then choked up into his lap, my moment of defiance, too little too late. He seized my jaw between thumb and forefinger, wiped my lip and pushed me away. "Get off," he said. "Little beast."

I sat in the truck on the way home, nose bruised by Schaefer's belt buckle, a white sugar pastry he had produced from a paper bag resting un-tasted on my knee, and we listened to the radio, a blurry station out of Portugal playing old songs for wounded lovers. I kept glancing sidelong at him, unable to help myself, unable to explain the stealthy ache of heightened life, the elation of having once again survived. I stole these glances at my rapist's face as if something in his aspect could explain this painful elevation; had he experienced something similar? But Schaefer didn't look at me once during the ride home. He drove with both hands on the wheel, his shirt marked with rosettes of my blood, and stared ahead as if he had forgotten me. Memory is imperfect, but if there had been any humanity in Schaefer, I would have eked it out. I would have held onto it like something precious. But he gave me nothing. There was no tension in his limbs that I could see, no hint of cruelty, passion or remorse, only a kind of lazy slackness. His fingertips tapped out mysterious messages on the steering wheel. He whistled. There was no talk of secrets; Schaefer knew I would never tell. "Have your mother take you to the doctor," he said gently. "You will need stitches. It will be alright." He stopped the truck in front of my house and said, "Wait fifteen minutes before you go in. Count them." Then he sat silently, waiting for me to leave, and I climbed out into the early morning, the air chilly and all the town's roosters crowing, and when he drove away I threw the pastry into the road. It left a white circle on the leg of my trousers, a dusty sporing of confectioner's sugar. I slapped at the mark, rubbing it deeper into the fabric, and sat down on the front steps, counting out the seconds.

In the still-dark kitchen, I washed my face, swished cold water in my mouth and spat it out. I sat at the kitchen table, looking down at my own hands resting in my lap, at the boyish grime of my fingernails, red and bitten to the quick. Even at rest, my hands were shaking.

My mother took me to the doctor while Santos still slept off the night, and he cleaned me up, saw to my wrist, which turned out to be sprained, as Schaefer had diagnosed, and used eight neat stitches to close a cut on my scalp. Months later, we noticed that the hair over the scar had grown back white. I would have a streak there for the rest of my life. My mother said it was handsome and unusual, and that it didn't matter. And I would never tell her or anyone else about what happened with Schaefer, partly because I was ashamed but mostly because I had no words to describe it and, like those African tribes who have no word for the color blue, could not really comprehend it at all. I was twelve years old.

A few months later, another boy pushed me in the schoolyard and I took him to the ground, pounding his face with both fists so that he coiled up under me, shielding his face in his arms. I had learned by then how to throw a deadly punch, knuckles supple and the thumb untucked, how to breathe into it, taking your time. I kept hitting him, my strength somehow multiplied but cold. He was unconscious by the time they pulled me off. I sat on a hard bench, winded, feeling the boy's blood dry and crack on my neck while the teacher shouted at me, the one we called Sister Lora. I was demure in the classroom. I can well believe my violence was a shock. Her hysterical voice was tuned to a dull static roar in the back of my brain, warped beyond distinction, like the sound of the sea heard in a dream. I was already paying for my rage, crushed from inside, losing my breath to a fit of torn, chaotic gasping. "Stop it!" Sister Lora shook me, I remember. "Stop it!" At the window, the other children clustered, staring in at us. Their eyes were hungry, fearful. I was no longer one of them. A boy pressed his nose flat against the glass, hands cupped up around his eyes. I lay down on the bench, turned my cheek against the wood. And I was crushed alive. I was thinking of the great Rodriguez, and of the grainy, flickering face of the monster in some old film I had seen at the mobile cinema, a pale, elegant creature of fierce appetites who had the shape of a man.

FOUR

His shame was a fat horse-driver.

The man drove a horse and cart loaded with furniture past the house of his childhood in the mornings, rattling the wheels. The cart was too heavy for the horse, and the fat man rode the cart. The horse was old. One day Tony saw the horse fall down in the road, and the man beat it with his whip. The man did not get out of the cart. He wore a vest with stretched buttons and a watch chain. His chins quivered with each swing. Tony held on to the curtain, and hugged the plaster with his knee, watching. Finally, the horse got up, and horse, man and cart went slowly around the turn of the road. When he told her of it, Tony's mother said that the man who beat the old horse was cruel. "It's a crime to ask too much of an animal, mon loup." Two days later, Françoise would take her morning coffee in the watchtower of the hacienda's compound, waiting for the cart and horse. At midmorning, she shot the fat man in the leg with a crossbow, tossed her cigarette over the wall, and went into the house to take a bath.

When Françoise gave him the white rabbit with pink eyes Tony hated it instantly because it was helpless, and did nothing but twitch and eat. Alone, he squeezed the white rabbit as hard as he could, and it squealed and kicked in his hands. The noise scared him and he dropped the rabbit quickly, and it went back to nibbling at grass clippings. In the following days, the rabbit grew a red mushroom behind its tail, and Françoise said it had an expelled intestine, and that it would die. "Did you hurt it, mon loup?" she asked, and Tony said, "No." He watched the rabbit hop and nibble on the grass, the bag bouncing off the backs of its legs. The next morning, he went to the hutch and the rabbit was dead. Tony dug a hole in the garden behind the swimming pool, while Françoise stood by in furry slippers, smoking her morning cigarette. "You don't know what happened to it?" she said, and he said, "No." They buried it. Françoise threw her cigarette onto the walk, and didn't grind it out. She would always throw them lighted on the ground, however dry the summer, despising the hacienda with its clipped paths, flirting with wildfires. Tony leaned his forehead against his mother's arm instead of squeezing her fingers, because her hands were in her pockets. He said, "I'm glad it's dead." He had meant that he was glad the rabbit wasn't suffering anymore, because that was a noble thing to say. But it didn't sound like that when he said it. Françoise looked at him for a long time. Tony was frightened of his mother's face, because he thought it would show how she disliked him. He had destroyed her gift. He had failed, once again, to be a good boy. She said, "That's cruel, mon loup." And he thought of the fat man with the whip. That was what he was. He was ashamed. Shame was fearing that others would see him for what he was. We must hide, to be loved. We are ashamed of our wants, and ashamed of our unwants. We hide them like the mouth and the anus and the rabbit intestine; it's the important parts that shame us. But could such things ever be hidden? The boy didn't know, and imagined himself gathering the rabbit's intestines, coiling them up and tucking them back inside its body, so that his mother would think he liked the animal. In view of Françoise, he would stroke its dry fur and let it clamber over his legs, scratching with its anxious little claws. It pained him that she would think he didn't appreciate the things she gave him. Françoise sighed, going inside to get her hat.

The house in which Tony had spent his childhood was a seaside fortress west of Playa Azul, in the Sierra Madre del Sur; seen from the road, little was visible but sand-colored walls and mission gates watched by armed guards in suits and smart sunglasses, a family crest more typical of a drug lord than a banana magnate. Tony, as a child, became so accustomed to the presence of these men that he stopped seeing them, was only peripherally aware of them as the clink of weaponry and whiff of colitas lingering on the borders of his nuclear family. The house itself, with its fresh-cut lilies and multiple wings, its balconies, swimming pool, and blooded Spanish horses, these things did not seem strange to Tony, and indeed were somewhat distant in the way that his parents were distant, inhabiting a world of their own. His father, Juan Caspar, was often gone, only stopping now and then for a brief respite with his wife and legitimate child, and when he arrived it was always as El Jefe, accompanied by a wave of lesser barons with their suits and pomaded hair, their German cars and Andean women. Tony could not remember ever having spent a substantial amount of time with his father. The older he became, the more it seemed to him that his father disliked having him in his presence. Galo Luna was the favored son, groomed to shoulder the empire, ten years older than Tony and child of a previous marriage. Tony viewed his older brother as a cousin and had few exchanges with him, fraught as they were with the knowledge of his father's uneven favor. In childhood, Tony had been hurt by this, and wondered what he had done, in his short life, to disappoint his father; this changed after the attack, when concern for his youngest son's safety caused his father to take possession of Tony's life.

When Tony thought of his mother, it was always with the blur of late morning in the stripes of a pale blind, when she would sleep wherever she had fallen the previous night, on a couch or a chaise or a deck chair, in a den with her head down on a table and the wreckage of the night around her, a stiletto dangling listlessly, seldom ever in her bed unless Juan Caspar was home. Tony would sit beside her sometimes and watch her breathing gently, the strap of her dress cutting into her arm and her makeup smeared, making the features of her face look indistinct and doubled, a dizzying affect, as if she were forever moving sideways and at great speed. She only wore the makeup after dark, softening her thin lips and wary, vulpine eyes. Without it, in the daylight, she looked severe. Tony loved his mother's hair, coppery, set off by the black, conspicuously French dresses she wore; in her husband's world, Françoise stood out. Françoise Renoult was a daughter of the old world, a writer and ethnographer, an escapee from graduate school who went to Michoacán looking for primal authenticity and ended up married to the plantation baron who would swallow her career, surrendering the world of ideas for children, horses and a heroin needle. She was never harsh to her son; distant, diffused, but loving in her clumsy, unyielding way. Even when she was bright and lucid, even when she laughed her strained, ironic laugh, kissed Tony and ran her fingers through his hair, or tousled the fur of the Newfoundland, he could not help but see her as she was on those blurred, blind-striped mornings, a radiant star exploding at some great distance from him. Sometimes in the afternoons Françoise would take out one of the horses, returning red-faced, whip in hand, black boots crunching on the granite paths and forearms green with froth. The horse legend ran deep in the family, Françoise having supposedly emerged from Lake Patzcuaro astride a horse the first time Juan Caspar saw her, all white, supple thighs and trailing foliage. When Françoise left them for an apartment on the Riviera, shared, Galo said, with her lesbian lover, it was only a mild blow to Tony, who felt that she had never quite been his, that beautiful stranger sleeping in the house.

When he was eight years old, his cousin Alvara was ten, and they played a game with the bedside lamp in his room: light dark. Light dark. Light dark. Alone in the seaside fortress, visited only by tutors, maids and riding instructors, the two children had made a smaller, more private home where they could hide together during a long summer visit. It was a white tent behind the garden wall, made of sheets. Alvara said Bedouins lived in white tents. Alvara the reader, wise beyond her years, who fell in love with Darcy in translation, later with English Rochester and Childe Harold. When Alvara's family came to the compound for the summer, she tried to lure Tony into literature, but he was unmoved, lacking the patience for these dramas, for the deciphering of French and archaic English. Anyway, he preferred to watch his cousin read, during those long, lazy visits in the heat of summer.

Alvara read lying on her stomach, chin pushed down and one leg kicked back, shoe dangling idly, under a white umbrella in the sun, the arc of a sprinkler flailing the wide, green lawns beyond her. When Tony wanted her attention he pulled her hair, sat on her, or grabbed whatever she was reading, yelling out manly curses picked up from the guards, racing to drown *Jane Eyre* and *Tess of the d'Urbervilles* in the swimming pool.

Tony was a lover of old horror films, both American and Mexican. His place of solace was the darkness at the edge of the projector's beam, close enough to smell the grease and feel the heat of the beautiful, clattering old machine. The projector had been a gift from his mother's sister, Aunt Yvette. When Alvara was not visiting, he would spend the heat of the afternoon in a dark room under the whisper of a ceiling fan, becoming, for an hour or so, a spy in the country of silver monsters.

What did the dead want? To explain themselves, it seemed. That, or company.

In the old films, it was the dead who could not forget the living, rather than the other way. The dead were vengeful, sometimes even selfish. The dead never forgave those who had wronged them, never deserted those they loved. Like children and old people, they were both lonely and single-minded. The dead wanted comfort, justice, fulfillment. Like everyone, they wanted symmetry. They wanted a living heart to draw them close. In the horror classics, Tony found a simple view of the world that confirmed what he had always suspected. In this world, nothing was ever gone for good. Nothing was lost, no one got away with their crimes, and the supernatural pervaded even the most mundane aspects of life. It was a world of justice, rules and sensibility. The ghosts of suicidal girls haunted boarding schools to avenge themselves on cruel headmistresses, and new lovers were haunted by deceased ones. Catacombs were guarded by the shades of lascivious monks. Children's invisible playmates were never the product of their minds. Cats were ill omens, but only to those who failed to respect them, and the black star, the mark of the wolf, always burned on someone's wrist. In this world, you never walked up the stairs alone. And there was never a soul so far removed from conscience that he might not return from the afterlife, trying to explain his sins. Tony approached the offerings of *Taboada, Libra de Piedra, Mas Negro Que la Noche, El Espejo de la Bruja* and *Hasta el Viento Tiene Miedo* with the same reverence as the American classics, *Wolfman, Dracula, Frankenstein*. This was gospel; there were no surprises. The dead wanted witnesses, and the monsters pined for love. Tony pitied the wolf man, who could touch nothing without destroying it, and the vampire who could never be sated. Even as a child he understood that blood was never really blood. He understood that the dead wanted to put on the skins of the living, and finish their own business.

When he was ten years old, he discovered the films of Buñuel. The first was *Susana, Demonio y Carne*, a melodramatic farce Tony mistook for a horror movie because of its title, its moral flavor, and the inevitability of the hacienda's ruin; all the inhabitants, mother, father and ingenuous son, overseer Jesus and an Arabian horse called Lozana, were brought low in less than an hour by the wiles of an escaped mental patient, the bombshell Rosita Quintana, a *rompe-huevos* if Tony had ever seen one. "God of prisons," Rosita whispered, kneeling in the straw of her cell, gown sliding perpetually from her half-moon shoulder, face crossed by the shadow of bars, "you made me, like the snakes and scorpions." Alvara explained that Susana was a proto-feminist, a modern Lilith (she then had to explain the biblical Lilith). "Susana wants to be free," she said. "That's all. But they leave her with no other way to achieve it; what can she do, but seduce the most powerful man she sees? She has to destroy the patriarchal family unit. Of course, in the end she gets dragged off by her hair, and the rapist Jesus gets his job back. They weren't ready for a woman like Susana in 1951." *Susana* led Tony to *Tristana*, a work far superior in his eyes and also more disturbing, involving a quasi-incestuous marriage between a waifish amputee Catherine Deneuve and her adoptive father, Hernando Rey. "Don Lope is basically a rapist, too," was Alvara's assessment of *Tristana*, but Tony would be haunted for years by the thump of the unhappy bride's crutches. His exposure to Buñuel not only gave him an abiding passion for film of all genres, but crumbled the wall between horror and melodrama. These latter stories had all the markers of the great horror classics, or so it seemed to him, the characters troubled not by ghosts, but by their own predictability. Men and women were the monsters here, though dressed in paler hues. All genres were at heart the same: the camera's invisible eye saw the weakness of our nature and turned it outward. And how helpless they all were in the end, these good women, these virgins, these *machos* once beguiled. They might have been the prey of vampires. To Tony, any monster would have been less frightening than the uncanny ability of adult men and women to become their own executioners. But the cautionary value of such tales was lost on him; he saw no trace of himself in these hapless *machos*, these men who lost the game, accepting so readily the suggestion of a vacant, feminine smile, the death-grip of *la perversa*, or even something as banal as money or power. To him, the weakness of such heroes was contemptible; he agreed with Alvara, there seemed to be no good men in melodrama. As in the realm of horror films, anyone toppled so easily, anyone so hung upon with lust, deserved their fate. But it seemed unrealistic; why were these people such easy marks? What caused them to feel so much, and why was Tony without this secret language? Watching the trials of these ardent people made him feel tone-deaf. "Give it time, *joven,*" Alvara said. Tony was thirteen years old then, and Alvara fifteen. "You shouldn't really be watching this stuff until then, anyway. Come back in two or three years, and then tell me you don't understand it." Despite her criticisms, Alvara's heart was pulled by the moralistic love fables, *Wuthering Heights* in cinema drag. She sat through *Susana* with him, and *Tristana*, and even the rather shocking, heretical Argentine hit *Camila*, in which a beautiful socialite runs off with a priest and both end up shot dead, thrown by Rosas' soldiers into the same coffin. "At least Susana and Camila have their way, for a while," Alvara said. "Who could help but admire Luis Lopez Somoza's ass? It isn't for his own joy *el patrón's* son wears those trousers. Viva Susana."

Unlike his cousin, Tony failed to identify with these rebellious lovers, and harbored no special pity for any of them. For him, the most sympathetic view was always that of the camera. It was the gaze that felt nothing but owned the passion of the audience, the invisible eye that played no favorites and couldn't be deceived. The need for distance always brought him back to the horror genre, a place of simpler rules, where the monsters inspired more pathos even than Camila O'Gorman, perhaps because they seldom wore the faces of men and women. He hunched down under the beam of the projector, a watcher, bodiless. *La Llorona, El Vampiro, El Fantasma del Convento*. By the age of fifteen, that threshold of understanding his cousin warned him of, Tony had decided to become a cinematographer. It was the only calling for which he felt qualified. He wanted to be that gaze, that remote, invisible witness.

Françoise was fond of saying that she saw no feature of hers in her only child. Tony inherited the olive skin and black mane, rusty in the sunlight, of the Luna clan, his father's heart-shaped face, and the sharp, grey-green stare of his maternal grandmother, or so Françoise told him. "Gra-mere had the witch's eyes, too," she would say, with a shrug. "Blood will out."

A female ghost haunted St. Ignatius. Tony felt her presence occasionally, at Mass and in the halls, a warm ghost, so incongruous in that cold, lifeless place. He would look for her in the stiff wind when he rode his bicycle on the country roads among the other boys, or would feel her at his elbow, slipping down the rows between the classroom desks when everyone else was already seated, sliding silently into an empty desk as Father Desmond tried to win them over to the charms of Pythagoras and the Golden Mean. He looked for the female ghost, a shimmer in the air near him; he could almost see her staring at the walls of the classroom, at the gray windows' rippled lead glass, her pale, luminous eyes reflecting nothing of the room, holding nothing but their own soft light. He felt her as a slight weight settling on the edge of his bed as his mother once had done, on nights when the drunks were screaming and rattling the floors below, or gunfire sounded in the hills beyond the compound. Now, in a dormitory full of the breath of sleeping boys, the weight was so slight that it scarcely disturbed the old, springy mattress, but he knew she was there, the female ghost. That special itch, that ache; there she was. With thin, cool arms around him, he would sleep, though only to wake alone. He wasn't afraid. He knew what she wanted. Like all ghosts, she wanted to get under his skin and finish what she had not done in life.

They were in Mexico City when the shots were fired, a rare family trip for the quinceañera of another cousin, Alma. Tony had been walking outdoors down a flight of steps beside his father, Juan Caspar "El Jefe" Luna, and Alvara walking behind with her governess, Inez, in the flash and snarl of camera fire; why so many photographers?

Hired, perhaps, by Alma's parents, to capture the event? In his memory, there were trees on either side. Tony remembered feeling blinded by the steady flashes, feeling hot and irritable, stumbling on the steps. Cousin Alma, star of the weekend, was walking behind and slightly to the right of Tony, chatting with her friends. He had seen her only a few times at family gatherings, and was always struck by her hair, silvery like Alvara's, proof that the germ of his favorite cousin's odd color existed somewhere in the Luna family, somewhere in his own blood.

The sharp, metallic pops had come from many directions, impossibly loud, echoing off the pavement. He was pushed to the ground, felt his cheek scored by glancing stone chips, and saw, rolling past his face and bouncing down the steps, pearls. He caught one under his hand, and saw that it was pierced with a tiny hole, one from the string of a broken necklace, a slight rosy glow about its surface. And he was crushed by the bodies of men, lifted, carried away from there, thrown with Alma and some other girl he didn't know into the backseat of a car, their heads knocked painfully together. He turned, squirming around on the slippery seat while the two girls huddled, shaking, looking for his cousin Alvara. She had been just behind him, close enough to touch. He could not find her, now.

There would be a funeral with white narcissi, attended by weeping strangers, the wives of magnates in Chanel and black lace, mounted police and what seemed like a hundred cousins, his brother Galo, his mother fresh from abroad, an unrecognizable woman with a black shawl over her head.

Françoise looked yellow in her mourning dress, pinched, her lips pale and tucked between her teeth. Tony thought it strange that his mother should be so affected by the death of Alvara, a girl she had never cared for and had once accused of being fat. He wanted to comfort her. In the black taffeta, Tony searched for his mother's hand, but couldn't find it; Françoise folded both arms under her breasts, and turned away from him, leaving him stranded in his own lack of feeling.

Tony's aunt knelt to kiss the lid of the coffin.

Throughout the ceremony, Tony, in a hot, black suit, watched his father's face for any sign of emotion, wondering what he himself should do, but saw only detachment; the dark glasses never lifted from before El Jefe's eyes, and even within their shield of darkness, he squinted and sweated in the bright sun of the churchyard. When it was over, Françoise left, telling Tony she would be back later that night, her heels wobbling on the churchyard's gravel path.

El Jefe offered the family home for the funeral gathering. That night, while the wake raged across the mansion's lower floors, Tony called Françoise at her hotel, addressing her as "mother", begging her to take him back to Europe with her. "I could live with you and Aimee," he said. "I could make you happy again." There was a long pause, and he could almost see Françoise at the other end of the line, sitting in a hotel bathrobe, her thin lips and distant, hollow eyes. "What's happening?" he asked her. "Who did this?"

"It was an accident, mon loup."

"I'm not an idiot."

"Ask Juan. Perhaps he will explain it to you."

"He doesn't care."

"Juan does care for you. He can't help being a son-of-a-bitch."

"Aimee is there with you right now, isn't she?"

"She's sleeping. Don't call again, it will make her upset. Promise."

"Why can't I call my own mother, if I want to?"

"Because she has her own life. So do you, mon loup. I know you're confused right now. The world is a confusing place."

"I don't want to live here with him. I want to be with you."

"Well, you can't." Another pause on the line, Tony listening to his mother's frustrated breath, the click of her fingernails on the plastic receiver. "Mon loup," she said, "you should understand that I have never been your mother."

He remembered a yellow day in summer, when he had rested in the grass behind the garden, using Alvara's hip as a pillow, listening to the pages of her book turning. He remembered the way the sunlight pooled above her collarbone, and the way her hair tasted, salty and taut as wire through his mouth. Her skin was cool, white, and chlorinated. He had used the hem of her skirt to shield himself that day, stretched it tight across his eyes till all he could see was blue light through the soft linen, felt himself dissolving in a bath of light the color of the sky, the spiny thumbs of mesquite shadows moving over them both, the grass sharp with drought, Alvara's leg soft and rounded through the linen. Juan Caspar had come home; Tony and his cousin could hear voices from inside the garden wall, urgent business of some kind covered by a radio playing old songs, Lara wistfully complaining over the state of his heart, *piensa en mí, cuando beses, cuando llores.* The night before, Tony had heard Juan Caspar talking on the phone to his mother, telling her that he had arranged for their son to go to a private school in Connecticut. "My father is sending me away," he said to Alvara.

His cousin rolled over on her elbow, gazing at him. "Well, that's good, isn't it? I wish I could go away to school. Not stupid Immaculate."

"There's snow in Connecticut," Tony had said, and they had both lapsed into silence. With his eyes pressed into Alvara's skirt in the blinding day, Tony felt the sweep and pull of hours against him, drawn to the edge of a well that spun like a cataract, and remembered a film he had once seen with some explorers thrown from a raft against the rocks of a wild river gulch, slick fingers torn from each other's grip, drowning, sucked down into the river's heaving frothy guts where there was neither heat nor light. Connecticut, he thought, must be like that. "I hate him," Tony said. "I hate them both. Fuck them."

Alvara shifted her leg against him, said, with an annoyed click and swish of pages, "Ouch, you're hurting." She looked away from him, off across the parched hill, where the distant pine trees hung in the still shimmer of the air. "Why do you have to ruin everything?" she said. "You're going to be a cinematographer."

FIVE

I can't remember when I chose the black. I told my mother when I was sixteen to make her happy, sitting at the kitchen table with our hands down on the scored wood in front of us. After I made my pronouncement she did smile, saying, "Praise God," and palmed her Saint Christopher medallion. Then we sat as before in silence, and I wondered if she had understood me, looking for some acknowledgement. "I will take care of you," I said. Santos was gone, working at the knacker's yard, and I wanted Ochanda to know that I was a better man than my father. And she did rally with a sharp glance, cutting her eyes to the side, a look that said it was harder than I realized to escape the natural order of things. My mother squeezed the medallion between her fingers, resting her elbow on the table, and took the golden chain for a moment between her teeth, drawing it through and through with a sound of dark porcelain, the sound of her perpetual worry. "God will prevail," she said. "Life is full of choices."

"Yes." And what I knew, but did not tell her, was that it was a choice that would protect me from other choices. I could only squeeze her hand, and say, "Mama."

My mother took to calling me Miguel, like the fighting angel, though my name had always been Xavier, after my grandfather. I worried that all the good in me had been snuffed out by those few minutes in Schaefer's truck, and this fear drove me into the church beyond the usual weekly Mass; I bowed my head to the rail as often as possible. That was how it was in those times, in our town, the church was a sanctuary to shelter any need. There was no more ardent lamb than I. The faith comforted me, the church smell of dust and stale varnish, the certainty and heaviness of its ritual gestures, the patriarchal affection and longed-for sting of purity. When I left home and became a novice, I found that the dreaded ascetic discipline suited me well, as did the distance from my family; Barcelona was as far from home as I had ever been in my life. I embarked on my spiritual education like a young man going off to war. I came home once at the age of eighteen, to celebrate Christmas with the family, and a drunken argument over a radio in the small hours of the night led to a quick slap across the mouth, Santos raging and my little sister Maitea cowering in practiced silence, putting her hands up to guard her face, and I upset my chair, landed a quick left hook and managed to dislocate my father's jaw. He was still a soldier, and I was trim and rangy, a runner, not a brawler. But I had grown in strength and moral outrage, and he was a man of fifty who had lived furiously. I could feel his bones under my hand. And I will never forget the murderous cold in his eyes as he leaned against the kitchen table, hunched in his failing body; it was so plain to me, his wish that he had never been part of my making. Watching my father, I thought that we all sow the seeds of our ruin, a truth I discovered but failed to learn, of course. I was eighteen, and had overthrown the man who made me. I spent the night with a childhood friend in town, reminiscing with little enthusiasm and icing bruised knuckles, and began the long journey back to Barcelona in the morning. As a child I had wanted to kill my father, had often wished him dead, but my victory over Santos had been hollow. Seeing him lose a fight was something I had not been prepared for. His defeat made him more human, and I less so. A week later I received a letter at school. "I pray that you will be happy," my mother wrote, "Whatever you do, don't come back here." I could smell my hometown in the creases of the paper, hayfield, horse and charnel house, the salt in the glue my mother's tongue had touched.

When I was still a novice, I took a weekend excursion, a drive in a rented car to a cheap beach house by the sea. I spent two days neither reading nor studying but simply living in my own skin, walking the beach, swimming in the mornings, turning over shells and exploring the seaside town. There was a hidden pleasure in being near other people while being distinctly separate from them, not a true part of their world. Accessible but remote. Untouchable. It was a safety I would wrap around myself, black cloth and a white collar, the dour costume of the neophyte halfway removed from the world. But today, in a seaside town, I still wore civilian clothes, still savoring my own young, fresh-faced anonymity and the possibilities it offered.

In a shop of old things I found a necklace for Maitea, soon to be married, a string of pearls on a tarnished silver clasp. "A present for your girlfriend," said the old woman who took my money, beaming at me with a look of nostalgia, and I had such a feeling of fondness for her in that moment that I asked her if she had anything for a son to give his mother; the woman showed me a pair of ancient lace opera gloves, fragile and the color of tea. "For you," she said, "half price." I would send these gifts, like the letters I wrote twice a month, but I would not set foot in Araba again.

In the evening, still aglow with fellow feeling, I swam out into the sea, fighting the surf until I outdistanced it and the ocean evened out, the large swells lifting me only occasionally high enough to see the beach over my shoulder. Before me and on both sides there was only water and sky. I wondered for a moment if I would be able to swim back, but reveled in the weightless feeling, the coldness of the water, its cleanness on my body, the sanctity of salt and its buoyancy. I alternated between floating and swimming, crawl and backstroke. If I could somehow stay in this remote world of sun and salt, I wondered, bathed in pleasant light, if I could make this moment last, might the darkness be appeased and go its way? The sun broke orange on the faces of the waves, and I turned back, climbing at last out of the surf in a pleasant exhaustion, seeing a blond-haired child playing with a red bucket, a black dog running circles around her.

Later I ventured out to the town bar where, in the hot summer night and the light of lanterns strung from the eaves, I danced outdoors with a girl named Veronica below a sign that said, "No singing, no dancing." When the music stopped, she kissed me on the cheek and went back inside, returning with a group of friends and glasses of tart red wine. I sat drinking with her and her loud friends, and every word we shared seemed so poignant to me that I found myself laughing with tears in my eyes, as if these people I had met that evening were old friends. We jostled together on the benches, which were too small for all of us, so that we sat with thighs and shoulders pressed. Someone punched my chest in a friendly way. When the group laughed, the ripples of it could be felt flowing through me from my close neighbors, so that we all rocked together, like a wave. Veronica, eyes shining, pinched my chin and slapped a boy's hand away from her skirt, why can't you be a gentleman like our Miguel, she said, such an agreeable young man. I laughed, pushed this way and that. Another boy dragged his finger through the spilled wine on the table, drawing the shape of a moon. And they did not know about me. They did not know that their affection, like the afternoon's surf, was a farewell. "Manresa. Isn't that a seminary school?" One of Veronica's friends, a skinny youth my age with brown eyes and a cap turned back to front, spoke the words softly from across the table, under cover of the noise.

I didn't know whether it was worth lying, and said nothing. He smiled and gave a low whistle, shook his head, abandoning me for the conversation of his neighbor. Shrill female laughter tumbled over us. Someone's shoe grazed my shin under the table. But the moment had passed; I felt so far from them all. Just before midnight, I shook hands with Veronica and her friends, and walked down the quiet road under a sky filled with stars, worrying the torn lining of my sleeve, drunk but unable to banish thoughts of another night road, another walk under those same stars, though this time I knew where I was going.

"Hey. Archangel." It was the young man who had sat across from me, cap now doffed and pressed in his hand. Before I turned, I knew it was him. His pale, widow's peaked face swam up to me from out of the darkness, something pulled from the depths of the sea. I could not remember if he had introduced himself, having only a vague idea of wicked, deep eyes and a chipped incisor. Beneath the lights of the bar I had thought him attractive. Now I shuddered at his proximity. I stopped, letting him catch up. "Hey, you," he said, "walk you home?"

"I'm drunk."

"Good." He fell in beside me, our steps matched on the white road, wild stars above us, the smell of sea life. He said, "What a tragedy."

"What is?"

"Watching you all night, dancing with the girls. Hey, don't be like that. Can't you see I know?" He looked desperate, starved, but showed me his most charming smile, friendly submission plain as a dog's. I had remembered the chipped tooth correctly, not a defect so much as a stamp of handsome trouble. There was no struggle to be had, because I had already lost, sitting at the table with Veronica's friends. I had gone looking for this, had I not? The young man wove toward me, cutting a crooked line in the middle of the road, the lights of town glowing faintly at his back. He said, "Don't play innocent with me."

"I don't know what you're talking about."

"No?" He had come up level with me now, and pulled my arm to stop me, circled me in the dust. "I should be more clear?" He put a hand up, scruffed the hair at the back of his neck. "You're killing me." He gave a low laugh, whistling through his teeth, and shook his head. "Say something."

"Go away."

"You don't mean that."

"They'll wonder where you've gone."

"I'm always going places, mozo. Anyway, they saw what they expected: Veronica, all over you. Poor Veronica."

"She's a nice girl."

"And wasted on you."

"Say what you came to say, and leave me alone."

"There's not much to do, in this armpit of a town. Unless you like fish, of course." And I remembered him sitting at the table under the lights, the dark curls and cap and chipped tooth, leaning on the table and watching me. The quick wink and lifted chin, a corrupt libertine salute. The infuriating knowledge of his smile. Now he circled nearer, city shoes sliding in the dust. He said, "You shouldn't worry so much about the things you can't change, mozo. See? I don't worry."

"Where are you from? Not here."

"Do you care?"

And I said, "You can't be seen around here in the morning."

"What are you so scared of? I'll make you forget all that." He clutched at my elbow, pressed in nearer, breathing out the Anisette shimmer of Pacharín, complaining softly. "I'm all feverish. Feel it? You've infected me." He did smell of heat, of leather jacket. "Don't pretend you're better than I am." He made bold with a hand, and I pushed him away, two palms slapped against his chest, the world spinning with me for a moment.

"Idiot! Are you crazy?" He stared at me, taken aback, and I added, "Anyone could be walking here." I continued down the road, briskly to see if he would allow himself to be shaken. He hesitated, and I expected him to curse me, and turn his back. But after a while his footsteps were audible, trailing me. I slowed, one shoulder hanging back slightly to include him.

Perhaps it made sense, I told myself, that this too would be among the evening's departures, morality slipping down the rungs of a toppling ladder. Night, an unfamiliar town. It was all so maddeningly easy. And I would never know who he was; the experience would remain here, behind a closed door, in this place I would never revisit. The jacket I wore was unseasonably heavy, but still I shivered. His eyes climbed my back, and I pulled him along silently, hating him.

The way home took us onto a sandy path away from the public road. He followed me between thorn bushes and tufts of beach grass, stumbling slightly in the sand. Even drunk, I could tell he was a creature of cities, unused to shifting ground, unused to the dark. I thought of Homer's wine-dark sea, feeling the aptness of this expression with the tremble of the hot night's drunkenness. I tried to navigate the unsteady ground as gracefully as I could, keenly aware of the warm, lank body behind me, of his eyes on me.

"You're killing me," he said again.

"Be quiet."

Where the path turned we could see the night sea, ships' lights visible far out beyond the surf, seeming, with the distance, to dance up and down, unmoored from the horizon. Yellow porch lights of the bungalows glowed from up the dunes. The key was in my jacket, strung on a ring with a partner of itself and a numbered plastic tag. I fished in my pocket and handed it to him, catching hold of his wrist, sliding the key ring over his index finger. In the windy, private dark, my hands crushed the lapels of his coat, releasing a squeak of troubled leather, and he breathed at me, "You're cold. Poor thing."

"Never look for me." I shook him suddenly and heard his teeth clip together, knowing I frightened him because of the way he cringed. The drunken nihilism of the whole evening had evaporated in rage, and I thought I would like to hurt him, or at least make him fear me. I was repulsed by his unjustified tenderness, this stranger who spoke endearments, as if he had mistaken me for someone else. His chest was thin, the hard ridge of his sternum apparent under my hand. He clung to my wrists, off balance and knees sagging, looking for a moment like a man begging for his life. He laughed nervously, breath quick against my face.

"Easy, mozo," he said.

I shook him again. "Say it."

"Whatever you want."

The keys in his hand clinked gently against my lips. "Easy," he said again. "Ah, you beauty. Let me make you happy." His fingers tasted of salt. A small, humped shape nipped my ankle in the sand and then rolled away. It must have been the toy bucket, abandoned by that little neighbor girl I had seen in the afternoon, she of the black dog. When he craned forward to kiss me I turned away, his teeth glancing my jaw, feeling under my hand his little sound of protest, a tremor climbing upward from the palm. "Don't," he said. "You're scaring me to death. You don't have to...I'll do what you want. See?" Abruptly I let him go, and he staggered back a few steps, recovering himself with the overdone ease of a clever drunk. In the dark, he kicked up sand, and laughed at me. He pointed to the light of the nearest rental, jingled the keys. "This one?"

I said, "I don't want to know your name."

There is only one way to sever our downfalls from ourselves. We who are torn by want must punish all objects of desire.

It was just before my first vows.

I am hesitant to talk about the making of a priest. That decade and its rites have little bearing on this story. And in truth, it is a thing I have never spoken of freely, a secret to be held. I chose the black. I put it on. I made my promises; take, Lord, and receive all my liberty, my memory, my understanding, and my entire will. Years of study, years of mystery, years of love. Is it surprising that, in this confession of mine, this story of a fall, I should avoid with pain the steps I climbed to achieve the spectacular height of it? I know where the fault lies. It is not with the Order that raised and sheltered me. It might have been other than it was; as a novice, as a scholastic, did I not feel supreme peace and even joy? Theology, philosophy, service, prayer. There are things still sacred to me, still beloved. There are memories I would keep separate from the rest. Or perhaps it is that I would not drag that other man, the priest, into this story, though he belongs to me, and I to him. Why hide that part of yourself, Father Wolf, when you would tell so many other things? But hiding is natural to me.

No one takes up the challenge of spiritual cleansing like a seminarian with everything to prove. I eventually concentrated on languages, and developed a reputation for the deftness and speed with which I acquired them. Spoken language and the translation of texts have always come easily. Since I was blessed with only an average ear for music, I attribute this ability to Ochanda, who spoke to me in the Basque, Romani and Spanish, giving me an early understanding of the shape and kinship of all language. But good translation, it seems to me, also requires the art of disappearing. One must fade into the visions and desires of another person, speaking his words as if they are one's own. It is a kind of acting. A putting on. I used this gift, not only garnering the respect of my teachers but dipping my toe into the waters of professional translation. It was an art I would pursue with wild inconsistency for the rest of my life, and I have sometimes wondered if, had I been of a more even temper, I could have satisfied myself with it as a secular career outside the Order, rather than for the Order.

Academics had always come easily. I thrived on the service, the discipline, the asceticism, even the lack of sleep. The initial drop-out level of any denomination is high, not because of the sacrifices required, but because of misplaced expectations; young men come looking for quiet, for an extended spiritual retreat, and this bears little resemblance to what they find. But I came to take a beating. During my novitiate, I even took up running, though such a pastime would seem unwise for a childhood asthmatic. There was a man at the track known by the regulars as The Coach, an old Argentinean with a palsy shake and rheumy eyes. "Walk it out, Chueco," he said, when I lost my breath and hunched, hands to knees, fearful of that old familiar catch in the chest. Chueco was his name for me, Lefty, twisted, leading always with the sinister foot. He never knew my real name; I never knew his. He said, "Pace yourself. Don't panic." And I was happy to be pushed, by him, by the brotherhood, by the enormity of the calling, hoping that this persistent pummeling would reshape me into something else. It was my reason for being there.

In this account, I speak of running more freely than theology. But for me, sublimation of the body's anxiety was a door to the spirit, a way in. To run without losing breath was to run without fear. To be free in the body was peace. I learned to breathe through the nose, careful, measured breaths, paced against my footsteps, to take my time. I learned this as I learned the motions of ceremony. I memorized, perfected, knelt for the host and the visiting spirit, and ran. In the rhythm of footfalls and slow exhalations I discovered that I could conquer my lungs and the impulses of my body to enter a trance state, a perfect blankness akin to spiritual vision. It was safety. To me, it was God. Years later, when Margaret Savage asked me about these spiritual mysteries, I would tell her my education was a process of discovering solitude, paternal love, and oxygen. By this I meant that running was as crucial in those years as any discipline, vow or spiritual experimentation. This I still believe. Every mile was a small triumph over myself, and proof that such a victory was possible.

At night I wrote letters to my mother, the side of my hand stained with the slow-drying ink I dragged it over, the *siniestro* curse. In every letter I would struggle to convey something of the gratitude I felt, this almost unbearable love for the forces that remade me. I was driven, humble, obedient. A shining specimen of would-be priesthood. I was happy. The battered running shoes retired to the bottom of a steamer trunk, replaced by a new pair, a gift from Agostin. Agostin, the Liberationist. "It's nothing," he said, and maybe it was nothing, for him. How difficult it is for me, to this day, to accept the slightest kindness of another man. And the things I couldn't say; I never could speak, while running. Agostin talked, and from the safety of the empty white, I matched my steps to his, and drank the wind.

In 1970, I was given a missionary post in India. South America was the place of action, but young priests who could tackle the more exotic languages were in short supply. When I left I intentionally lost everyone, friends, colleagues, teachers and mentors, even the old, palsied Coach, who would have affectionately called me Chueco, no doubt, forever. And Agostin, who yearned for the foreign fields. The things that matter have a way of following, no matter how hard we run; they don't allow themselves to be lost. Agostin would get his wish, dead three years later somewhere in the Amazon, pushing too hard for Liberation Theology. I never learned the details. The news would reach me at St. Ignatius, where I would mourn him, locked behind an office door with a bottle of straight bourbon whiskey and a pile of student papers, mourning and scribbling corrections in red pen on the last night of term. "Here's to you, you damned savant," he said, the night before I left, and clinked my glass. "I won't pretend I'm not jealous." The last time I saw him, we were standing under trees in the three a.m. darkness. We had wanted to watch the sun come up one last time over the spires of the city, but it was snowing, and Agostin had only a thin jacket. The night was very cold. As we said our goodbyes he put his hands into my coat pockets, which makes me think he must have been drunk. "All good things," he said. Then, with a twisted grin, he added, "In paradisum." I remember that my face hurt from smiling, that the wurst of his coat left an impression on my cheek. And then we went our separate ways, and I tumbled face-first into the dent of my own head on a pillow, bed, alarm clock, Bengali phrasebook and breviary the only things in an empty room that hadn't been packed or dispensed with.

SIX

"Xavier Ochoa is marked by the Lady of the Seven Powers." So said Lupe María, the old woman who smelled like meat and mopped the floors at St. Ignatius and never swallowed the host when she took communion on Sundays, but slyly spat it out into a plastic bag and put it in her pocket. "He will have trouble with her." She pushed Tony into a broom closet on his second day of school, got out her oily Rider Waite cards, and showed him The Tower with its flames and double bolts of lightning, while he leaned against a shelf full of Clorox and stared down at the wiry grey hairs that sprang from the top of her head.

"Great calamity," she said. "*El regalo de las lenguas.* Change." She showed him a little figure of Oxossi, the Divine Hunter with his arrows and iron bow. And she licked her dark lips with her little cat's tongue and put away everything and made Tony promise not to tell. He hated the way she singled him out from the others, though perhaps it was simply because he reminded her of her own long ago children. Tony promised, and silently vowed that he would never cross Lupe María, who was, he thought, undoubtedly either a *curandera* or a *bruja*. He knew she would empty the wastebasket from Ochoa's office, steal the clippings of his hair from among the apple cores and crumpled student evaluations. She would tie them to the branches of trees in the dark of the moon, muttering the Lord's Prayer backwards, and birds would make nests out of them, soft as silk and curiously warm. The clippings would, like the hair of a dead person, grow continually with the secret, hidden will that remained in them, until they would hang from the trees, long as the tails of horses, dark with the fragrance of cedar. Tony knew everything he needed to know about witches, and what they could do. This Jesuit would do well, he thought, to keep out of the hands of Lupe María, even though the other boys knew her as Mrs. Ruiz and tracked through her mopping, never giving her a second's thought. Tony knew a *bruja* when he saw one; when Lupe María was near, he could feel Alvara twitching in his rib. A priest would not believe in such things. But it might be that Miguel Xavier Ochoa was already cursed, a windblown soul, wandering the school with unbuttoned cuffs, his shoes etched in mud.

"He was struck by a bolt of lightning in Quito," said Big Andre, a junior who knew everything. "Billy Cato told me. That's what made the white stripe. That's why he's sad."

Ochoa shook his hand, standing under the sky between Father Desmond and another priest whose name, Tony thought, was Leo Carol. "Hello," Ochoa said when Desmond introduced them, adding vaguely, "Basic Italian, next semester?"

Unsure of what he was being asked, Tony remained silent. At Ochoa's elbow, Carol made a small, impatient movement, and Ochoa turned back to him. "But what of our long-term goals?" he said. "Vigh believes a message of inclusion…" And Tony found himself dismissed by three benign Jesuits, who closed ranks and drifted off across the lawn of St. Ignatius, under the dripping locusts.

The St. Ignatius boys, mindful that the Connecticut fall would be brief, took advantage of any break in the weather by playing savage and ruthless football. Tony had played more soccer than football ("the American football," his relatives in Mexico called this sport) but he was an eager athlete, and was soon in the thick of the game, sprinting down the field, glorying in speed and the way it made his thoughts go white, which was when he felt the twitch of Alvara beside him. It was in looking for his cousin that Tony saw the language teacher, a smudge of black on the sun-warmed wall of the building, squinting in the light, holding an apple in his hand that was half red, half yellow, reading de Vaca's *Adventures in the Unexplored Interior of America*. Tony came to a halt twenty paces from the end zone and stood as if struck dumb in front of the priest, and Ochoa, distracted from his book by the frenzied yells of Tony's teammates, looked up at him. Ochoa smiled, amused, and raised his eyebrows, and then Tony felt all the air leave his lungs as he was broadsided by Michael Nunzio. By the time Tony climbed out from under the heaving pile, Ochoa was gone, and Tony had to go to the infirmary to have a bandage called a butterfly applied to his chin.

He had only ever known the study of private tutors, vacuous and cowering in the shadow of his father. His math skills were abysmal, his knowledge of the sciences scant. He would have failed that first semester, if Matt had not befriended him, patiently coaxing him along. Though his English, at least, was nearly perfect, he began to feel that Matt was acting the part of translator, and he stuck by the other boy's side, even accompanying Matt to choir practice, though his own voice was husky as a rusty swing;

he sat in the back, among the basses and the ne'er-do-wells, picking at the scab on his chin and irritably watching as Father Vigh coaxed Matt and his clear countertenor voice into one solo after another in praise of the Almighty. Tony was not a large boy, but he was agile, fast and strong, and it gave him vicious pleasure after hours of study to exact his vengeance on Matt on the football field. Matt seemed to accept this with neither grudge nor comment; Matt was, at the best of times, apathetic toward sports, cultivating it as part of his personal mystique. He was also the first avowed atheist Tony had ever met. "Seriously, Luna," he said. "Don't tell me you believe that crap."

The St. Ignatius boys had names for all the teachers. The favorite ones had several. Father Ochoa was known as "Stripes" and "The Ghost", the last partly because of the air of spectral sadness that surrounded him, but mostly because of his nocturnal wanderings. Ochoa, as far as anyone could tell, never slept. He wandered at night, walking with a ponderous tread at odds with his daylight grace. Sometimes Matt and Tony, also stricken with insomnia, would hear him pass by their dormitory in the night, and the sound of his measured step would spread a pall of holy fear over them that would cause them to stop breathing, as if the Angel of Death were passing over, and then, as his footsteps faded into the distance, they would shiver and laugh quietly at each other, their eyes pressed down by the dark. It was in the middle of one of these nights, when they had just listened to the footsteps passing on the other side of the door, that Michael Nunzio slipped into their dorm and sat down on the edge of Matt's bed, turning on the bedside light.

"I'm going to follow and see where he goes," said Michael.

"Don't," said Matt Kelly.

"Jesus, Matt. Could you be any more of a pansy ass?"

Tony snorted into his pillow, and Matt caved in, blushing. Nunzio looked around at Tony, and smiled slowly, his wicked, stallion's eyes uplit and narrowed. He jerked his chin in Tony's direction. "What's your damage?"

"Nothing."

"You coming, or what?"

"What's happening?" It was Andre Macarios, slipping in through the door behind Nunzio. He pushed his glasses higher up on his nose, blinking in the light. "Are you all going somewhere?"

"Not with you, Fatty. It's just me and Luna." Michael's Bronx accent flashed full of scorn and courage, and his eyes blazed at Tony in the dark, and Tony felt a flame of pride at having been chosen over Matt and the third-year boy.

"Just like a bunch of kids," said Matt, and nobody looked at him.

"Stripes is alright," said Andre slowly. "He's kind."

"Come on," said Nunzio, and he stood, tousling Matt's hair, and started for the door. Tony threw off the covers and followed him.

Andre said, "But what's the point?"

"It's a pissing contest," Matt told him.

Nunzio eased open the door. "Scared?"

"Chingada," said Tony. "Of what?"

Just before they closed the door, Tony caught a glimpse of Matt's face, his luminous eyes, and knew some frail thing for which he had no name had torn between them. Nunzio paid no heed to Andre, who loitered uncertainly in the dark hall and finally went back to his own room.

"If we get caught," said Nunzio, "No matter what happens, no matter what they do, you can't tell them what we're doing, right?" He whispered in Tony's ear, so close that Tony could feel his hot breath.

"Right."

They walked in their polyester pajamas down the deserted halls, shivering with nerves and cold, straining to hear that recognizable tread somewhere ahead of them. But The Ghost appeared to have stopped; they heard no signs of his movements in the dark. They passed by the doorway to the chapel.

"Come here. You stand here and keep watch." Michael grabbed a fistful of Tony's pajamas and pulled him to one side, planting him by the chapel door, pressing into his collarbone with his hard knuckles so that it made Tony breathe in very quickly through his nose. "Ow," he said, pushing Michael away. "Fuck." One had to endure a certain amount of pain, it seemed, to be in Nunzio's circle. "Where are you going, anyway?" Tony said.

"I'm going to go inside and see if he's in there." Michael said boldly. He peered at Tony. "But if you're scared..."

"I'm not scared. But why..?"

"Good. Wait for my signal." Michael edged the door of the chapel open, and the red sanctuary light spilled across the dark corridor. "Wait," he whispered. He smiled and tossed his head, and Tony smiled back, and then Michael slipped into the warmth and light of the chapel and closed the door behind him, so that the light was extinguished.

Tony waited in the dark, leaning against the doorframe, listening to the steady beating of his own pulse. It was right, he thought, that Michael Nunzio had chosen him from all the others, because he was different, like Nunzio was different; he had heard the stories. Tony knew that Michael's father, like his father, made deals, and though he still did not know exactly what this meant, he knew that it was the source of the danger and dark glamour he had been born into, and that he and Nunzio were not like the others, soft and complacent, but were in a class of their own. He respected Nunzio for his daring and toughness, and was glad that Nunzio recognized him, too. He thought briefly of his father, who seemed to think he was weak, of his mother who feared him, of Galo's admonition, given at the airport in Morelia, that there was no trusting these people, and crushed it down. He would outlast them all.

Then, as Tony continued to stand alone in the dark hallway, he thought of Matt, of his blank face and betrayed eyes, and he felt a ripple of anger, because Matt was back there in the darkness, waiting for him to return, and Tony would have to get free of him somehow, if he wanted to be friends with the likes of Nunzio. He felt sorry then, almost in the place where Nunzio's knuckles had bruised him, and he hung his head and clung to the doorway, blinking his eyes in the dark.

Tony had only just started to wonder what was taking Michael so long when he heard the sound of footsteps approaching rapidly. He knew from the sound of them that they were not Ochoa's, for they were heavy, and slightly uneven, even shuffling, as if one of the approaching legs had been detached and then sewn on again. Not knowing what else to do, Tony slipped into the chapel to warn Michael, but couldn't see him. The steps paused in the corridor; Tony ducked into a pew seconds before the door opened, revealing the blunt, pitted face of Father Farriday. The priest shambled heavily into the red square of light, pausing to listen.

Tony watched him through a gap in the wood, at once frightened and intrigued by Farriday's ugliness. Jealous, too, in a way; the man's misshapen ears and crumpled nose, which sat slightly untrue above the slit of is mouth, told of his years as a bare-knuckle boxer, fighting for glory in midnight car lots and pub basement rinks filled with bloody sawdust in Halifax before he came to God, and he wore the wounds like trophies now, carried into a tamer life. He was famous for his foul temper. He had been known to let fly with a cane. Farriday moved forward in the direction of the altar with a rolling, stalking gait (stalking God, Tony thought wildly), resting his hand on the back of each pew in turn, until Tony found himself staring up Farriday's nose. It seemed only loosely attached to his face; Tony wondered if the man could actually smell him. But Farriday's heart didn't seem to be in the chase tonight; abruptly as he had entered, he retreated back through the chapel door, letting it close behind him.

When the shambling steps had faded, Tony uncoiled himself from the cramped space between the pews. He didn't bother looking for Michael. He knew he had been had. Humiliated, he made his way back to the dormitory.

Michael had not chosen him for any other reason than to make a fool of him. That was clear. Michael, like the rest of the St. Ignatius boys, was foreign, treacherous, a bloodless enemy without honor. Tony could befriend none of them.

Strangely, he found he was unprepared for the sight of Matt sleeping peacefully, as if nothing had happened, as if Tony's pointless betrayal of him had also meant nothing.

Tony climbed into bed and pulled the blankets up to his chin. He tossed on his side, grinding his teeth together, and his eyes burned with furious tears. He would be an outcast here, an eternal emigrant, and there would be no solace to be found; he could not even speak and be understood without the harsh language of his enemies in his mouth, could not eat without accepting their ashen food.

Then, as he lay on his bed and burned with rage and sorrow, he thought of the female ghost. "Stay, if you want," he told her, whispering the words into darkness, and luminous arms snaked around him, his vision dazed with the fading blue burn of her eyes.

SEVEN

On the train from Delhi, weary with travel, I shared a cigarette with a man who pulled my sleeve and said, "Are you a priest?" When I said yes, he told me he was a murderer. He described to me how he had killed his own sister because she had committed adultery with a Swiss businessman. He and the girl's husband strangled her with a silken scarf, cut apart her body and threw it in the Ganges. He told me this in detail while we passed a damp cigarette back and forth. At the next station he left, and I felt my way to what passed for the train's lavatory, a rocking, closet-sized compartment with a hole in the floor, and was violently ill. Vedic sciences would hold the gut, not the heart, to be the center of all passions in the body. I have never been a good confessor. I still avoid it when I can.

It is a strange phenomenon that, during my time in India, people with no vestige of Christian belief would confide in me all sorts of things. I do not know if so many non-Catholics were driven to confide in me because I was available and patient, or because I was seen as less than man, devotee to an order of virgins and eunuchs with a frowning, solitary god, an empty shell of gentleness cast up in a foreign land. I am reminded of the old fable of the king's barber, who, on discovering that the king had the ears of a donkey under his crown, could not contain the secret even on pain of death, and whispered it into a hole in the ground. "Wait," I said to the man, before he left the train, "What of your absolution?" But he just turned his back, melting in among the other passengers on the platform.

In India I found two Indias, one a place of cities, of Bombay and Delhi and Calcutta, with pavement, hospitals, taxies, electric lights, tenements and Nepali prostitutes, the latter of which accosted me at an unwary turning down an alley, girls squawking, to my ear, like birds, clustering around me so determinedly that I came away half crushed, snagged by dirty fingernails; at the time I could only think of Agostin, and how he would have laughed. Every city I stopped in smelled the same, of petrol, joss sticks, sewage and cookery, smelled of death and rotting flowers.

The other India was rural, a place of villages and farmland, with thin boys riding water buffaloes, women who squatted in the dust and stared at white men like me, Sadhus decked with gold carnations, malaria, leprosy, sewers in the streets and benightedness, smell of incense, smell of rot. In the India of electric lights I saw long-haired Americans smoking hash and children in back alleys burning plastic to keep warm at night. I saw a smiling woman with no legs and no arms begging on a railway platform, and crowds of people walking by. I saw roadside shrines full of gods and rats and sleeping cattle, the divas with twisted limbs and eyes painted closed, and a sudden horde of monkeys stealing bananas from a truck, dodging boys who beat at them with canes. Once, while in the middle of a crowded street, I felt a tug at the strap of my bag, and turned to see a pickpocket with a razor in his hand; it was a strange moment, the two of us shocked, staring at each other. "It's alright," I said. "I'll give it to you. What do you need?" And he ran, and did not cut me.

I was not yet thirty. I imagined a place of absolutes, where doubt did not enter. I wanted to be simple and pure. Among innocent people, I told myself, I, too, would be an innocent.

Benedictines welcomed me to their rural monastery on the last leg of my journey to the eastern border. I would rest with them for two days before meeting a local guide, a man called Rohan. A young French novice was charged with showing me around their grounds, practically falling over with excitement; visitors were rare, I gathered. I followed him around through the vegetable gardens and outbuildings, Ora et Labora, trying not to look as jet-lagged as I felt. The novice had weak grey eyes and a dimple in his chin, a red forelock peeking from under his hood, a nice smile spoiled somewhat by the way he blinked at you, using his whole face. He spoke to me politely in halting Spanish, though I could just as easily have addressed him in French. He chuckled to tell me of their ongoing difficulties with monkeys climbing over fences and absconding with yams. "You do good work here," I said, rather blandly, and he inclined his dark hood, looking pleased. "How long have you been here?" I asked him. His name, appropriately, was Beauclerc. "I mean, you, yourself?" He had been there only nine months, three as a postulant, but already had perfected the Benedictine way of standing, I thought, on the rare occasions when he was at rest, gingery head tipped forward, hands clasped and hidden in his sleeves, anonymous as a goose. It was a sublime kind of humility that I, in my own training, had never known, and I found myself both touched and jealous. "I will pray for the success of your mission," Beauclerc would tell me, before I left. "And I for yours," I would say. The first evening I spent in the place I bowed out of the service with an apology, saying I had a headache, and Beauclerc brought me a carafe of cool water, beaded in the heat, and two aspirin. I knew it was a part of his novitiate, looking after the guest, but I was grateful, and said so. He nodded silently. He hovered in the doorway for a moment with a look of submissive concern and then left me alone; Beauclerc was under a vow of silence during dark hours. From the windowless sleeping cell I could hear them all singing together in their chapel, an order far more ancient than my own. They would have sung just those words a thousand years ago while peasants trembled in fear of Mongols or a solar eclipse, the brothers clustered in their togetherness, their humble, simple love, their garden hoes and salt-less food and awe of the unknown, singing for the traveling sun. *Libera nos*, I mouthed along with them, bitter aspirin dissolving on my tongue. *Salva nos*. The heat made it impossible to sleep; I would never grow used to it entirely. In the daylight I shared their Liturgy of Hours, and sat with them at meals. The abbot asked me some questions about Manresa out of politeness, squinting up his yellow old eyeballs. He said, "Leave us to our labor. You rest until you feel better, Father Michael," anglicizing my name. "You look tired." I thanked him for his hospitality, relieved to be in the presence of a fellow initiate after days of solitary travel. If I encountered a monk on the garden paths, he would draw aside to let me pass, smiling, never failing to acknowledge me as an outsider.

When I first came to the Sundarbans they told me I was not to go among the mangroves alone, because of Dakshin Rai. I was not to leave the compound at night, for a tiger had already killed nine souls and a water buffalo that year, and Dakshin, furthermore, hated Europeans. Only the honey hunters and the fishermen entered the mangroves, Rohan said, and the women gathering firewood, and never without first offering prayers to the forest goddess Bonbibi and Dakshin Rai, the tiger god. Besides that, they all wore masks on the backs of their heads so that the tigers would not attack them from behind, a tiger's favorite way of attacking; though they are all-powerful, they have a distaste for looking into the eyes of their prey. Shy killers, so it seems. Here was a strange distinction that confounded me, though most likely it was because of my imperfect command of the local tongue: Dakshin Rai was both the tiger god, and the tiger, any tiger, and when a human life was taken, it was both tragedy and necessary sacrifice. One did not tempt such gods. Other than those who were required by necessity to do it, no one ever went into the mangrove jungle alone. It was a place of death.

The village had no name I was ever aware of, and was on the edge of the great tidal mangrove forest. Rohan came to collect me at the Benedictine monastery. We took a truck, then a cart, and then a boat to reach the village, navigating a maze of drowned forest and overgrown waterways dotted by islands. We passed one such island where the bushes were hung with scraps of colored fabric, waving in the breeze like tiny flags, and I asked Rohan what they were. He would not tell me, saying only, "These are tribal people." By this he meant that they were neither Hindu nor Muslim, devotees to a far older faith. Mosquitoes savaged every inch of exposed flesh, so that I eventually gave up and let them have it. I held onto the side of the boat, balancing myself against the gentle rocking, wondering what level of hell the Order had sent me to.

We arrived at the village late in the evening. It was a scattered collection of huts on stilts, the windows covered by bars. Behind these bars, a multitude of dark faces peered down at me like silent, caged birds. Rohan told me Sundarban tigers are fierce because they drink only salt water, which makes them hungry for man's flesh. I do not know if this is true, but the compound he led me to, the place where I was to live for the next eight months, was girdled by a fence of corrugated tin, nine feet high and strong enough, he said, to fend off a tiger. The mission was the only building on ground level; the Western missionaries who built it had not listened to the advice of the local people, and had built it as they would any building outside the tiger country. The iron fence had been added later, after a young nun from Uppsala was pulled from her bed at night and eaten, tattered threads of black cloth hanging in the low branches of the mangroves the only trace that remained. I listened to these and other warnings about cobras and malaria, crocodiles and militant socialists, but if Rohan was trying to frighten me he did not succeed. Cast adrift so suddenly in this strange world, I saw only an opportunity to prove myself.

In the compound, I had a small room to sleep and pray in, with a hard bed, a picture of St. Ignatius nailed to the wall, and a cross. There was nothing of beauty or comfort, just little sundries left behind by previous missionaries, a clock, an ash tray, a few books, *The Bacchae*, Dante and *King Lear,* all in the Italian, their inner covers bearing the signature of a Father Domenico Falco. I suppose the last missionary, this Falco, thought that I might be lonely, and want to smoke or read. There was an old piano, out of tune, a turntable and a small stack of records. I went through them, mostly classical with the odd addition of Nina Simone; Falco grew more and more interesting. I had never had occasion to read Shakespeare or Euripides in Italian. In moments of solitude, when my thoughts should have been turned to God, I was more likely to read of Lear and his treacherous daughters. I tried to be upset only out of view of the Indians, in the mission kitchen, painted dull yellow with its fan and dirty screens, or the windowless bathroom. Insects immolated themselves every night in the flickering light fixtures, huge moths and iridescent beetles. I was unable to sleep for the first few nights in that place. So I prowled, opening drawers and cupboards, listening to Nina's reedy howl. "*Ne me quitte pas*," she moaned, Americanly, in her pained, throbbing voice. I wondered if Falco, the owner of the record, was proficient only in Italian, since most of the songs seemed to be about those husky love-struggles of men and women, an odd choice at best for a priest (such were my purist notions at the time). Perhaps Falco, like me, had simply lain with his ear on the floor to feel the quake of Nina's voice, filtering out the words; *don't leave me, don't leave me, don't leave me. Everything can be forgotten.*

For some reason, Falco had left behind his Spiritual Exercises. I stalked him through the margins of the book, reading his cramped, womanish handwriting, his youthful, rather pedestrian insights. "To what do I cling too tightly?" he had asked. This must have been a first assignment, I thought, a missionary priest in his twenties like me, an Italian with a taste for American jazz. Where could he be now? The book smelled of cigarettes. A snake fell from behind the stove, a gentle black thing with dish-like eyes that slithered along the baseboards, giving off an acrid reek of fear. They had issued me a prescription of tetracycline pills I was to take in preventative doses, against malaria and God only knew what. In a moment of theatrical martyrdom, I gave the pills to Rohan, and told him to make sure they found those who needed them. Drugs of every kind were almost impossible to come by.

A few days after my arrival, Priya came to the little open-air chapel, which I was in the process of scrubbing. She went barefooted, as all the village women did, and I was kneeling on the floor so that the first thing I saw was her right foot, slight, dark, the ankle cuffed with a string of small glass beads, and the edge of a green sari. She greeted me haltingly in Italian, and I watched her smile in surprise when I answered her in Bengali. She had brought me a gift of carnations to welcome me. She had come with her brother Lal, the two so alike they were probably twins, though Lal was less trusting than Priya and hung back in the doorway, like a Chital in the shadows of the jungle, watching. Priya was shy, and kind to me, though we could hardly understand each other at first, my Bengali being what it was. Falco had baptized her Catherine, after Saint Catherine of Siena, by which I was, of course, expected to call her. But in my heart she was always Priya. Priya, she told me, meant "Beloved." It never suited her, the name of that young Italian stigmatic; ah, Falco, you poor devil. Is it not human arrogance to name something that does not belong to you? But Falco, it seemed, had fallen into the trap of Adam, naming according to his need.

It had been a while since there had been a priest at the mission; my predecessor Falco had apparently left over a year ago, and I learned from Rohan that it was because of the cholera outbreak. All the whites, he said, had left the area at once when the locals started dying. He said this without judgment, as if such a thing were expected, the way of the world. Rohan had lost a young child to the cholera, and Priya and Lal had been left orphans, the sole survivors of a family of six. This, too, he related to me without a trace of blame for the missionary who fled when most needed, for the aid that never arrived, for the drugs that never reached the countryside; the village's sole defense against the cholera had been the drums they beat to drive out the evil spirits. He added only that many other children had died as well, and many elderly. In India there are no graves. The dead are burned, the ashes thrown into running water, every trace carried away.

Though Rohan did not seem to hold any ill will toward the mission, I felt a strangeness toward me from the people, a withholding, and I thought that when they looked at me they must see the face of the man who came before me, Falco, who I was told hardly spoke a word of Bengali and fled when the cholera came, another ill-informed stranger in their midst. They were tolerant of my presence, curious about my religious practices, and hesitant to reveal their own to me. As Rohan had said, they were tribal, speaking both Bengali and an older language specific to their village. Their religion, as far as I could ascertain, was an animistic one, preoccupied with forest spirits and the phases of the moon. They did not seem to have high hopes for me. The first month I said Mass in the little chapel, which was really just a roof of corrugated tin raised up on six rough-cut poles, there were only six or seven curious villagers in attendance, Priya and Lal among them, squatting on the ground and fanning themselves in the oppressive morning heat. It felt wrong to stand above them on my little platform, saying Mass over the tops of their heads. So I said Mass seated as they were, with my legs folded over, and in Bengali, if awkwardly. They seemed to like this, though the first time I sat in the dust among them they were shocked, looking at one another, and then beginning to laugh, eyes crinkling, teeth flashing. Also, there was no wine in the village to make the sacrament, India being under prohibition. For the host, we used ashy flatbread, baked in the Indian manner on the inside of an oil drum stove, and the milk of a white cow. I felt in my heart that this was right, for what better to serve as the blood of our savior than the milk of a sacred animal? Priya and Lal assisted me in my duties after Mass and often ate with me in the evenings, sharing whatever simple food I had on hand.

Nights, I would sweat under my mosquito nets, listening to the forest noises carried in by the sluggish breeze, the yap of rhesus monkeys, the calls of night birds, and often the drums of the village. I went to bed with Falco's spiritual exercises, his humble, charming stupidity accosting me from the margins; "Do I accept the edict of God in my heart, even when I am sick, or otherwise suffering?" Rohan gave me a pistol, and I kept it beside my bed next to the breviary, though I didn't like to look at the thing. "What am I supposed to do with this, Rohan?" I asked him. But he wouldn't take it back.

I decided that the soul of the village was in the river. Along the riverbanks, the women walked all day, dragging nets to catch fish for supper. At midday, clothes were washed in the brown waters, and laid out on flat rocks to dry. When I went down to the river in the mornings, there would be mist rising from its waters, golden clouds of midges, and boys watering their buffaloes and white, sloe-eyed cattle. Girls washed their hair and bathed, wearing plain white shifts that floated around them, calling out with laughter while they wrung the water from their hair. A month after my arrival, I forsook the stagnant, lizard-filled shower at the compound, and washed instead in the river every morning. This simple act won me more converts from the village than anything else I said or did there, for though I was initially a source of general wonder, wading into the brown, crocodile-infested river in my underclothes, they soon became used to me and welcomed my presence among them. I believe they saw my daily bathing as a sign of reverence for the reality of their lives. I started seeing new faces at Mass. From time to time, there would be a handful of flowers waiting for me at the compound gate.

The malaria caught up with me after two months. I had not been prepared for the harshness of the disease; I hear it is worse for some constitutions, and I have never been resilient. For days I was consumed with fever and fits of shaking, and could take only milk and water. Priya nursed me, coming every day to attend on me (I did not know at the time that she actually never left my side, sleeping on a mat outside my door). In the depths of fever there were many visions, but what I dreamed of most often was Araba, snow collecting in the cart tracks, the neighing of the horses in the knacker's yard. I must have described the scene in my sleep, and in Bengali too, for Priya asked me later about snow, which she had never seen even in a picture and could not readily imagine. I told her it was like white ashes, but had no way to describe cold. I did not tell her about the horses. Priya touched my hair, the white streak that stood out in the black, and asked me if it was from the snow. I told her no, I had been marked that way by an accident. To this she said, "Poor Father."

"No," I said, "it was a very long time ago. I don't remember it." She held my head up and fed me congee, wiped the sweat off my forehead, listened to my raving in Spanish, English, Italian, Bengali and, when I dreamed of Araba, Basque. Sometimes Lal would come, and sit like a ghost in the corner of my room, a dark phantom, indistinguishable from the shadows.

I dream of those butchered horses, and the twins, to this day. Though I try, I cannot say what it was about them that affected me so powerfully, except for the simple fact that I was jealous of them. I thought of them as innocents, a girl and boy who wandered blithely through the world. I should have asked them many things, I should have seen the sadness in their shared being. Instead, they threatened me. I was jealous of them, a stranger in their home, and I meant no harm. These are the stories I tell myself at night when I am not sleeping, when the horses whicker in their pen and churn the snow.

When my sickness came to an end I went to the river, supported by Priya and Lal, one on each side. All along the path to the river, people approached, hesitantly at first and then many at a time, touching my hands and my clothes, even the stripe in my hair, whispering in Bengali. They welcomed me with whispers back to the living. I was exhausted by the time I got to the riverbank, and stood for a time, leaning on Priya, staring into the water. The river showed me a face no longer pale but tanned by the sun, with a week's growth of beard, gaunt cheekbones and blazing eyes, hair grown wild as the mane of a horse. The river showed me my face, and then it told me who I was; in its waters, at the end of the time of fever and visions, I had arrived in India, no longer held apart by memories of the world I had known before.

Lal began to speak to me. He told me there was a man in the village who said I knew nothing of sin, because I had never seen a tiger. This was so curious that I asked Lal to bring me to this man, which he reluctantly did. The man looked to be in his fifties, possibly older, though really it was difficult to tell. He was sitting outside his hut braiding a snare to catch birds, and his body was black as a stick and so thin that his chest was concave, pressed in on itself.

There were scars on the side of his face, parallel slashes of raised silver, one of which ran through his left eye, a great white demon eye. The other eye was wary, and flicked between me and the grass strands he was braiding; all the while we spoke, he never stopped braiding the snare. Lal and I sat on the ground, and I asked the man about tigers.

The man answered my question with a question, a trick I associated with my own order. He asked me if the Jesuits thought it was a sin to kill a tiger, and I said no, strictly speaking it was not a sin to kill any animal, though it was not virtuous. "But without the tigers," I reminded him, "the Sundari trees would all have been cut down generations ago, and there would be no livelihood for the village. In a way," I concluded, "it is a sin to destroy God's noble works, like the forest and the tiger. The Jains are learned, and they believe it is a sin to kill an ant." As soon as I finished speaking I realized that I had contradicted myself.

This was not lost on the man; in fact, he seemed to see me as rather simple, or at least deluded. "You do not talk like a priest, Father," he said, stressing the last word with a slight smirk, and I knew that this was true.

"I am not much of a priest," I said.

He gave a dismissive grunt. "You are very young." In the tribal language, he muttered something, and I looked at Lal.

"He said, 'They've sent us another milky-faced boy to do the work of a man,'" Lal said. And he couldn't help smiling. I bowed my head. It did seem ridiculous to pretend that I knew more of the world than this man, who was twice my age.

He said, "The Jains may be learned, but they do not live here. How can it be a sin to take your own life, as the missionaries say, and also a sin to kill death?" Then, before

I could answer, he said, "Until you feel a tiger, you don't know. Feel Dakshin Rai's breath, Father," he said ironically, glaring through his good eye, "and then tell me about sin."

I asked him to help me understand. He pointed to the scars on his face, to the white demon eye, and said, "This is where they stitched my face in the hospital. I was in a truck to get there, but I don't remember. I only remember how the tiger felt."

Lal and I sat in the dust, waiting till the man continued. "The tiger was hot," he said. "Its windpipe was hard but its belly was soft, spongy. When its claws were in me I knew I could not escape so I did not fight. You understand me?"

"Yes."

"I hugged the tiger, I threw my arms around it."

His hands went still on the grass rope, and he looked at me with his proud, wary eye. "I do not know why, Father, but Dakshin let me go. He let me go."

Lal walked me back to the compound at dusk, and before he turned to go I stopped him at the gate.

"Lal, thank you. What do they call that man?"

"He is called the Tiger Prince." And he flashed a brilliant smile like a star, hidden away just as quickly, and turned from me into the darkness.

I saw them by the river in the morning, Priya and Lal, together as always. Priya had just emerged from the river, her skin sparkling with the drops of water, and Lal stood behind her, combing her hair with his fingers. I was struck by the careless intimacy of the scene; how close, how natural they were. They appeared like pagan gods to me, a pair of deities unspeakably beautiful, oblivious to my presence. I watched them together, splashing in the water, and my heart turned over as I withdrew into the sheltering trees, the panic so immediate I could taste it, black and bitter on my tongue. At night the drums in the village beat into the first hours of morning. I took them into the compound the very next day, and, with the accompaniment of a badly tuned Spinet piano, warped by damp and pillaged of ivory, I taught them to sing a few simple hymns. Lal refused to take part but looked on, sitting in the window, the pale soles of his bare feet dusty and gripping the sill. Priya learned by ear with amazing speed, both notes and Latin text, *Agnus Dei, qui tollis peccata mundi*, and sang while standing on one foot as I struggled away at the battered piano, her naked voice joyless and veiled in a kind of shadow, like a grief cry. She made me a bracelet of crimson thread and tied it around my wrist. In the evening it rained, and the young people and I ran around the compound, finding leaks and catching them in pans and buckets. We ate our dinner standing in the kitchen. I put a record on while I washed up, and they both sat near the turntable, heads tipped to the side in a fair impression of the Edison-Bell dog. After some coaxing, Priya stood on the tops of my feet, and we circled the room, waltzing to Valse Triste. "Why do you know how to dance?" she wanted to know. "Priests do not dance."

"Who told you that? Was it Falco?"

She shrugged.

I told her that my mother had taught me, not so long ago when I was small as Priya, dancing in the kitchen just like this. My young, lonely mother, waltzing with her eldest son. "But we had no turntable, not even a radio," I said. "She used to hum, and count out the time."

And was she pretty, Priya wanted to know?

"Yes," I said. "She was the prettiest, kindest person in the world. Except for you, little bird."

Priya tapped my shoulder reprovingly. "You say it was when you were a child, small as me. But I am not a child."

"Silly me. It's because you are so small and light, and I forget these things. Have a care, or I'll step on you with my clumsy paws."

"Feet!" she said. "Not paws! The word is feet! Paws are what a dog has." Priya laughed at this, turning with me around the room. Lal sat on his haunches in the shadows, watching.

In the night, I was awakened by a series of taps. At first I thought them part of my dream, or the sizzle of rain over sheet tin. Eventually I realized that someone was tossing stones over the compound wall, some of which were striking the screen. There was smoke in the air. At the gate I found Priya, soaking wet and shaking. Behind her I could see the edge of a red sheet of light moving up and down beyond the trees, where I knew the village to be; without the scent of smoke, I would not have realized the gentle motion was fire. Her words were too fast for me to understand. She kept repeating something about the "other village." Peering through the rain and low-hanging smoke, I could see figures running to and fro.

"Is it bad?" I asked her. She stared dumbly at me. "Where is it?"

"The house," she said, and I knew she was speaking of the hut she shared with her brother. Her face pulled tight at the edges, as if fighting down laughter, and she put out a hand to the rain. "It won't spread further. Too wet." She gestured and spoke in short bursts, trying to make it easier for me to understand. But her hands flew; she couldn't seem to slow them. "Stay here tonight," she said.

"Where is Lal?"

"In the forest. They wanted me to come here. They would have...I had to come here. They won't find him."

"Who wanted you to come here? Have you been attacked?"

"The other village," she said again. Her hand flickered out to the north. I had never been to the neighboring community, knew of it only because of something Rohan had said in passing. I knew it was a village larger than ours, and not easily accessible. I knew there was a strict panchayat, a council that, as I understood it, oversaw domestic issues and matters of family honor. But why anyone from the neighboring community should concern themselves with ours was beyond my understanding.

Looking back on that evening and the things Priya tried to tell me, I can no longer be sure she intended to say "the other village." It could have been that her meaning was more complex than I could grasp at the time, given my shaky understanding of the language, that there was a fault line dividing our village into two separate places, that no threat from a neighboring community existed. It could have been that the "others" Priya spoke of were not strangers to her.

"They wanted me to come here," Priya said. "They told me, 'Run to him.' "

I started forward from the compound gate, and she threw her weight against me, pushing me back inside. "No!" she said. "Everyone is safe; they will stay out of sight. They wanted me to come here. You are not safe. You must not go down there tonight. Do you understand?" She was crying softly in the tribal language, a low muttering I couldn't untangle. "They want to frighten you, so that you will leave. You should leave. But not tonight."

"People may be hurt." I was still trying to move past her in the gate. "Go inside. Turn the lock behind you. There's a click, when it goes."

"You stay here!" she said, three sharp words in Italian. There were tears on her cheek. She smudged them off with the back of her hand, violent, exhausted. I realized that in our shared panic I had fallen out of Bengali and had been speaking whatever language presented itself, that she had answered me in kind as best she could.

"Why is this happening?" It was all I could think to say.

She cast her eyes down, rain dripping from her lashes. Her voice was scarcely audible over the tumult. "They say you have come to possess them, and I am your whore." She looked up at me, face carefully blank. "They say I am not a good woman. They say I should go and be with you. Do you understand?"

"Who are they?"

She didn't answer.

"Listen, the monastery has a telephone. We can go when it's light. We can send for the police."

"Please," she said, "They say you are a devil." Her eyes pleaded with me, large and glassy in the dark. "They do not know that you are a good man. You are not like him."

"But who are they?"

"Listen!" She gave a low sob, pushing at me, her feet sliding in the mud. "They say you are a devil! They say you should be driven away, like the other devils."

"Surely the council..."

"Listen to me!"

"But..."

"Go in!"

"Catherine," I said, clinging, for some reason, to her borrowed name. As if a tame name would make the village a tamer place. It had never seemed more hollow and contrived.

Priya seemed to sense my uncertainty, or perhaps there was something else in me that frightened her; she stopped shoving at me, pulling away instead. She was going to run. I could see it in her face, her eyes roving over the tree line, plotting an escape, and there was no time, I thought, for any of that. As she turned I caught her wrist and pulled her back toward the gate, hard, so that her light frame snapped against itself, all her weight swung out against her wrist, and we clung together like two acrobats falling from a height, leaning, connected at the pivot of our hands. My grip dwarfed Priya's wrist, thumb overlapping fingers. She was fighting with me; it was ridiculous, she was so small and weak, and I couldn't understand why she should resist, perhaps wanting to flee to the forest with her brother. But she flung herself away from me in the gate, making a high, frantic braying, hair swung back in an arc around her face. She was pawing her heels into the wet ground, crying pitifully; I didn't know what else to do but hold on. I couldn't understand her. She struggled with me, and then I caught hold of her other arm, walking her backward into the gate. "Stop it," I said. "There isn't time." I had to drag her the last few steps, holding her up. She sagged, refusing to walk, wrists held out pleadingly before her.

When I had gotten her inside, I closed and locked the gate, and she stood there dumbly in the compound, head down in the rain. The loose fabric of her garment, spotted with rain, shivered across her breast. "I can't let you go back out there," I said. Her resistance annoyed me; couldn't she understand what was happening? "Look, it doesn't matter what they think." From the village came the sound of laughter now, singing, jeering, the small crowd of men drinking contraband liquor, trying to burn Priya's house in the rain.

"Priya," I said sharply. Her face snapped upward, huge, calf-like eyes, swamped with fear. "I can't let you go out there. You understand me? But you're safe here. I won't let anything happen to you, not ever. Do you understand?" Black, blank eyes.

I extended a hand to her. "Will you come with me?"

We spent the night sitting side by side on the floor near my bed with our backs to the wall, Priya wrapped in blankets, me with the heavy pistol in my hand, an unnecessary precaution since no one tried to enter the compound. We sat close together in silence, listening to the shouts and laughter from the village, until the night was nearly over, and the only sound was the hush of warm rain.

The sky paled. In the hours before morning, Priya's exhaustion slowly overcame her terror, her head rested on my shoulder, and she slept while I kept watch. In sleep, she reached her arm around me. The heat in combination with the girl's clinging proximity made me feel twitchy and slightly nauseous, malarial. I was frightened and I wanted to be alone, as if being touched in a weakened state would only add to all the hysteria. I dozed off under the reproachful eyes of St. Ignatius, the books of Falco who had run away, watching lizards climb the mosquito netting, clutching the absurd pistol. This is how we were in the morning, when Lal found us after climbing a tree and dropping in over the compound fence; Priya with an arm around me, and I with my cheek fallen to the top of her head, pistol in hand. Lal stood over us, wordless, and I looked up at him, feeling slow and stupid with sleep. His expression was unreadable. After a while he simply said, "They've gone." And he looked at the floor, backed slowly out of the room.

Priya stirred against me, and I touched her hair, its heavy

locks, tangled. It was pleasant, the weight of her head against my chest. "Priya." I whispered Basque she could not understand into the damp curve of her ear, little endearments, not with any real intent but because I wanted comforting myself. Who hears the confessions of a priest?

She nestled closer, soft and heavy with sleep. And I felt, truly for the first time, the full extent of what I had given up. Not sex, not love, not a family. But that particular gesture of physical reassurance. Someone's heavy head on the middle of my chest. Just then, it seemed important.

"What did you say?" she mumbled.

"I said, 'Sleep, little bird.' That's you. You're a sleepy little bird. Go back to sleep."

I watched her fluttering eyelids as she struggled to wake up.

It was as if a curtain was suddenly drawn aside in my mind, and I saw my greatest fear spread out before me, a vast nothingness, void, in which all faith and striving vanished in a blink like oceans pouring through a hole in the world. It shocked me; as a young priest, I was not used to that place, looking over the edge of doubt's well. There was no barrier between myself and it but the soft little person sitting next to me, this person who needed me. I understood something about Priya, the full weight of her sadness and the things she had chosen not to confide in me.

Priya opened her eyes and looked up. "Lal?"

"He was just here. He's alright. They've gone."

Priya let out a sigh and grasped my hand, pressed her forehead against it. She was muttering, making a strange chant, half singing what I realized were Hail Marys in Bengali. On her lips, the familiar words sounded eerie, pagan and exotic. I felt like a fraud sitting there, Priya's hand clasped in mine, listening to her recite the words in her strange way with more sincerity than I had ever had myself.

"Priya," I said, "are you going to tell me?"

She said, "You are a good man."

"I am your servant, and your friend."

The man had followed her down to the river and caught her in the woods. He would not always wait for night to fall. He said that if she didn't, he would kill her. No one would look for her, when she was gone. He said he could hurt her brother, if she didn't. She spoke on, in a steady, low, relentless voice, until I could hardly bear to hear any more, but still she went on. When she finished the story, she told it again, repeating it over and over, until I stopped listening, watching the movements of her face. She nestled close to me, her fingers curled into the fabric of my shirt. The girl did not cry. She leaned on me, morning light bleeding in at the window. She was small enough to be held by me completely.

In the room, insects fled from the sunlight, following the night into the wall's deep seams. I held Priya's head and kissed the crown of it. "I'm sorry, Priya, I'm sorry," I said, unable to summon a customary blessing. "It's not your fault. This will pass." How well I knew that this would never be true. I had shed the confessor's code, among other things, seeking comfort in the offering of it. I spoke the words I longed to hear. "There will be a reckoning for this." But this place was far from the sunlit walks of the Spanish seminary, far from any notion of what I knew as justice.

I wondered what it would be like if this child were mine, and taken away from here. Mine to comfort, mine to spoil, mine to protect. My daughter, my own child. We could set the world right. I had a sudden deranged image of us, walking together through a summer street fair, a tame

European city and the girl younger than she had ever been allowed, bright smile and a colored pinwheel, a white cotton dress and white socks, my indulgence, applying lotion to her nose, her skipping. I could be good because she would demand it of me. A view of the sea, a sun-warmed boardwalk, and all that was good and innocent in the world. I needed her to need me. I needed all of them to need me. I found myself wishing she would cry, because anything would have been better than that awful silence of a child that suffered like an animal, without grudge or hope, as if she didn't know another way of being. "Little bird," I said, rocking, "hush, I'm here."

While waiting for my placement, I had spent time as the assistant to a parish priest in Barcelona, Father Derosa. Among his many objections to me, he said I was too soft as a confessor. "It's all gone to the dogs," he said. "People come looking for a shoulder to cry on, but what they need is a guide. The troubled ones will come to you like flies to honey because you're young and not bad looking, and they will mistake that for the mark of a kindred spirit. It strokes your vanity, being liked. There's nothing more despicable than a narcissistic priest." He was one of the old guard, brusque, moral and ugly, like an unfashionable saint. He snapped his fingers under my nose. "Wake up, dreamer, there's a war on," he said. "Vale, vanitas." But his kindness ran deep. He brushed breadcrumbs from his soutane, and I remember sitting there, looking at his sad eyes and hairy nostrils, and thinking he was old. What can we offer, if not solace? Now I saw the wisdom in it. My experience had changed the way I listened, but I couldn't save any of them. I was in my twenties; what did I know? "God takes no half-measures," Derosa said once. We were sitting together by the radiator in the Barcelona rectory. I remember that I was looking down into the street, trying to seem politely heedful of his words, which, in the way of Derosa's sermons, wandered slowly and in ever-widening circles, like a horse dragging a broken plow. I remember a radio playing faintly in the background, filling up the silence between the words. I remember that I was surreptitiously flexing the toes of one foot back toward my shin, stretching a sore Achilles tendon.

Derosa said, "God does not creep in, like a beggar on La Rambla, to coax us one penny at a time to sanctity. He will ask for your entirety, and when you give in He will consume you. God has more hunger for us than we for Him. We take little bites, but God devours. That, mijo, is what ordination means."

"What remains, after this consumption? We have our will. Ordination is to become one's self an act of will, loving God. It is to serve with every breath, every thought, and every physical act. A burden? Why so? It is easy! You do not spend all day continually reminding yourself of your own name, do you? You simply are. It is like that. Give yourself, give your life. Illuminate every action with your love of God. For you can be sure that God has chosen you. That is why it is a state of being, not just a vocation. To be once a priest is to be a priest forever, because God is not like man, and He does not abandon one He loves."

He said, "Serve God. It is an active state. You have come here empty, thinking, like some Agnostic, that God lives inside the gaps. You think He will contain you, and provide you with that sense of self you lack. But when I look at you, I see a man so hollowed out, so frightened of his own existence, I wonder that there is anything left to offer God in return. I've seen it before. With you, it is like spiritual psychopathy. And so this sacrifice that should be joyful will be, to you, a sanatorium. How do you serve God? Where is your joyful, active humility? That is what you should be thinking. Until you meet God blow for blow, there will be no haven for you. Until you see the flame of God in every face, there is no haven for you. Don't pity this old man, don't smile at me like you know better; save it for the ladies of the parish. You don't fool me."

I held the dark image of a man without a face. If he had existed outside of me, I would have taken pleasure in hunting him down, indulging all the violence in me, wrapping myself in the mantle of avenging another child. Vanity, Derosa would have said. Vanity. I was not in the business of revenge, or personal scores, or even justice. My duty was to feel for Priya's rapist the same love I felt for her. The same love I felt for God.

This I know; the years have only proven it to me. If God is not behind the eyes of a sinner, He is nowhere.

"Don't tell him," Priya said. "Don't tell Lal. He wouldn't like it if you knew." She turned her eyes up to me, and brushed the tears from my lashes, salting her knucklebones. And she said it again, as she had when I was sick: "Poor Father." She leaned, head heavy, and the air was thin, that asthmatic, frightened little boy pulling in the darkness at my sleeve, still there. I didn't like to remember how he had wept without sound, that boy who had been me, thinking he was too grown up for all that. How he sat under a dark porch light, counting off the minutes. Counting, waiting until it was safe to return to himself. He had never stopped counting.

I said, "Tell me who. Give me a name."

She didn't answer, speaking to me only with her stillness. With my thumb, I traced the sign of the cross on her warm forehead.

"Priya," I said, "did you tell this to Falco?"

A sudden noise from beyond the compound made her sit up, one hand against my chest, and said, "Where is Lal?"

She left me there, just like that, narrow calves flashing as she fled. She left me with the scent of her skin on my clothes and all around me, clean as rain, and a profound feeling of exhaustion. It was Sunday morning, and the feast of St. Cecilia. In an hour or so, I was expected for Mass. When I emerged from the compound, I saw smoke still rising from among the huts, and people clustered just outside my gate, men with adzes, plastic buckets, stick bundles, fishing nets, and women clutching children, all hanging back and watching me with wary eyes. I searched those eyes, rage and contempt building in my heart. And suddenly I was shouting at them. "Who was it, which one of you?" I drew myself up, taking advantage of my height to stand taller than them all, face raised to the light, feeling for a moment capable of bringing down the thunder of God. "Who knew, and did nothing?" They looked at me with mistrust and uncertainty. Someone had splashed red paint on the compound's tiger fence, a garish smear in the sunlight, dripping in long streaks into the dirt.

When I was ten years old, my father took me to his place of work to see the horses being killed. I was afraid of my father, his bigness and his rage, his dark-haired forearms and the mean slant to his left eye, the grisly badge of having once been kicked by a horse. He came home in the evenings smelling of blood, and would hang his leather knacker's apron on a peg by the kitchen door. He hated my delicacy, my snagging breaths. He hated the way I avoided other children, my precise speech, the way I was always hanging on my mother. He was the sort of man who never showed his anger, but would strike suddenly and without warning. Or it would be all warning, and that was the worst, a cool and methodical torture, when he would withhold punishment, saying, Tomorrow morning. Just wait. You'll hear me climb the stair, and know it's time. The coolness of his rage was the most frightening thing. The day he took me to the yard, a horse managed to snap one of the ropes that tied his leg, thrashed free and bucked through the mud, dragging the men at the ends of the remaining ropes. He crashed against the fence where I stood, my father's big hands clamping down on my shoulders. He must have looked like he was embracing me, a proud, paternal hand on the shoulder, but I knew better; the hands were cruel. He touched me, and I froze, a fawn ducking low in the grass. And I heard, over the shouting and gong of sheet metal and groaning boards, the animal's panicked breathing, saw the blood come with the steam from his nose. He wheeled around, screaming at the sharp goads, a spirited, beautiful animal, prancing, cresting his neck, and for a moment I hoped that he would somehow escape, scatter his tormentors and tear down the fence to run away through the fields of snow beyond my village.

The fence was weak, already falling in places; why did the horse not run away? He turned helpless, demented circles in the mud until they cracked down on his skull with a hammer, and when his knees buckled they held his head up and cut his throat. The blood came all in a rush, like a heavy sigh, and then in pulses, staining the white fur. He quivered, hide twitching. They hoisted him up by the hind legs, so that his head lay turned on its side in the mud, turned toward my father and me, white eyelashes still fluttering. My father's hands squeezed my shoulders, not to comfort but with painful force, digging in the tips of his thick fingers under my collarbones, perhaps because he thought I would fall or cry. But I stood, though my knees almost folded with the stench of blood. I stood, concentrating on my breaths, not letting my lungs tense and seize, not giving Santos a reason to be angry. The only thing I asked of God in those days was to protect me from my father.

Santos was a madman, a casualty of war. It wasn't his fault, and I know it. But I think he was also what a father must be. The father stands above us. He starts our life, the force that quickens and then throws us from the nest as far as we can go, from blood and fear into the beginnings of freedom. He throws us every which way to knock the world into us. The father is a jealous god.

I was the eldest of six children. When I left home for the last time, I left my brothers and sisters vulnerable, no longer protected from the notice of Santos, even by the weedy strength of an adolescent boy; it was not much, but it was all they had known. When I looked back at them from the road, it was to see those empty dark eyes, half mocking, saying they had always known I would fail them eventually. But the older I become, the more I believe that distance is my gift to all those I have loved. As much as I would like to think that, by some happy secret, Santos was not my real father, I see his indelible trace in me. We tell the same lie. We stand with our deceptive physical graces, our charm and lunacy, our passion for hiding, our mania for power, our savage, dread addictions, our scars. Perhaps it was the same deep lack, Derosa's spiritual psychopathy, driving Santos Lopez to violence and prompting my lifelong rush into the arms of God.

Is it any wonder my father hated me?

That night, the drums sounded in the distance, as they had many times since my arrival, but this time the noise filled me with a sense of rage and urgency. I dressed quickly and ran, armed with pistol and flashlight, to the mission kitchen where Priya and Lal had come to sleep. They were both there, curled next to each other on straw mats near the stove. I exited the compound, locking the gate behind me, and made my way down the packed dirt road between the stilted village huts, greeted by nothing but the bark of emaciated dogs. I saw no one stirring in the village, no lights behind barred windows. The drumming came from the mangroves, the forest alive with dangers, unthinkable to enter alone at night. With a soft curse, clutching pistol and flashlight, I traced and retraced the boundary of the village, where the tree line had been pushed back. The drums called to me, the sound rising and falling on the night breeze, seemingly coming from many directions at once, and I strained my ears to make out any other sound above the dense, barbaric symphony, the cry of human or animal. But the drums grew only louder the longer I listened, drowning out every other sound, it seemed they came from within me, inside my skull, under my skin, invading me. But I could not enter the tangle of trees. I continued, for the rest of the night, to pace the beaten mud by the tree line, raging and helpless, pointing the beam of the flashlight into the mangroves until the beam dwindled and expired. A man with a gun, standing in the pre-dawn rain. A man who must have resembled my father very closely. I returned, defeated, to the compound.

We had to rebuild Priya and Lal's house. This took only two days, because their house had been simple, little more than a one-room hut, and the frame of it, though blackened, still stood. Lal and I worked side by side with the other men of the village, Priya never far away, but I sensed that they were all ill at ease with me, sensed Lal's anger and jealousy though he showed nothing; I, too, am a jealous man. I wished I could have told him that he had little to fear from me, that his sister's confidence in me was just that, confidence. That I, of all people, was not a threat to her, no more than a castrated dog. But I would never truly understand them, or know how to talk to them, no matter how many languages I might learn. There was not enough space in the twins' interior world for anyone but each other. I was, and would always be, a remote object of reverence, at best a guardian for the two outcasts, a delicate illusion that would shatter as soon as I left. I would be transferred in a few short months. As for the other villagers, I felt I could no longer trust any of them; every smile, every gesture of kindness from them, now struck me as false. They plotted behind my back, or so I imagined, tolerated my presence among them, made a mockery of the Mass and everything I had done to help them. With the host on their tongue, they lied to me. One of my lambs was not what he seemed.

I gave my obsessive nature over to protecting Priya. Fear for her safety consumed me constantly. I followed her to the river one morning, when she went there alone, carrying a basket of clothes for washing. I took care that no one saw us go. I watched her from the trees as she laid out the clothes in the water, beating them with stones to clean them, placing them on a flat rock to dry in the sun. Then I stepped out of the trees, softly calling her name, and my heart clenched at the way she gasped and recoiled from my outstretched hand, dropping the hem of her sari in the water.

"Don't be afraid. It's only me."

With some effort, she smiled at me, though her eyes still darted, searching for her brother no doubt. "I am not afraid. You are a good man."

"Priya…" I faltered, realizing there was nothing else I could say. "Why are you protecting this person, Priya? What good is it?"

She gazed steadily at me, and said nothing.

122

"How can I ensure your safety, if I don't know who it is?"

Still nothing. She was never going to tell me, just as she was never going to release me from the seal of confession.

I took a little package from my pocket and held it out to her, the German pistol wrapped in green silk, heavy with bullets. "Take this," I said. "Be careful with it, it's loaded. Use it to protect yourself and Lal. In case." She took the pistol from my hands, and I knew she could tell from the cold, metallic weight of the package what it was. "God knows I shouldn't have it, anyway," I said. Her smile slipped, and she held it back out to me, not accepting my gift, though I could not tell from her expression if she was afraid of the weapon, or me, or simply rejecting the idea of the thing. I raised my hands, palms outward, and backed away from her. "Take it," I said. "Please. It will comfort me, knowing you have it." She stood in the river, holding the pistol in its wrappings like an infant. "Yes, Father," she said quietly. "Thank you." And then, as I turned to go, Priya spoke what I recognized as that famous Deuteronomy passage, thirty-two thirty-five, of vengeance and repaying. It must have been learned by heart from the dry New International we had distributed in the village. She called it softly after me, the equivalent of a gentling hand.

"Priya," I said, turning back to her, wanting somehow to justify myself. But there was nothing else I could say.

In the light of day, seen from the river's water in the morning, the village appeared peaceful, simple. I became obsessed with the idea of its secret life. I felt that if I could shine a light on the people's hidden corruption, I could somehow put a stop to it, for I was there to save them all, even though they deceived and thwarted me like willful children (such was my thinking at the time), and I was still determined to do so. Now, with a transfer looming, the situation seemed more and more urgent. I asked Lal to take me into the mangroves. He went there himself to gather wood from time to time, and sometimes to gather honey. I was cautiously flattering, suggesting that Lal could be my guide in the jungle, that he obviously knew what he was doing and could keep me safe (how must I have seemed to him, to all the Indians, a childlike giant, lost without constant guidance). I didn't think that he would do it. But the day before Diwali, he found a wild hive hidden among the mangroves an hour's walk from the village. He found it by following the line of bees; as we walked through the jungle, Lal told me that Kama, the Hindu god of love, strings his bow with such a line. "But those are not your gods," I said, and he looked away, slicing at the undergrowth.

"Lal," I said, as we walked along, ducking tangles of vine and branch, "Are there religious rites of some kind in the forest?"

He didn't answer at first, and I watched his thin, brown back as he continued to walk ahead of me, striped with sun and shadow. He moved with such a thoughtful grace, not like a stumbling, disembodied European. It was as if he spoke in movement, thought with skin and fingertips, with the pale, flexible soles of his feet. Priya had tried to explain to me the language of movement, the subtle meaning of gestures in the traditional dances of the village. "This is the chital," she had said, throwing up her head above splayed fingers, showing the wide, clear whites of her eyes. "This is the moon." They spoke a language of physical consciousness that excluded me. Lal moved between the trunks, rolling silently heel to toe; this is the hunter prince, drawing his bow in the green leaf light. This is the prey, his quivering eye. He loped ahead of me, all finely-tuned ease, machete in hand, a satchel of threadbare canvas bouncing against a dark flank. With outsized gait I followed him, feet damp in a pair of old running shoes. He watched me with his back.

"There is nothing in the forest," he said. "Only the tiger. And he will not take two together."

We said nothing more, tramped along in silence, splashing through low, standing pools and salt bogs, climbing over the spiny tangles of mangrove roots. A chital broke from the trees near me once, startling and filling me with thoughts of tigers. I saw nothing in the forest to shed light on the secret doings of the village; it seemed to me nothing but a damp, confused hell of salt-loving trees. Lal stopped once to let me catch my breath, and he showed me a tiger print in the mud. The print was deep, and wider than the spread of my hand. It made my skin sing, that physical reality of the beast, as if I was freshly aware of the limits of my own body. Lal watched my expression, and said nothing.

I was scratched by branches and sticking to my damp shirt by the time we came to the hive, a dead tree with a long split in its trunk from which the bees came and went. We drove the bees off with the smoke of green leaves. Then we broke open the hive's warm chambers, and caught the red honey as it poured over our hands, bright as the vermilion paste women use to color the part in their hair. It was so sweet that it made my head spin when I licked it from my hands, and Lal laughed and smiled at me, that quick flash. Had I been forgiven so easily, with sweetness?

"Lal," I said, "what is the significance of the drums?"

"They drive away the evil." Lal's eyes were bright, one hand reaching into the heart of the tree where the warm hive dripped out, honey on his lips. He looked at me as Priya would never look, not with blind faith but with knowledge, with a bold challenge, as if he saw my innermost secrets and shone a light into them. He dared me to meet him with the same intensity. "The spirits come in with the silence. That is what some people believe. Is it not the same for you, with your holy noise? Your Agnus Dei?"

"It was Falco, wasn't it?" I said. "He was the one, and Priya couldn't tell me. And now the village thinks I'm a devil, because I'm like him. Those drums are meant for me."

Lal stared back at me. "Not everything here is for you," he said.

No more mystery, then. Only an ugly truth. What came over me was not shame, or horror. If anything, it was a powerful urge to sleep. The green sun and tree shadows were on us, the light of early evening. And secretly I felt relieved, knowing it had been Falco. It made me a better man than him.

"Lal," I said, "I don't know what to do."

But Lal appeared to have spoken his last on the subject. He held up the jar of honey we had gathered, amber when the light shone through it, little bubbles suspended inside, bits of pale wax. He leaned back against the tree, licked the honey from his fingers. He seemed careless of my confusion. It had nothing to do with him; I had come there, a young fool in paradise looking for evil, and I had found it. "We must go back now," he said, as if to reassure me. "It will be dark soon." He brushed a bee off my arm with a sticky hand, glancing at my face as he did so. "Father?" he said. I could not remember if he had ever called me that.

"Yes?"

"You do not belong here."

"I know it. I'll be leaving soon. You have no reason to fear me."

"I don't." He tipped his head to the side, plainly weighing me. "I will be sorry when you go."

"Bless you, son."

"I am not your son. But I think you mean no harm."

"Will you give me a chance?"

"Priya trusts you..." he faltered, then gave up, shaking his head, as if he had decided that what he had been about to say was beyond my understanding.

"Lal," I said, "wait," and as he turned away from me, as I reached to pull him back, a great, flared whip rose up from the darkness and flashed, one two, across his thigh, the honey jar smashed down against a tree root, and the boy fell against me and into my arms.

I have been told that the bite of the cobra is often fatal, that a person who has been struck has only a short time before the poison reaches his heart, and nothing can be done. I tore the sleeve from my shirt and cinched it around the top of Lal's leg above the snakebite, as I had been taught. He fought with me, his hands pressing down over the bite and slapping at me, fingernails tearing my wrist, pushing me away with his knee. "Be still, damn it," I said. It was horrible; his throat rattled in fear, and an exhausted sob, and he turned his face from me into the dirt. I picked him up, thrashing limbs and all, and ran with him toward the village. It came effortlessly, the runner's pace, footsteps measured against deep, steady breaths. I carried him like a bride. He was light; in the terrible strength of my panic, it seemed that he weighed nothing at all. I ran, whipped by branches, splashing through marsh and fetid water, and as I ran, I prayed.

But I couldn't find the way; every tree looked the same to me, as if I ran in a nightmare, forever in place. The boy panted in my arms, and after an endless span of minutes that was perhaps half an hour his chest began to jerk with spasms, and he fell still. I lay him down on the leaf bed, called to him, begged him, shook him. "Lal," I said, "talk to me. I can...let me absolve you." His eyes focused on me, and then looked past me, and I saw no light there, no revelations, only confusion and pain, an animal in a snare. A breath rose to his lips in an iridescent bubble, tears cutting tracks from the corners of his lids. He thrashed backward once, a hand catching my chest, and I caught and held it, though I knew he was no longer even aware of me. I spoke the words to him, fumbling with haste, the Latin tumbling over itself into an incomprehensible mess. What sins could he possibly have had? I licked my thumb to trace the sacred sign in water on his hot brow. I picked him up again, and kept running. His head lolled against my shoulder, moisture spreading on my shirt below his open mouth. Then, as the branches slashed my face and I knew I had lost my way in the mangroves, my rhythm fell apart, and the gasp caught me. I slowed from a run to a lurching walk. Flies settled on Lal's throat, and buzzed around my eyes.

It was dark by the time I found my way back to the village. I staggered down the packed dirt street, Lal's limp neck and legs hanging backward over my arms, swinging with my motion. Dogs barked at me, and first one person came out of their house, then another and another, and bright torches came, and cries went up in the darkness, until it seemed the whole village was pressed in around us, so close I could not fall, but only stagger forward toward Priya's new house. And then Priya was there, standing in front of me. When she saw her brother in my arms, she began to shriek, and fell to her knees in the dirt before me, her hair thrashing loose in the night wind. "Priya," I said, but my throat was raw, and my voice only a cracked sound, a hissing. "Priya." Nothing would quiet her screams. There was torchlight in my eyes, and more eyes all around me, black, Indian eyes shining out of the darkness, one among them white, the dead glow of the demon eye. I thought they would kill me. But a strange passivity surrounded them, a hum of electricity and expectation. Two men lifted Lal's body from my arms, and I backed toward Priya, reached for her, but she thrashed me off, crying out in a language I did not know, older than Bengali, the tribal language, calling on tribal gods. When I caught her in my arms and raised her from the ground, she looked on me without comprehension, seeing someone other than me, seeing Falco, perhaps. Her face was as alien and unknowing in its suffering as that of her brother. I backed away from her and fled into the mangroves.

Dakshin Rai would come, if I waited for him. In the mangroves, I ran until I could run no more, and then I dropped to my knees at the foot of a tree, pressed my back up against the trunk, my hands clasped around my up-drawn legs, and listened, panting, for death. It would come softly. I knew that tigers were more dangerous at night than in the day, and that my crashing flight through the mangroves would surely draw one to me, as would my panicked breaths, my scent of sweat and blood where the thorns had scratched me. Like any predator, Dakshin would be drawn to the weak, the isolated. As I waited, I tried again to pray, and then realized I had not said my office that day or the day before, could not remember the last time I had said it. And strangely, though the words were there through repetition, I found I had forgotten what they meant, as if I had purged myself of every language I knew. Unable to pray, I became lost in the taste of salt in my mouth, in the snap of a twig and the silence of the forest around me, not a deer, not a bird, as if all the animals had fled. It was a silence that waited, like me. And I could not pray. What was I, a priest with no words, no gestures? The ritual of death was there: Thou shalt sprinkle me, O Lord, with hyssop, and I shall be cleansed. Thou shalt wash me, and I shall be made whiter than snow. Another priest would have had to anoint me, hands, feet and senses. But I made the sign, touched the backs of my hands.

What are we, without these words, ancient words of many languages we repeat until they become ours? Language had been my earliest bond, the vow between my mother and myself. The secret Basque, in which my father never rose beyond basic, tying us together in mutual resistance. Words had been my shelter. In that empty space where the words and image of God and all my obsessions had lived I saw only my mother, sitting at the table. She brought me back to the beginning of myself. Her wan face, her childish hands, how quietly she accepted life's pronouncements. The dying always called out to their own mothers, at the end. Not the Holy Virgin, but Mother. Little Mother. Taken back into the darkness before we began. I had never been comfortable outside it. And I had built structures around myself, artificial bonds to hold me, a thousand denials to tell me who I was. Had I ever had more fervent proof of God in all that time than my mother, sitting at the table? What I had thought submission had been her strength, her realism. She had tried to tell it to me then: how hard the innocent fall. Life is full of choices, must you run into them so quickly? But I was ready now. I had come all this way not to regain, but to shed the last remnants of an innocence I had always held too tightly.

I was sitting in the dirt when the tiger finally appeared. My tiger. It was a relief to see him.

Tiger, I said, addressing him in the language of my childhood, the only one that would come.

In the darkness he came as a giant, sinuous shade, eyes

collecting light where there was no light, gleaming, a black tiger made of shadows. He stood on the edge of the clearing ten feet away, and looked at me with lazy, golden eyes, so close I could hear him breathing, feeling the warm stir of the air. I could smell the tiger, damp, dog-like fur and saltwater and another tone still deeper, a hot smell, a musk. He flexed his paws against the ground, each paw the size of a collection plate. He flicked his shadow tail. He considered me. Dakshin Rai, prince of the south. A tiger, large as God.

It would be quick. A tiger would go in for the back of the neck, long teeth on either side of the spinal cord in the nodes and arteries, the tender sides of the throat. With six hundred pounds of muscle he would pin me until the shock set in, the staggering, velvet weight of him on my back, waiting to have his way with my flesh. Through the roots of his teeth in my neck, he would feel the slowing and the stumble of my heart, and, with firm patience, give me time to exit. His tail would play gently over the ground. That was what they had told me. Rohan had explained it in the boat before we even reached the village, trying to frighten me like Santos, laying it all before me so I would know what to expect. I found myself strangely comforted by this subtle apparition of my father. I thought of the scraps of dark fabric, left in the low-hanging branches, transient monument to the way of things. Flags, touched by the wind. A nun from Uppsala, an orphan girl collecting firewood, a sad, deviant Jesuit. A savant of tongues. A man who, without words, was nothing much at all. And the tiger, the tiger. Was this the very animal who had killed the others, who had inexplicably spared the Tiger Prince? All tigers were Dakshin Rai, and every god a tiger. This tiger was mine. I shivered with the anticipation of his claws. He revealed a tongue, pale against the great, black lips, as if he were about to speak or roar into my face, and I caught the moonlit flash of teeth, each one perfect and the size of a woman's finger. The sad eyes, far from human, containing all the mercy and inevitability in the world. I knelt against the ground. It was the purest resignation I had ever known. The way was suddenly clear to me; I had no fear of death. And I had never been afraid of pain.

The tiger huffed a great breath; it was hot against my face, and smelled of meat and animal. His whiskers quivered, wrinkling the scarred velvet of the muzzle, tasting the air for me.

He took a step closer. I bowed before the tiger, showed him the nape of my neck, and closed my eyes. With my forehead pressed to the salty earth I made offering to the tiger god, the only offering I had. I wanted him to rend me open, wanted to feel that power overwhelming me, so badly I was shaking with it, leaning into an ecstasy beyond fear; here it was, the blood gift, action of a supreme will. Out of the darkness, out of the void. I would see beyond the animal inside.

Mercy, have mercy upon me, O God, according to Thy great mercy, Thy most tender mercy, I give You my heart and my soul.

But Dakshin Rai did not take me. He made a deep sound in his throat, a huff almost like a soft bark, as, I have learned since then, a tiger makes to another of its kind. When I looked up, it was to see a retreating haunch, long and muscled, a paw scraping once at the earth to leave its mark, a swinging tail live as a viper, bright tip quivering, following into the shadows. He turned, dissolving like a dream into the mangroves. And I was left alone with my own darkness, the darkness that would not consume its own. I followed the dull sound of drums back to the village.

Strange, but it was Beauclerc who greeted me at the monastery two days later. He looked older than I remembered, more of the world on him. "You've had your vows," I said, and he bobbed his head in assent, peering at me. "Ah. Congratulations."

He was concerned for me. "We did not expect you for some time, Father. Are you well?"

"Well enough. Is the Abbot here?"

"Please sit. Forgive me, but you look like death." I dropped onto a convenient bench and leaned back against a warm wall in the sun, waiting for the young monk to return. But when he finally did, he was alone. "I'm sorry, Father," he said. "The Abbot is out of pocket. Can I help you in any way?" His eyes wandered over me. "What has happened?"

"I had a struggle getting here. Is there a telephone?"

He shook his head. "No, forgive me. The lines have been down for a week."

"Then I need to send a telegram immediately to…to the nearest provincial. It's very urgent. And there's someone else, too. Her name is Ochanda Lopez. Tell her…." My tongue was heavy, eyes dazed with sun, the first soft ache of what I knew to be a malarial fever creeping in my limbs.

The young man looked confused. "Désolé. A telegram?"

"Non, oublier…I ask for your help, Brother." There was no dignity left for me to pull around myself. I could hear the whine of begging in my voice. "Je suis très soif."

"Je vais apporter de l'eau."

"Did you know Domenico Falco?"

To his credit, he was not frightened of me, but on my behalf. He made the sign. "Cholera."

"No. Just hear me." But how could I have made him understand? I stretched out my hand, then dropped it.

"Stay close. I need you to hear me."

"You are not well," Beauclerc said decisively. "Your lips are cracked. You are dehydrated." He glanced over his shoulder toward the other Benedictines, who had paused in their work, watching the two of us.

"I've made a terrible mistake. Let me tell you." I stared at the young man in front of me, the hollowing cheeks and recently shaved scalp. "You're all I have."

He turned from me, calling out to his brothers.

"Wait," I said, "don't go. Never mind about the telegram." But there were his hasty footsteps flying from me on the warm path, his calls for help, the sound of a hoe dropped in turned earth as the monks came to my aid.

EIGHT

Mrs. Ong, Tony's cleaning lady, found the tabloid with the story of the tiger. "The poor thing," she said, in her flat, squashed tone, denoting more impatience than pity. "His foot's hurt. And he's old. How will he survive?"

"He's a tiger," said Tony. "Pity the hikers."

"You're going to find him, and take his picture."

"For you, Mrs. Ong. If he was really out there."

"There's a tiger in Hoboken. If not Raj, some other one."

"You know the Sanskrit word for tiger is 'viagra?'"

She issued a high squawk, and clicked her tongue.

"So you think I can just walk into the woods and find a tiger?" he said. "I'm more likely to find a tweaker."

"No," Mrs. Ong said, "a tiger. You have good luck. What is a tweaker?"

This was their weekly game. Mrs. Ong would clean the apartment, in her strange, unhurried way, sometimes humming out a thin treble through her nose, and Tony would follow her around as she moved from room to room, talking to her, receiving her gentle scolding. "You've been smoking," she said. "You stink like sidewalk."

"Yes. It's something I do when I'm anxious."

"What happened?"

"Work stuff."

"Do you enjoy it?"

"Work?"

"Smoking."

"Of course. It's a vice."

"Is that why your hands shake? Nicotine?"

"My nanny kept a bead of mercury in a bottle, and I would pour it onto the floor and play with it."

Mrs. Ong was not impressed. "How will you find a nice girl, when you smell so nasty?"

On Mrs. Ong's last visit, he had given her a copy of his recently-published book, *Tresses*, and she had frowned, saying, "I have no coffee table."

"Neither do I. Keep it by your toilet."

"Pictures of what?"

"My main interest with this series was hair."

And Mrs. Ong shook her head at him.

"I forbid you to use it for wrapping paper, or to prop up the leg of your table. Come on, just look at it. You might like it. Anyway, I have more of these than I know what to do with."

She shrugged, sitting down at the kitchen table with the book. From her purse, she took an orange, peeled it, split it with her long, spatulate thumbs, and set the sections in a row to eat them. "Thank you," she said. Her hands were dry. With her head bent forward, he had a chance to examine her scalp, thinning slightly, powdery, emitting an interesting, mustardy smell. Mrs. Ong's hair was dyed to a flat, slate-black, grey at the roots, and she wore it in a perennial knot piled on top of her head, adding two or three inches to her height. She had the unusual habit, he noticed, of licking her finger periodically as she leafed through a book, catching the slick page with her saliva. Tony excused himself, went to his office and locked the door. He unlocked it and locked it again. And he thought, for some reason, of Lena, as he did from time to time in these last weeks when tired, drunk or rattled. Lena, that bundle of kinks and vulnerabilities. How she had insisted on calling Valentine's Day *Lupercalia*, how she had said she didn't care if they actually made love, how she had leaned across a café table and misquoted Mayakovski, saying, "In the church of my heart, the altar is burning," and it had all made it easier for him to be cruel to her.

NINE

It was a tiny rural town not without charm, with languages
to learn and woods to wander. A community of what
Spaniards would have called dominguistas, decent, white-
bread individuals bled of religious passion, attending the
occasional Sunday Mass to assuage their need for
communitas. These townies bore no resemblance to our
boarders, who were upper-middle class, urbanized boys,
mostly from Irish and Italian families with a smattering of
exotics, creatures of moderate privilege or notable talent,
blue uniform sweaters, regulation cropped scalps. Amazing
how similar most of them seemed to one another, mixed
around in the crucible of that special teenage
exceptionalism that seemed, to me, very American. In any
case, if there was anything remotely intriguing about them
when they arrived, it was stamped out by the time they left.

St. Ignatius was a dreary institution on the verge of
decline, but more comforting to me for that. Alexander
House was toward the edge of the school grounds, one of a
row of faculty housing, drafty and built in a previous
century, but home. There I lived, in an upstairs apartment
that looked to have been furnished long ago by an elderly

woman, sharing the house with three other teachers. Alexander House had been built, like many of the campus houses, in the shape of an equal-armed cross, a grand old lady of a house, steep peaked roofs and high ceilings. The basement flooded annually in the spring and teemed year round with mice, who seemed unbothered by the immortal grey cat who preceded me as a tenant of the house; we became friendly, Sigil and myself. He would wind around my ankles, arching up his narrow back, and would have slept in my bed had I allowed it. A chandelier, grey with age, hung in the stairwell, and gas brackets, no longer functional, lined the hall. One had the impression of a slowly graying monument. The face of the house was a cascade of wild roses, gently crumbling the siding and climbing all the way to my window, reaching in to me over the sill in the warm months so that I had to clip them back to close the shutters. The front gate was hung with the school seal, a lion for valor rearing against the black Jesuit wolf, Scientia In Honore.

It was perfect, all of it.

In the house and in the classrooms, in the dark halls of an old academy, weighted down by books and student papers, I settled into a life pleasantly devoid of choice. My reality became one of endless students, lecturing and grading interspersed by church duties, the chapel with its scent of leather and wax varnish, stone and moldering velvet, the winters, the summers. I learned to avoid the town, preferring my own company, that of colleagues, and the students themselves, a cultivated world that seemed safe, except when it wasn't; adolescence is a force at war with all the other forces of the world. It becomes impossible not to take sides.

I have been guilty, famously so, of playing favorites. Every so often, one will catch my eye, breaking my routine and stirring those old waters. I remember one senior with particular fondness, a young New York Medici, son of a shady demolition tycoon, quick darkness, that unmistakable aura of masculine danger. Mauro, that was his name, though he called himself Alex. I'm afraid he exploited his power over me; what was I to do, but give him high marks and glowing references, and send him off into the world? He left us for Dartmouth, and I fell back on other pastimes, secretly relieved. On the wooded trails around the school, I could run as hard and punishingly as I cared to. Five years passed, and I required a pair of glasses when reading. I learned the school's secrets, and the names of local flora and fauna, kestrel, tamarack, fall aster. My work on some Trappist manuscripts created a mild, pleased stir among my colleagues, and even bled for a while to the outside world, before being quietly forgotten. I strained a tendon in my knee and cut back on the running. After ten years, my fingers took on the scent of old books. When Father Clarence retired, they made me the prefect of discipline. It was a title, Alomeda explained to me, often given to a well-liked, gentle teacher, in the hopes that he would be seen not as an enforcer so much as a guide. A father figure, to use Alomeda's words. "Just speak to them in their own language," he said, meaning, I gathered, the language of protest. "They trust you. They won't want to disappoint." So I taught the boys Spanish and Italian, and held the scales of justice for that quiet institution. I imagined I had left the world of sun and salt behind.

It was his solitude that made me notice the boy from Michoacán; I knew nothing about his family, other than that they were wealthy, as anyone could have guessed by his behavior. But he had never, I think, been overmuch adored by anyone, no mother who petted, no father who cherished; he was alone as any boy could be. He walked among the others as if they were hostile animals, dangerous and sometimes contemptible. There were fights in the halls and on the sporting field, for he would fight any who slighted him regardless of size, ever conscious of his foreigner's honor. He was not yet aware that he was beautiful, blind to his own power and made all the richer for his innocence of it. He was through and through a child of privilege, bearing himself with a careless arrogance as if the world belonged to him; who were we to contradict?

Beauty is a form of rightness, regardless of its ends. Call it God's little joke: beauty's unshakable tyranny over age.

He came to me full of rage and with a bloodied lip, smelling of torn grass, seeming too familiar, even from the beginning. A slender receptacle of anger and loneliness so powerful as to be almost infectious, making it difficult to be near him. He came in, the boy with green eyes, announcing his presence like a wild animal caught in a house. And I slipped, fumbled and lost the counterweight of the world. Four years or more since Mauro spat out his wintergreen gum, stuck it to the underside of my desk, took his letter of recommendation and left for Dartmouth. A whole rotation of students, gone. I was blinking stupidly, tongue kinked in anxiety at the back of a mute throat. This is how I remember it, anyway. Choked, with no particular desire to be saved.

He stood there frowning, rude and exquisitely spoiled, daring me. And I was convinced for a terrifying instant that I had actually been transported back to my own adolescence, that I was somehow seeing my young self through my father's eyes, thin-armed and defiant, fist raised and shoe untied. This ludicrous notion passed as soon as it came, but the flavor of it lingered. Though I did not know the details of his story, I had been warned about him, a foreigner, a troubled youth, one in need of careful, steady guidance.

And here he was.

He said, "I was fighting for my honor," an excuse I had never heard before from an American student. How could I have failed to be charmed? I believed him, too, the way he stood, straight-backed and proud; he still believed in honor.

Don't ever lose that, I wanted to say. Keep fighting. Fight for all of us. Fight like hell.

I don't know why he chose me, for he was too intelligent to trust me; was it the shared language? That may have explained, in part, what drew me to him as well, the boy being an alien, like me, giving every interaction a clandestine charge, as if we had formed a rogue cell between the walls of the monolith, bound by secrets. And maybe the unsuitable nature of the whole thing was what he enjoyed. Maybe, like all gods, he simply needed a votary. In truth, I've never known what he saw in me, or what it was he needed. A sad fact. How could I not know? It haunts me now, more than any notion of wrongness; I was so inattentive at the time. A cruel lover to a cruel idol.

But it was everything, to be the focus of such a heavy attention. It was like slipping back to a past I had never lived, to be a lonely, wild boy myself, playing wingman to some bad and dashing friend. It was like becoming young, filled with mystery and deeper stirrings of the promise he saw in me, a self I had never been aware of. Over the years, I had become adept at the mechanics of denial, realizing it was a matter not just of strength but perspective, that given enough time, I could talk myself out of almost anything. Tempted by a new possibility of self, I crumbled; nothing is as stirring of one's own vanity as love.

How extreme, my use of this word. I know it. In this language, I am aware of no subtlety that will allow me to distinguish, in that one word, between, "I loved him," and "I was in love with him," though these are two very different things. And can a boy of fifteen, an almost-child, be loved without cruelty? Can I speak further, without contradicting myself? My ruin stood in the doorway glaring, plainly hating me.

He had a way of asking questions, of throwing me off balance, often taking pleasure in giving voice to the things I wanted least to hear. "So how old are you?" He asked me this on one of our walks, when I had taken him to see a certain place in the woods beyond the school, a Native burial ground; what boy could resist that? I had hoped, as I often did, to cheer him, but he seemed immune to the adventure of it all, wrapped in a deep quiet of his own. We stumped among the little mounds in the earth, hardly perceptible now, scarcely larger than sleepers bedded in the leaves we kicked through. I noticed how solemnly he regarded them, not clambering over them as another boy might, how he retreated further into himself, looking at me and the ancient graves as through a curtain. He wanted to know my age, and it stung me just a little, not for vanity, but because it set me apart from the pleasant, companionable illusion I was in whenever we were together.

"Forty-six." No reaction; I never could read his thoughts entirely.

He blinked, and said, "Because we thought, you know, that you were younger than that."

"That's kind of you." Was he being kind, I wondered, or was my age simply outside his reckoning? I remembered a time in my own youth when anyone over the age of twenty had seemed ancient, back when I myself had planned to be dead by thirty-three; I had overstayed my welcome by a decade. Little difference between thirty and sixty to a young person, and in a way this was true. A light goes out. But it was still present in him, a warm vitality that I could feel but no longer possessed. It must seem to him that my life is over, I thought, and then wondered if I had wasted it. It seemed only yesterday, the heavy book bag, those gravel walks of the seminary; in truth, I was still the youngest priest at the school by at least ten years, with the exception of Mark Desmond, but I wondered if this boy, too, thought I was wasting my life, here at the edge of nowhere. "But these," I said, gesturing to the mounds, "these have been here for many hundreds of years. There were others on the land where the school chapel is now." I was, today, a guide in the land of the dead, a Virgil, perhaps no more substantial than a spirit myself. The woods themselves seemed bleak, their color fading with the afternoon.

He said, "When I think of time like that, I can't. It just seems like outer space."

"Full of stars? It doesn't seem so bad."

"Heavy. And cold, I guess." He was quiet for a time. A red leaf clung to his sweater, just above the St. Ignatius seal, wolf and lion. He said, "Who built these things?"

"A mystery. Most of the known tribes in these parts didn't bury their dead at all. They put them in trees." Slipping into lecture mode. The sound of my own voice exhausted me. I shuffled my shoes against the leaves, leather oxfords, the black earth. "They put them up there on twig platforms for the birds, and the picked bones eventually fell down until nothing was left."

"So they were eaten by birds."

"Yes."

He turned impertinent, narrowed eyes to my face, regarding me with sudden anger, a flat, dark hostility. He would have attacked and wounded me, I thought, if he could have gotten away with it, not for anything I was, but because I was there. His hands, jammed far down in his pockets, were fists, the knuckle ridges visible through the fabric. "Your accent is strange. You don't sound like a Spaniard."

"I come from Araba, in the North. You've heard of it? I was raised speaking the Euskara and Kalderash Romani. My mother used the Romani and Basque interchangeably, when she wanted to talk to me. My father only spoke Spanish, you see. It was a secret my mother and I shared." For years I had fought to eradicate the provinces from my speech, in vain; no matter how formally I spoke, in any tongue, the childhood language tinged my words, haunting me like an unwelcome ghost, the last vestige of home.

He said, "What do you know about man-wolves? Like Lon Chaney Jr. and things?"

"Well…"

"Never mind."

"You like the old films? We have quite a good movie house in town, you know."

"I want to be a cinematographer."

"I've never understood the difference between that and the director."

"The cinematographer is the gaze of a film."

"Omniscience. I see. Do you dislike being surprised, in general?"

He glared at me. "They say you've got twenty languages."

"That's wildly generous."

"French?"

"Vous me comprenez?"

"Not really. My mother is French."

"C'est bien. You can practice at home."

"She doesn't want me to live with her. She sent me here. I thought maybe…I don't know." We went along for a while in silence. I could see something was worrying him; he kept nipping convulsively at the front of his sweater, whenever he thought I couldn't see. He said, "You could be anywhere. You could be doing something important. Why did they send you here?"

"A demonstration of good will."

"You *wanted* to be here?"

"I was ill-suited to missionary life."

"You'd rather spend ten years walking around in the woods, teaching idiots like me?"

"Something like that, yes. Teaching manners to young werewolves."

"What's the point?" He kicked his sneaker suddenly at the leaves, which flamed up in a splash of crimson, said, under his breath, "What's the point of you?"

"Tenacity."

"Goddamn this place," he said, and turned his back on me.

"Look here," I said, "language," and he rounded on me and said, "Just cut it out," in the harsh cadence of someone punched in the throat, nostrils flared and eyes spilling over. "Cut it out. Can't you leave me alone?"

He didn't know or didn't care that the charm he wielded so carelessly, this glamour dark and perilous, was a power that would not be his for long. But at this moment, light slanting through the birches on an autumn afternoon, leaf like a burning heart clinging to his shoulder, he was a being so perfect in that fierce, liminal grace of youth, so, I admit, vulnerable, that I could only turn my gaze away from him into the shade between the trees, offering up in silence one of the most earnest prayers of my life: see me. Witness me.

"Let me help you," I said to him. "It's what I'm here for. Whatever it is, I'll listen." He hung there for a moment, and I reached a hand out, brushing the leaf from his shoulder. He stiffened but held his ground, shrugging my hand away, his fingers against mine for an instant, calloused and slightly cold. Then he shook his head, confusion showing through. "I'm sorry," he mumbled, and scrubbed at his cheeks with the sleeve of his sweater. "I didn't mean to be like that." He shifted for a moment from foot to foot. "I'm an idiot."

"It's alright," I said, breathless. "It's alright." But he turned wildly and ran into the trees, leaving me alone. And I stood hand to solar plexus, reeling in that ridiculous, mortal feeling of absolute joy, joy to the point of agony, disarmed, leaning back into nothing while the woods spun around me, reckless and out of control.

Walking back to the school alone, I came upon a ragged, black shape stretched out across the path. When I stood over it, I saw that it was a murdered crow. Its head and claws had been torn off and set in a row, the body arranged with wings outstretched and pinned by small stones, a crucifixion. Black feathers curled around my feet and blew away, scattered down the trail through autumn's leaves. And in my heart I knew it was a traveled letter returning home at last, not from the mother dead six years but from some demon of conscience, could almost hear the scratching radio and smell the powdered sugar, the press of my ear against a steering wheel, Gaivota, Gaivota, floating to me from across the starless void.

TEN

The restaurant Matt had selected for a meeting place was called Cannibal. On the street a gas lamp burned, and a white wolf-dog crouched in a recess by the door. As Tony came closer, he saw that it was a German Shepherd. It waited, patient, un-collared, ignoring all passers-by. A perfectly trained dog, Tony assumed, waiting for its master. He edged past it, heading for the door, and its wolf's ears twitched, luminous blue eyes following him, brush tail thumping once.

Matt, who apparently worked in Soho, was already there when Tony arrived, and he rose for the greeting, opting for a manly handshake over an embrace, as Tony thought he might. He looked strikingly truthful to schoolboy memory, still slender, blond and affluent, but longer of hair, wearing a pale blue sweater and odd, emerald-tinged sunglasses, though it was evening, so his eyes could be seen as only a faint glint behind the lenses.

Tony smiled. "Soho," he said. "I always wondered if you were a genuine trust-fund kid."

"Wrong. I deal in antiquities," said Matt. "As for my ingenuousness, I'm afraid that's sadly deceased."

148

He was, Tony noted, already three quarters through the bottle of wine on the table, and had been picking at a plate of rocket. They both sat. Matt had chosen a seat with its back to a fireplace, so that Tony saw him ringed with pleasant, mannerly, gas flames. Everything he knew or had ever suspected about Matt, Tony thought, could be summed up by this, and his aristocratic use of a fork, all idle flourish, the prongs turned upside down. He felt suddenly charmed, as he had at the age of fifteen, by Matt's valiant obviousness. "Forgive me for starting without you," said Matt. "You're late."

"Sorry."

"Salad? Amuse-bouche?"

"No thanks."

Matt pushed his plate to one side, folded his napkin in front of him with a smile. "Hello, stranger," he said. "My. Aren't you stunning, all grown up."

"Thanks."

"You're welcome."

"I guess there's a lot of catching up to do," said Tony.

"Yes. But I don't feel like filling you in on my adult life thus far. Do you mind if I just allow you to make assumptions? You're not here for me, anyway."

Tony smiled. The green glasses annoyed him. "We could start over fresh."

"No," said Matt. "Sometimes that's just not possible."

"You summoned me," said Tony.

"Well, I'll get to the point. He died in a Scranton hospital, and was cremated on Monday. I guess that's what they do with dead priests, nowadays."

"Scranton, Pennsylvania?"

"I know, right?"

"Is there a headstone, or something?"

"Could be. I wouldn't know. But I bet what they really do is dig up a square inch of ivy in the garden behind St. John the Divine every once in a while, dump all the ashes in there, and then put the ivy back down."

"John the Divine isn't Catholic."

Matt shrugged. "Have a drink."

Tony looked down at the menu, glancing over an array of beasts, rabbit and quail and duck stuffed with chanterelles and swallows. He couldn't have eaten anyway. After a minute, he said, "And you thought I would just like to know."

There was a single white hair threaded to the fabric of Matt's sleeve, and Tony thought of the white dog waiting outside, somehow chilled by the idea that it would belong to Matt, blue-eyed man and blue-eyed dog, the absence of a physical leash. Matt leaned back in his chair, eyeing Tony over the tops of his glasses, a flash of palest blue. "Well yes," he said. "Was that wrong of me?" He gazed steadily at Tony. "Odd, isn't it, the two of us winding up here." He glanced down at the menu clutched in Tony's hands, unopened. "What's the matter? Too nervous to eat?"

Something about the prim twist of his lip and the arch of his blond eyebrows made Tony feel he was being mocked. "I'm a vegetarian."

"Oops."

"Is that your dog out front?"

"Dog?"

"I appreciate you telling me, I really do. Look, I don't want to be rude."

"Oh, stop." Matt sighed. "If there was anyone else I could talk to, don't you think I would have? Have yourself a nice salad, and stop whining. If you didn't want to talk to me, you wouldn't be here." He leaned forward and smiled,

TIGER

running his fingers through his golden hair. "You really haven't changed that much, have you? I'm glad."

Tony had never, as a boy, been able to keep up with Matt Kelly's convolutions, and should not have expected this to be any different now. But looking back on their schooldays, he suspected he deserved whatever resentment Matt held for him. He said, "Kids are cruel. Whatever I did, I'm sorry."

Matt said, "Look at you and your pouty face."

"I assume you're eventually going to tell me what you want."

"When you left, after the fire, we didn't know what had happened. We assumed you went back to La Familia."

"You could have found me. You could have written or something."

Matt made a dismissive gesture, closing his eyes. "I could have, but there was the matter of the predatory psychopath." He leaned back with a look of satisfaction, watching Tony's face. "Don't you know how obvious it was, to everyone? No one did anything. Not a damn thing. Including you. It left a bad taste in my mouth, you could say." He was, Tony thought, a perfect imprint of that vulpine schoolboy, one of those people who become more themselves with time, rather than changing. "He really did a number on you."

"I don't know what he told you..."

"And that must really cook your noodle. That's why you came here, isn't it? 'What does Matty know?' It's quite a story. I don't think I've ever heard such a moving account of Stockholm syndrome. I hope for your sake that you've explained it to a professional. And by that I mean a therapist, not, obviously, a priest."

"Experimentation is the artist's prerogative."

"I'm a fan of your work, by the way. *Tresses* was beautiful. Eric likes to call you the Hair Guy."

"You didn't used to be such a bitchy Machiavelli."

Matt's smile stayed in place and it was hard to tell what went on behind those green glasses. "I didn't used to talk," he said. He poured wine from the bottle into his own glass and Tony's, spilling a few drops in the process. Tony watched the red stain spread on the tablecloth. The waiter was eyeing them from the corner.

"That's not how I remember it," Tony said.

"Well. Too little, too late."

"What happened," Tony said, "after I left?"

"Oh, you know. There was some kind of enquiry, but they didn't tell us anything of course. That was the end of St. Iggy's, as I'm sure you know. I expect there were other troubles as well. For whatever reason, they never rebuilt the place, couldn't even be bothered to tear it all the way down; insurance doesn't pay off in cases of arson. I'm sure they must have been dying for an excuse to write the whole thing off. We don't really stay in touch with one another, or have reunions or any of that. God, can you imagine? We all went to other schools, the priests transferred. The usual bit. I think of you so often, you know. I thought about calling, but I just never…and then years have gone by."

"You said arson. Is that a confession?"

"Say it was; so what? Secrets from back then don't weigh on me the way they used to do. I sleep like a baby. Statute of limitations, blah blah blah."

"What happened to him?" He avoided the name deliberately, trolling for a reaction, but Matt kept his poker face.

He said, "Dragged himself off and bit the big one. Like people do." He looked away from Tony, straightening the edge of the tablecloth. "He's been under a different name, though. Xavier Lopez. If you were looking for him and found nothing, that's probably why."

"But how did he…? I mean how, exactly."

"Shot through the heart," Matt said seriously. "By a man with a white hat."

"Don't mess with me."

"You're right. Sorry." He looked sideways into his plate of salad, adding quietly, "But wouldn't part of you like that?"

"You're such a shit."

"Watch your mouth."

"Matt," said Tony, "I get it. This is your revenge, but for what?"

"The boy in the aquarium."

"Who?"

"I'm drunk. Care to join me? It's nice here."

"I have this rule about drinking with enigmatic people. Do you mind?" He gestured to the glasses. Matt did not remove them, only leaned forward slightly, and Tony found himself drawn across the table, hands going up to the corners of the emerald glasses, pulling them gently from the bridge of Matt's nose while Matt sat still, chin forward and eyebrows raised. Matt blinked in the light. His eyes looked tired, exposed, shadows beneath. He gave a tight laugh and cleared his throat, stared down at the spot of wine on the table, taking on a fixed, glassy look.

"Sorry, Matt," said Tony, "hey, buddy," and he flopped his arm in an awkward, halfway gesture, reaching and then pulling back. And Matt looked up sharply at him, that azure stare, pink at the corners.

Matt said, "Sarcasm is a replacement for disgusting shows of feeling. Don't let it bother you."

"It doesn't bother me, Matty. Be whatever you want."

"I think it was pneumonia or something."

"Or something?"

"I don't know. I read an obituary. Alright? That's how I know. I didn't see him."

"But you knew he'd changed his name."

"Xavier Lopez *was* his name. His real name, I mean." He settled back again, regaining his look of superiority. "Go ahead. Ask me how I knew *that.*"

"I'm going with private investigator."

"That sounds like a good guess. What? You were hoping for something more scandalous?"

"So you don't know anything. About me. You never spoke to him."

"Sorry."

Tony wondered how he could leave without being rude, and if it mattered. He wanted very much to be alone.

A young man in a white shirt and long black apron emerged from the shadows at Tony's elbow, bobbing demurely, saying, "Good evening."

"Not now," said Matt. "For God's sakes, this man's heart is breaking. Go away until I call for you." The waiter melted away. "Anyway," Matt went on, "I always thought it was odd, you know, how your family couldn't manage to find him. They would be baying for blood, if they knew. You must have a few secrets of your own to keep. I hope it's a nice closet, with a view. Good light in the afternoon."

"Jesus, Matt."

"And here we are, sitting here, after all this time. Both of us looking at the road not taken."

"You don't know anything about my life."

"Lord knows it wasn't easy for any of us."

"Us? What does that mean?"

Matt tossed his head, swinging the hair out of his eyes in that old rebellious gesture Tony knew so well. "Oh, please. What do you think?" He watched Tony's face with his crafty, brilliant eyes, and Tony felt a soft pang for the lines at the wings of his nose, for this flushed, drunk blond in a cashmere sweater who would not age gracefully. But Matt had never particularly enjoyed being young.

Tony said, "Antiquities, huh? How does a person get into that?"

"Free fall. The family business was repairing antique clocks."

"No way."

"Yep."

"I had you pegged for a white-collar asshole," said Tony. "Kind of useless, everything inherited. Sounds more like me, of course." And Matt smiled, delicately not saying the obvious; you never asked. Tony imagined him as the boy he once had known, placing him in a childhood room alive with soft ticking, the scurrying of tiny metal claws in a place never silent, never still. Singing the chimes under his breath maybe, marking time only for himself. Another lonely, vulnerable boy. Tony picked up his glass. "Matt, I wish…"

Matt gazed across the table, glass in hand, mirroring him. "Cheers."

The waiter made a pass, and went away again. Tony said, "So it was a music scholarship to St. Ignatius?"

"Yes. Dear Father Vigh. I thought it was expedient to let you all believe I was rich, like you."

"Smart kid."

"Oh, you know. Kids are such shits."

"And you went on to another school. And college, art history or medieval studies or something. You dealt in antiquities. Lost your ingenuousness."

"I wanted him to suffer," Matt said. "That's why I didn't tell you sooner. You understand that, right?"

"And 'the boy in the aquarium'?"

The hardness of his smile. "He can see everything. But he can't be heard."

"So the boy in the aquarium sets fire to the sacristy," Tony said.

"I don't suppose I'll tell you."

"I don't suppose you will."

Matt busied his hands, picking up his fork, turning it over, putting it down.

After a while, Tony said, "Why didn't you tell me?"

"Tell you what, champ?"

"That you found him. I mean, before."

"Because I didn't want him to see you, idiot. And I already said that."

"I could have handled..."

"It isn't about that," Matt said. "I wanted to win."

"Win?"

"I don't know. It doesn't..." There were little worried creases between his eyes. Tony remembered that look; it was the expression Matt wore when he slept. "I always knew another lost boy when I saw one. I guess I just wanted to see if...I don't know. If you were..."

"Real?"

"Something like that." He laughed quietly. "God, I sound so...I mean, don't you ever wonder about back then? What was real? What we just tried to make ourselves believe?"

Tony stood up, digging in his pocket for his coat tag.

"Wait," said Matt. "Where are you going?"

"I just can't help but think..."

"We're next?" The hollow, tired eyes accosted him.

"I'm sorry," said Tony, not without kindness. "I have to go." He leaned in quickly and kissed Matt on the cheek, a quick dry peck. "Take care, Matt."

"Tony, wait." Matt actually extended his hand, though he didn't pull Tony back. He dropped his arm, the hand remaining open on the table, gold cufflink winking in the flames, a tiny, dull window into another room, convex and upside down. "He wasn't a good person."

"I know," Tony said quickly. "You don't have to keep saying it."

"It was the right thing. What I tried to do, I mean. Even if it didn't…" He paused again, then smiled, shrugged his shoulders. "I wanted to win," he repeated.

"Win what?"

"Don't be obtuse." He shrugged. "I wanted to win you. And I did, in a way. Didn't I? Here we are, the two of us. Still breathing the same air."

At the door, Tony was greeted once again by the white ghost Shepherd. It stood and confronted him, tail wagging, smiling its black-lined eyes. And without thinking, though he avoided the touch of animals, he placed his hand for a moment on its broad, wolf's head, wide as his hand between the ears, and muttered sweetly to it.

He sat on the subway, ignoring the child who danced in front of him, shaking a bucket of change. Emerging into the night at Morgan, he realized that Matt's emerald glasses had somehow made their way into his pocket.

A black, lithe shape unfolded from the shadow of his front door. J Schwartz regarded him solemnly, one elbow propped on her huge military duffel, gnawing at a frayed cuticle. The girl smelled, he thought, of peanut butter and melted plastic. After his evening with Matt, the specter of the wild girl crouching in his doorway, scowling her J Schwartz scowl, filled Tony with a wild, almost painful sense of relief, and he said, "This is strange, but I like it."

"Out late?"

"You should call your parents."

"And you should pull your head out of your ass."

"Nice."

"Where were you?"

"I had dinner with a friend."

"A gay dinner?"

"I guess that's a fair assessment."

"What kind of friend?"

"An aquaintance more than a friend. Possibly an enemy. To be honest, I don't really know. It surprises you, does it, that I have friends?"

"No," she said, scowling. "I don't know anything about you, do I? I have zero opinion."

"Yet here you are."

"Yeah." She pushed her back against the door, boots sliding on the checkered tiles of the hallway, levering awkwardly to her feet. "Don't make this harder than it has to be."

"You need a place to stay. I understand."

"I don't have anybody. Get it?"

"It's cold out."

She frowned, looking him over; she was chewing her cuticle again. The black kohl she wore around her eyes appeared to have run, dried and resolved into a dust across her cheeks, a grey, porous bloom over her skin. The colorless hairs above her upper lip were damp with sweat. She didn't look healthy; not that she ever had. But there was a brittle desperation in Schwartz he didn't remember from before. She nodded quickly, accepting his charity. Her boot slipped again on the tiles, so that she clipped the toe of his shoe and pitched forward slightly, presenting him with the crown of her head and a faint, oily whiff of New York subway.

"Hey," he said, catching her arm. "What did you take?"

"Why would you let me into your house?" She snarled at him, baring her teeth, scrubbing the back of her sleeve across tearing eyes. "Suppose I bit off your ear while you were sleeping? Did you ever think about that?"

"If you behave badly, I'll send you to the pound for girls." He cast his eyes down the empty hall. "Come on, Schwartz. Don't be an ass. It's cold. I mean, really, it's nothing. Don't cry."

"Do I look like I'm crying? Fuck off."

"You're right, by the way."

"Yeah?"

"I have no friends. Only lovers, clients, and strays."

She sniffed, dragging the dirty sleeve across her nose.

In the warmth and harsh light of the apartment, Schwartz closed her eyes. She stood in the entryway, swaying slightly, letting the duffel bag drop to the floor, as if she had exhausted whatever reserves she had in getting over Tony's doorstep. Her skin had a definite greenish palor, the cheeks hollow, nostrils rimmed in pink.

"Schwartz," Tony said. "Jesus. You look terrible."

"You're supposed to tell me I'm pretty," the girl said. The corner of her mouth twitched upward, and she regarded him with a damp, pink sliver of eye. "Isn't that what happens now?"

ELEVEN

In class he was easy to miss, because he would insist on lurking in the back, and so it was two or three sessions before I realized he was there at all. He never contributed anything; it must have been ridiculous for him to listen to the other students' butchery of his mother tongue, their cracking, uncertain voices and tin-ear pronunciation. He seemed simultaneously bored and amused, his chin sliding lower and lower in his hand until it rested on the top of his desk, and I wondered why he was there at all; this boy from Michoacán was obviously not studying Spanish. I supposed he felt lonely, and so I decided to ignore him and let him stay. A week later he was still there but becoming more disruptive, pulling threads from his sweater and glaring at me from the back row, chair tipped back, holding himself in place with one toe on the ground and a knee braced under his desk. Poor posture has always bothered me, my being of the belief that a sluggish appearance leads to sluggishness of thought. He wasn't the kind to slouch, and as soon as class was over he would unwind himself like a spring, loping off through the halls, backpack hanging from one shoulder. It was almost as if he could sense my disapproval of his trick with the chair, and did this intentionally to provoke me. I sensed that he was not accustomed to obedience, and naturally assumed that he would give me trouble if I let him. So I opted for a strategy of aggressive strike. I waited for an excuse to confront him, and eventually he obliged. Nothing outrageous; in fact, it was a zipper. He was wearing an outdoor jacket over his uniform, some sort of horrible synthetic windbreaker, its fibers making a slick, watery sound in time with his wiggling foot. He was tipping the chair again. He had caught the zipper of the jacket in his teeth, and was pulling it from side to side, sometimes nudging his face all the way down into the collar, leaving only his eyes exposed. But rather than seeming manic, he had a calculated air about him, and I had the impression that, under all the external fuss and restlessness typical of schoolboys the world over, he was not only calm, but poised. The students were working on conversational Spanish at the time, as I said. They had been paired off for the early part of the class, practicing the basics; the boy from Michoacán displayed a bizarre patience, dutifully and slowly mouthing these phrases to his partner: *Hola. Cual es tu nombre?* The Kelly boy, next to him, had turned bright red at some comment of his, evidently off script, and buried his face in his hands to stifle a laugh. When the rest of the room started to fall apart I had them break it off, turning their attention back to me. The Kelly boy was still trying not to laugh, looking helpless and pained, his eyes now filmed in tears. By his side, the other fixed me, for some reason, with a look of cold satisfaction.

As I demonstrated, I paced; it is difficult for me to speak without moving around the classroom, a habit that, I know, has an unfortunate soporific effect on my students. Back and forth, back and forth, hemmed in by a desk, a window, and the warm, humming box of a slide carousel. At the far end of the room, he tipped his chair and hauled on the zipper with his teeth.

Was this the first time I actually spoke to him? I don't remember. The importance of any first meeting is only ascribed later. In the way of all memories it is cut and cheated, turned this way and that to gleam with fullest effect, until its aspect satisfies us, and we take from it whatever we desire.

Still addressing the class (was I conjugating a series of verbs, to be droning on so long without interruption?), I made my way down the middle row between the desks, until I was standing over him. He reacted not at all. Biting the zipper, tipping the chair. He refused to look at me, staring instead at the space I had vacated in front of the class. Elsewhere, a quiver of interest animated the room; the boys followed my progress, eager for any kind of diversion, their chairs squeaking as they turned. The blush receded from poor Kelly's cheeks, leaving blotchy, yellow outlines, but the other boy gave no sign that he was aware of my presence or the reaction of his audience, supremely unimpressed by all of us. Balanced on its rear legs, the tortured chair gave up a thin, dry sound. The jacket slithered to the relentless pull of his teeth, though his foot, at least, had fallen still.

"Take it off," I said. Quiet, in Spanish.

The corner of his eye tensed. He gave no other indication of having heard me.

"You can have it back at the end of class."

Still balanced on the back legs of the chair, still avoiding my gaze, he shook his head.

No show of teeth from the Prefect of Discipline. No rage, not even a growl. I set my foot on the rung of his chair, which thumped gently back to earth and stayed there.

I could feel every eye in the room on us, and the anguish of the Kelly boy biting his lip, torn between laughter and horror, but the focus of all the attention seemed strangely calm, as if he alone were the center of the room, and I was no more important than any of the boys, spinning in the Ferris wheel of his self-assured gravity (I can't resist these evocations of a carnival for some reason, carousel and Ferris wheel, ooh and aah, the mindless, animal pacing). He did look at me then, not fully, but from the corner of one long eye. And I knew he was dismissing me, or at least my authority. Nothing I or anyone else could do would be a punishment. Cat's eyes, my mother would have said. Green, flat, and depthless. I waited, one foot planted on the rung of his chair, and after a while he faltered, or at least had the grace to look embarrassed, staring at my shoe holding him down. But he was still pushing backward with his toe on the floor; if I had suddenly removed my foot, he would have fallen over. I was tempted to do just that. The other boys were watching this incomprehensible exchange with wide, back-and-forth eyes, following each serve and silent return; they could understand little, if anything, of what I said to him, and couldn't see whether or not he was complying. It I let him win, they would have no explicit knowledge of it. But I was suddenly set on having my way, with the chair if nothing else. As if the chair, the zipper, and my will set against his, had attained a sudden significance neither of us could fathom at the time.

But the truth was he impressed me, showing up for my class, refusing to answer, tipping the chair. His destructive sangfroid was dashing, in part because of the rage it hid; rather than simply thinking him rude, one had no choice but to feel sorry for him, even to be concerned on his behalf. He seemed unwilling to save himself. The others waited for something to happen, for a sign of acquiescence from him, for the unleashing of my displeasure. They were all in on the joke of course, the presence of a native speaker in my class, sitting here when he should have been off studying somewhere or, for all I knew, in someone else's classroom. They had no doubt been waiting for my reaction. Whispers and rustling came from the far corners of the room with the snap of a dropped pencil. But the boy himself seemed to have lost interest in the outcome of our contest. He lowered his head into the jacket collar. His eyes sank. He stopped pushing back. At his side, Kelly appeared to be engrossed in his own fingernails, but the blood flamed up under his skin from brow to collarbone. I smiled for the room at large. I lifted my foot from the boy's chair and turned my back on him, this small, though significant, victory allowing me to let him keep the jacket, further establishing myself in a show of largess. There was a feel of tension ebbing from the room; I could almost hear the collective sigh. But the boy's sudden passivity made me feel ridiculous. As if I had been caught swinging at shadows. As if I had not only expected him to fight me, but had wanted it.

At the following class he was gone, and never came back; I could only imagine that I had hurt his pride, and inquired with the registrar. He had, of course, never been assigned to my class in the first place.

Before India, Derosa had faulted me for my personable nature, seeing it as a weakness. "*La Pietà,*" he called me, grumpily. I accepted his condemnation; he was old, and snapped, as an old dog will, at the sleek young puppy frisking around its master. To him, the calling was all tradition and stern obedience, or so he would have others believe. For my first two weeks in his company Derosa insisted on answering even the most casual questions of mine, how to work the sticky catch of the window, for instance, or where to find a spare lightbulb, in Latin, as if hoping to scare up the laxity of Vatican II. But there had been real horrors in his life. I knew, from having shared a house with him on the downtrodden side of Barcelona, that he slept poorly. He prowled around the rectory; in the small hours, I would often wake to the working girls shrieking at each other in the street beneath our window, screeching tires and the crash of bottles, cats knocking the lids from rubbish bins, metal gongs ringing the night like alarms in the bare, brick alley. Most nights, Derosa would already be moving through the empty rooms, muttering over worries of the day, over an arthritic hip, and I would listen, lulled, to the sounds of his nocturnal life, the singing of brandy into a crystal glass, the breath whistling through his copious, hairy nostrils. I ran five to eight miles each morning then, slept the sleep of the righteous and never touched alcohol. I knew as well as he did that I had been sent to pique the interest of a flagging congregation; the faithful, like everyone else, are slaves to youth. Derosa seemed ancient to me, the product of another time, turned over its harsh lathe. I was afraid of him, and his sore, grumpy age. I humored him, and convinced myself that he had nothing to teach me. My heart was already in the foreign fields.

But I think Derosa saw me clearly for what I was, a Gide-like Achilles puffed with virtue, limping piteously around religion's circus ring. He saw me as a well of solace for hire, at a cheaper price than the women on our street. He was right, of course; I have made it my business to be sympathetic. But at heart, I was always out of tune with people, too much of a worrier to be suited to parish or missionary life, wary of a handshake, afraid of public speaking. It wasn't until the teaching position that I felt somewhat comfortable in my role.

Because of his difficulties sleeping, Derosa was a late riser. He would lumber down the stairs in the morning to find me in the rectory kitchen with a towel over my neck, hair damp from the morning run through the city, eating cold cereal or toast. He himself was too ascetic for breakfast. I can imagine the irritation he must have felt, because, years later, I felt it myself, slumping into the kitchen at Alexander House, watching Desmond optimistically gird himself against the day. Derosa, long gone to your reward, to you I light a candle; what would I say to you now, had I those years back again?

"It's a game to you," he said once. I watched the liquid in his glass, held between thick old fingers and tipping perilously close to the brim, but his eyes were shrewd as ever. My inability to charm Derosa was always unnerving. He cleared the phlegm from his throat. "You made a choice to be here, but it's not a choice you've ever had to defend. You haven't examined it. Just a nice thing for you to do. A respectable job, to please your mother. Or perhaps you think black suits you. You've spent more time flossing your teeth than contemplating God, isn't that right?" I started to protest but he plowed on deafly. "When you stand in the street with a tire around your neck, soaked in gasoline, and they bring the torch, and ask you if you still serve God, that will be a calling well examined." He huffed again, swirled the glass.

I have no business to be lonely. Loneliness is akin to despair, a shameful downfall, useless. Derosa said this often. But I have never been a good priest, only, occasionally, a likeable one. Loneliness draws itself, and all illusion shatters. It is the dilemma of anyone who wears a mask, and for me the collar is a mask. In such a wilderness, does loneliness speak of weakness, or humanity?

"Parasite," Derosa hisses at me, even now. "Animal."

My prelude was Hyska. I was two or three years into my post at the Academy, had left Europe and my twenties behind. Hyska was a scant twelve years younger than I at the time, the despised pleb of the senior class that year, the kind you see in every bunch, knobby throat and a bird-like chest and nervous, pale eyes. There was nothing particularly attractive about him, except his desolation. And in the way of the desolate, he latched onto me almost immediately. He would come find me two or three times a week and hang there with that kicked look, talking about nothing just for the pleasure of speaking to another person under the age of fifty, smelling of wool and toothpaste, freckles on his nose.

The year was 1973. The culture of revolution was in full flower, as was youth's distrust of the old; Hyska probably identified me as a member of his own tribe, young as I was at the time, the foreigner, the modern priest, as close as he could get to an actual friend. No doubt a boy like Hyska should have been living on the land as part of some socialist collective, or writing a treatise on Arctic wolf behavior, not mired in Catholic school. But the church was enjoying some political notoriety at the time, our pacifist stance aligning us for a brief golden hour with the interests of the young. Hyska could comfort himself in his unpopularity with the idea that he was not only bringing the war home, but bringing the war to boarding school. For my part, I didn't mind him, and let him bend my ear about the WUO, and the National Forest Service; Hyska had ambitions to be among trees, and to give up the corrupt race of man entirely, an idea I never thought was wise, judging by how much he liked to talk.

We were walking in an abandoned stretch of hall one afternoon, my sleeve white with chalk dust, his arms filled with books. Hyska, as usual, was complaining about something, "the Kids" this and "the Establishment" that. He was walking quite close to me, speaking in a low voice, as if the halls of St. Ignatius might be wiretapped. The physical proximity would have made me nervous, but my mind was elsewhere. Besides, it was only Hyska. In all innocence, as if he were a dog or a much younger child, I put my arm around his shoulders, thoughtlessly tugged at his ear, said, "Chin up, it's only…what, six months? You'll be able to vote, at least. That's something."

"For who?" he said. "I don't see that it makes a difference."

"For whom, Martin. For the anti Nixon."

He let out an exhausted breath. "Sometimes I get so frustrated I could just…"

"How would you change things, if you could?"

"The people who run the world have forgotten what it means to be human."

"Old, jaded people, you mean."

"Yes. I mean, don't you think? They're just old men, they're fearful because they've disconnected themselves from the source of common humanity."

"And you think the world would be better run by young people like yourself."

"My experience is more pure. Therefore, I am more qualified to speak for mankind. QED."

"And you will put the old system in a canoe, and push it out to sea."

The rhythm of our walking knocked his shoulder back into my chest. My shoe grazed the inside of his ankle. And whether by accident or forgetfulness, or simply because he was young and lonely and at the mercy of opportunity,

Hyska settled back for a moment. We hung there in mutual shock, leaning, ever so gently, in the empty hall. There were windows behind him. I remember an afternoon sun lighting through the red of his ear, his gingery lashes and slight odor of sweat, the motes of gold dust in the air. A vision suddenly rich in color. It lasted for a second, no more, and then someone slammed a door open further up the corridor, voices tumbled out, Hyska was only himself, and we both recoiled, painfully aware. I laughed, pushing him, he blushed, and that was that. "Eyes on the prize," I said, and he nodded, mute.

Ours is not an era of innocence. There were names, and not pretty ones, that were no doubt resting on Hyska's tongue; the ache for human contact is no match for that kind of conditioning. Every touch divorced from the world of sport was covert to boys like him, unthinkable, the red thorn of male paranoia. I knew this, sure as I could stand in the woods and point north; it was the kind of knowledge that came effortlessly. Late for some class, Hyska shot me an apologetic smile and rushed off. It was alright, he wanted me to know. Nothing had happened. Nothing could. In my mind, I found myself quietly writing him off.

I nodded goodbye, and went away to be upset in private.

Hyska's grades were excellent, for all his moping. I believe he went on to become an attorney, with a wife and family. I say I believe, but I actually know quite well; Martin Hyska has two daughters, and lives in Maryland. A civil rights lawyer, bless him. I am happy for him, in that I believe the Hyska I knew at St. Ignatius would have admired the man he became. Once he sent me a card at Christmas with a picture of his family and the decade's pet, all very cheerful and vacuous. He wore glasses. They gave him the look of a Marxist. Probably our strange moment was not an encounter he remembers, a worry seen through the dark haze of adolescent fever, a ripple in the glass, no more. But it was a signpost in my life; I felt I had been called out. It was a serious defeat, one I worried over. What I had not managed to quell now followed me, keeper of the secret that made sensible Hyska fall mute. Every so often it made itself known like the breath of an invisible horse, warm on the back of my neck. According to our nature, denial can be either the most abiding or the most delicate of illusions.

Mrs. Savage lived on the outskirts of Birnam, and Mark Desmond and I would drive there occasionally to join her and her husband for dinner. I did not often venture into town, and didn't like to go alone without another priest; there is a way that American secular people look at a man in a collar outside of church, half pitying but also with disdain, as if we are the butt of our own joke, and it was nice to have an ally like Desmond. Desmond's car smelled of cigarettes, the old Honda being the only place he actually allowed himself to smoke them. I gave him grief about his habit but rather loved him for it at the same time, the one flaw in the perfect Faberge that was Desmond. Without the cigarette, he would have been a fatally nervous driver. We drove without talking usually, Mark holding his cigarette out of the window. Trees would race by on either side of the narrow, country road that led into town, Indian Lake glimpsed through the bare forest in the distance, shining in the setting sun. White birches, red lake, the graceful, spreading trees locals knew as white oak, quercus alba.

When I first arrived at St. Ignatius in the autumn, the beds and gardens of Alexander House were all wild rugosa roses, growing in large, sprawling banks around the house's iron fence, heavy in that season with plump, orange hips, which were too tart for my taste, a bundle of seeds in a waxy skin. These plants needed no attention from me; in the spring they would be thick with pink roses, each five-petaled and blazing, yellow in the eyes; Margaret Savage called them "the wild star of the woods." I would never have the heart to prune them, so they grew increasingly leggy. They would, during the time I lived at Alexander House, be an ever-encroaching tangle, gnarled and thick in the trunk, having ringed the fence for decades. In the autumn I tucked the old stocks in with straw, if I remembered. I was, at best, an apathetic gardener, following fits of passion with months of abandonment. Mostly I fed the roses on crushed eggshells, and left them alone. Mornings in the warm months would find me in the garden with spray can and trowel. It was Savage who pointed out the other plants to me; this is digitalis. This is caradonna. This is monkshood. Here is a scarlet trumpet. But the roses were the main attraction. In the warm months their scent would carry across the campus, dark, old-fashioned, feminine. It was not uncommon for me to return to Alexander on a warm Saturday evening to find students loitering with stunned expressions by the fence, having been distracted from some other outdoor goal, drawn to the source of the fragrance like flies to a pitcher plant; somehow, I could only view this attraction in a sinister light, as if faulting the roses for their immaculate charm, forever mistrusting it. Or was this mistrust of mine a point of envy in disguise? Sometimes I was tempted to show them the edge of the lopping shears.

The roses were how I met Savage, walking home to Alexander on a Sunday to find not dazed, nostalgic students or the odd priest, but a middle-aged woman in a flowered dress and a sweater with artificial pearl buttons, sitting by my gate. "Hello," I said, and she looked up but didn't rise. She wore a distracted look, and a smudge of dirt on her cheek; she had been weeding. "Would you like some company?" I asked, and she said she might; scarcely had I sat down when she began to pour out confidences to me in a dull, perfunctory way as if we were in confession, a chilly marriage, no children of her own, that sort of thing. "And then," she said, "a few weeks ago, I was mending a coat of my husband's and found a letter in the pocket. It had no return address, so of course I read it. It was a woman's writing."

"Well, that's..."

"Anyway, it was something silly, to do with a reunion. The sad part is I felt the need to open it. Though he really isn't the type, I don't think. It's been a long time for us. I thought that might have been why, that there was someone else. I almost hoped there was someone else. It...I feel rage, honestly. That's what I feel. As if..." She took my hand suddenly, clutching it with force as if to prevent me from leaving, but then changed her mind and settled for picking a bit of lint from my sleeve. "I know, of course, that he had other hopes as well, things that didn't include me. And he doesn't include me now. Why should I have expected different?" She took her hand back, leaving a coating of dirt and the fine, grainy dust of her skin.

"It's not uncommon," I said, feeling wrong-footed as usual by this call for psychotherapy. "Have you spoken to him about meeting with a marriage counselor? Sometimes a conversation between..."

"Someone other than a priest, you mean?" A quick smile. Even in her trouble, she never made a drama of herself, never leaned on me with her ego; with Savage it was one friend to another, as a rule. There was not a gram of pity in her, for herself or anyone else. Empathy, but not pity. "It's the way time passes, and you realize that every experience you have takes you further apart from each other. You have a marriage, say, a list of experiences you think are shared, and every time you turn them over in your mind they change a little. We live alone, don't we? All of us?" She eyed me beadily. "Are you going to stop me, and say I'm wrong because God holds it together?"

"No. I think you're right."

She laughed. She gave me the richness of her smile, earthy and plain. Plain as paint, as she liked to say. "It's the damn roses," she said. "They make a person melancholy." She stood, dusting the grass from her skirt, and I followed. "I'm sorry, springing on you like this, you not knowing me from Adam. Is it alright?"

"There must be some reward for the trouble it takes to cultivate a garden."

She smiled, tugging at the sleeves of her sweater. "I suppose." She offered her hand again, for a shake this time. "Margaret Savage. I know who you are, of course."

"Oh?"

"My husband, Jack, is groundskeeper here."

"You don't come to Mass with the other staff families."

"I'm an old pagan, at heart."

"A garden witch."

She laughed again. "I will say, though, watch the watering." She reached down, thumbing one of the lower leaves. "You're spotting them. We don't want blight, do we?"

It was then I remembered her. She was the part-time hygienist of Dr. Salmon, the town dentist to whom I made my biannual pilgrimage (I have always been horribly vain of my teeth). She it was who had polished and impearled my teeth with cinnamon-flavored paste, while I stared past her at the framed Waterhouse on Dr. Salmon's wall. I had never looked properly at her, just accidental glances, close and out of focus, of her eyelashes turned down, far less demanding of my attention than the instruments she wielded. Rude, to stare at one's hygienist; I had pictured her as a bird, in fact, the kind that gets its living cleaning between crocodiles' teeth. It seemed amazingly arrogant of me, not to recognize a person who had spent so many collective hours caring for me, her fingers in my mouth, no less. She had known all along, and been too kind to point it out. And I, of course, had pointed her to a marriage counselor rather than helping her in turn.

She crooked an eyebrow, admonishing me with a slightly acidic smile, turned and made her way across the lawn, heels trailing in the damp grass. The roses nodded around me in the breeze, coloring the air with their breath.

Savage and I became friends. I would join her and her husband for dinner, or accompany her with the shopping. It was through my observations of Savage that I came to realize how insulated I truly had become. A priest does not have a car payment, or a mortgage. A priest does not worry about employment, an alcoholic spouse, varicose veins or a retirement fund, let alone the worries of family life; though there were no children, the complexities of Mrs. Savage and her husband and their reportedly sexless marriage were intimidating enough. I simply could not imagine it, and said so.

"Well," she said, "That's internment in the marital institution." I admitted that I had not struggled overmuch in my adult life, not in any way resembling that, and wondered if what I had could then be called an adult life at all. In the presence of a woman like Savage, sharp and glowing with life, her well-pared hands boldly touching every surface in the room, my solitary experience seemed cold, and I was perplexed that she should enjoy my company. Her house was exceedingly female, a cottage filled with brightly colored trinkets, hot as a rule and smelling of sawdust, a curiously circus-like odor, the windows always fogged. I found little trace of her husband, Jack Savage, in the house beyond a pair of Wellingtons in the mud room, his toothbrush sitting next to hers, a man's razor tucked away in Margaret's medicine cabinet. The garage was Jack's domain; I used to peek in and wonder guiltily over his half-finished projects, disassembled lawnmowers, stacks of boards. But the matriarchy of Margaret was much more welcoming. There was a red tea-cozy on her teapot, a hooked rug she had made showing a white bull in a bank of flowers, a cushion on every seat. It charmed me, how she talked too loudly, how she laughed from the gut and only ever listened to half of what I said, as if I were a great black, ill-starred dog she was fond of, Savage's own Black Dog of the Hanging Hills. Because she loved exotic words, I bought her a Royal Quiet typewriter I found in a Birnam junk shop. Because she loved to garden, I bought us tickets to a flower show. I remember this vividly, wandering around with Margaret under the fluorescent tube lights, looking at the African Violets in their plastic terrariums. And though she wore a game face, I remember how quiet it left her, that mockery of a garden, bleached with sterile light.

At some point, Savage decided in her perfunctory way to mother me. She had a habit of dropping by Alexander on Saturday mornings, the time I put aside for gardening and other chores, and would usually find Desmond and myself, the late risers of the house, sitting in the kitchen. She would join us in a cup of coffee, chatting while she swept the kitchen with her eyes. If we sat too long, she would leap to her feet and carry on the conversation while absently tidying the kitchen; she was not one to sit still for long. Her presence would fill a room in some mystical way I never understood, bringing life and humor. If we tried to stop her, she would tease us for our bachelor housekeeping, "Men without women. What a disaster." She reorganized the junk drawer, dusted sills. She ignored our protestations that we actually had a housekeeper, Mrs. Ruiz, who came by once a week. "I'm not a domestic person in my own house, you know," she said. "I enjoy looking after you, that's all. I enjoy playing Woman. It's something I can do that you won't do for yourself. If I had a son living on his own, I'd do the same. Think of it as a gift of hand."

"So you've adopted us?" I said.

"And why not? You need someone like me around. Some sensible female person, clearly."

"Someone turn this woman out of here," Desmond said. He adored Savage as much as I. "She's hardly old enough to be our mother."

"I claim the privilege of a staff wife."

It was not a romantic vision in any way, nor one tied to Savage particularly, but I had flirted with the idea of a settled life. I couldn't decide if such a life would have made me happy, or if I simply lacked the courage and the fortitude to live, as she did, within the loud, tactile stream of things. She had a St. Christopher medallion hanging from her rear-view, and a plaque in her kitchen that said, "Bless This Mess." We never discussed our friendship, for which I was grateful; everything would have been ruined, if it had ever been declared. Savage's bossy mothering was how it was expressed, but I always felt her truest affection was in her frankness with me. It was Savage I would call, on the night of my exodus. It was she who would tell me, on learning the reason, that she would not forgive me for my own good, and that I was never to speak to her again.

"I envy you," she said once. We were in the garden, and she sat back on the grass with a little sigh, palming her lower back. Savage had arthritis trouble, for which she refused to take painkillers. "It'll still be there," she had said, when I asked her about it, "I just won't feel it as much. So what's the point of pretending?"

She said, "I would like to have some quiet of my own, someday. Something just for myself."

"Everyone wants to be alone, until they are."

"Hyperbole," she said, waving her hand. "Try picking up someone's shoes for thirty years, and say that again." It was summer and she wore a wide-brimmed hat. Strands of hair stuck to her face, and she wiped them away, trowel in hand, leaving a smudge of dirt.

I gave her gloved fingers a squeeze, and she smiled, went back to digging in the flowerbed. "Don't be like that, now."

"Like what?"

"Superior. That looking down fondly thing. The 'one' pronoun. You can't get away with that, not with me."

"How superior?"

" 'Poor old provincial Margaret.' I've not been across the pond, but I know a thing or two, Father Polyglot."

"Polyglot. What a word. Like a fat chimera."

"It's a good enough word."

"That's why I tolerate you."

She laughed. We crouched there side by side with the sun on our backs, and said nothing more for the rest of the morning, often the case with us. We were comfortable enough to be quiet together, Savage and I.

A few nights after the arrival of the boy from Michoacán, I was disturbed by a soft scratch and pinging at my window, as of large moths or some night bird drawn to the glow of my bedside lamp, a sharp, intermittent tap that went on until I opened the window and looked out. There was no one there. In the morning, I would find the garden littered with small stones beneath my window, glancing white on the black, damp earth between the roses, the soil trampled down by the prints of a boy's athletic shoe.

TWELVE

Tony waited for a week to avenge himself on Nunzio, and the opportunity finally presented itself on a rainy afternoon when the St. Ignatius boys were once again on the field, playing the ubiquitous American football. American football, in Tony's opinion, did not present the same opportunities for moments of standout athletic grace as football elsewhere in the world, which here was called soccer and relegated to the fringes of the sports pantheon, occupying a similar place to lacrosse and cross-country skiing, a curious import (like Tony himself), not a red-blooded American sport. But though Tony considered it graceless and wanting in beauty, there was ample opportunity in American football for vengeance.

The weather that afternoon was chill and opaque with rain. The boys on the field steamed in their wet sweaters, and slogged with red cheeks and mud-spattered thighs in the drowning grass. The ball was in play; the quarterback made a long, heroic throw (blindly, because of the downpour) that Michael Nunzio (with a cry of "Mine!") ran to intercept. He jumped to catch the ball, fumbled it in his wet fingers, and then caught it again, momentarily surprising himself, then went pelting down the field with his head down. Three different boys tried to tackle him, and he managed to shake them off. A fourth boy was trampled, and a fifth, acting, perhaps, out of a desire for self-preservation, veered out of the way at the last second.

This was Tony's opportunity; he was sprinting across the field at an angle to intercept Nunzio. And though the charging Nunzio had almost crossed the field, and though he outweighed Tony by a good twenty pounds, Tony was both fast and motivated; a sudden rage took hold of him, lengthened his stride, and he managed to outstrip the others, so that there was nothing between him and Nunzio. Michael looked to the right and saw Tony bearing down on him, and his eyes widened in surprise and then narrowed as he charged onward toward the touchdown. "Come here, *cabrón*," Tony panted, running to burst his heart, "Come to me," and as the gap closed between the two, Tony twisted his body around and thrust out his arm. Michael, who had been bracing to meet Tony shoulder to shoulder, instead met Tony's elbow with his face, and the full force of his charge behind it. His head snapped backward, and he landed with a solid thud at Tony's feet.

The other boys suddenly ceased yelling and came to a halt. Tony's wrenched shoulder throbbed, and he felt the rain roll down his chest and back, into his eyes and down the bridge of his nose. Michael lay in the mud without moving. Tony could sense the other boys' fear, was vaguely aware of someone running off toward the school, perhaps going for help. Then Michael stirred and sat up heavily, shaking his head. He was still clutching the ball. His eyes traveled around the circle of boys standing over him, and when they rested on Tony, he hurled down the ball and heaved himself to his feet. "Son of a bitch!" he yelled, swung back, and caught Tony with a right hook across the jaw. It was an uncoordinated punch, owing, no doubt, to the fact that Nunzio was still unsteady on his feet, so it only caused Tony to stagger back a few steps. They lunged together, and the other boys jumped out of the way as they went over in a pile. Tony found himself crushed facedown between the mud of the field and Nunzio's superior weight. He knew nothing about fighting. For a moment he wondered if Michael intended to drown him by holding his head down in the mud, but then he felt Michael's arm hooking around him, flipping him over, so that he was on his back with Michael straddling him, rain falling into his eyes and mouth. Michael seized him by the hair, and hooked his hard, mobster's fist into Tony's face, once, twice, like a movie cop beating a confession out of a suspect. "Take it," he said, "fucking trash."

Tony thrashed under the hailing blows, putting his hands up to guard his face, and when Mike bent forward over him he lunged upward with a scream of rage, catching Mike under his already mangled nose. As Mike crumpled away from him in agony, Tony, still on the ground, reached forward, grabbed hold of Mike's leg and laid into him again with his own furious fists, until Mike, cursing, got him in a headlock, tried to get up, slipped, and fell once again on top of him.

"You're dead," he screamed, "motherfucker!"

It was Farriday who broke up the fight, managing with deft arm holds to subdue both struggling boys. He twisted Tony's arm behind his back so that Tony went up on his toes, felt the joint of his shoulder grinding against itself, and smelled the tobacco on the man's breath as he growled, "That'll do."

This was how both Tony and Nunzio came to be sitting on a bench outside the infirmary, soaked through and covered with mud, Tony's eye swelling and Mike breathing loudly through his mouth, cotton protruding from his nostrils.

"That move was fucking illegal, asshole," said Nunzio, his m's and n's sounding like b's.

"You deserved it, *cabrón*," said Tony. He was probing the inside of his mouth with his tongue, looking for loose teeth, but did not find any. They had given him ice in a plastic bag for his eye, but his fingers were too cold to hold it there.

"Maybe I did," said Nunzio, "but you fight like a little whore, *cabrón.*"

Tony gave a snort of laughter, and looked at Nunzio, who was eyeing Tony, his head thrown back under a distended nose.

"At least I'm not ugly," Tony said.

"Right," said Nunzio. "Whatever. This is nothing, you piece of shit."

They sat for what seemed like a long time, listening to Farriday's muffled voice through the door as he growled into a telephone.

"Farriday gave me six good ones last year for climbing a fucking tree," said Nunzio. "You can only imagine what happened when they found out it was me that smeared the toilet seats with poison ivy."

"What happened?"

"What do you think? Stripes talks all high-minded about how we're a modern school, but he doesn't give a fuck about Peg Leg and his 'student handbook'. This place is going to shit. Somebody's going to get sued."

"What are 'six good ones'?"

"Shit, Luna. You don't know anything, do you?"

Farriday emerged and frowned at the boys. When he frowned, the skin of his face was all pulled downward in folds, so that his misshapen ears twitched forward. Tony narrowed his eyes at him. Farriday seemed not to notice.

"Michael," he said, "you can go wait in my office."

Nunzio gave Tony a sidelong look, winked, and slouched off down the hall. Tony wished he could have gone too; after everything that had happened, he somehow didn't want to leave Nunzio's side. It was as if he had lost his only ally.

"You," Farriday growled at Tony, "you come with me."

They walked together without speaking, along halls and flights of stairs, past a trophy case with tarnished plaques and the glum, mealy tintypes of long-dead scholars, boys a few years older than Tony who looked like grown men in their neckties and jodhpurs, and a set of barred windows from which Tony could just make out the trampled football field in the rain. "Please, sir," he said, "where are we going?"

"Prefect of Discipline," Farriday grunted.

Tony had never seen this so-called Prefect. Was he perhaps about to be expelled? Well, what did he care? He wished, suddenly and with passion, that Alvara was by his side.

"Here you are," said Farriday, and steered him by the elbow toward a heavy, wooden door, black with age like the rest of St. Ignatius and carved with a sinuous tree. The priest gave Tony a gentle push toward the door, said, "Well, then," turned on his heel and stumped off down the hall back in the direction of his office.

Tony stood alone in the hall for a few seconds. There was nothing to stop him running away altogether, except that he would then look like a coward, besides being stranded in Birnam, which, aside from a couple of abandoned textile mills, a movie theater and the Black Bear Soda Fountain, manned by a girl called Bernadette with gaps between her teeth, was something of a charmless wasteland in Tony's eyes. He put his hand to the door, and knocked.

"Yes."

The office was large but oppressively dim, with two windows letting in only the most smudged and sluggish light. Perhaps it was actually not an office but a prison, Tony thought. Where else might a Prefect of Discipline keep himself? His eyes came to rest on the man behind the desk at the far end of the office, head bent over some document, black hair, lustrous even in the anemic beams of light from the mullioned panes, crowned by a white stripe.

Ochoa was wearing glasses with thin wire rims that caught the light from the window, glinting slightly. In their lenses, Tony imagined he could see the contents of the room, books and walls and straight-backed chair, his own pale face and a bronze sphinx, an ormolu clock, a carved wooden mask and a pair of ornate Turkish scissors, a glass paperweight with the cosmos inside it, all distorted almost beyond recognition in the convex glass of the lenses, phantoms and funhouse mirrors, the rumors of ships in a fog.

"I'm here to see the Prefect of Discipline," Tony said.

"Well?"

The realization that Ochoa could possess such a title as Prefect of Discipline, in addition to being a language professor, left Tony feeling disoriented, as if he were spinning inside the glass paperweight on the priest's desk.

"I would be remiss," Ochoa said irritably, "if I did not take your situation into account, but..."

Tony looked up at him quickly, "Sir, Nunzio..."

"When I want you to speak I shall ask you a question. You have held our rules in little regard, but interrupt me again, and it will be the last thing you do."

Tony fell silent.

Ochoa sat back in his chair and looked down at his folded hands. An intelligent face, as with most Jesuits, turned inward, aquiline. A wistful something in the eyes, a flicker of dark humor, there and then gone. There was a scar below one cheekbone, smaller than a dime, a curious hook shape like half of an eye fastening. It seemed at odds with the man's careful way of moving. Tony wondered if Ochoa, like Farriday, could possibly have been a fighter once, and found it difficult to imagine; his hands were too pristine, his bones too fine. A flight animal. Ochoa said, "Violence is the realm of beasts."

"Yes, sir."

"Tell me, Mr. Luna; if reason can't impress on you the importance of rules here at St. Ignatius, what, in your opinion, can?"

When Ochoa spoke, it was with great care and formality, his accent blurring the hard edges of consonants, and Tony could tell that, despite his command of the language, English was distasteful to him. He felt sympathy for the man, who was even more an alien than Tony in this grey country, eternally other, profoundly alone.

"Well?"

"I don't want to be here, either."

Ochoa took off his glasses, folded them and put them in a drawer of his desk. With thumb and forefinger, he rubbed the bridge of his nose, under the corners of his eyes where the glasses pressed down, right where the tear lines would be, thought Tony, if Ochoa were a jaguar. He wondered why they were called tear lines, and he wondered if jaguars wept.

"Come here," Ochoa said. His eyes were still pinched. Tony wondered if the man had a headache. "Have a seat. You're hovering."

Tony approached and gingerly lowered himself onto the straight-backed chair on the opposite side of the desk from Ochoa. Up close, he smelled strangely sharp, a warm juniper fragrance. Tony raised his jaw, feeling suddenly defiant; he was of the outside world, the world of crisp air and youth and field brawling, everything this man was not, and wanted him to be aware of that.

Ochoa said, "I saw you on the field. Weeks ago. You were running. You would have gotten away, but you stopped. Why did you stop? It was as if you wanted them to catch you."

"I don't know. I saw the de Vaca. I thought...I don't know."

"Fond of the classics?" It was odd how when he smiled, his eyes looked sadder. Tony noted, with an inward shiver, his sharp eyeteeth, the clean trace of licorice on his breath, the way his fingernails over the years had scored nervous half moons in the leather of the chair's arms.

"I guess," said Tony.

"Of course you are. It would be too much to ask, that you also be well-behaved."

"I'm not..."

"Hush. That is why you're here. To learn to behave. We have no other distinction, you know."

Tony fixed his eyes on the grain of the desktop, listening to the loud ticking of the ormolu clock, tasting the ferrous remains of blood in his mouth, feeling the stir of hair on the back of his neck. "Can I go?" Tony asked.

"Not until I say."

"What are you going to do?"

"I don't know. What would you advise?"

"Me? You can't ask me. I don't know." He stared at Ochoa, confused. "You're supposed to know what to do. Sir."

"You can go."

Tony stood, moving in the direction of the door, but Ochoa said, "Did he insult you?" He said it in Spanish, with its dry, continental flourish, and Tony stopped, his hand suspended over the doorknob. "What did he say?"

"Sir?"

"You gave Michael Nunzio a bloody nose. What did he say to you?" There seemed more reproach there than anger, and Tony was suddenly frantic that he not be the cause of this sad man's disappointment. He was touched and strangely thrilled, as if he and Ochoa shared a secret.

"I was fighting for my honor."

"Fighting for an abstraction. I see."

Tony shrugged.

Ochoa turned to the shelves behind his desk, removing a thin, green-bound volume. He held the book out to Tony. When the boy grasped it, Ochoa did not immediately release it, and he could feel the slight worry of the priest's hand. Ochoa frowned at him, offering no explanation.

"Thank you, sir."

"Lay a hand on one of my students again, and you'll be sorry. Do you understand?"

"Yes, sir."

Ochoa reclaimed his seat behind the desk, set the reading glasses back astride his nose, looked up at Tony, and said, "Well?"

In the hall outside Ochoa's office, Tony rounded a corner and came face to face with Lupe María, smelling of meat, standing beside a mop bucket, chewing on a mouthful of leaves. Her eyes widened at the sight of Tony.

"*Ay, María purísima,*" she whispered. She came at him, fingers writhing in some hideous parody of the sign of the cross, her mouth opened wide, shawls flapping, lungs filling with the air of malediction.

Tony ran. He did not hear her speak. He ran and didn't stop until he found himself by the trophy case with the plaques and tintypes. Then he looked both ways down the hall, making sure that he was alone, and stepped back into the angle that the trophy case made with the wall, hiding himself in the small space. There, he was able to examine the book Ochoa had given him, and found it to be a collection of the works of Lorca.

In the trophy case, there was a tintype of a boy's football team. They wore no helmets or padding, just shorts and knee socks, showing the white skin of their virginal thighs, and sweaters emblazoned with the seal of St. Ignatius. All looked steadily into the camera, with the dead eyes and rigid mouths of boys who have been forced to keep still. But one boy, at the end of the second row, had turned his head while the slow film was gathering the light, and his face was a ghostly blur of motion, without form or substance, a laugh frozen forever in collodion and silver nitrate.

Dear X,

In the beginning, the sun and the moon were lovers, el sol y la luna. But the sun came too close. He was kissing the moon, and his mouth burned the moon's neck, and the moon cried. The moon was on fire, and the earth was on fire. And there was no peaceful night on earth. It was the end of dreams.

That senior boy says I must go to confession. Just look at you, he says. You must be guilty of something. He laughs at me, and I hate his dumb, pink face. What does he know of guilt? Go to the chapel, he says, and confess.

They take me to the chapel. They take me to the confessional. The curtains close, and I sit in the warm, dark box. I hear their shoes on the flagstones, growing fainter and fainter. And I am so small. They are leaving me with him. Do you understand me? They are all leaving. And I sit in the dark, and wait for what will happen. And the window slides open. Bright, like the sun. Bright, the light of the world.

Yours,
Tony

The wild girl was desperately ill for three days. During that time, she lay on Tony's couch, curled in the same tight ball, alternately clutching the blanket and throwing it off again, shaking, burning, and sometimes at night making mewling sounds of despair, rattling the windows with a liquid, mortal cough. She refused to call her parents. Refused to even acknowledge Tony's presence in the house, and didn't eat but drank massive quantities of water and orange juice. Tony hovered around her, refilled her glass when it was empty, plied her with cough syrup, and offered repeatedly to take her to a doctor, until, delirious, she screamed at him.

"Fuck off, fuck off, fuck off!" the girl howled. "And don't touch me. If you want me gone, I'm gone." She got up unsteadily, pulling the blanket around her and spilling a cascade of wadded tissues over the floor, and he followed her to the kitchen where she sat on the tiles and sobbed. Her hair was damp with sweat. He could see the plume of blue veins on the edge of her forehead, pulsing with fever. Shushing, he helped her back to the couch, and when he did she leaned into him with her full weight, which wasn't much.

On the second night of her illness, the girl's sobs reached such a pitch that he was afraid Mrs. Kauffman downstairs would hear. He went to the livingroom and knelt beside her. He said, "Just let me help you. Please."

189

"Go away," Schwartz said, her voice weak. But he stayed. She let him stroke her hair until she fell asleep, the hot crown of her head dipping under his hand.

He sat there for hours, a hand on the girl's tangled, oily locks and the light of morning creeping across the floor. By the time Schwartz woke, Tony had decided to let her stay with him for as long as she wished.

PART II

SAMBAR, ATTACKED BY
WILD DOGS

THIRTEEN

On Saturdays, the boys of St. Ignatius could do, for the most part, what they pleased. Tony, Nunzio, Macarios and Kelly would ride their bikes down the pitted road that led to Birnam, and once there, carouse through the town. There were a couple of movie houses, one of which featured pornography and the other of which carried a strange smattering of blockbusters, old films, and comedies aimed at lonely women. The boys would go to the second theater (only the seniors ever succeeded in getting into the pornos, sandwiched companionably among the truckers, mechanics and undesirables of Birnam). They would bounce into its well-sprung, moth-eaten seats, the sticky velvet so compressed by generations of backsides that it would mould to your shape, reluctant to let you go at the end of the film. Many of their precious Saturdays were spent slouched in the back row of the theater with their sneakers up on the seats in front. They would see, in the course of that semester, *Lethal Weapon* and *Good Morning, Vietnam, Moonstruck* (which they attended ironically, having nothing else to see, and mocked for weeks), *The Untouchables* (which Mike Nunzio said was all true) and *Fatal*

Attraction (which Tony found utterly terrifying, mostly because of Glenn Close's shoulder pads). Tony loved to be hidden in the sticky darkness under the beams of the projector, his fingers buttery with chemical yellow popcorn (in Mexico popcorn was called *palomitas*, or little doves, and it was white and tasted like popcorn), squeezed between Matt and Nunzio, blissfully absorbing American culture with the occasional interruption of Mike drawing attention to an actress' "hooters" in the dark of the dormitory after lights out, Tony had to ask Matt, in a buttery whisper, what "hooters" meant. In his reverence for the screen, Tony could not readily distinguish between good films and films that, in Nunzio's words, "sucked". Nor did he always grasp the difference between horror and comedy; Glenn Close's insatiable pursuit of Michael Douglas, for instance, did not terrify him nearly as much as Nicholas Cage's wooden hand. For weeks after seeing *Moonstruck*, the wooden hand would haunt Tony's dreams, resting, when he least expected it, ice cold on his shoulder.

Besides the movie house, there was the Black Bear Soda Fountain, home of the "triple fudge sundae" and, more importantly, Bernadette, who stood behind the counter, leaning on her elbows, popping her sour-apple gum. Of an age with the St. Ignatius seniors, Bernadette had predatory, bottle-green eyes, horsey buttocks and lascivious gaps between her teeth. She was said to be a nymphomaniac, though none of the boys that Tony knew had so far had the courage to test this theory. Nunzio said that a few had tried, but none had lived to tell the tale.

On Saturdays, the town was swarming with girls; Birnam contained the Belham County Public High School, and was within easy distance of Sacred Heart Academy for Girls, and it was thrilling, after a week of almost exclusively male company at St. Ignatius, to see real live girls passing by in their swinging skirts and wellingtons. When they weren't watching movies, the boys would sit in the Black Bear Soda Fountain, flirting with Bernadette and staring immoderately out the window at what seemed like an endless parade of brunette hair caught and subdued in little plastic clips, blond ponytails worn jauntily on one side, lambswool breasts and sapphire eyelids, and undulating rumps in pleated skirts. Their presence caused Tony to feel a homesick nostalgia for the world of women, which appeared to have banished him. Women's voices, women's footsteps, the fragrance of hairspray and floral, naïve perfume. The St. Ignatius boys would watch and listen to the girls until they were too restless to stay on their swiveling Soda Fountain stools. Then they would ride their bikes down the road back to school, pedaling feverishly and shouting across the wind at one another various stratagems for securing a girlfriend (or seducing Bernadette), none of which were plausible.

The road between Birnam and St. Ignatius passed through gray fields and bare trees. Tucked back among the naked oaks just off the road, by a stone bridge and an historical marker bearing a faded legend about the French and Indian War, stood a massive ruin of brick and timber, an abandoned textile mill, which for some reason had come to be known as the Slaughterhouse. It was said to be haunted. Saturday afternoons would occasionally find the boys holed up in the Slaughterhouse, red-faced from their ride in the brisk wind, sitting on half-broken chairs or reclining on heaps of ancient sacking. The Slaughterhouse was by far the best place for the drinking of pilfered booze and the smoking of forbidden cigarettes, either of which, if done under the eyes of the priests, would have earned the offending boy a few good ones if Farriday had his way, or a sorrowful shake of the head from Ochoa. It had also become a cache of comic books, dirty magazines, and other forbidden reading material; Tony, on his second trip to the Slaughterhouse, had found a moldering copy of David Hume's *Dialogues on Natural Religion.*

The works of Lorca, Tony thought, were unlikely to be St. Ignatius-approved reading material, and he had no wish to augment his reputation by reading Spanish poetry around the other boys. Since Ochoa had given him the book, he had taken to carrying it around on his person, and had not yet found a solitary moment to read it. So the next Saturday, he did not join the other boys in the movie house to see a limited release of the old classic, *Crossfire* ("Hate is like a loaded gun!"), but slid the book into the inner pocket of his jacket, where it pressed against his chest and made him think of Nicholas Cage's wooden hand, and went alone to the Black Bear Soda Fountain.

He was surprised to find the place almost empty, just three girls in a booth in the corner and Bernadette, leaning, as usual, on the bar with her pink, eczematic elbows.

"Hey," she said. "Are you all alone today?"

"I have reading to do," he told her. "Lorca."

"Wow," she said. "Racy."

"What do you mean?"

"Nothing." She leaned farther over the bar, so that he could see the tops of her breasts, straining to free themselves from her flimsy diner uniform, which did not seem to have been designed to contain such strong stuff as Bernadette. She snapped her gum between her horsey teeth, and Tony caught her scent, mustang and grassfire, wreathing up to him from the darkness at the neck of her uniform, smelled her sour-apple, mentholated breath. Tony thought that when she stood up straight, in the red cowboy boots she kept behind the counter during working hours, she would be significantly taller than he was. As it was, she towered over him; the floor was elevated behind the Soda Fountain counter. The menthol on her breath was making him light-headed, clinging to the bar and grinning nervously.

"Well?" she said. "What is it?"

"I'll have a sundae, please."

"Don't you ever want to try something else?"

"Alright. How about an ice cream float?"

She leaned back with flared nostrils, veined, pale forearms and hands on hips, and shook her head. "Kiddo, you're catnip. You know what that means?"

"No," said Tony, not really listening.

Bernadette rolled her eyes to the corner, where the high school girls in the booth were stealing glances at Tony, giggling, whispering together.

"That's what it means," said Bernadette, and gave a neighing laugh that made one of the girls in the corner drop her spoon. "You're a lady-killer."

"I don't...a what?"

Bernadette's jaw paused for a moment in its mechanical gum chewing, then she smiled and turned briskly, seizing the handle of an ice cream scoop. She made him a float, and Tony sat under the covetous eyes of the high school girls, eating ice cream and Coca-Cola with a long-handled spoon, feeling the hard edge of Federico García Lorca press against his body through his jacket lining, waiting for Matt, Andre and Nunzio to rescue him.

The last film Tony had seen with them had been *Nosferatu*. Andre said it was the town theater's annual tradition, running *Nosferatu* around the end of October. "We have to go," he had begged.

"Give me a break, Fatty," said Nunzio. "It's a stupid silent film."

"I want to go," said Tony. "I've never seen it."

"We should definitely go," said Matt. "For Tony's sake."

In the end, Nunzio said he would only go if they could get drunk first. Pressed in the darkness between Matt and Nunzio, both reeking of purloined liquor, Tony put his feet up on the seat in front of him, laughing at first at the werewolf that was clearly a hyena, the gamboling music and the mincing demonstrations of Hutter, only to fall into a tight silence at the introduction of Max Schreck, Nosferatu himself. Seen through the haze of too many swigs of whiskey, Schreck's black figure, thin as a Judas effigy on Holy Thursday and preternaturally tall, was somehow impossible to mock. "Beware," the script said, "so that his shadow cannot burden your sleep with horrible nightmares." At a pivotal moment of the film, when Hutter was attacked for the first time, the sound cut out and did not return for several minutes. In the dark of the theater, Tony had hidden what Nunzio referred to as a boner during that scene, much to his own horror. But it wasn't because of Schreck or the doughy, childish Hutter himself, so much as that revelatory look on Hutter's face, as, with no hint of a struggle, he gave up. A man confounded by the sudden presence of a grotesque, erotic dream which, he realizes, is his own.

In silence, the monster advanced on hapless Hutter, who cowered under the shadows of his fingers, and miles away in her bed, Hutter's equally child-like wife reached out her own white arms. Her eyes were those of a dead person, Tony thought. In the dark, Tony felt Matt grip down on the armrest they shared. "I hated the wife," Matt admitted later. "All those hysterical fits." A hallucinogenic montage of amoebas and Venus flytraps rolled across the screen. "From this time, I am recording that Professor Bulwer explained to his students the gruesome manners of the man-eating plants," the caption read. "In horror, they looked at the mysterious ways of nature." The theater did seem to be spinning, between the flashes of warm and cold hues Murnau used to indicate the passage of daylight into dark. Hutter's wife sleepwalked only on her toes; Tony wanted to laugh at this, as the woman drifted around in her nightgown, but could not, and realized that none of the others were laughing either. The woman was inviting death. You couldn't really laugh at that, even drunk. Tony thought, with a shock, that the actress playing stupid Hutter's wife was beautiful, small-breasted, eyes fringed with black. He squirmed in the seat, bothered suddenly by Nunzio's alcoholic mouth breathing. Words flashed across the screen. "In the morning light, Hutter decided to explore the horror of his nights." Hutter was a moron, Tony thought. He deserved to die. But the fate of the wife pained him. "That's the thing about the genre," said Matt, later. "What is it with women and the undead?"

In the final sequence, when Ellen and the vampire stared at each other from their opposing windows, Matt was sick in a popcorn bucket, and the boys left quickly, before the old woman who ran the theater had time to notice. Tony never saw the end of the film. The last thing he saw was Ellen, dark hair stirred by the wind, throwing back the shutters of her window.

"Jesus, Kelly," Nunzio said, as they dragged themselves down the sidewalk in a bright late afternoon. "When she finds a bucket of vomit, she's never going to let us in there again."

"They won't know it was us," Andre said reasonably. "We could have stayed for the end."

"What happens?" said Tony. "Does the monster die?"

"Yes," Andre told him. "Ellen dies, too. They kill each other, sort of. Ellen lets the vamp drink her blood, and

ASHLEY MAYNE

Nosferatu gets so carried away sucking on her neck that he doesn't realize the sun is rising. It's kind of beautiful."

"It's a cheesy old movie, Luna," said Nunzio. "Who the hell cares?"

"Tony feels sorry for the vampire," Matt said drunkenly, and laughed, though Tony couldn't understand what was funny about it.

"Cop," said Andre. "He's looking right over here."

"He's your type," Matt said. "Tall, dark. Undead."

Nunzio punched Matt in the side. "Try to at least walk sober, Matt. Jesus. You're going to get us all in trouble."

"Okay," said Matt, "okay." But he kept bursting out in strange laughter.

It was the way he just gave up, Tony decided. Hutter and his look of dumb arousal retreated from the monster, but only as far as the nearest corner. Ellen's offering had been a kind of saintly sacrifice. But what of her weak-minded husband, and his failure to escape?

"Tony knows what I'm talking about," Matt insisted. "Don't you, Tony?"

"Shut up, idiot," said Nunzio. "What's wrong with you?"

"You've heard the call of the death bird," Matt gabbled. "Already, Nosferatu spreads his wings."

"I think I only feel sorry for Ellen," Tony said. "She didn't do anything wrong. I thought she was brave."

"The master approaches!" Matt yelled, to the street at large.

"Rule one for horror movies, Luna," said Andre, hiccoughing. "Only the virgins survive."

"Sometimes even the virgins die," said Tony, thinking of innocent Claudia, host and first casualty of the blond schoolgirl ghost in *Hasta El Viento Tiene Miedo*, a girl whose only crime had been her gift of perception. He had momentarily forgotten that Claudia was resurrected in the end, her life exchanged for that of the cruel headmistress. The image of the broken girl sprawled at the foot of the stairs was what remained in his mind, Claudia and her lonely ghost.

"Well, in America, they don't kill the virgins," Andre insisted.

"So you'll be fine, Andre," Nunzio said testily.

That had been a week ago. And though he would never have admitted it to the others, Tony didn't go to see *Crossfire* because he hadn't wanted to spoil the memory of *Nosferatu*. He stared at Bernadette, puttering with a chrome blender on the other side of the counter. On the radio a man was singing something about lipstick, and Tony said, "Bernadette, is your sleep ever burdened with horrible nightmares?"

Bernadette stared at him. "You're a weird kid. Anybody ever tell you that?"

"Yes," said Tony.

Wider baby, smiling, you just made a million, groaned the radio man.

"So do it, Kim!" he heard one of the girls in the corner say, followed by laughter from the others. The little bell on the Fountain door tinkled then, and Nunzio, Matt and Andre came in with a blast of cold air from the street, Nunzio swaggering as if he owned the place, Andre wiping steam from his glasses, Matt holding a baseball and a catcher's mitt.

Seemingly influenced by the old movie they had just seen, Nunzio hailed Bernadette with the tip of an imaginary fedora and a "What's up, doll?" to which she replied, "Nothing much, little boy."

"Hey you," said Nunzio, kicking Tony in the shin by way of a greeting. "You done? I've got a surprise for you."

He hooked his arm around Tony's neck, pulling at him roughly, and Tony shook him off. "Hi," Nunzio said baldly to the girls in the corner, who turned their eyes on him in a single, withering motion of disdain. The freckled girl caught Tony looking at her, smiled and lowered her face, fiddling with the strap of her monogrammed backpack, jiggling her knee like a dog chasing squirrels in its sleep.

Tony said, "Are you Kim?"

"For crying out loud," Nunzio muttered. "Sacred Heart sapphists."

They clambered out into the crisp afternoon (Tony knew from the electric sensation creeping down the backs of his legs that the girls and Bernadette were watching him leave), unchained their bikes from the lamp post where they had left them, and set off down the road.

"So," Nunzio shouted into the numbing wind, "When are you gonna French her?"

"Who?" yelled Tony.

"Bernadette, obviously!"

"Do what to her?"

"French her," shouted Matt. "It means kissing with your tongue."

"Bernadette probably bites," said Andre. "She's a bad girl. Everybody knows that."

"Yeah! She might bite it off! You'd be conjugating Latin with no tongue! Or worse."

"Knock it off."

"Woohoo! Bernadette!"

They pedaled madly down the road, zigzagging from shoulder to shoulder, almost getting flattened by a passing blue Ford with a dog leaning out of the window. When they got to the Slaughterhouse it was late, the sun slanting through the bare branches of the trees, and the boys were red-faced and panting. They dropped their bikes in the dead leaves in front of the building and went inside, stomping their feet and rubbing their wind-raw hands and noses.

Nunzio's surprise turned out to be a bottle of Wild Turkey, stolen from the shelves of a Birnam liquor store and hidden in his backpack between workbooks of algebra and Latin. He uncapped it and raised it in the air. Tony could practically see the shimmer of the fumes escaping from the mouth of the bottle, and wondered if it would taste like gasoline.

"A toast," said Nunzio, "to…" He faltered.

"Bernadette," said Andre.

"To Bernadette!" said Nunzio, and turned the bottle up, his white Adam's apple bobbing as he swallowed. When he surfaced, his face was contracted in a look of pain as he fought to keep the liquor down. He handed the bottle to Tony.

"Whew," Nunzio said, "That's a man's drink."

Tony swallowed the whiskey, which was, to his surprise, much smoother than the last liquor Nunzio had pinched, and handed the bottle on to Matt, who drank, and coughed, and drank again, until Andre shoved him in the ribs.

"Don't hog it," said Andre.

"Matt's Irish," said Nunzio, "he needs twice as much as you do, Fatty. He needs to put some hair on his chest."

"Yeah, like that's ever gonna happen."

"It's going to be dark soon," said Tony.

They sat for a few minutes, waiting for the glow of the 100 proof to warm them. Nunzio drank and pitched a small stone at the brick wall of the Slaughterhouse.

"So, Luna," he said. "Time to come clean."

"What?"

"You've been very circumspect. Dish. What's with the Prefect?"

"With who?"

"The Prefect, moron. The good Praefectus."

Tony glanced at the others, and saw Andre's glasses flash red in the waning sun. He shrugged into his jacket and pulled it closer around himself, so that the book's spine dug into his ribs.

"Nothing," said Tony.

"Bullshit. Matty says Stripes gave you a book of poetry. So, why are you holding out on us? Let's have it."

"I did not," said Matt, coloring.

"Nothing," Tony repeated. Nunzio glared at him.

"How do you explain it, then? Farriday had my hide, after the fight. The Ghost doesn't ever have the stones to do it himself. Gets Peg Leg to do the dirty work. You must be a very special case."

"That sucks for you, *pendejo*. We just talked about literature. Yeah, about Lorca and Cervantes."

"He doesn't believe in corporal punishment," Andre volunteered. "I heard him say that once. Said it's old-fashioned, and almost nobody still..."

"Old-fashioned, as in ancient Greece?"

"Oh, come on," said Matt, "you're such an idiot, Mike."

"You're telling me Farriday's gone postal?" Nunzio shook his head. "God, this fucking school."

"I don't know. It's in the rulebook. It's The Ghost who's out of line, probably. Maybe the other teachers don't respect him."

"Yeah, well. He's a freak, isn't he? *La mano, Nunzio. Non dimenticare di alzare la mano.*" He held his hand out before him, an imaginary pistol tipped to the side, squinted, and hooked his index finger. "Pow."

"Shut up, asshole," Matt said. "It's not his fault you're a dick in class."

"Yeah, well we all know you've got a soft spot for the old queer, Matty."

"You're an idiot," Matt said again.

Nunzio threw another stone, skipping it off the bricks. "Yah!"

"Farriday's awful," Matt said with conviction. "Awful. He shouldn't be in a school."

"Tell it to the crows, Matty." Nunzio grunted and swigged from the bottle. "Well, Luna has nothing to worry about, it would seem. Your ass has an advocate, pretty boy. Literature," said Nunzio, lip curling. "Which is it, Luna? Top or bottom? 'Cause I'm no expert, but I think the Prefect looks like a top."

Matt laughed, and covered his face, nipping at the cuff of his sweater. "Oh, God," he said. "Don't. I'll puke."

"You already puked," Andre observed.

"Fuck you, Nunzio," said Tony

"No, fuck you, *cabrón!*"

Nunzio pushed the bottle into Andre's stomach and lunged playfully at Tony, making mock jabs, cuffing his ears. "Whoa there, big boy."

"Qué idiota."

"Don't drop the soap."

"Tony," said Matt, "do you know the term 'switch-hitter?' "

"No, *pendejo.*"

"How about 'catamite?' "

"Fuck you, Matt. Know what that means?"

"Anybody got a cig?" said Andre.

Nunzio's magic backpack came through again, producing a half-finished pack of Marlboros and a lighter, which Nunzio gave to Tony and Andre, and Matt declined (he never smoked, for fear of roughening his voice). Matt tossed bottles into the woods, coiling and uncoiling his thin frame in slow-motion pitches, and Nunzio, Tony and Andre sat smoking as the six o'clock sun went suddenly dark, leaving them freshly aware of the cold that seemed to radiate from the ruin's scant and broken bones. Tony squinted through the smoke and watched the red tip of Nunzio's cigarette, raised and lowered, illuminating alternately his denim knee and his square face. Nunzio's nose was swollen across the bridge from some recent mishap, making him look more like a mobster than ever. This thuggish quality in him would only increase, Tony imagined, as Nunzio got older and lost the lingering traces of boyish padding that softened his fierce cheekbones and sledgehammer jaw. He imagined Nunzio in a three-piece suit with a tommy gun propped jauntily on his hip, one foot on the bumper of a sleek and feisty car. He imagined him in his coffin, an outsized, man-sized coffin six inches too long for him.

One of Matt's bottles hit a tree trunk and exploded like a green firework, bringing whoops of appreciation from the other boys. They stubbed their cigarettes, and Tony passed around a pack of wintergreen gum to remove the last traces of sin from their breath. They mounted their bicycles and headed for St. Ignatius.

In his bed that evening, before lights out in the dormitory, Tony made a tent of his blankets and, with a flashlight, finally read from the book of Lorca. He read in Spanish, whispering its round, heavy-throated vowels and lugubrious consonants, savoring the familiar feel of it in his mouth and chest. He saw a broad, slow river, and the murdered poet watching a boy eating lemons from a balcony. He saw Lorca's owl, and the cosmos under glass. He saw a bicycle that became a horse all made of metal, spurred by bayonets, bitted with a piece of gleaming steel that was Ochoa's pair of Turkish scissors. And he saw Ochoa himself, dressed not in clerical robes but in a dark suit like one of his father's entourage, and Ochoa touched his forehead, saying, "This one shall live," and he sent the soldiers away, and he placed the bread that was Christ on the tip of his tongue and blessed him. But when the bread touched his tongue, it was not bread. Tony fell asleep with his cheek pressed against the book's pages and the flashlight dimming to a dull flicker. He woke on Sunday morning in thirst, with a splitting headache and fingertips that smelled of cigarettes and lemons.

FOURTEEN

At St. Ignatius, Tony and Lupe María were the only ones who had known about *brujas*. Perhaps Ochoa knew of them too, but Tony never asked him. When Tony was a boy, his half-brother Galo had told him the story of the *bruja* who appeared as a bird, *el pájaro negro*. The bird had the power of human speech, and whoever heard it talk was cursed. Galo had recounted his own close encounter with the *bruja*, how he had been a kid younger than Tony, walking alone down a dirt road with a melon balanced on the seat of his bicycle; why Galo should have been walking around with a melon somehow never came into the story. The black witch bird had suddenly landed in the middle of the road, shaken its feathers and opened its beak to speak. Galo, fearing the curse, dropped his bike and took off running across the fields, and thus didn't hear what the bird said, but it was something beginning with "Haaa..." This was the point in the story when Tony, as a boy, would always start to tremble, eliciting either a grin of satisfaction or a disparaging comment from the storyteller, depending on what mood his half-brother was in. Tony didn't know what it was about the story that terrified him so much (and still did), but he suspected that, more than the fear of any curse, it was the wrongness of the whole thing, the wrongness of a bird talking like a human, the wrongness of something that was not what it was. Galo would always end the story by telling how, when he came back for his bicycle the next day, the melon had rolled across the road and broken open, black and rotten and covered with maggots.

Alone in Morningside Heights, Tony stalked around the Cathedral of St. John the Divine with a cigarette between his lips, squinting through the cold and his own smoke. The cathedral doors were closed. He wondered if there was a service going on, and realized it was indeed Sunday, nine-fifteen. Tony prowled the church's immense perimeter but made no effort to go inside; he had no wish to. He strayed awhile by the grey gardens of the Peace Fountain, an artificial grove holding the battle of Good and Evil waged on a crab's carapace. Gaunt, comely Archangel Michael beheaded Lucifer for his viewing pleasure, witnessed by nine peaceable giraffes. On other days, Tony had seen a white peacock roaming the grounds by the fountain, but there was no sign of it today. Even so, the grove and its statues put an itch of excitement in his fingertips; he had a camera with him, and he didn't want to go home. From the base of the bronze sun and Michael's ankle, the little lion glowered at him. Tony finished his cigarette, ground it out below Lucifer's head, and tamped out another but didn't light it, turning instead back to Amsterdam Avenue, hand in the air.

The cab driver was surprised that he wanted to be driven out of the city. "You want to go where?"

"Just someplace outside. I don't know, someplace with woods. I'll tell you when I see it. The woods, you know?"

"What are you, dumping a body?"

"Looking for a cat."

"Damn," said the driver. "Talk about a needle in a haystack."

The city rolled slowly by, all steam and bridges, and Tony found himself snatching glimpses of his own eyes staring back at him from the window, flickering on and off in the shadow of buildings and overpasses, a face that suddenly struck him as totally unrecognizable, seeming in this cold light to be all substructure, fierce bones and wild forelock not unlike the two beings wrestling in the Peace Fountain, every feature exaggerated. Could a face, he wondered, express what the ego shied from, all our outer layers giving the lie to what we wished we were? Because he didn't feel that he recognized this person who stared at him, certainly had not cultivated or asked for this person, the half-starved, deviant glare, all hunger and cruel eyes; it was a face he would have steered away from in a crowd, sharp chin hunched into an upturned collar, fresh cigarette, unlit, hanging from his lip, an effete, toothy decadent weary of the daylight, a dilettante slumming for a fight. It was the face of a doomed person; everything about his life, he thought, had been calculated to avoid just that. But was it not Ochoa who had voiced, once upon a time, some epic pronouncement in his strange foreigner's phrasing, how life conquers all desire, even our greed for life itself, death becoming less of an outrage over time? "Resignation is a supreme grace, not a failing." Tony had never understood this, not then, not now. Life was, in his view, nothing if not the constant reach. Neither grace nor resignation had shaped the man he was, and the face in the window showed it. Old charm, but not grace.

Lena had once said, half seriously, that she had thought when they first met that Tony might be a killer of women. "It's something about the way you look at people," she had said, "like you're amused, but separate from the rest of us. Like you're just holding back and waiting for your moment."

"And you took me home with you."

"It's what I liked most about you." Lena's killer fantasy was not a death wish, she said, so much as a desire to shed personhood. "The salty communion of bodies," she proclaimed, her use of the word raising Tony's hair and then making him laugh, though it was, he thought, as honest an interpretation of the mystery as any. He remembered thinking how sad it was that they lived in such an age when one would feel obliged to die a horrible death in order to feel release. It spoke of Lena's fear, that she wanted to be consumed but could not bear to be actually loved. Hence, her need for him. She said, "Don't we all want the desire that kills?"

"Sometimes I think I might love you," she would say. "Other times, you're just nothing. A collection of fetishes."

He spread out over the seat, fingers snapping out nervous cadenzas on his knee, voices crackled over the cab's radio, and the iron bands of the bridge flashed past. Beyond the city, the first sight of trees and mountains, or the gentle hills that his city-starved eyes perceived to be mountains, the wild of wilds, set his heart to racing. He waited until they were beyond the arm of the city's sprawl, where the traffic thinned and the bare forest stretched itself, leaned forward, and asked the driver to stop. "Here's fine," he said.

"And I'm just supposed to wait for you?"

"I appreciate it. Money's no object."

"Suit yourself." The driver pulled off the road, the car sandwiched between the shoulder and a rocky bluff, and as Tony stepped out into the cold the man stretched his back and slid a cassette into the tape deck; Tony heard the first few seconds of the recording, a calming male voice with a rolling accent, what must have been a self-help tape. He zipped his coat against the wind, climbed the leafy bank, and loped into the trees, leaving the road behind.

He was not really looking for the tiger. He only half believed in it, but wondered idly if Raj had been there, if he had left some trace of himself in these woods, some tuft of orange fur caught in the bark of a tree, some mouthed old bone. He didn't want to find Raj, but to see the landscape that the tiger's eyes had seen. Somehow, knowing that it was a possibility, however remote, that he, Tony, was not the most deadly creature in these woods, made everything look different to his eyes, the air crisper, the golden haze of pine needles more inviting. He slipped while clambering up a rock-strewn incline, bashing his camera, and thought, with the shock of cold ground on hands and knees and wet forest scents filling his nose, come on Raj, come on, I dare you. Take your best shot. But of course, Raj didn't show, leaving him stranded, cold and ridiculous. A fugitive tiger wouldn't prey on a wary adult stumbling around a forest, he would comb the roadside scavenging for carcasses, trash, lost children. Tony couldn't even say why he had brought the camera, but ended up snapping some forest shots, a torn plastic bag caught in the trees, blown over from the busy road and filled with wind like a black lung, the white vapor trails of jets through the branches. He wondered over the mechanics of a tiger's eye, and how many colors Raj could see. At one point he came upon a leathery mass lying just under the leaves, what he took to be a dead animal, though it turned out to be a pair of men's trousers with a belt still threaded through the loops. In the woods where Raj ran wild, Tony wavered, kicking leaves and wiping his nose on the back of his sleeve, until he found his way back to the cab.

The driver leaned back, eyeing him. "No joy?" The man in the tapedeck said, "And now, with two fingers in the middle of your chest. Uuum...sahhh."

"Let's just go," Tony said.

"Coyotes," the man said.

"What?"

"I hope she didn't get eaten by coyotes. Your cat."

"I doubt it," said Tony. They pulled back into the road, Tony slumped, looking up at the receding shapes of trees.

He lay in the backseat and the cab rattled and purred slowly back toward the city, Tony imagining some catastrophe, an accident or a hunter's shot, his innards disgorged across the frosty ground. And he hoped Raj would keep running. He hoped Raj would never let anyone lay a hand on him again.

He knew Schwartz was well again on the fourth morning. She had coughed and moaned and sobbed all through the night, so weakly this time that he half expected to find her dead when he entered the living room. But J Schwartz sat sideways in his favorite chair, reading, bare legs a-drape over the chair's arm, nervous foot twitching from side to side, twisting a strand of hair through her mouth like a thick black licorice stick. The book was, he thought, his old written-in school copy of *The Quiet American*, though he couldn't be sure because the cover was pressed down across the tops of her thighs. *Tresses*, the coffee-table book without a coffee table, lay on the floor, ignored. Schwartz looked up at him when he came in. "This guy," she said, indicating the book, "has a drug problem."

Tony took the blanket from the couch, covering her naked legs, and she protested but allowed him to do it. She smiled at him, what appeared to be an honest smile, and her gums were a healthy pink, though the shadows beneath her eyes lingered.

"Welcome back," he said. "I thought I'd lost you."

"Don't be weird," said Schwartz, but he could tell that his concern pleased her.

"Why?" he said. "What's wrong with weird?"

She laughed suddenly. "You'd think I'd come back from the dead, the way your face was just now. You should relax, you know."

Tony laughed with her, laughed and shivered and laughed again.

Schwartz wouldn't go home, she said, until her mother stopped drinking and got rid of her new boyfriend, a locksmith who assembled bicycles as a hobby and had stuck his tongue in the girl's ear. Tony listened to the story with some reservations, not sure if any of it was true, though it did seem more plausible than her previous claim that her parents were both dead.

"What about your father?" he asked. "You could have gone to live with him."

No, Schwartz's father had left when she was four years old and now resided in Oregon, a place where she refused to go. "It rains like nine months out of the year," she said. "You put an orange on the counter, and in two days it's moldy. Gross."

When Schwartz left home, she had spent some time living in the woods near her house. She had a tarp, stolen from her mother's garage, a blanket to keep her warm at night. She stole food from the local corner store, ate Snickers and peanut butter and cold beans out of a can. It was amazing, she said, how long you could get by without any money at all. But Valencia, PA, was a small town; the local kids found out where she was camped, and when they did they attacked her and stole her belongings. After that, she fell in with a bunch of hippies, "Real stoners," she said, who were driving to a music festival upstate and offered her a ride. But they drove off without her at a pit stop, leaving her at a gas station in Scranton. She had nothing but the clothes on her back when she hitchhiked from Scranton to New York City. Schwartz appeared to be undaunted by the dangers of hitchhiking. "It's about confidence," she said. "Crimes don't happen without a victim."

"I'm not sure if that's true," said Tony. "I think that sounds pretty stupid, actually."

The girl shrugged. "Right, Mr. Expert. I guess it would have been smarter of me to buy a Jag."

Once in the city, it had not taken her long to fall in with a gang of other runaway girls — were there really gangs of runaway girls in this city, Tony wondered — and they looked out for each other. She mentioned a few names of people who had helped her, giving her clothes and food and a couch to sleep on now and then, but she had adopted an independent strategy for survival: sleeping in Grand Central Station, which was warmer and safer than the places the other girls slept, carrying everything she needed in her backpack. She never asked for anyone's charity, but had discovered that if she stood long enough outside a deli, some man would eventually buy her something to eat. In case this failed, she still had half a jar of peanut butter in her backpack. Not much of a long-term strategy, Tony thought, but kept his opinions to himself. Her strategy had worked well enough, in any case, to ensnare him, so much more the fool than those men who had offered the girl their sandwich meat and a grin.

"What's your five-year plan?" he asked her.

"Fuck off," Schwartz said.

To celebrate the girl's return to health, Tony took her out to dinner at the Starr Hotel. It was a long way from the corner diner, and clearly not the kind of place Schwartz would have chosen on her own, but Tony was curious to see how she would react to such an incongruous environment, and how it would react to her (there was in Tony more than a little of the provocateur). Besides, the last woman he had taken to dinner was the insane and broken-hearted Lena. This seemed to him like a good way to start over.

"Jesus Christ," the girl said as they walked into the candle-lit dining room. Tony wore a suit and tie, Schwartz her jeans, boots and lumberjack shirt, which, though it had been washed since her arrival, was unmistakably the only shirt she owned. It had occurred to Tony to buy the girl some new clothes, but he couldn't imagine her any other way than she was at that moment, tromping across the dining room of the Starr Hotel in those ridiculous man's boots and foul shirt. Besides, given what the kids were wearing these days she was almost fashionable. He reveled in the discomfiture of the maître d', fully aware of the happy irony that required Tony to wear a tie but could not dictate the wardrobe of his young companion; Tony could have paraded a string of prostitutes into the place if he had wanted, and the man would not have challenged him. Thank God, Tony thought, we live in such an enlightened age. They were seated at a window, where they drank champagne from gaudy flutes, giggling at the stares of the other diners in the place, at the prices on the menu, the waiters who bobbed sleekly out of the shadows at their elbows, the lack of ketchup. They ate oysters and tomatoes, caviar, which the girl soundly rejected, steer served in its own blood, seared eggplant, broccoli rabe, asparagus in orange sauce and salmon, chocolate mousse and butterscotch crème brulée and panna cotta with Concorde grape preserve (the closest thing, they decided, to Jell-O).

Another bottle of wine followed dessert. Schwartz, Tony noticed, would scan the menu each time and order the most expensive dishes, order for both of them, glancing sidelong at Tony in a kind of dare, testing the limits of his generosity. She also ate well beyond her need, wrestling down enough food for three girls her size, as if unsure when she would eat again, and talked all through the meal about someone called Providence, some redneck bitch from Bumfuck Nowhere who stole cash from Schwartz's backpack ("a bonafide harlot," Schwartz said). But it pleased him all the more, every detail; she was the most delightfully unsuitable dining companion he had ever had.

"So," she said, halfway through the third bottle of wine, "I bet you don't know anyone else like me, huh?"

"I wouldn't say I know you. Jessie."

"Nope."

"Jane."

"Cold." Even so deep into the wine her eyes were still sharp, calculating. She said, "You like me, don't you?"

"I don't like anyone."

"So why are you being so nice to me?"

"I don't know." It was true, and she seemed to accept it as the truth. "When I was your age," he said, "I had a bodyguard. She flew with me once from Morelia to JFK. She cursed out some guy at baggage claim, in English. She drove me to boarding school in a black Camaro."

"Bullshit," said the girl.

"The boys at school thought she was my mother. I kind of wished she was, right then."

Schwartz was quiet, pondering, perhaps, the reality of boarding school and children with bodyguards. "So you're a cartel kid."

"No. The family business was bananas."

"Seriously?"

"Largest producer north of Guatemala. Crop dusting airplanes, strong-arm tactics, chlorpyritos bags, refrigerated trucks, slave wages. I know almost nothing about it, actually. The plantations were mostly in Chiapas, and we grew up in Michoacán, and my father made a point of never taking us there. I mean, I barely left the compound. Then he packed me off to boarding school, and I never came back." He shrugged. Schwartz stared at him with round, glassy eyes, a little too fixed. She looked drunk. "Anyway," he said. "So I was a banana prince. Don't bother with the jokes, I've heard them all."

"I wouldn't mind being a banana moll," Schwartz said. "You're still a banana prince, right? Wait. You said, 'we grew up'. Who's 'we'? You've got siblings? There's, like, other banana royalty?" She laughed.

"I didn't say 'we'."

The waiter brought the check.

They were both unsteady by the time they left the Starr, laughing and cursing the cold, and fell together into the back of a cab to be whisked away through the crowded night. Schwartz threw her head back on the seat rest so that she could watch the streetlights and buildings bend around the rear window, the lights crossing in stripes over her throat. When she closed her eyes, she leaned with a sigh into the space between his arm and chest. It was effortless, natural; Tony rested his cheek on the top of her head, and they rode like that for what seemed like endless blocks, eventually past the little park and the awning that said RALP, past the pompadours, Justice and the iron fence, all the way back to Bogart Street.

"J Schwartz," he said, the cab spinning, her hair finding its way into his mouth, "you're going to try something, aren't you?"

She snuggled in deeper, little claws digging into the

220

leather of his Hugo Boss jacket. "You smell good," she said. "Like leather and oranges."

On the stairs going up to Tony's apartment, he missed a step and caught himself against the wall, laughing, and the girl was suddenly in the hollow of his arm, pressed against him. She stood on the step above his, pushed him back against the green wall, and his free hand slid down to the curve of her hip below her ribcage, resting there. Dimly, he pictured the two of them plunging over the handrail and into the dark space below, for the walls and stairs seemed to be buckling under them, wheeling and shining with unearthly color, and it would be impossible, he thought, to endure such a thing without falling. He muttered something, some kind of protestation or dire warning, but her mouth was soft and hot, tongue fluttering in some expert, girlish way. The wall slid upwards under his back until they were both sitting on the steps.

"Well," she said at last, leaning back and wiping a string of saliva from his lip, "that's over with."

He looked up at her, haloed by her black hair and the stairwell light behind her. He said, "You haven't really thought this through, have you?"

She leaned in close, not for a kiss this time but to extract the keys from his pocket. She held the key ring in her fist with the tines spiking outward. She said, "Are you coming up, or what?"

"I object to this," he said.

She threw back her head with an exasperated sound, tottered to her feet, and smiled at him. "Oh, listen to that," she said. "The banana prince objects."

She extended her hand to him, and he took it, falling to his feet in a rush that nearly sent both of them down the stairs again, found the door of his apartment, which she unlocked. He switched on the light, locked the door again behind them, and shot the bolt, fending off Schwartz with his elbow. "Can we talk about this?" She was, he thought, much drunker than he was, which made sense because of her size. Perhaps that was why she was leaning so insistently, with her full weight. "Hey," he said. "I mean it."

"You've been so nice to me."

"Come on, Schwartz. We're pals."

She tugged at the zipper of his coat, and he realized she wasn't smiling anymore. She said, "It isn't only that."

"No way," he said. "Forget it."

"Fine," she said with a hard laugh, and he could tell she was humiliated. "I'll see you around, I guess." She turned away from him, off balance but ready to storm away.

"Come on, don't be stupid. I didn't mean…. You'll freeze to death." He grabbed her arm to stop her, and she threw him off with a violent movement, cheeks flushed and mouth open, and he could see her pink tongue, crouched behind her teeth.

"I feel sorry for you," she flung the words at him. "You're scared of women. It's so obvious. Do you even think of us as people?"

"What…?"

"That's why you have that fucking neuroses book. Pathetic psycho."

"You're not a women," he said, and squeezed his eyes shut, willing the dizziness to subside. "What's wrong with you?"

She was shaking, hair crackling with rage. "You can't keep me here if I want to leave."

He was fighting it, but the darkness was coming, the light patterns dancing, narrowing around Schwartz's furious face. "Of course you can leave if you want to," he said. That would be better, yes, better for both of them. He reached for his wallet, all thumbs, fumbled out the entire contents, and held it out to her. "Get yourself a room. Some place safe. And use the rest to get home. Don't hitchhike, take a bus, for God's sake. It's more than enough."

She took the money. "I'm not paying this back."

He gestured impatiently, leaning against the wall, said, "Yes, I know it." He could no longer see her clearly, was aware of her only as a shadow, a small dynamo of anger standing in his hallway. He left her there, following the wall to the bathroom, aware of the weight of his limbs and the sounds of J sniffing as she collected her things from the living room. The wall was cool against his cheek, and pushed back the darkness momentarily, leaving him feeling dizzy and nauseated, but able to follow the wall to the bathroom, to turn the tap and lean over the sink with his forearms pressing down against the porcelain, the water cold against his face.

He had time to note the scent of the inside of his own nose, bloody, and to find the floor with his hands and knees. Then the fog came into his eyes and over him, and he let go of his toppling body and sank down, down, to be among the eyeless fishes and biplanes and rotting whale bones of the deep. He saw the tiger, decked with dew, moving through trembling grass. In the manner of dreams, he could not move his body, but watched as the tiger approached, its shoulders rising and falling over its neck like sets of tawny waves, or no, something more solid, sliding mountains and movable hills, rippling sand dunes barred with jet, sliding cairns and traveling glaciers whose claws tore and scraped away the hide of the earth, all this seen in accelerated motion, millions of years in a moment, and the tiger's paws, big as God, molding silently to the ground. When the tiger was close enough that he could feel the rank, beast heat from it, smell its meaty breath, and see the floating shards of sea glass in its lazy, pitiless eyes, his skin quivered and jumped and then went still. Something in him surrendered. He knew the relief of the prey, the helpless relief of having no fears left anymore. The thing he most feared had come to collect. When he looked at the animal, at the shape of it under the stripes and under the skin, at its black lips, what he felt was a desperate and heedless desire to be consumed. To be tossed and torn and plundered. To be wrecked. To be the weaker. He wanted every choice to be removed.

"Hey," he said to the giant, breathing thing, to its amethystine eyes and the growl that issued from the depths of its chest. "Hey, you." And he closed his eyes and bit down on his lip until he could taste himself, and found that he was sitting on the floor, looking at the rusted metal pipe behind the toilet.

"Oh, fuck," the girl said. "Holy shit." She was standing in the doorway, staring at him in the bathroom mirror. His first thought was that she looked tired. He could see his own face framed beside her, the tracks of blood seeping from his nose. What a pair, he thought.

"Hey, you," he said again.

"Your nose is bleeding," Schwartz observed. She sounded irritated, as if it was something he had done intentionally. "Are you snorting coke now?"

"No. It's just something that happens."

"Can I sit down?"

"Please."

The girl sat and leaned against the bathroom wall beside him, tucking back her hair behind her ear. "Sorry about saying those things," she said, after a while. She hugged her legs, resting her ear on the battered knee of her jeans. "Is it going to be okay?"

"Yes. It's going to be okay."

"I really do like you." Her shoulder pressed briefly against his. Then she leaned across the tiles in front of him, gathering a wad of toilet paper. "That's gross," she said. "You're fucking up your shirt. Here."

She helped him up and led him from the room with her arm around him, her shoulder snugged under his armpit, arm squeezing his ribs. She led him to his own bed and turned it down for him. He sat down on the edge, letting her remove his shoes. Looking down at the top of her head, he noticed for the first time that her hair was dyed, roots showing not glossy gun black but pale. She tried to use the sleeve of her shirt to wipe the blood from his nose, and he resisted, asking for a fresh tissue. It was unexpectedly moving, being cared for. "Go to sleep," she said, and gave his foot a squeeze. She tucked his shoes under the edge of the bed, doused the light, and went out.

Tony knew he couldn't let the girl leave, though he was sure she would, eventually. He would have to keep her there somehow; he could not let her leave, because if the girl left he would be alone with himself.

In the early hours of the morning, exhausted but sober once again, he woke to find that the girl had crawled into bed with him. Schwartz was lying with closed eyes, curled fully clothed on her side in the huge, white snowdrift of a bed, hair spread around her, small, closed hand tucked in against her mouth. Asleep she was disarmed, a worried little animal couched in a down comforter. It was as if her skin had lost its waking ability to hold out the world and was instead completely permeable, giving and receiving light, a pliant, supple barrier. The absence of her unnerving hostility made her younger asleep than she was in waking life, and somehow smaller as well; it was easy to curl himself around her, to hold her in the hollow of his arm.

With care, Tony reached around the sleeping girl, one slow inch at a time, until his arm rested around her ribcage, her back against his chest, the tops of his thighs tucked in close against her, the girl's rump digging into his lap, and his chin on the warm top of her head. She stirred, but slept on. Outside, the muted sound of traffic crept up from the street, and with it, the unexpected sound of winter rain. Rain would fall in every part of the city that night, in every borough and lost neighborhood, until every tree and guardrail, every sidewalk and loading dock and monument, bronze horse and cemetery angel – all were covered in a mantilla of ice that would last, in the sudden, breath-taking cold snap, for a whole week. No amount of salt would cause the ice to melt. Pigeons were frozen in their sleep on ice-hung fire escapes. In Brooklyn, grown slick with fractured glass, old couples were afraid to leave their homes, and a green Cannondale bicycle stayed locked to an iron fence. The city slowed and came to a halt, still and strangely quiet. Pipes burst and power lines came down, causing several neighborhoods to darken. In the frozen dark, people wandered the streets with flashlights, lanterns and even candelabra, speaking quietly and with warmth to one another, marveling at the sudden confluence of stars. Tony slept a delicious sleep without sound and without dreams, an ice-bound sleep oblivious to the coming and going of sun and star and the slow procession of hours.

FIFTEEN

The boys lined up outside the doors of Wolf Chapel, bleary-eyed and shivering in their uniforms and shined shoes, and when the doors creaked open they came pouring in to take their places. That Sunday, as usual, there was a scramble at the back of the church as the boys fought each other for the choice pews closest to the doors. Tony found himself sandwiched between a yawning sophomore called Ross and a senior with a pockmark on his cheek whose name, he thought, was Seamus. He did not see Nunzio, but as he craned his neck around he caught Andre's red and baleful eye, and he nodded to Andre, who looked down and turned away, facing the front again. His fat hair was shiny with pomade. From where Tony was sitting, he could make out the back of Lupe María's grey head, rocking gently backward and forward under its covering of black, motheaten lace. She had a space around her; no one liked to sit too close to Lupe María if they could avoid it, partly because of her alarming smell, and partly because of her habit of muttering tunelessly under her breath when the congregation knelt to pray.

The St. Ignatius chapel was the true heart of the school,

for the whole complex had been built around what used to be the Church of Ignatius Loyola of the Wolves. As a result, the chapel did not match the rest of dour St. Ignatius. It had thick beams holding up its lofty roof, carved into arcs from trees the like of which no longer grew in New England, and strange paintings in alcoves along its walls that, due to over-painting, extreme age and the corrosive damp of Connecticut, had ceased to resemble what their artists had envisioned, showing not the warrior saint preaching in India, but conquistadors and naked Indians with peeling faces kneeling in the midst of wolves, presided over not by doves, but feathered snakes. It was a church that, Tony would not be surprised to learn, had been built on a Native burial ground. It had been built badly. Cracks appeared regularly in its lime, running up from the floors and crossing the massive ceiling; it was as if the once Jesuit, now school chapel did not desire to be a church at all, but would rather have been a ruin open to the sky, termites gnawing in the heart of its lectern, pagan poetry living inside its walls. If a building can be said to have yearnings, the St. Ignatius chapel, it was clear, longed to give up its many ghosts. Even when it had been the Church of Loyola, no one had ever called it that. The townies, the St. Ignatius boys, and even the priests all knew the place by the name of Wolf Chapel. In the vaulted stained-glass window overlooking the crumbling nave, beneath the feet of Jesus ascending, Ignatius himself, blank and Spanish-faced, stood between his two wolves. On one, his hand rested, fingers curled into the grey neck-fur. To the other he offered an open hand, as if to feed it. Matt said that the second wolf looked as if it hadn't decided what to do, whether to suffer the saint's touch, or eat him.

"Maybe he'll lose the hand," he said, hopefully.

"But we know he didn't," said Tony. "It's history." And

Matt had looked at him pityingly, said, "It's an archetype. That means it has to happen again and again. It never stops happening."

Tony sat on the hard pew and marveled, as he did every morning, at the coldness of the floor, which seeped into him from the feet up and worked its way through his entire body, and at the light passing through the main window, painting the first three rows of the congregation red. The sophomore called Ross leaned across him to show something drawn on a piece of paper to the senior named Seamus, who stifled a laugh and pushed his hand back. Tony caught a glance of the paper, a roughly drawn cartoon of Farriday with flames coming out of his ass. He squirmed irritably inside the cloud of his own hangover and Ross' oniony breath. His mind wandered from the snickering boys and dry sermon to the saint and the wolf, and then, quite naturally, to the wandering moon, and Lorca's owl, the wailing of gypsies and the argentine glint of scissors. He thought of de Vaca the madman, wearing deerskins. De Vaca the slave, lost in America.

In the Slaughterhouse, Ochoa had told him that the bottles in the trees were there to trap evil spirits, but that he didn't know who had put them there. He had made him a gift of de Vaca's *Adventures in the Unexplored Interior of America.* "Take this. A gift, from an idiot who admires you. And I do. From the other world."

"I didn't say..."

He had extended the book. "Go on, give me the satisfaction. It won't bite, I promise." Between the fingers of his other hand he turned a dry oak leaf, gently shredding it down to the veins, bending the thin, soft spine. He said, "Sometimes I think I was assigned here, with all these books, just so I could give them to you."

He had overtaken Ochoa by accident on a late Saturday

afternoon, walking the path into the woods, the priest dressed in a long woolen coat with large pockets and a red scarf around his throat. And it had seemed quite natural that they should fall in side by side. They continued down the path, coming into a place where the trees thinned and gave way to an open field, and Ochoa broke the silence, saying it had once been a hay field, but had been fallow now for many years. When they moved through the long grass, clouds of white, floating seeds rose around them, touched their cheeks and lashes, bright in the waning gold of the air. Just ahead of them, the forest closed in again, and among the trees stood the huge, dead husk of an oak. Tony recog-nized it, and knew that if they continued on their present course they would soon come to the Slaughterhouse.

"Why do you walk here alone?" Tony had said. "There's nothing here."

"There's an old bicycle just over there. Someone chained it to a tree when the tree was just a sapling, and left it. Now the tree has grown around it. Would you like to see?"

Tony shrugged. "Not really."

"Why do you come here, then?"

"To hide things."

A disturbance in the woods caused Tony to stop, catching his breath. A group of deer watched them from among the trees. Tony raised his hand, watched them scatter in a tangle of legs and flashing tails.

"You must know the place the students call the Slaughterhouse." Ochoa said. "Though I doubt it was anything so funereal. A cannery, maybe. It always surprises me that the students believe they live in a different world."

Tony said, "André Macarios says that your hair keeps growing after you die. Is that true?"

"I believe so."

"So some part of the person is still alive."

"Well, I don't really know if you could call it alive. What an interesting thought. Perhaps it takes some parts of the body longer to realize that they are dead. Of course, when I say dead, I mean the physical body exclusively. Perhaps the will remains for a time."

"In the hair?"

"It's possible. Why do you ask?"

"No reason."

"You're too young to be thinking of death."

"Young people die."

"Of course."

The Slaughterhouse was empty, as it would be on a weekday. There were more colored bottles tied to a sapling that grew in the middle of the ruin, its branches leafing the open sky; somehow, on all his previous trips to the Slaughterhouse, Tony had failed to notice this. They stood together under the tree in the leaves and rubble, watching the blue sky turn and the bottles swing, glinting and chiming in the light.

"The others don't understand you, do they?" Ochoa had said. "How could they?" There were tiny lines in the shadows beneath the priest's eyes. Black, as if all iris. Always a hint of apology there, Tony thought.

"You've seen things that frighten you," Ochoa said. "Are you ever going to tell me?"

"I don't know." Tony's palms felt their way over the rough bricks behind him. He felt unable to do anything but stare at those friendly, pitying eyes. Past the shutter, down to the points of black space; there was nothing in the center of a man's eye. It was like falling, seeing past humanity.

"Why be alone," Ochoa said. "You don't have to be." There was a scurf of stubble on Ochoa's jaw as if he had shaved carelessly, his attention, Tony thought, in some world beyond his own imagining. He listened as Ochoa told him what to feel. "You know you can always come to me," said Ochoa, and his knuckles, just for an instant, were warm against Tony's cheek. Did he lean into them? Did it matter? "I want to help." He must have sensed Tony's paralysis. He changed course. "There," he said. "Don't be...it's alright." He retreated with a laugh, shuffling his feet, black oxfords, the bare earth. And Tony had pitied him, a grown-up man in grown-up man shoes, standing in the leaves. "It's nothing," Ochoa concluded, smiling. He crossed his arms, as if feeling the cold of late afternoon, politely staring off into the trees while Tony leaned in the doorway, waiting for his breath to return.

When he offered the book, Tony had taken it from him. It was a thing of beauty, worn, peeling gilt leathers, clearly valuable. Tony had tried to speak some word of gratitude, but found himself strangely mute, and stood there, disoriented, clutching the book to his chest. Ochoa made a dismissive gesture. "Just promise you won't do anything unspeakable to it. It's a sin, to deface a book." He had extended a hand, rested it briefly on the book's cover; Tony felt the subtle pressure of it on his breastbone. "I read it when I first came here. The New World. De Vaca spent years here, you know, wandering, as a slave, as a shaman among the tribes. Read it, and tell me if it gives you vivid dreams."

And Tony had nodded, tucking the book inside the inner pocket of his jacket, feeling, as he did so, a sudden breeze through his hair, and realized that Ochoa had ruffled his overgrown forelock.

"Your hair is too long. Shall we go back?" he said. "What time is it?"

After Mass, Tony found Matt, Andre and Nunzio on the playing field. Jangling with reckless energy, he ran laps around the goal posts, until the cold burned his lungs and he went to sit on the bleachers next to Andre. Matt and Michael were on the field, Mike swinging a baseball bat, Matt with a ball and leather mitt. Matt was not an athletic talent, having little passion for sport. But his pitching was reminiscent of his singing, executed with care and technical skill. It was mesmerizing, watching him step to the side and paw the dirt, focus the glare of his blue eyes on the batter, curl his body up around the ball, eyes unwavering from their goal, glove brandished, and then release with a graceful sweep and pointed toe, uncoiling in one strong, smooth motion. Usually his pitches were too swift and deadly for Mike, who would grunt with the force of his swing but hit only air, and Matt would smile and look down while Mike then cursed and hocked spit into the grass. That evening, Matt was wearing a baseball cap decorated by a pair of red socks, which, he told Tony, were a symbol of his team. Tony found it curious that Matt, so apathetic to sports in general, should have a chosen baseball team at all. "The beautiful losers," Matt had said, when Tony had asked about it.

"You can't resist the sadness," Tony had said.

"That's right. Someone left my cake out in the rain."

The cap was dark blue, and when Matt stood on the mound to pitch that evening he turned its brim to the side and squared himself, glaring into the distance at Michael, who waved the tip of his raised bat and shifted from foot to foot. Matt glanced for an instant at Tony and Andre in the bleachers, glove raised to his chin, and Andre called out some word of sarcastic encouragement while Tony stared back in silence. Then Matt coiled and uncoiled in a rush, the ball flew true, Mike swung with his usual grunt of effort, and the crack of the bat rang across the field. Mike whooped and took off for a victory lap, fist raised in the air. Matt watched him cross the field. Then he glanced again at Andre and Tony, and came slowly toward them, shoulders hitched awkwardly. "Well," he said, "he had to get lucky sometime."

"You gave him that one," Andre said.

Matt sat down next to Tony, and took off his blue cap, picked briefly at the stitching. No one said anything; they watched Michael come running out of the woods with the ball in his hand, and when he reached them, glowing and red-faced with cold, they all went inside.

In choir practice, Tony heard Matt sing the counter tenor solo of the Agnus Dei. Matt's voice was both sustained and weightless. He knew how to throw it into a room, to make the air thicken until the sound was nearly visible and then hold back, disappearing, casting circles of endless dark. "What do you think of, when you sing?" Tony asked him that night. Matt said, "I stop thinking." De Vaca, stranded in a cold desert, found a burning tree by which he warmed himself.

Dear X,

I do not remember how it was I came to find you in Wolf Chapel, or why you should have been there yourself, in the middle of the night in November. The red sanctuary light burns, casting its many shadows, playing games with the building's murals. "Come here," you say. "Sit down." And I do, of course. We sit an arm's length distant in the second row, staring forward at the Christ writhing horribly on His six-foot cross, dark, lank thighs somehow appearing far more aged than they have any right to be, older than civilization itself, worm-eaten. Because of the length of the artificial nails, He appears to float in front of the cross rather than hang from it, projecting outward into the room, or perhaps he lunges straight for us with outstretched arms and is held back only by those nails, a holy high-diver caught midway into a fall. Behind Him, the Ignatius wolves are black, and can be seen only by their leaded outlines, softly throwing back the light. It is a strange place to come dodging nightmares. "Can't sleep?" You are in fine form tonight, all kindness, with a whole salvation's worth of concern lining your forehead. And I can only nod, the tongue-tied kid. "Neither can I," you tell me. "You can stay here, if you like."

And I do not know how it is I come to be lying with my head in your lap. The moment stands out for me because of its innocence. Truly. I can see it as if from beyond myself, a boy lying on a church pew, curled knees to chest, eyes drifting closed, held by a larger, darker figure, one hand on the boy's head, all serenity. We are a black pietà, you and I. This cannot have happened, but I remember it as if it were yesterday. The room is cold, even in the dull glow of fire, even as we are, practically in each other's arms. Your fingers play with my hair, twisting and smoothing, as you would tease the fur of a dog you aren't sure you can trust. You ask if there is something on my mind, and I say, "Not really."

You offer me licorice seeds from your pocket – there it is, the mystery of your sweet breath and immaculate teeth, snowy, radium-white – but I decline. After a while, you simply rest your hand on my head, welcoming home the prodigal animal, this erratic, dangerous creature that is both your son, and anything but. Sleep comes stealthily, rat-like, without my will or permission. I sink into this oily sleep. And in your lap I dream, and pull from my lips the hard, black feathers of crows, erupting like secret language under my tongue.

Watcher of nightmares. The bones of the old chapel creak. We are another word for silence.

Yours,
Tony

In the middle of the night, Tony felt a weight descend on his dormitory bed that was not his, and felt a hand grip him by the wrist. He knew, by the cool, shallow breaths, that it must be Alvara, that his isolation had somehow summoned her there, and he reached out in the darkness for her, his hands finding folds of fabric and grazing, for an instant, a collarbone. Alvara was a silhouette against the perfect dark of the dormitory (which might have been the bottom of the sea, touched by no sunlight, stirred only by Matt's sleeping breath), the shape of her somehow darker than the night, as if she were a hole in the world.

"Where were you?" Tony tried to say, but he was still mostly asleep.

Alvara's arms were around Tony, coaxing him from the bed, and Tony felt himself half carried, helpless, stumbling from the dormitory in a fog of sleep and out into the hall.

"Where are we going?" He did not want to look at Alvara's face, somehow fearing what he might see, for he recognized no trace of the summer cousin he had known in this presence that surrounded him, though it was true, thought Tony, it had been a long time since he had felt her there. Alvara was stronger than him, as she always had been, steered him irresistibly forward through the halls, and Tony went, not knowing where, and not caring.

"I looked back and I couldn't find you," said Tony, half in Spanish and half in English, and shook his head in confusion; it was as if a heavy curtain blew suddenly behind his eyes, snapped by the wind, leaving him dizzy and weak. He leaned against the one who held him, and let himself be led. "They told me you were dead."

La Capella de los Lobos felt larger and more cavernous in

the nighttime. Tony knew it when they arrived in the chapel because of its scent, like cool earth, the hum of the vast space, and the red flame of the sanctuary light that flared behind his closed lids. He remembered that the last time he had been here at night he had been betrayed by Nunzio, under the wolf's black eye. He stiffened for an instant, resisting.

Alvara would not be resisted. She dragged Tony forward so that his sock-covered feet slipped over the tiles. She was pulling Tony past the pews and the altar toward the sacristy, its mouth a vast empty socket, a void in the red dark. There were shapes moving all around them, wolves and serpents and conquistadors in a tangle of flames, bared teeth and weeping jaguar eyes. De Vaca, wandering foot-sore in the wilderness.

Tony did not know why he was begging, or why he was suddenly afraid. He struggled, hanging back, slipping forward in his ridiculous socks.

And then they were inside the sacristy, pressed close in the tiny space, and when the door closed the darkness was absolute. He was panting in terror, he could no longer see Alvara even as a shadow, could only feel her, with him and under his skin and all around him, arms tight around his body, heart beating quickly against his. They pressed together into the soft dark between the walls, fell helplessly and wildly against it until he could no longer discern the limits of their bodies, and Alvara kissed him on the neck in that room of holy things, as if telling him that this was the safest place, that here he was not alone, that no one could see them but God.

SIXTEEN

He understood power. He understood it the way I understood violence, because it was what we had been born to, what attracted us, what we knew. The birds knew to fly along the earth's magnetic lines, and we understood power and violence. That was what he saw in me, the mystical authority I wielded, the danger I possessed. How strange, that he would see me in this way; no one else did. But he didn't want me to wear the face of benevolence, the priest face. He knew it was not true.

Why play innocent, Father Wolf?

I let him peel off my skin with his pale, glass-like eyes, knowing his perception made me honest. This is the main peril of anyone two-faced: it is so exhausting. And such a relief, being seen.

Had I come into the fold to hide, and to be human? What better reason could one such as I have had to be a priest than to be driven, again and again, back to the fount of human misery? I took comfort in the charm and gentleness demanded of me. I had the power to empathize. But when I had run that race, when the day was done and everything gone quiet, when no one was watching, the

Other would be there. He didn't care how long I buried him. He had no respect for time, just as he had no trace of human kindness. What mercy he had was of an ancient streak, a quiet, inexorable patience. An animal's patience. Say what you will about me; I am a patient man.

Is anything more commanding than a hidden struggle? In the manner of beautiful people, the boy had grown used to the affect he had on others, used to being unattainable. But who can deny anything to a saint? I was both kind and remote. I gave him things, cuffed his hair, squeezed his shoulder, little suggestions of the physical presence. In mirrors, I avoided my own eyes. It was not that I feared the law, expulsion from the Order, or any extrinsic coercion; these things seemed not to matter, when my own will did not, and anyway he wasn't the kind to tell. It wasn't necessary to play such a careful game; likely enough it was always in my power to lead him into anything I imagined, in such a way that he would never know who led, and who had followed, because he was already in such a state of conflict. It wasn't difficult to see. These days I like to think I didn't, when I could have, because I was afraid of hurting him.

Fall drew on. In November the cold deepened and the skies bled white, though Jack Savage, always ready with predictions of the weather, said the snow would be late in coming. Afternoons in the quad, the boys donned sweaters under their uniforms. When I went out in the mornings on the forest's well-run trails, I would find my footprints of the previous day edged in frost. I placed my feet into those old wounds, but there was no quiet to be had now. The stranger planned, and I moralized. Even this mental clangor was sweet, restraint and elevation; such snares we set to tangle our own feet. I was a good man, because I didn't. It was intoxicating. One might say the sin was not in the want, but in the pleasure I derived from it, morose delectation, the vanity of struggle. And I would always fail to drive away these unsuitable visions, because I needed them to tell me who I was.

I once heard the confession of an unhappily childless woman. "Children fill the soul," she had said. "One needs purpose." I had advised her to take up volunteer work; what an idiot she must have thought me. But I had been barren myself, without purpose. Now the struggle filled my life. In silence, I lit my candles to Schaefer, and he rattled through me with every breath and footfall.

The boy hung at the edge of the playing field, face red with cold, waiting his turn at something or other. There was a small crowd of students pelting back and forth across the field. He spotted my approach, and looked away, as if I were a person of no consequence to him. So I went straight to him, planted myself before him with my back to the others, watching as shock overtook indifference, and he drew into himself, fearful of me; would I ruin everything? I shed my scarf and hung it around his throat, tucking the stray ends in at the gap of his blazer. "There," I said. "Keep it. I have others." Against my knuckles, the skin of his windpipe was hot and unexpectedly rough, not with stubble but with a grainy residue, clean, like chalk dust. He didn't thank me. His eyes faltered, slipped down my shins and fell into the dead grass, trapped. And I walked on through the locusts bordering the yard and down toward Alexander House, the wind cooling my neck, unable to think of the last time I had been so blithely fearless. Behind me, the game raged on without interruption.

For years I had avoided thinking of Schaefer. Now it occurred to me that he was probably dead. As a young person, he had occupied my fantasy life. He had been the subject of both rage and pity. In my mind, Schaefer and my father were the same; it was Schaefer I fought, Schaefer's aging bones, creaking under my hand, his defeated eyes glaring from the shadows. I grew strong, overpowered him and replaced him. I stepped into his skin, because there would always be a Schaefer, or a Santos. That man who stood tall with the stars around his head, bitten nails and a dark overcoat. The stranger, looming large in children's nightmares. A man with the heart of a predator.

In Araba I had avoided him, because I did not know what I would do if I were ever close to him again, no easy feat in a town small as ours. I let him near me only once after that night in the truck. I was fifteen and it was Sunday, and I sat in my best clothes on the steps of the church, waiting for my mother so we could walk home together. And there he was. He turned a corner a hundred yards down the street and slowly approached, hair so pale it would never show his age, limping like a chained dancing bear. I stopped breathing, helpless in the grip of the old spell. I had lost control of my own body; his proximity made it not mine anymore, as if our moment had been yesterday, not years distant. He hugged the wall of the church to avoid a group of women passing by. He would come near enough to touch me, and I knew I was still his, a thing, a toy, a prey animal. I imagined his hot handprints would rush to the surface of my skin for all the world to see. I watched his eyes dart from side to side under the brim of his hat. He passed right by me, his elbow brushing past my knee, glanced at me and then away, murmuring an apology. I will never know if he recognized me then, sweating in my ill-fitting suit, gangly and razor-burned, a broken-voiced scarecrow improbably striped with white, stranded halfway between boy and man. He made the end of the street and turned the corner, hands in his pockets and one foot dragging, passed forever out of my life. How heavily he moved. I shrank into the shadow of the church door, pressed myself to the warm stones until my throat relaxed and I could breathe again.

The boy from Michoacán would leave little trophies, cat-like, to be found. A gallery of destroyed things. Textbooks with the pages shredded. Boys coming in from the playing field with sprained limbs, complaining of the Mexican terror. A prayer card of St. Sebastian, tied to his tree on that Roman hilltop and pin-cushioned with arrows, sheep in the field beyond him grazing obliviously. The boy had gouged him through the eyes with a pencil, so that you could look through the skull of the saint to see a narrow view of the world, two holes of light. But it was brutal and messy, the point stabbed in many times. His aim, I thought, was not so true at close range. I had begun to tell myself I knew what he wanted. I had begun to feel stalked.

I have always survived on very little sleep. Sometimes my dreams are of mangrove swamps. Gauche, maybe, to chronicle the landscape of my dreams. But I will say I dreamed of India, and of the boy from the New World, somehow in conjunction. Teasing dreams, because in them I never managed to escape from that unpainted mission bedroom, the torn screens and St. Ignatius nailed to the wall. Visions to wake me, grasping after the shreds, industrial cotton fabric shrugged aside, a shoulder grazed by a kiss, trails of iridescent water, a wandering moon come home to me. Moon, moon. He said, what was the point of it, all that running? I dreamed him up against a wall, loosened tie and uniform button-down so incongruous in that imagined setting, never letting me forget it was a dream. The prep school slang, the shirt untucked, the cast that carried, so subtly, the badge of his distress, and of course those pale eyes — they haunt me still — all of it impossible. But still I dreamed. And sometimes he was that other boy, the one who had led me into the mangroves so long ago. The boy I had carried who turned his face from me, who had stared past me with indifference, slipping quietly out of my arms. In a borrowed room, a borrowed bed, the shape of love held me at a distance, foot in the middle of my chest. A size eight American athletic shoe. Green, cruel, salacious eyes. That way he had of glancing up, of feigning innocence; how I hated him, as if he were the only thing between me and simple grace. Which was this current visitor, the dead or the living? It hardly mattered anymore. The Malinche, reborn, placed a foot on the neck of another conquistador.

Beyond my window, the stars made themselves known, each one held gently in its solitary sphere, hinting that there were many worlds, not just the one, that everything I dreamed was given form. In one of them, the nun from Uppsala might not have been taken by the tiger, or even Falco might still have been lying in that other room, with his books and his records and his sad ashtray, not me. In one of them, a borrowed car sat under a covered bridge, the engine ticking softly as it cooled. In one of them, a horse ran across a field in Araba, trailing a broken rope. In one of them, Dakshin Rai had claimed what should have been his, and I had thrown my arms around him. One little man in one little world held his place in the universe, assuming he was alone, struggling to lift his tiny weight of loss. One little man making gestures, making sounds, pointing his finger, naming the family of stars. I would wake up still smothered with mosquito netting, breath harsh and the hollow of my arm empty. And I swear the moon was brighter when I dreamed of India, the belly of a drowned, white cow, that same moon that made the village dogs bark, hanging low enough to crush the huts on their knobby stilts. The dogs, semi-feral, skulked around the walls, fighting and rutting and digging for the scraps. The bones projected from their collapsed flanks. I had been told never to feed them, that sometimes a dog would bite a man and the man would lose his mind and become like an animal.

Even the quarter moon was too bright for me to sleep. I walked the school; I knew they called me The Ghost, and it was fitting. Ghost I was, no comfort could be had. His shape in my doorway; but whose? Which of my bad, black lambs in the three a.m. darkness? A glancing kiss turned at the last moment, my tongue shot with the salt of his upper lip. I prowled the school as I prowled the compound, or wherever I was, asleep or waking, re-learning how to breathe, waiting for the heat to break and the night to die. Waiting for a reprieve, and dreaming of him. Dreaming of him.

The day of the covered bridge, the boy from The New World was throwing rocks by the school's western wall, and somehow struck a small bird. It fell to the ground and lay dying, and he bent over it, seemingly surprised by his luck. When the creature stopped fluttering, he picked it up. The bird fit easily in the rosy sheaf of his hand. He studied it curiously. Then he looked up and saw me.

I said, "Shame on you."

He stared at me without expression or apology. It was after the point in our relationship where he had discovered he could push me.

"Why did you do that?"

He said, "I wanted it to be mine."

"Bury it."

He did, kicking aside the leaves, scraping a shallow trough in the earth near the wall. He lay the bird in it, and covered it over, looked up at me expectantly.

"Come with me," I said.

"Where are we going?"

I didn't answer, because I didn't know, and he trailed wordlessly after me.

At Alexander, no one was home. I made the boy wait by the front gate while I went inside, rifling through Mark's coat pockets until I found his keys. It was a silly, overly large key ring with a pewter disk commemorating the "Sheep and Wool Fair." Mark only had the one key, for the car. There were no locked doors in our faculty house. By the time I returned to the front yard, Sigil the cat had found the object of my worry, and was in the process of stropping his ankles, mewing, while the boy stood uncertainly, fists tucked in against his chest. He was, I thought, refraining from kicking Sigil, and I quickly said, "This way."

"Are we supposed to be doing this?" He looked quizzically at me as he dropped into the passenger's seat of Mark's car. "It smells like cigarettes in here."

"You won't get in trouble if you're with me. Seatbelt."

"Will you get in trouble?"

"No."

"Where are we going?"

"Please put on your seatbelt."

"This is crazy."

Yes, it was. There was dirt under his fingernails from burying the bird. He had somehow acquired scrapes on his knuckles, and grass stains on his knees. I could hear the click of hard candy, worried behind his teeth. "Spit that out," I said. He shrugged, and complied, leaning out of the open door, coming back with lips red and sticky. He glanced at my face, wiped his mouth on the sleeve of his sweater. The red scent lingered in the car, fighting with the reek of Mark's cigarettes. I had long since fallen in love with all his vices, long since fallen for all of it, but there was no sense in gilding the lily. I was agitated enough. A headache started at the corner of my eye, then passed. His breath was sharp and spicy. "What is that, anyway?" I asked him. "What are you rotting your teeth with these days?"

"Pop Rocks, and Cinnamon Imperials."

"Both? Mixed together?"

He shrugged. "What?"

No one saw us leave the school. We drove down the country road, passing few other people. I didn't know where I was going, and took strange turns that looked promising. There was a house painted yellow beside a leaning fence, faded washing luffing in the cold breeze. An old man stood by the mailbox, hunched in an overly large coat. His thin neck and upper lip poked forward, giving him the look of a turtle. That could be me, I thought, in twenty years, if I chose it. The American disillusionment. It would be easy to slip away quietly, to mix with other people, a solitary house on the outskirts of some pretty, nowhere town. People like me were seldom allowed to be alone in old age, retired to a single room in a house of worn-out God servants. The idea of being cared for, fawned over with that soft, false veneration, was repulsive to me. "Nothing like the last cigarette," Mark always said, one hand on the wheel and the other angling out the window, smoke torn from his fingers in the wind. "That's why it's never really the last." Mark was slowly killing himself, deliberate about it. As much as he insisted that cigarette smokers don't believe in the future, it seemed to me he knew where he was going. I had lost the feel of a manual transmission, and kept grinding gears. The boy at my side nipped his chest strap nervously. "This isn't your car, is it?"

"It belongs to Father Desmond."

"So, priests can have cars?"

I said nothing.

"Are you angry with me?"

"Disappointed. You shouldn't have done that. It was cruel. You're better than that."

He fell silent. Then he said, all in a rush, "It would be unwise of you to kidnap me."

"Unwise?"

"Very."

I glanced over at him, and saw that he was grinning, hoping to lighten my mood.

"I've seen troubled boys like you sink, and ruin their lives," I said. "You have such potential. It would hurt me if you squandered yourself in that way. I worry for you."

He continued to stare at me, the grin slipping a little. "This is so weird," he said, lapsing into English as he never would have a month ago.

"Why?"

"I just never imagined you driving a car." He was working on his American accent. It was jarring, as if he was not only making light of the situation, but deliberately putting distance between us. I was the only foreigner in the car.

"Of course. What did you think?"

He shrugged. "I don't know. Hey. Let's go to New York City."

I didn't answer him. He sighed, slipping down in the seat, and tapped the center console. His fingers looked red and sticky; I wondered if there would be cinnamon fingerprints all over Desmond's car. Our tiny crime scene, stolen, sticky, smelling of hard candy and the unthinkable.

He said, "People are scared of me. The teachers and the others. It's like they think I'm dangerous or something."

"You are dangerous."

He laughed. "Come on."

"I thought you were proud of your danger. You said so, just now. Is it so terrible, to be feared?"

"You're not scared."

"I'm indestructible."

"Come on."

"Who said it was better to be feared than loved?"

He rolled his eyes. "I don't know."

"Machiavelli. We can only guess at how he fared in high school."

I was relieved when the town unfolded before me, my strange route having led us in a giant circle. We stopped at the one traffic light, no one but us on all the street, and I saw him lean his forehead on the window, breath misting the glass, eyeing the blinking lights around the movie theater marquee. His hands were folded in his lap, fingers laced together, white around the knuckles giving the lie to his careless posture. His denim knee lay near the clutch; I could feel the warmth of it in the back of my hand. A girl stepped out the door of a shop, wearing a uniform and carrying a broom, and he must have known her, because he hunched down lower in the seat, raising a hand to the side of his face, making a sound of mortification like a soft growl. The mystery of his secret life. The light changed, and I continued on through town.

"Acquaintance of yours?" I said.

He shook his head.

"Don't lie to me."

"She's just this girl I talk to sometimes."

"You're sweet on her?"

He was silent. It was none of my business.

"Will I be forced to revoke your town privileges?" There were no solid rules about girlfriends, but I was unable to say anything reasonable. "Shall I have you stay here over the holidays? I could, you know."

"No, sir," he said quietly. He glanced at me from under his lashes, and then looked out the window. His sudden meekness baffled me, and I was amazed to find myself stung with jealousy, the situation spinning out of my control.

"I am trying to help," I said. "These people will only waste your time. They don't understand."

"Yes. I know."

"You shouldn't associate with people like that."

"Like what? Female people? Older people?"

"You need to be careful."

"Yes, sir. You're absolutely right, sir."

I glanced over at him, and surprised a wicked little smile on his face. He was not quick enough to hide it. He was playing with me, the devil. "Look here," I said, and he cut me off. "What's that?" he said, pointing ahead, sitting up straighter. We had just passed the outlying houses, had crested a little rise and dived into a wood. Where the land dropped away, a stream wound through the oaks and birches, having cut itself a deep channel in the slate. Downed trees lay half out of the water, black and swift with small white curlers. A bridge spanned the river, one of those wooden covered bridges from another time. We plunged into the darkness of its insides, the boards thudding rhythmically beneath our wheels. I stopped the car in the middle of the bridge, and cut the engine. When the instrument panel had gone out, there was nothing but the dim, green light of the river. "Wow," the boy said softly.

We sat together in the darkness, steaming the windows with our breath. Beneath us, we could hear the river; its light came dancing up in thin pale ribbons, snaking across the timbers. They lit the side of his face. I knew that it was not a place to linger, that we were likely to be disturbed by another car, or a pedestrian. But it was dark, and we were alone. We were hidden. I swallowed the water in my mouth, not knowing what to say. The boy fixed his eyes on the dashboard.

"I didn't mean to be so harsh," I said at last. He didn't answer. "Listen. I care for you, is all. I care what happens to you. Don't you know that?"

And he replied, in a strange, flat voice, "Feels like a cave in here." His lips were stung with fake cinnamon.

"Can I ask you a question?"

"Knock yourself out."

"Do you trust me?"

"No," he said, staring into the lights of the dashboard.

He refused to acknowledge me as I leaned in toward him. He smelled of Ivory, Pop Rocks, and the damp, clean wool of his sweater. I found myself wanting very much to rest my head on his shoulder, and I did. He let me, or rather froze, like a startled deer. The river made its muffled curling sounds, the stripes of sun licked over the darkness and the tensed cords of his throat, and I rested there with my head on his shoulder, and he let me. His heart fluttered under my ear. It was hopeless, hopeless. I felt very tired.

But my thoughts moved fast with those crackling strands of light. I thought that I would like to build a giant fire. To come alive in that way. And in my thoughts I had killed him, again and again. That was the true sin. In the woods, in the fields, on the stone altar of some desolate mountainside, wherever he would consent to follow me, a blade driven in up to the handle where he would never see it coming; not because he was innocent, but because he would look the other way. He had always known better than to trust me. His pulse would bounce and falter and then slither away under my thumb in the way of a grass snake. I saw it gilt in lurid colors: the death of a catamite. In the woods, in the fields, in the guts of a covered bridge. With every word I spoke, with every touch, I killed him a little more. But he would get away from me, what was essential to him, the purity I coveted expiring. They could never be mine, not any of them. They, not he, a plurality now. I saw them as a parade of shadows, the clean and smiling faces of my doom. Every one of them died in my arms.

I felt diseased, contagious. Alone, in physical hunger, my mouth filled with dark juices. But not alone, for there was the stranger, that ghost-pale creature, always awake and planning, ever present. He sported Schaefer's square palms and bitten fingernails; the tame details of his physicality, the way he tapped the steering wheel and whistled through his teeth, had become the man for me. He was the voice soft as cotton that came to kill my silence, ending my life of quiet. I leaned there with my head on the boy's shoulder, soft and weak, felt the tendon in his neck stiffen as he turned his head slightly, his face pressed into my hair. For a moment, I gave him the whole weight of me, and he held me up. His whisper was a roar beneath my ear. "Please," he said, "please don't," and I said, "It's alright." And there we were, alone in a dark car surrounded by the scent of Desmond's cigarettes, the covered bridge, the lights. Hopeless, hopeless. I sat up, turned the keys to start the car. We left the covered bridge, came out blinking in the light. The boy leaned against the window. He wouldn't look at me, eyes fixed too intently on the passing scenery. I wondered if he ever would look at me again. On the window, blue mizzle now against the open sky, I could see the quickness of his breath, coming and going. He looked more crushed than I had expected, all his show of boldness come to nothing. We took the country roads in silence, but it seemed to upset him. A mile or so before we arrived at school, he started to tell me he was sorry and seemed unable to stop, though I told him there was no need for that. "Sorry," he said, "I'm sorry."

"Don't," I felt numb and tired, and had nothing to offer him. I just wanted him to be gone. "What do you have to be sorry for?" But he just went on repeating it.

"I don't want this to change things," he said, at last.

"Don't want *what* to change things?"

And he just looked at me, helplessly. If I was not going to speak it, he had no way to put it into words.

On the grounds, I pulled the car into its place, and the boy leapt out without a word and bolted away, his sneakers throwing up birds of damp turf, and it was just as well, I thought, leaning across the seats to pull his door closed. I walked back to Alexander House alone. Mark had not returned yet, and I slipped the keys back into his pocket, secret safe for the time being. But it was an ugly secret. I wanted to call it out, the horror of my true identity. To build a giant fire.

This is my body, broken for you. Said often enough, do the words become mine? Bow the head, strike the chest, wrestle the bluntness of the world. Isolation has made me a heretic.

"You look wrong," said Savage. "You look like you've seen a ghost." She sat in my kitchen frowningly, Old Savage, with her softness and her solicitude. Her hands were around a cup. Vermont, it said, with a scene of autumn leaves. Dear Savage, her hands like trowels, short fingered, mother's hands. The nails of them were battered

with dirt from the garden. Our garden. There was a smudge
of latex dust on her wrist, where she had peeled off her
hygienic gloves earlier in the day. Ah, I thought, what did it
matter, now. But it mattered, it mattered, and the weight of
it would crush me. So many secrets. "It's not a very long
story," I would say, and start talking. My own voice would
find an echo in my ear. I could taste the bitterness of her
instant coffee. She had that paleness around her eyes, that
tension, so I knew her arthritis was acting up. And I loved
her, I really did, then more than ever, an equal and a friend.
After a few minutes, I couldn't bear to look at her face. I
would confess to Savage, it wouldn't take long to cover the
essentials, perhaps it would even bring relief. I would
promise to try harder, to do my best not to do it again, or
something of that nature. And when I stopped talking, the
click of her spoon would sound on the table as she put it
down. She would get up with a sigh, carry her cup to the
sink, rinse it out and set it lip-down in the dish rack. She
would leave my house forever, closing the door softly
behind her. I smiled at Margaret Savage, saying, "Oh, you
know. Just tramping around the woods."

Unbearable though it was, the secret was now my
companion.

I knew I would not sleep that night, and so I planned to
spend it in my office. When all were asleep, I would wander
the halls of the school, as was my habit. At three in the
morning the school was a different world, soft light left on
at the ends of the oak-paneled halls, shadows pulling on the
edges of my vision. Shadows wandering, like me. In one of
the gardens there was a maudlin stone angel leaning on an
urn, ivy pooling between her knees, an angel hiding her
face, a little plaque below, *Donated in Memory of Thomas
Mattheson, Loving Husband and Father*. The boys called her
Saint Hangover. Sometimes in darkness I could have sworn

she changed her position slightly, as if stone itself and the nature of things could become fluid. Darkness would soften the edges of the world, and the rigid shapes of day could change their forms. I would be there when it happened, walking through it, past altar and classroom and dormitory hall, the door where the green-eyed boy lay sleeping. But I did not go wandering that night, because he chose that night to give up. He came to me, as I had thought he would. Where else would he have gone?

SEVENTEEN

When dawn came Tony found himself alone in the sacristy, though he could not remember having fallen asleep, and could not remember being abandoned. His limbs were cramped from the night spent in the cold space; it was with the movements of an old man that he pushed open the heavy door and squinted out into the white light of morning, the chapel's huge windows ablaze with sun. Wolf Chapel was empty, its black, whale-rib timbers still holding up the Indians and conquistadors, who, in the waking world, were stationary beings once again. Tony wondered why no one was in the chapel, and then realized how early it must be; the entire school was still asleep. He clutched his clothes around him, and shuffled to the chapel door. When he turned his back on the altar, a chill caused the hairs on the back of his neck to rise, but he did not turn, only moved more quickly. Only when he had closed the chapel door behind him did he dare to draw a breath.

His body felt strange, somehow no longer his. It was as if he had grown smaller in the course of the previous night, and no longer filled the boundaries of his own body. His ribs ached slightly, and his jaw; he must have been clenching his teeth during the night, but could not remember doing so. His mouth had the taste of wine and pomegranates.

In the hall just around the corner from the dormitory, he felt water seeping through his socks, and realized the floor was covered in wet, soapy streaks. He smelled Lupe María's alarming scent before he actually saw her, but by then it was too late to turn back. Lupe María leaned on the handle of her mop, chewing leaves, a rosary dangling from her belt under her black shawl. When she saw him, she clutched it.

"*María purísima,*" she hissed, her eyes narrowed.

"*Lo siento,*" said Tony automatically, forgetting to speak English. It was different with Lupe María, different from Ochoa, who somehow made him feel that he was chosen, a part of something. Lupe María made him feel afraid; it alarmed him that he could speak to her in a way the others couldn't. He didn't want to look at the old woman with her rosary and black shawl that, Tony could see at close range, was covered in cat hair, and so he looked at the floor and tried to edge around her. But she moved toward him, blocking his way to the dormitory, and said, "You look like the devil."

She leaned in close, so that he was almost overpowered by her meaty smell, her licorice breath, her sly smile, curved up and then down at the corners of her mouth, like an iguana. "Last night, I saw *El Morro* walking," she said. "Dark of the moon, time for secrets. Where were you last night, Lunito? Not in your snug boy bed? You can tell me." She grinned. "Yes?" Her teeth were small and perfect, like a child's. Tony was frozen in place, could only stare into her shrewd, veiled eyes.

"Lunito," she said in a whisper, "*los muertos nunca se van.*"

He stared at her, feeling stubborn and reluctant to speak. Lupe María reached into her pocket and brought out a little cloth pouch, placing it in his hand. "Keep it," she said. "Don't let them see it." By "them," he thought she must have meant the priests. She pressed her thumb to his forehead, her other hand clutching at her *curandera* beads, and her eyes crinkled with what looked like sympathy. "*Pobrecito*," she murmured. "Poor boy."

Her eyes focused on something beyond Tony, sympathy vanishing, and she was backing away from him. He slipped the little talisman into his pocket. Behind him, Tony heard the heavy tread of a man, and turned to see Father Carol.

"What is the meaning of this?" Carol said. He looked from Tony to Lupe María. "Mrs. Ruiz, is this boy bothering you?"

Lupe María ducked her head, flashing her clever, iguana smile. Tony did not know why she should be afraid of the priest, but she was. "*Lo siento, Padre*," she said, retrieving her mop and bucket and backing away. "Lord bless you, kind *Padre*, and keep you in good health." And she was gone. Tony and the priest listened to her brisk, retreating steps until they could not hear them anymore.

Carol said, "Where are you going, son?"

"Back to bed," said Tony.

"I should hope so," said Carol, and he stood at the chapel door, following Tony with his eyes as he made his way back to the dormitories.

That evening, Tony found his bicycle and left the school alone, pedaling quickly down the dirt road, still with no clear idea where he was going when he found himself stopping at the Slaughterhouse, the evening red and wild with electricity; there would be an ice storm later that night, and young trees, the pliant ones, would be toppled and broken all through the back country by morning.

Tony dropped his bike in the dead leaves, and followed

the side of the building to the door, his fingers lingering on the stained brick. He stood in the factory's inner sanctum, open to the sky, amid piles of rubble and birch saplings. There were pale blue and green bottles, the detritus of generations of contraband gatherings, and they rattled together when he kicked them. All day, he had been hiding the little bag Lupe María had given him. He took it out now and looked it over, a bladder of plain white cotton half the size of his palm, stitched in red around the edges, smelling of cedar. It appeared to be nothing more mysterious than a sachet, something the old woman would use to repel moths. What had he been expecting? Angrily, he put it back in his pocket.

There was a pack of Marlboros hidden behind a loose brick in the wall, Nunzio's cache. Tony held the damp pack in his hand and laughed, though there was no one to hear him. "*Pobrecito*," he muttered. "Keep it." He took a cigarette and held it gently between his lips, turned in place, and squinted into the winter sun. He thought of Nunzio, who had crowed at his own cleverness the day he hid the cigarettes in the wall, and then, inexplicably, thought of Françoise, of her idle hand in his hair. He squeezed his eyes tighter, till the light broke into pieces and went white. He discovered that if he kept turning slow, three-step circles, if he kept his eyes on the sun, it was almost like flying, optical sunbursts and all. It was a pleasant sensation. He stopped spinning and stood, cigarette in his mouth, blinded.

From the woods outside the walls, he heard footsteps, and squinted through the green haze to see a woman in a black coat standing framed in the Slaughterhouse door.

"Hey you," she said. It was Bernadette. She wore red cowboy boots and a black wool coat. Her cheeks were flushed with cold.

He said nothing, and she smiled. "Did you think you

were the only ones who knew about this place?"

"No," said Tony truthfully. "It seems like everybody does."

"Should I go?"

"No," he said. "Stay, if you want to." He could not decide if he was happy to see her. It seemed unreal to see her without her uniform, away from the Soda Fountain. She might have been a ghost, but a warm, solid ghost.

She came closer, peered at him from under her russet hair, and he thought of a red filly hiding among trees in a forest, and felt the weight in his chest turn over and ease slightly.

"Do you need a light?" she asked.

"No. I mean, yes. Yes please."

She smiled and fished in her coat pocket, brought out a lighter, and cupped a hand to Tony's face, shielding his cigarette from the wind while it took the light.

"Would you like one?" Tony said, and coughed.

"No," she said. "Cigarettes kill. Didn't you know that?"

"No," said Tony. "They're glamorous."

He smiled half-heartedly at the weak joke, and then inhaled as she touched his face, flinched away from her outstretched hand.

"Easy," she said. "You've got something. An eyelash."

He swallowed and looked at his shoe, laughed quickly, one short bark. He looked at her, turned his face to the red sun. "Is it gone?"

She was very close. Too close, really. There was an invisible barrier they seemed to be leaning into. He had kissed a girl, a shipping magnate's daughter in a white frothy dress, larking through the darkness by the swimming pool, the night alive with hissing sparklers in the hands of children. Alvara had mocked him for it later. "When can we expect a happy announcement?" she had said. "Or did you choke her to death with your tongue?" But this was a different world, now, these stones and cold light. He could still feel the weight of Ochoa's head resting against his collarbone, and the *bruja* talisman in the pocket of his jeans. Bernadette turned her face slightly to the side, and pressed closer. Her eyes held the light of the sun, gleaming gold and yellow. "It's still there," she said. "Would you like me to get it?"

"Yes."

"Yes, meaning no?"

"Yes."

She plucked the cigarette from his lips and took one drag of it before tossing it aside. Then she took his face between her hands, leaned far in, and swept the rim of his eyelid with her tongue.

Kissing Bernadette was like the way he had always imagined it, except that she was actually the same height as he was, not taller, as he had thought. It was like kissing anyone, really. Bernadette was rough. She grabbed his lapels with large hands and pressed against him, pushing him back to the brick wall, and for a while he simply let her handle him, shy of his own comparative lack of experience. But there didn't appear to be any secret in it. When he pushed back and pulled her around, so that her coat was catching on the dead vines that covered the bricks, she laughed, and made an odd sound like a sigh, the exact sound Matt Kelly made when he was exasperated, a synapse on which Tony did not want to speculate.

There was suddenly something frantic in his need to kiss Bernadette, to taste her salty mouth, smell the coffee grounds of her hair and press himself against her, it was the most important thing, like breathing and forgetting, and he kissed her hard and punishingly, but Bernadette was too soft to wound with kissing. It left him feeling clumsy and aware of himself, concerned with the mechanics of tongues and teeth. Her hands were suddenly fussing with the front of her coat, with the buttons of her shirt, and he was overwhelmed by her fiery scent, by the warmth that escaped from the opening of her shirt, surrounding him. "Come here," she said, and placed one of his hands firmly on each of her breasts, holding them in place with hers. He stopped kissing her then, and when he looked into her face he was shocked to see the stony blankness. She leaned against the wall, hips forward, shirt unbuttoned and his hands on her, and her eyes were closed, there were creases between them, her neck was tensed, her head tipped back. She looked like a perverse St. Agatha. He stepped back from Bernadette, hands still held out before him as if clutching something hot and precious. "Sorry," he mumbled.

Bernadette nodded and looked away from him, looked over his shoulder, toward the setting sun, blinking her eyes. "Sorry," she said. "Sorry. You're a fucking kid. What do you know about sorry?"

"Alright. I'm not sorry."

She leaned forward, and he hardened himself inwardly, thinking she would strike him, but she only grinned at him, showing her gapped front teeth. "Sorry is what you say when you leave. You say sorry when someone dies." She pinched his chin. "Just my luck. It's always the pretty ones, isn't it?"

"I'm lost, Bernadette."

"That's a bitch."

"Bernadette," said Tony, "why are you a bad girl? Why do they say that about you?"

It was such a naïve and childish-sounding question, Tony felt his face heating and felt like a fool, but she gave him a long, considering look, and said, "Give me one of those."

Tony withdrew a cigarette from the damp pack in his pocket and handed it to her, watching her eyes narrow through the smoke. She was a surprisingly elegant smoker, holding the cigarette with a strange wrist flourish, exhaling in plumes from her nostrils. Her shirt was still open to the navel, as if she had forgotten it, revealing her black, workman-like bra and something Tony had not noticed before, a long scar, a sickle moon running across her abdomen.

"What do you think, kiddo? Do you really want to know?"

"Yes."

"You're not much of a liar." Her eyes softened again. "You remind me of this boy I used to know, before. Same pretty eyes. He was a tease. Is that what you are?"

"No," said Tony. "I mean, I don't want to be."

"You don't know what you want."

Tony leaned against the wall, not knowing what to say.

"It's not a crime, or something," she said. "Don't sweat it."

"Bernadette," he said, "were you thinking of that other boy while we were…just now?" She raised her eyebrows, and he amended quickly. "I mean, it's fine, but…did you feel like you were with him, just for a second?"

"Get over it."

"I do know what I want, Bernadette."

"Uh huh."

"You're beautiful."

Bernadette sighed, shrugged and flicked the cigarette. "If you wouldn't mind… this is a small town."

"No," said Tony, "I won't tell anyone."

She nodded, fixed her hair, buttoned her shirt, and walked off into the woods the way she had come.

"Bernadette," he called after her, "were you with that other boy, when you were kissing me? Could you actually see him?"

"Mystery is everything, kiddo."

"Hey! What am I supposed to do?"

He heard her horse-laughing sharp through the dusk as she called back to him, "Figure it out, Lorca."

He looked down at the twist of his un-smoked cigarette, trampled in the dirt. The sun went down. He collected his bike, and rather than take the road back to the school, walked it along the forest track, the one Ochoa had shown him. He tramped through the deep leaves, leaning forward into the handlebars. He wondered about Bernadette's scar and how she had gotten it, wishing he had asked her and knowing he would never be able to do so; the scar would haunt him for years to come, when he would make up stories, each one more elaborate than the last, in order to explain it and what Bernadette had done. But he knew he would never be able to talk to her again.

There was a photograph in Tony's portfolio, one of his early pieces, black and white, of a girl smoking a cigarette, leaning against a brick wall. The figure in the photograph was a girl, not a woman, which is what Bernadette had been in the fall of '87, just a girl, she couldn't have been older than nineteen, though she had seemed like a woman or a monument to Tony at the time, some fierce Venus of meat and bonfires and aloof intimacy. She would stalk his relationships for decades. Bernadette, who had done him no harm.

He walked past the dead oak and checked at the sudden snap of a twig. "Hello?" He waited, stomach fluttering, as the leaves crunched beneath somebody's shoes on the other side of the tree. A shock of blond hair poked around the trunk, and Matt Kelly's shy, penitent smile followed it.

"Tony," he said, "I hoped I might find you out here." Matt seemed nervous, grinning, twisting his foot in the dirt, hands stuffed deep down in his pockets, the crooks of his elbows turned outward in a kind of shrug. "Hey, listen, I need to talk to you. I just want to say sorry. For being so weird. And if there's anything you want to talk about…"

He stopped, peering at Tony. "You okay?"

"What are you doing here?" Tony's voice sounded angry, though he wasn't sure why. Matt's smile slipped.

"Nothing," he said. "Looking for you. What are you doing?"

It wasn't too late, Tony thought, for him to return Matt's gesture of friendship, to smile at him and say, "You wouldn't believe what just happened." They could walk back to school together, laughing about it. But what Tony said instead was, "You're creeping around in the woods like a… a creep. No wonder nobody likes you."

Matt's face colored. He opened his mouth, but no sound came out.

"Just leave me alone," Tony said. "I don't need you."

Matt's eyes glistened. "You'll be sorry." He turned from Tony and ran further into the woods. Tony reached into his pocket, took the little pouch from Lupe María, and tossed it after him, a scrap of white lost among the leaves.

At St. Ignatius, Tony chained his bike to the rack among the others, climbed the steps and pushed through the heavy doors. The heat of the inside made him sleepy, and he turned away from the dining hall and the echo of boys' voices there, making his way instead toward the dormitory. With any luck he would be able to catch an hour of sleep before lights out, when the darkness came. And when it came, he would be hungry but somewhat rested.

EIGHTEEN

Privately, Tony thought of Lena Schaefer as The German Commandant's Granddaughter. It began with a story she told him about herself, one of the first, unfolding a map of atrocities, the guilt of which Lena believed she had somehow inherited along with the man's surname. "It means 'shepherd,'" she told him. She had never met Grandpa Schaefer, so she said. But she dreamed of him often, a quiet man with a Russian bullet lodged in his neck, false papers in his coat pocket, limping into old age under an assumed identity somewhere in the chaos of post-war Europe. Perhaps even as a shepherd. Her eyes grew round, the morbid, squirming joy of this association plain, however she tried to disguise it. "I try to imagine the karmic enormity of it," she told him, "but of course I can't. I don't have the right to even try to imagine it."

"You're going to wind up an academic," Tony said. "That should get you square with the universe." He was fairly sure the story was a lie, one more of Lena's bizarre, self-mutilating habits. "Is that why you're sleeping with me? Atonement?" But he liked to imagine it; The German

Commandant's Granddaughter, and her cloud of karmic guilt.

It was always a certain kind of woman. They were like sea creatures; they smelled of the sea, of wildlife. Their flesh was ghostly flesh. Their depths were unknowable. They enraged him, enthralled him, alarmed him too; he knew they would, because he chose them carefully. He didn't want to deviate from the formula.

"Do you hate us all?" Lena asked him.

He denied it; ultimately, what he felt was a bitter cocktail of envy and pity, a tug-of-war that Lena mistook for misogyny. It struck him as unfair that she should think so. "I love women," he said. "You're out of your mind."

Not surprisingly, his relationships with women never lasted very long, resembling brief forays into a hostile encampment. He would occasionally think of them, a parade like Christmas reindeer traipsing across his roof: On Sophie, on Haley, on Laura, on Nina! On Shawna, on Sarah, on Sasha, on Deena! They were usually young, though youth itself wasn't the object. It was their neutral quality that attracted him, college and conservatory girls, really a separate gender altogether and therefore slightly more accessible: Clair, who had played her cello naked sitting on the edge of Tony's bed, Margot, with her flat breasts and accent so suppressed he never placed it, Samantha the budding photographer, whose limp and stiff left side had caught his eye, and Jane, the so-called bisexual.

"You set us up to be stereotypes," Lena said. "You choose people who confirm your view of people. You're curating."

It was Lena, the tragic, red-haired philosophy freshman and clerk in the Bobst Library who introduced Tony to the concept of Catastrophe Theory, a mere three months before Schwartz entered his life. Lena told him, after Tony kissed her in the library stacks, her thin buttocks pressed against the works of Edgar Allen Poe, that life was defined by a series of irrevocable acts, so dire in nature that they redefine our lives from that point onward. These acts, or catastrophes (she said it with the Greek stress, "catastrophe"), then become signposts, moments after which nothing is the same ever again. It is possible, Lena breathed into his ear, to chart the course of one's life as a series of catastrophes (this should have been a warning to Tony, but he was much more concerned with Lena's skin, soft and crimped with red under the band of her underwear, than with the fact that he would soon become one more catastrophe in her life). In the stacks he explored the taut strings hidden up in the front of her coiffed, feathery pubic bowl, a black taffeta skirt bunched high around her waist bringing to mind varsity gropings behind the stands at a high school football meet circa 1960, while somewhere nearby a clerk pushed a book-laden trolley cart with a squeaky wheel. It was Lena who eventually brought the Hall of Asiatic Animals to his attention. She said, "It should be 'Sambar, Attacked by Wild Dogs,' not, 'Sambar Attacked by Wild Dogs,' all piled up with no breathing room."

Of the very young women, Lena Schaefer was the most recent and memorable. He had first sighted her at an exhibition of his photographs in Chelsea, new tintype photography, a series he had done of steel workers, all oil begrimed and oddly posed against clean, grey scale backgrounds. Lena had come leaning on the arm of an incidental person twenty years older than she, her dark-green dress making her red hair stand out like a signal fire. In the gallery full of grey people and pictures, she was the point of convergence. Tony had been busy schmoozing, and after her arrival he did not see her until she left, exiting, as she had entered, dramatically.

"Fuck you, Reuben!" she cried, causing an uncertain silence to descend on the room, in which a champagne glass fell to the floor. "The *Inferno* is poetry!" And she left. The next time Tony saw Lena was behind the counter of the Bobst Library. He recognized her immediately. He hesitated for a few minutes in the checkout line, wondering if he should speak to her, trying to gauge how upset she still was about Reuben. It had been a week. Her nails were painted red, and her pale throat was adorned by a silver mechanical pencil on a ribbon, dangling threateningly like a railroad spike above her breasts. She wore a mustard yellow cardigan and black taffeta skirt, hemmed halfway down her calf, revealing black suede pumps and nylons, like a slightly naughty soldier's girl of yesteryear; Tony always noticed clothes. When she looked up at him and recognized his face, she glared, dropped her eyes, and dug in the countertop with her thumbnail, chipping the lacquer. She asked him if he had managed to find everything he wanted. "You were at the Chelsea show," he said. "You left in a hurry. Was everything alright?" He watched her eyes widen, and thought that there was something of a gawky animal about her, in her expressive nostrils and the softness of her eyes, a giraffe-like quality. She balked under the weight of his recognition, blushed all the way to the pale, freckled skin at the shadowed cleft of her shirt collar, where the oily ribbon crossed between her breasts, and his thoughts drifted wide, caught up in the conquest suddenly. Would she let him, he wondered, take pictures of her back, shaped like a viola (he had a weakness for that curve, at the narrow of a woman's back). He thought that if he asked her in the right way, she might let him. Her redness emanated from a point at the base of her throat, filling with each blush and then receding gradually to that spot. The curls of her ears were inflamed with blood, as were the lids of her eyes and the long, flared edges of her nostrils, as if these places would be hot to the touch.

"I'm sorry you had to witness that," she said. "I was embarrassed about it, later. About making a scene at your party."

"It's fine."

"It's not. But thanks for saying so."

"I like a good scene every once in a while."

Tony had gone to the Bobst Library to pay the fine on a long overdue book on Schiele he had eventually lost. The girl raised her eyebrows at the amount, and the two of them joked about it. Her fingers brushed his as she handed him back his card, and there was a tiny shock between them, maybe from the magnetic scanner, maybe from the charge of her wild hair. "I can't believe I'm saying this," she said, "but I love your work."

"Really?" he said.

"The black art."

"What?"

She shrugged. "The tintype series, the wet plate collodion stuff. Isn't that what they call it? The black art?"

"Those are your favorites? That's...thank you. Why those?"

"You sound surprised. It's your fingerprints, actually, along the edges."

"I always feel like what I'm seeing in the collodions is time. Like it's the only way to photograph time, with a long exposure." The black art, he thought. Of course. "There was a man on your arm, in Chelsea."

"Was," she said. " 'Was' would be the key word."

"He was too old for you, anyway."

She tilted her chin back slightly, putting on a brave, sultry face, the way shy girls did when they decided to wade straight in. "How about you?"

"I'm also too old for you."

"You know what I mean."

"Unattached."

"That's funny," she said. "You don't seem that way, somehow."

"What way?"

She shrugged, smiling at him. "Sorry, but you seem sort of...you know. Taken. That's what I was thinking at the Chelsea show. I was thinking you looked taken. It made me jealous, actually. I was thinking you knew something I didn't."

He laughed. "What does taken look like?"

"You know what it looks like. Can't you tell?"

It was September, raining. Tony had an umbrella, and shared it with the red-haired girl; he wished he had thought to read her nametag in the library, before she covered it with her coat. He didn't like asking names. She had ten minutes to go for a coffee, she said. They moved briskly, pressed close together to keep out of the rain and to make way for other people passing on the pavement with their umbrellas. Her hip knocked against his at every other step. He switched his gait so that their movements would be more compatible. When they crossed the street, stepping together over a rill of black water, she reached up to grip the handle of the umbrella with him, subtly steering them both. They passed by the coffee shop and went on without stopping.

The corner of the park she chose was plastered with yellow leaves. Trees surrounded them, black, naked. The rain faded to a drizzle. The sky was white. They were near the fountains, but the jets of water were still that day, the air still, the noise of the city lessened. The leaves stuck to their shoes like sodden paper. No one else was under the trees.

"What do you do?" he said.

"I work in the Bobst Library." Her tone was of playful, mock exasperation. "I walk in the rain. I befriend strays."

"You walk in the woods with older men."

"I don't like young men. I don't like older men, either. I don't like men much at all, in general."

"You like me. I can tell. You should have dinner with me."

She shrugged.

"Come on," he said. "Why not?"

She looked away, toward the open space around the fountain, where the pale, damp light was stronger. Her breath was white. "I think I want to go back now," she said.

"The rain's pretty much finished," he said.

"I only have a few minutes. I'm already late."

But when they were back, she didn't go in. They stood together near the doors, hidden from them by one of the huge, brick shoals that lined the entryway of the Bobst Library.

"Have dinner with me," he said again.

"You don't know anything about me."

"Just say yes. It doesn't have to mean anything."

"You should ask me something about myself first."

"Do you think I'm a narcissist? Just kidding," he said quickly, at her look. "What's your name?" She didn't answer, but she had worked down the zipper of her coat while they stood, sheltered by the bricks, and he could see the plastic nametag she wore pinned to the mustard cardigan. "Lena? Is that it?"

"Yes."

"Is your break over, Lena?"

She glanced down at a slender, gold-faced watch. "A

while ago."

"Believe it or not, I actually need help finding a book."

"Oh?" She smiled, a flicker of amusement, and some of the stiffness left her shoulders. "What book would that be?"

He thought quickly. "Poe," he said. " 'Ligeia.' "

"The saintly dead girl?"

"I guess that seems like a red flag," he said. "You should still let me take you out to dinner."

"I'm probably going to take you home with me," Lena said. She actually sounded annoyed by this admission, as if by the disruptive antics of a roommate. Her eyes sharpened on him, searching his face. "If there's some reason why I shouldn't, you should tell me."

"You seem like an honest person."

" 'Ligeia,' " she said. She was smiling again. She reached toward him in a sudden, perfunctory way as if to shake hands, but touching the arm that still held the umbrella. Her fingers skated hesitantly down his sleeve from elbow to wrist, rested for a moment on the bare joint of his thumb, then fell away. She looked embarrassed. Her flesh was warming again, even in the cold of outdoors. Blood spread from the low point in her throat, covering her breast and neck, her cheeks, nose and ears suffused with soft, red warmth. Her fingers, though, had been unexpectedly cold. He could still feel the spot on his hand, the skin tingling, somehow more aware. "You know that's just one story, right, not a whole book?" Lena moved away, looking back after a few steps to include him. "You'd better come with me." And he followed her back into the library, followed the excited lash of the black, taffeta skirt. "How lucky," she said, "that the stacks are so quiet today."

Lena's shift ended at six, and her roommate worked

evenings. In her kitchen there were potted cacti, and every appliance made a sound like some other appliance. A framed vintage of the Coppertone Girl loomed above the sink, pouting orange child, white buttocks, black spaniel tugging away. "Don't be a paleface!" the caption warned. Lena allowed Tony to photograph her lying on the kitchen floor with her red curls fanning out around her, a pool of operatic gore, a matador's cape. From the floor she said, "You're so handsome, it makes me not trust you. Like you'll lie every time you open your mouth. Did I tell you how much I loathe handsome men?"

"You said young men. Or men in general."

"Handsome men are the worst."

"I can't lie to save my life. I wish I could."

She had an odd body, long in the torso and milk-skinned, spangled with an explosion of freckles, that made Tony yearn to buy her things, emerald cuffs and diamond collars, fox furs and Italian boots, if only to watch her fling them off. He had always been drawn to the distant, alien beauty of a redhead. Lena said she loved the collodions; given that treatment, the silver would make her eyes ghost pale, and her handsome freckles black. There was a tattoo of cursive script high up on her inner thigh that said *Never*. The fur there was darker than her hair. She stared at him as he hid behind the lens. "I can believe that," she said. "You do this thing, when you focus the lens, where you bite your lip just a little. It's a tell."

"You like that sort of thing?"

She wrapped her long legs around him, pulling his face down to hers. Her tongue crept into his mouth, pushing for a moment against his. Then he pulled away, sitting back against the refrigerator, and she stared at him with a look of empty questioning.

"It's not you," he said. "Oh, God. I'm sorry."

There was a long, incredulous pause, and he could almost feel the girl's outrage turning on itself. "Hand me my purse," she said. She sat up, knees drawn to her chest, long toes splayed in front of her, digging in the purse until she produced a lighter and a packet of cigarettes, which surprised him; there had been no taste of cigarettes, no scent of it on her skin. Her hand was shaking when she set one between her lips, and she couldn't get the lighter to produce a flame.

"You're upset," he said, reaching out to touch her knee. "I'm sorry. I hate myself right now." In the shadows over the sink, the black dog and the Coppertone Girl went at it.

"Good." She gave up on the lighter, sat with the cigarette dangling from her lip. After a minute she said, "You liked me better in the library. I guess it was safer."

"You're beautiful, Lena, and obviously intelligent. It really isn't you." She gave a hard laugh. "Please, I mean it with all my heart. It's not your fault."

"Right."

"Lena," he said, "I didn't want to humiliate you."

"It has nothing to do with me at all. I know."

"Lena," he said, and produced his final card, the broken heart. "The truth is I'm a little at sea, right now."

The muscles of her abdomen began to jerk. The sobbing shocked him. He tried to comfort her by putting his arm around her, and she looked confused and offended. "What are you doing?" So he backed off, and watched her cry. She said, "Don't think for a minute that this is about you, asshole. I don't give a damn about you." He told her how beautiful she was, and that he was an idiot, repeating it in both English and Spanish, knowing it meant less each time. "That's not the point," she said. "Why are you saying that?"

Lena's crying was so violent as to be almost like an act of religious flagellation; he worried she would actually harm herself, rupture something, perhaps, or slam her head against a cabinet. But after a while she finished, got up, and put on a turquoise kimono. Instead of asking him to leave, she said that she was hungry. They ate punishingly spicy Indian takeout, cold from her refrigerator, and drank red wine. She asked him about photography, and he asked her about philosophy, both with only passing interest. When she asked him if he ever missed his home country, he said, "I live in Bushwick." Unlike Lena, he was far from eager to embrace any family identity, whatever that entailed.

"Mexico," she persisted, and he said, "Mexico is a country that has betrayed itself, again and again." And she gave him a look, but didn't say anything.

From the street, he saw her shape in the window, a shadow against the orange light of her room, though it might not, he knew, actually be Lena, as he didn't know her window. It was just a shape, a woman's shape. He went home that night and slept like a baby, deep and pure and dreamless, slept hard, as if all his sins were forgiven. He called her the next day, said he was sorry, and asked if they might have lunch. "I don't think that would be good for me," Lena said, and hung up. But it wasn't the kind of "no" that really meant "no," he decided. Two days later he received a postcard of Arizona, showing red stone, a scorpion, and a cryptic message: "Sambar, Attacked by Wild Dogs. Saturday, four-thirty."

This was how he came to be loitering in the Hall of Asiatic Animals at the Museum of Natural History, parting a flood of screaming, post-schoolday children, "ooh," and "aah," and sugary breath on the backs of his hands, glared upon by women with perambulators, back offered to the family of Bengal tigers, while the sambar deer, glass eyes rolled and crown thrown high in panic, fought off a gang of nondescript tan coy-dogs. He noticed immediately that

Lena had added a comma to the title of the exhibit, and smiled at her editing. A small hand had left a grease print on the glass level with Tony's elbow. Somewhere in the bowels of the museum, alarm bells rang for a while, then fell mute.

Lena was late, but determined. She came dressed as a pre-war starlet, famous shades and a green silk dress, drawing stares from stroller-pushing mothers. He admired the cross of her elegant heels in the doorway where she paused, scanning the crowd for him, the miles of feminine leg in sleek, seamed stockings, her toe cocked like a sharp hoof. No denying it; The German Commandant's Granddaughter was a beautiful woman. He approached and offered her an arm. "You look famous," he said.

"You look hungry," Lena replied. In heels, she was taller than Tony. She slipped her fingers into the crook of his elbow, and they walked out together past pardus fusca and the Asiatic buffalo, turning heads. Tony thought it was because of Lena's clothes, but would discover in the ensuing weeks that he and Lena turned heads wherever they went together, whatever they were wearing. Lena would enjoy pointing this out, teasing him by speculating on the attractiveness of their theoretical future children, causing him to plead with her: "Never say that again, ever."

"I don't know what happened to you," Lena would say to him, weeks later. "I don't think you have it in you to love another person without torturing them. Why is that?" He had balked at the love word and at the presumptuousness of this, wondering how it was she sounded so sure of herself, having known him for only a few days. He decided that the girl must be crazy. He made no reply, and after a while she had sighed, and folded her napkin on her plate, staring out the window of The Horus Cafe.

There was a certain nervousness about young girls, an insecurity even in girls like Lena, as if they had not quite discovered how to inhabit their bodies, and might as soon fly away as allow themselves to be held. A young girl's conduct with an older man was characterized by stock gestures, the light touch of the wrist, the quick glance from under her hair, as she tried to determine the effectiveness of her beauty, the quiet apology for that same beauty, as if she were wielding a weapon that was not entirely under her control, the light-hearted laugh, the playful slap, the myriad charming deceptions as she danced circles around the minotaur, dodging his shambling advances. And always, there was the inner absence of her, youth's invitation to jealous age, a vacuum of will begging to be filled. Lena couldn't help being young.

In the days counting down to the final struggle, or Lenapocalypse, as Tony privately called it, she rarely spoke to him, though she slept at his apartment every night and took to wearing his shirts. She was an avid reader, and read compulsively, picking up whatever was close to hand. He could follow her changing moods by the reading material he found abandoned in the living room, the kitchen, even in the bathroom, soggy books perched on the edge of the bathtub. The whole thing had the feeling of a waiting game, an intermission holding space before the *tercio de muerte*.

Who had the upper hand? In a moment of weakness, Tony had invited her into his life. In another moment of weakness, he had given her hope, perhaps, that she was wanted there. And Lena, the virus, the small-breasted diva, now inhabited his sheets, his shirt, his apartment, and him. His was the absence, his the vacuum to be filled; how could she have lodged herself so firmly in his life, he thought, if there had not been a gaping space inside it? It made him uneasy that Lena had so neatly turned the tables on him.

One night he woke up shivering; he had left the window open, and the space next to him in the bed was empty. Lena must have gone off to read, he thought, or take a midnight bath, as she did on occasion. He was about to climb out of bed to close the window when he became aware of breathing, not his own, close beside him in the darkness. He felt a shock of fear in the middle of his body, knowing that the Commandant's Granddaughter was standing at the foot of his bed, watching him as he slept. He didn't move, but lay still, feigning sleep, listening to her gentle sounds for what seemed hours. The curtains streamed into the room with cold air and the rumor of the street: a garbage truck, a homeless man, someone's desperate laughing, the three a.m. train, passing far away in the night. It came through in a deep, slow pulse, as if the city itself and its millions of dreamers were breathing with the girl into the damp hair at the nape of his neck. The room was cold, and he felt the heat of her body. Before the green of dawn, she got back into bed and curled in behind him, drifting quickly into sleep.

There was a delicate shadow on her neck that he at first mistook for a love bruise, only realizing by the mark's persistence that it was really just a place where the blood ran close to the skin. In the morning, when he stood at the kitchen counter making coffee and she sat at the counter, he could see the life in the love bruise; it quivered and jumped, as if she had a restless fish under her skin. When she stood by him invisible in the night, he sometimes thought he could hear it pulsing. He imagined he could hear the blood whispering smoothly down her long blue arteries, and the pernicious will that drove it. The room always grew hotter the longer she stayed; it grew so hot that an ordinary human body could not possibly have generated so much heat. He feigned sleep and drenched the sheets with sweat as she kept her vigil beside him. He listened to her breathe, inhaled the air that she exhaled, and knew that there would be steam on the windows in the morning, that water would be dripping down the walls, peeling the paint, corrupting the hardwood floor.

His days and nights fell into a fevered insomniac rhythm; he got out of bed in the late morning, drank his coffee, smoked his forbidden cigarette, and pounded the typewriter keys aimlessly, not having any idea what he was producing; it could have been *Hamlet*, a novel about Victorian botanists, or his own obituary. And these were the boundaries of his empire. He, and she, and the apartment. A moth stuck between windows. Typewriter, takeout, coffee and cigarettes, and the untouched pills in their bottle. Nothing else. He thought of calling Lena on her odd behavior, but didn't, afraid of what she would say. He suspected that he was not completely awake, but he never wanted to sleep. And his monkey's paw tapped the hot keys. Easier, in the end, to get rid of her.

"I think I have a fever," she said one morning.

"Come here."

She crossed the room and stood by his desk, and he rested the back of his hand against her forehead like a mother. His hands were too big and clumsy, too stupid. He set his cheek against her forehead instead.

"You don't have a fever."

"Are you sure?"

"If you do then I do, too. I can't tell. You've been using my shampoo."

"You don't mind, do you? I like the way it smells. Not sweet."

"I don't mind."

She was wearing a slithery night dress, dark blue, leaving her legs bare, and he ran his hand up the inside of her leg, over the tattoo, before steering her away, giving her a little pat. "Run along," he said.

She sat down on the windowsill, and watched him as he stared at the page in the machine, and he noted her perfect posture, how she sat with her hands folded in her lap and her knees pressed together, as if she were sitting on a hard church pew or a dissection table. A bizarre image flashed through his mind, Lena gazing at him from a stained butcher's block among pheasants and wild onions and opened hares, split wide from throat to pubic bone, her glistening organs garnets and precious rubies under the white, cold lights.

He said, "Can you leave me alone for five minutes?"

She met his gaze, and he felt for an instant the heat from the love fish that pulsed in her throat. Then she shrugged and left the room. Later he heard the bath running, and a few minutes after that he heard the bathroom door open, and her bare feet padding down the hall. He brought his fist down on the typewriter keys, so that the metal arms all came down at once and tangled like a nest of snakes in the machine. In the hall, he found a cloud of steam and a trail of small, wet footprints. And when he passed by the open bathroom door, he saw that she had drawn with her finger on the fogged mirror, the figures run with long drips down the length of the glass, painfully childish, a stick man, a house, and a tree.

NINETEEN

It was a night cold as any he had ever known, Matt Kelly sleeping in the next bed with the light left on and that worried ridge between his eyes, the halls of the school empty. Tony dressed against the cold but wore no shoes, so as to step without sound, creeping not to the chapel this time but to the door with the carved tree. There was a light beneath the door. He lay his palms against the wood, resting there. His fingers traced the whorls of the tree's branches. When he lay his ear to the door, he could hear a soft tick and rustle, the pulse of the old building. Tony opened the door without knocking, stepped into the office and closed himself inside. Ochoa did not look surprised to see him. He did not look angry, or reproachful, or anything Tony would have expected. Wary, more than anything. He put down the pen he had been using, placing it next to the paper. Tony said, "You're left handed." He hadn't meant to say it, or to attach any importance to it, but the air in the room seemed to thicken; the sudden ringing in his ears was deafening.

"You never noticed?" Ochoa said. "Of course not. Why should you?" The white streak caught the light, and the collar clean as bone. "Does it scare you?" said Ochoa, and Tony shook his head, said, "Don't be stupid."

Ochoa removed his reading glasses, rubbed the bridge of his nose. "I assume you came here of your own volition this time."

"You know that girl from the Fountain, Bernadette? I went to the Slaughterhouse today. She was there. She showed me her breasts. That's got to be a venial sin at least. And we were smoking, too. Now tell me it was wrong, and tell me what to do. And it will be like it didn't happen."

"Don't patronize me." Fumbling with the pull of a desk drawer, bright slivers of glass still in his hand. "Go away."

"Why?"

"You know why."

"Does it make you angry?"

"You're being difficult."

"Matt Kelly says I should stay away from you."

"Probably. Yes. He's a smart boy. Perhaps he has a better measure of me than you have."

"He thinks I don't belong..."

"What do you want me to say, exactly?" Ochoa stood, empty hand coming down on the desk so that he leaned forward on the knuckles, eyes vivid, and Tony flinched at the sudden motion. "You can't do this. You can't come here, and talk to me as if you know everything." He straightened, tossed the folded wires of the glasses down among the papers. His voice was quiet when he spoke again. "Show more respect, or leave."

Tony felt the heavy wood of the door against his back, and little tremors of electricity in his fingertips and knees and down the backs of his legs. "Don't you want to know what happened? With Bernadette?"

"Tell me, then. If you're so brave."

"Nothing."

The old building made its soft night sounds, copper pipes groaning, the growl of boilers, the soft settling of stones. The school breathed and shifted in its sleep. Ochoa's desk was littered with student papers, an empty cup, a letter opener, its bright edge catching the light.

"So," Ochoa said. "Should I bother asking why you're here? Or am I to be met with more of this arrogant stupidity?"

Tony left the door and drew closer to the desk, reaching out to touch the edge of it. It was a bolder move than he had imagined, and for a while he paused, not knowing what to do next. Looking down, he saw, of all things, what looked like an essay with Matt Kelly's name on it. The glister of the blue ink, that neat, old-fashioned signature, made him feel suddenly ill, and he took two steps back again, averting his eyes.

Ochoa said, "Take a moment. You're pale as a ghost."

"I don't know what to say to you. I'm sorry." His voice was worried with quick breath. "I don't know what to do."

"Come here." He could see Ochoa's eyes dilate, falling into their own black centers to leave the golden iris flaring, the heart of a collapsing sun.

"What will it mean, if I do?"

"You foolish creature," Ochoa said. "Come here to me."

Tony drew closer, until his hip was pressed against the desk edge and he could go no further. Ochoa leaned across. His hand was preternaturally warm; in the cold of the room, Tony could almost smell the heat emanating from the crisp fabric of his sleeve, and thought for a moment, cheek turned into Ochoa's palm, of resting his cold face against the neck of a horse. He was overcome with an unexpected sense of relief, now that it was done. He leaned his cheek into Ochoa's hand, resting there, taking in that extraordinary feeling of collapse. For a moment, nothing mattered.

"Come closer," said Ochoa. And then, wearily, "You're impossible. What am I to do with you?" His hand fell to the knot of Tony's uniform tie, nudging it down with a soft tug. He loosened Tony's collar next, a gesture methodical but almost motherly, as if the good son, pressed and spit-shined, were being sent out to greet guests. His fingers lingered on the starched tongues, unhurried. He brushed something from his shoulder, lifted his chin. "You're perfect, you know," Ochoa said. "I wish..." his voice trailed away. With fingertips he traced the structure of Tony's throat, in the way of a blind man, heat blooming up at his touch, circling the cartilage in the center. His breath was warm, fingers learning the shape of trachea, jaw, closed lips, each fingertip a soft, marveling eye, straying down to the space where the white cotton now gaped at the top of Tony's chest, letting the palm of his hand rest there.

Daring to look up at him, Tony saw a face carefully emptied, the gaze wary, fixed. He dropped his eyes again, finding it easier to focus on the joints of the leaded window at the far end of the room. Ice feathered the glass tonight. It lay in the hollow of every seam.

Ochoa ran the pad of his thumb into the trough below Tony's collarbone. "What do you see in me?" He set his lips against his cheek, then mouth. Tony leaned into the kiss, opened to it, face tipped to the left, a taste shot with metal, clean and faintly sweet. He could feel the ridges of teeth, blind and hesitant, the warm weight of hands cradling his jaw. As with Bernadette, he worried over the mechanics of the act, and not the implications. It seemed nothing more than a confirmation of something he had known. His ankle rebelled suddenly, setting him off balance so that his hip jarred the edge of the desk, and he turned it, the hard lip nudging at the crook of leg and body. It threw his weight forward so that he leaned in, giving more of himself than he had intended, dropped abruptly into the physical experience, Ochoa's teeth bruising his lip, a falling swoop of adrenaline. A soft sound, coming from his own body.

In that white instant, when his mind was a perfect heat, Alvara slipped in. Fingers between his fingers, cold and damp with chlorinated water, a yellow day of dappled shade, her skirt cut from a piece of the blue sky. She was there with him in the room, that ache of unraveling in the middle of him, pulled off balance, desk edge catching him in the groin, his body springing painfully to life. With his mouth parted to the force of a kiss, she was as near to him as she had ever been. The garden wall was warm with summer.

He didn't know where to rest his hands, or what to do with them, a schoolboy appalled by this outrageous fact, the dignity of the cloth defying touch. He settled at last on Ochoa's elbow, other hand braced on the desk between them. But he was gone, anyway.

When they broke apart, Tony put out a hand to touch the other's cheek, the right one, with its half eye fastening. He did it without thinking, as if he had forgotten all the reasons why he should not have been there, why such an act was forbidden, why it was brave. But Ochoa turned his head, avoiding him, and Tony retreated, feeling somehow more exposed by his gesture than by the kiss. Whatever this exchange was, it was not supposed to be a thing of sympathies. Tony would never be allowed to pity him.

From across the desk, Ochoa watched him. His face gave away nothing. "You brushed your teeth," he said.

"You need a shave," Tony replied. He gave a strange, abrupt laugh, one small burst of sound.

"Does it burn you?"

"It's not that bad."

"You disappear, when I get near you. Come closer."

"Aren't you worried about...?"

"No."

Tony edged his way around the desk, so that they were on the same side, shifted aside some papers, and sat down. It was a substantial desk; his bare feet hung down a few inches above the floor. He had meant to be deliberately casual. He wished he had remained standing.

"What happened to your shoes?" said Ochoa, fingers nibbling softly at the hem of Tony's shirt.

"I forgot them."

"You remembered a belt, but not shoes."

"That's right." He laced his fingers together between his knees, feeling, perversely, like a child sitting on a too-tall bench, and found he couldn't look Ochoa in the eye. His palms were damp. Ochoa loomed, resting a warm hand on his knee, and Tony said suddenly, "Do you mind if I smoke?"

"You'll not do that while I have anything to say about it."

"Don't touch me."

"Perhaps you should leave." And then, "Perhaps you should forget this."

Tony's lips burned, scratched by a whiskery kiss; at this hour, Ochoa looked slightly grey in the jaw, and Tony wondered why this should be, when there was not a thread of grey in his hair. But none of it worried him, just now; the dizzy fear had been momentary. None of it seemed wrong. It was nothing, really. He was left with a curious blankness after the fact, feeling his way around the edges of a blind spot. And he thought of Ellen, Hutter's wife in her white nightdress throwing open doors and windows to the night. Pretended it was this, or the blankness itself, working changes over his body while he himself was elsewhere. That this hard knot of anxiety and want could possibly belong to someone else. Ochoa had moved away from him now, anchoring himself at the corner the desk, evidently waiting for him to leave.

"You don't really want me to go," Tony said. He shifted a knee and hunched, trying unsuccessfully to hide the sudden, alarming cry of his flesh. He looked away. He tried to fix his eye on something safe. The ledge under the window was dusty. There were dead moths. His breath was quick. "I want to stay here. Just let me."

"To what end?"

"I need you to be...I don't know. This."

There was a rustle, Ochoa piling the essays to one side of his desk, making a neat stack, squaring the edges. "You seem confused."

"Don't tell me what I am. If you pretend this never...that you didn't..."

"What? You'll ruin me?"

"I'll have you killed."

A sound beyond the door of the office caused them both to go still, then resolved into some tiny scurrying, no more than the claws of a rat behind the paneling. They both hung there for a moment, failing to breathe. Ochoa's eyes were fixed on the door. He said, "I must terrify you."

Tony shook his head.

"Don't lie." He leaned in abruptly, grasping Tony's polyester tie between his fingers, leashing him. Ochoa gave the tie a gentle shake, the corner of his mouth flickering up. "You have only ever been yourself."

"I want to be a cinematographer." Tony didn't know

what made him say it. He felt the blood rise to his face. The absurdity of it, reminding himself of his own identity, or bargaining for it with Ochoa. A school uniform in the middle of the night. The absurdity of the desk on which he braced himself, covered with student evaluations, with bad translations of Spanish poetry. Ochoa loomed over him, chin level with his eyes, pressed in against Tony's knee.

The white stripe glowed. He wanted to lay his hand on it.

Ochoa let the tie slide through his fingers. He held him steady with a hand on the back of his head and pressed Tony's mouth with a kiss, more lightly this time. Almost chaste, were it not for the pressure of his body and the way it trapped him there. Tony pulled him in closer, tightening his knee against the black flank, reaching up to put his fingers in Ochoa's hair, felt him shiver, held on anyway. He gripped the white stripe. A hand grasped hold of his side and strayed down further, half-slipping onto the desk, the carefully stacked papers cascading off the other end and onto the floor. Hasty fingers pleaded with the knot of his tie, and he went under piecemeal, in little staccato gasps, wrestling with buttons and hauling at endless fabric, feeling the click of tooth against tooth, pinned by Ochoa's body against the table. Sinking into touch. And was it really a lie, his lack of fear? He wanted to be touched.

The warm breath of an exhalation filled his lungs. A hand wandered down the front of his sweater, past his heart and the St. Ignatius seal. He grabbed the wrist to stop its progress, held on with a vise grip, the hand pressed down against the seal. His fingers found the gap he had created in the black, knotted buttons, and wandered into the warmth. Hard ribs there, sliding back and forward under the skin. Damp under the arm, modest streak down the middle of the chest. And it seemed the world was splintered, so that each physical fact stood out, the prickle of sweat under Tony's arms, the struggle of two tongues in one mouth and his own hardness, the texture of someone else's skin under his hands, his knee jutting up against a trim, male haunch. The eminence of things beyond himself, of objects, fractures in the paint and ticking clocks. He was aware of a worried, purr-like tremor, a warm forehead resting on the hollow over his collarbone, his hand slapping down to find the cold, sharp edge of a letter opener, student papers sticking to his sweaty palm. Of a bruising kiss where the shoulder met the neck. A syllable flew from his mouth, a protest lost somewhere in the air of the room, unheard or unheeded. It came out scarcely a whisper. No surprise, he thought, if it could not be heard. And did he really want to stop? He didn't have the power. He was a thing without form or impulse, a thing, a mass permeable as water in which a stranger's body thrashed and fought against itself. And somehow, the loss of control calmed him. His body did not seem to be his any longer, populated not just by Ochoa but by a host of others; neither panic nor pleasure at the deep end of things. Alvara moved in his skin. Trails of electricity followed every touch. But the lines that tied him to himself had slipped away.

Ochoa freed his arm from Tony's grip and reached for him with sudden, decisive force, knocking something over with a dry clatter, nudging between Tony's knees where they hung down over the desk's edge, laying hold of his belt, pulling him in closer. Tony let him. He set his palms back further on the desk, elbows locked to hold himself upright. When he turned his head, the room seemed to move with him, and he closed his eyes. "Look at me," Ochoa snapped. His voice was harsh. Nothing mattered. "Don't just disappear." There was an agitated scent about the man's hair, salt at his upper lip. Tony opened his eyes to stare at the dark window behind Ochoa, the ledge where the moths were and past it. Hard fingers struggled with the catch of his lap. He turned his face into his own shoulder, away from the rasp of Ochoa's chin, away from his patient rage. Eyes open and dead. And if he didn't take another breath, if he couldn't see what was in front of him, it was because he was dead and sealed in under the lid.

"Look me in the eye."

But he couldn't.

Through the forest of legs and arms that held him, he had seen the red pieces of his cousin's skull among the hair that didn't know when it was dead, his throat scorched with blood. Alma's fine-boned knees, crossed by scars and clutched against her body, her head heavy on his lap in the backseat, the rhythmic shudder of her crying. The car sped away, and on the hot vinyl seat, he comforted Alma as she sobbed. Holding the weight of her, he was peaceful. "Hush," he had said. "Don't cry." Bending, he tasted the salt of the blue, transparent tree, branching at the corner of her forehead. He licked her tears. Alma turned up to him, sunk in a pool of green froth and the light stuff of her gown, face burned red with crying. Yellow hair, like Alvara's. She clutched at the hand of the other girl, the two shrinking from him in the backseat. He raised a hand to his neck, feeling it sticky, hot, his fingertips coming way red. Alma said, "What's wrong with you?"

He would be a child for eternity, under the thorny mesquites.

Something slipped from under Tony's palm and sent him down, papers flying, the man's weight sliding with him, a shape suddenly vague and washed, trembling as if seen through water, black hair, white teeth. The wolf, not what it was, stood on its hind legs and acted like a man. Coaxing, pleading, threatening.

This will happen again and again, Matt had said. That's the difference between history and archetype. He floated, pulled beyond the limits of himself. "You hypocrite," he said. "You can't." Pinned against the top of the desk, someone was making the sharp, drawn sounds of laughter.

Ochoa shushed him suddenly, a palm coming down over Tony's mouth, smothering the laugh. There was that sound again, something in the hall beyond the door, they both heard it, not the scrabbling of a rat but the harsh, uneven tread of a pair of ill-matched legs, Farriday somewhere nearby on his midnight rounds, and they stared at each other over Ochoa's stifling hand, neither moving until the steps had passed away again. Ochoa lifted his hand slowly. The black, dilated gaze flicked from side to side, boring in on one of Tony's eyes, then the other. Somewhere to his left, the clock ticked away on its dusty shelf. Water pooled at the corners of Tony's eyes, shed with the effort of strangling that high, hysterical sound that still wanted to come out of him. He said, "What's wrong?"

"You have…"

"What?" Tony said.

"Your nose is bleeding."

There was a soft metallic clatter; it must have been the letter opener, falling to the floor. "It doesn't matter," Tony said. He put a hand up, feeling the warmth spreading at his upper lip.

"Don't move. You'll make it worse." Ochoa's weight shifted. A thumb unhooked itself from Tony's belt. "Here," he said, and levered himself back on his elbow, rummaged in a pocket somewhere, leaning in again to press something against the base of Tony's nose. A handkerchief, plain white. "Hold that." He raised Tony's chin. "Here, like this.

Would you like the chair?"

"No."

"Tell me you're alright."

Tony slumped back on the desk, and didn't answer. His eyes traveled to the mullioned window to his left, where the round, cold moon floated in the night above the trees, world without end. He wondered about snow, and when it would begin. He thought that he would like to see it. Ochoa's hipbone was pressed too near his erection, and he pushed him off slightly, not wanting him to know. As if he didn't know; he pushed him off but held him by the sleeve, so that Ochoa hung over him uncertainly.

"It's fine," Tony said. "Cut it out." The humiliation of being caught like this made him feel suddenly numb, but he didn't know what else to do. He pressed the cloth against his nose with his free hand, and cleared his throat, tasting metal, hearing nothing now but the two of them breathing and the soft pinging of steam heat in the copper pipes. Even the fear had been lost somewhere. Tony felt tired. He gazed at the ceiling of the office. There was a crack in the paint, a long, wandering seam traversing the room. He let go of Ochoa's sleeve.

"Just stay there," Tony said. "Don't say anything." He sniffed, trying to clear his nose.

"You'll make it worse," Ochoa said again. "Stay down. It will stop in a minute."

Tony felt a tug at the hollow of his neck, Ochoa's fingers loosening the top buttons of his shirt to let him get his breath, raising gooseflesh.

"It's fine," Tony said. "I should go back." The gestures of concern struck him suddenly as pathetic. He shrugged his head free of Ochoa's hand.

"Are you dizzy at all?"

Tony ignored him, scrubbed roughly at his nose. He

thought of the last rites, and the heavy lid of Alvara's cement crypt with its elegant cedars. All of it futile, empty gestures, solace for the lonely living. There was no crossing to that other place. And he too would die, without reason or belief. It meant nothing.

"It will probably have stopped," Ochoa said. "It was just a few drops." He took the handkerchief and showed it to him, stained with a spot of his blood. "There. See? Hardly anything." But he sounded unsteady, the levity false. "We should probably...it would be best..."

Tony stood up slowly, his eyes filled with clouds of fractured light.

"I understand," he said. He noted the sound of these words, solemn, flat, too distant to be his own.

"Let me walk you there."

"No. Are you crazy?"

"Let me help."

"Stop it."

Tony felt again that strange responsibility toward him. "It's okay," he said, "really," and knew he sounded dishonest again, as if he were speaking to a child.

"I can't just let you leave."

"Why?" Tony said. "You're going to try to stop me?" His lips felt strange. Part of how it was with a man, he decided, and a fresh jolt of electricity reared in him; he was elemental, trapped in the room, bounding around the casement like a black squirrel. He pushed Ochoa away. "Leave me alone. I can't breathe." He slid forward, pushed his bare feet into the carpet, and moved around the desk in the direction of the door. He was dizzy; he couldn't seem to set his feet in a straight line. Still hovering behind the rifled desk, Ochoa gazed after him. There was color in his face, and a sere, collected smoothness Tony would take for shock or dismay, remembering this as having defined that moment in the office with Ochoa; shock, and his grace after the fact, a gently countenanced slip. He would decide as an adult that this was a false memory. Why, after all, should Ochoa have been surprised by any of this? Instead, he would see pained humor in the man's face. Ochoa, grimacing at his own audacity. Ochoa, spinning the wheels of remorse.

A moment of insanity, Tony would say years later, at a loss for any other way to explain. A slip. And then another, and another. Given enough distance, even he could appreciate the comedy.

"What happens now?" Tony said brutally, turning back at the door. He wanted to take control of the situation by saying something shocking. But it was an honest question. What happens now?

A soft breath of laughter from Ochoa. His fingers closed over the handkerchief, its incriminating mark now hidden.

"I have to go," Tony said. "Sorry."

Ochoa nodded, handkerchief crushed in his hand. And it seemed to Tony that it was all someone's mistake, this room and the two of them in it, Ochoa's abject slump and kicked-dog eyes, that it was something not meant for him to see, and he wanted not to see it; he retreated quietly, edging toward the door.

"Sorry," he said again. He thought Ochoa would call after him, but he didn't. He looked beaten. There were light scratches on his cheek, and a delta of thread-like, broken veins. Tony said, "I'll see you around."

"Yes," said Ochoa, just before the door closed. "Yes."

The light of the office had made the hallway nearly black to his eyes. Tony could see the red, illuminated fire exit at the end of the hall. He made his way toward it, though he knew the dormitories were in the opposite direction. He had no intention of going there.

TWENTY

God never made a place so beautiful as those hated tidal mangroves, the sun falling on green water, catching in its rays floating golden clouds of insects, glittering on iridescent wings. Spotted chital deer turn their heads all together as they run, black, liquid eyes, white hindquarters, flashing tails. The tiny lapis fisher bird, bright as a scarab, riding a bending reed. Always, there is a gold-soaked, nearly equatorial light, a bright, slow haze, a honeyed richness, full of being. Had I been a naturalist, less absorbed by myself and all my little troubles, I would have filled notebooks, gone blind, spent a mile of lead. Just beyond the village was a shrine to Manasa, goddess of snakes, remover of poison. An unhappy goddess, Lal told me, owing to her rejection by her father Shiva and her stepmother Chandi's cruelty, hungry for human devotees, gentle with her faithful, harsh to her detractors. Our Manasa stood beneath a stone shelf, bowls for offerings scattered around her feet, holding such little things as her faithful could afford her, sometimes catching only dew. The shrine had been carved out of the side of an embankment, a mud wall pocked by roots and little holes, the nests of shy, nocturnal kraits. Painted blue and scarlet, eyes cast down, the goddess looked to me like an appropriated Virgin. As such, I found her comforting, despite her semi-nudity and fierce teeth. Her shrine was almost always isolated and quiet, away from the worry of the village. More than once, I placed a flower or a morsel of food in the goddess' empty bowl. It seemed natural, an act not inconsistent with my other duties. Lal and I talked about Behula, heroine of the Manasamangal, whose devotion to her husband Lakhindar defied both gods and death. "Behula is the best of women," Lal said, surprising me with a moment of candor. "When I am married, it will be to such a woman."

"I hope so, Lal. Behula was virtuous."

"Yes. She is strong."

"The story must symbolize the human spirit's dominion over nature," I said, and Lal shrugged, as if I were revealing my ignorance again, and said, "It just is." The forest grew up and around Manasa's shrine, saplings sprouting on the rock shelf over her, hair-like roots dangling around her scarlet, plaster crown. The paint was peeling from her hands, white under blue. Lizards lived inside her open mouth. This was what I saw of that beautiful Eden, a mouth like a dark inverted star devouring air and space, chewing and devouring, greasy lizards scampering between its teeth, life poring into a mouth, out of a mouth, a nest of blindworms writhing in hot, selfish bliss. Every creature a beast of prey, from tiger to chital; even a chital has his weapons, will slice the ribs of a wild dog if not a tiger, and other predators will turn on their wounded kin. I saw a dead fox on a refuse pile, consumed in a rage of heat and biology, sinking into a nest of its own fur, stripped down to the clean bones in less time than it took Lazarus to rise. The monkeys laughed and screamed, yes, an animal can laugh, dark, twisted faces flashing above me through the trees, walking upright in the trees on black, grotesque hand-feet, branches rattling their passing. Golden, celestial light. Never again will I see a place so beautiful, so cruel, cruel because remote; I glimpsed it as a stranger peeking into an illuminated window from the night, stealing glances of a beauty that does not belong to him, hating the desired object that does not belong to him.

The tigers of the Sundarbans did not always prey on men. I am told they learned to eat human flesh because the bodies of the dead are carried downriver by the Ganges in flood, bodies of men and bodies of cattle, all prey for the unsmiling, unloved gods, all meat, all food for tigers.

The cobra growled. I remember that it was not a snake hiss, but a growl, a low frequency, felt in my chest. And how slowly it swayed, horrible flared head on its stalk, slick black hide and creamy underbelly, slimy, roach-like. In my imagination, I give him round, amber eyes and forked black tongue, though I did not have time to see these things. So I know I have invented at least some portion of the snake, if not all. And where did he go, after? Why am I so sure of the snake as a 'he', as if all snakes, being phallic, were male? He disappeared in the dead leaves, so quickly I could almost believe I had imagined him. He vanished as quickly as the shadow tiger. What tiger? Dakshin Rai, a real tiger, or a dream, what force held me under its terrible eye? What snake wrapped the youth's bare leg to plant its fatal bite?

Years later, Lal is more real to me than the cobra. The silky pliance of skin, his warm, anxious scent, damp of sweat, the froth at the corner of his mouth, muscles roped with little tremors, all more vivid to my memory than the growling cobra.

A growl; of that I am sure, I felt it in my own chest, buzzing the hollow spaces in my chest. Why a growl? How can that be? Does any snake growl, like a dog, like a wolf, like a man? A black snake, rearing, streaked with white. Lather of salt on skin. My hands on Lal's bucking throat, shaking him as he fought to breathe, fingernails scrabbling, ineffectual, clawing death from out of his throat, a wet rattle, the kick of his bare foot in the leaves. His clouded eyes, flown past me into the spinning well of green. His eyes. How sleep-like he lay beside me, slack, spent, dead. And Falco's sins will die with me, the lone survivor of our trinity of secrets. It seems unlikely that Priya still survives.

You are unfit for my blood sacrifice, the tiger's gaze told me. You are unfit, because you, too, are a god.

There is no pain as pure and despairing as that of a young person. Being ephemeral, he does not know that the pain will eventually dull with time, and become less. He sees the injustice and the wreck of his world, and he can't see beyond it. I was afraid the boy from Michoacán would do himself harm, because he had that look of despair on him. He plunged blindly through the school, looking for fights, he wandered the halls at night, he desecrated hymn-books; you knew it was him, the torn leaves, profane phrases scratched in Spanish, pen pressing down through the page. When we walked in the woods together, he talking and I listening, our steps would often take us to the abandoned factory, where he would yell and snarl demonically to frighten the birds, smash bottles, hurl himself at the brick walls trying to scale them or tear them down. He wanted to feel, I believe, that something he did would change things. He had no idea how powerful he actually was, how he personified change, how the world and everyone in it leaned back to get out of his way. And I was hopeless, already lost to the dark spell of the rampage, destroyed like every other object. The bottles smashed against the factory wall, the sharp pop echoing and spinning, the explosion of a million green shards dazzling my eyes.

Love is a form of vanity, a form of blindness; he reminded me of myself. I was the only one who could understand him, this displaced foreigner struggling with the ruin of his life. I told myself that I knew that kind of pain. He could have been one of Santos' brood, slender, dark-haired, scratches on his arms, alert as a bird of prey. In his desire to destroy I saw a body struggling to make sense of what the mind could not. And I wanted so desperately to feel that we understood each other. I wanted some of that rage and luster for myself. I wanted not to be alone.

We were not alike. He was born to an era out of step with God that was, like him, somehow both guileless and corrupt. It was an age staggered with its own speed and arrogance and magnificence. Where I had been poor he was a child of privilege, wild in a way that I had never been; no one in his life had ever refused him anything, and it had made him dangerous to himself and others. But is this not the essence of attraction, that feeling of pure danger? In him I saw the age I had been thrown into but to which I was a foreigner, all decadence and death and wish fulfillment. He was the New World to me.

In the abandoned factory, he threw punches at the crumbling plaster until his knuckles bled. When he kissed me…despite the direness of this story, I almost laugh to think back on it now, how he kissed like a teenager, all torturous technique, all punition and fear and thrusting tongue. When he kissed me, he leaned into my lips, then pulled away, then leaned. It was sometimes painful if I failed to hold him still, if he was in a vengeful mood, a lip lacerated by the bruising contact of his jaw. In the rain of sharp fragments I pulled him near, and held him fast, trying to re-remember my own history.

In 1971 I boarded a plane in Barcelona, fell asleep crossing the Atlantic, and woke to see dawn breaking over the Americas. At the airport there was a riot on the tarmac, young people with linked arms screaming at police in blue. Still weak from malaria, I waited for the bullets to start flying, though of course they did not. They were students gathered in a show of support for the American soldiers on the plane, and to protest the war that had deployed them. I felt a surge of awe and terrified admiration in my heart for the protesters, many of whom were not much younger than I was then, throwing their bodies against the cold iron of authority in a way that I never would have dared. They screamed and raged and pelted us with daisies, and everything about my world had taught me to hold my silence. That was the moment I fell in love with the Americas and their youngness and their dreams, how they all believed against all odds they were immortal. The passengers filed out of the airplane, stiff-limbed and blinking in the light, the protesters chanted and the young soldiers pulled down their green caps and averted their eyes, and I was pushed in the chest by an American policeman; step back, sir, the terminal is that way. We don't want any trouble here.

A priest from the local chapter met me on the sidewalk in front of the airport, exchange of names and the customary embrace, and he hefted the suitcase with all my earthly possessions into the backseat. "Quite a welcoming committee they gave you," he said, but I was lost already, the sun of a new country warm against my face, and scarcely heard a word he said all afternoon.

The year after I arrived, one-hundred-sixty-six people, many of them seminarians, would be arrested for circling the Harrisburg Federal Courthouse with a chain, protesting the trial of the Harrisburg Seven. University students across the nation went on strike. And as Nixon escalated bombing in North Vietnam, the Sisters of Notre Dame de Namur fell to their knees in the White House, praying for peace. Even prayer had entered the language of resistance. The war they despised would come to an end, Nixon toppled in disgrace, and America would lick its wounds before slouching into the self-absorbed drama of the eighties, and I would watch it all unfold as if from a distance, soft-eyed and nostalgic for the time I lived in, loving its innocent rebel spirit from afar long after it lay down in corruption, the pilgrim's soul in the New World.

All this somehow led to an extreme loss of prudence and a troubled youth standing in my office, all wildness and trembling destruction, tossing the hair back from his face, nervous fingers wound up in the frayed end of his sleeve, his eyes, green as Calvary, seeing something beyond what I had tried to become. My heart was already broken for him. I pressed his lips with a traitor's kiss. And I will not dwell on this, nor make excuses, except to say my downfall was a long time in the making.

I left the house still dirty from the garden work, and wandered through the woods below the school. There was a stand of birches, white roots in the wet, swampy ground. Beyond them lay the so-called Indian Lake, really a large pond, deep sluggish water rimmed with tall reeds and stirred by the wind, visited by redwing blackbirds and a pair of wild swans. The swans were still there, even so late in the year; strangely, I don't believe they ever left, even in the winter when the pond froze over and disappeared in snow. Perhaps someone fed them all winter. I watched the swans glide around the lake, leaning into each other, reminding me, despite their whiteness, of serpents, sinuous necks reared back, red beaks, black, beady eyes. I stood there inhaling the marsh scent of rotting leaves. In my confusion, I found myself returning to the Spiritual Exercises, that most basic of Jesuit texts written in Loyola's limping Spanish, hand laid over my heart as we are instructed to do to remind ourselves to rise above adversity; over the years the gesture had become habit with me. Loyola, like me, had come from the Basque country. I needed to feel that weight on my chest, bringing me back to myself. Soul of Christ, sanctify me. Passion of Christ, strengthen me. From the wicked foe defend me. Permit me not to be separated from Thee.

The swans ducked their heads, rifling back their feathers, pluming and shaking their wings. Years ago there had been another pair as well, but they were gone now, one shot, we thought, by some youths from the town. The swan's mate had lived there by itself for a time, calling its fluting cry. But a few weeks later, some of our boys rushed in to say that they had found it hooked by a discarded fisherman's line, and I had gone with them to the lake to see if we could save it. The poor swan had expired by the time we got there; it must have struggled for a long time, because it had been completely wrapped by the line and had managed to strangle itself, the hook buried deep, feathers bent, dirty and broken. It had taken us half an hour to untangle it. It was a much larger and heavier bird than I had always imagined, observing them from a distance. One of the boys, a kind-hearted freshman by the name of O'Neil, had been so upset that he was nearly in tears, causing much derision among his friends, and I had said, without thinking, that the swan was with her mate now, that it was a terrible crime to hurt a defenseless living thing, which had resulted in a conversation about the sentience of animals and the church's stance on this, and was I a heretic for suggesting that a swan should have a soul.

The first time I had seen this landscape was from the car window in 1971, when that kind priest whose name I have now forgotten drove me from the airport to the school. "Cortez," he muttered, as we sped into the Northeast woods, their wild hills touched by sun and cloud shadows, ragged strings of mountains, trees in the first flame of autumn. The man glanced at me with a small smile, and I saw that he was trying to make a joke of my European bedazzlement, that he had not missed the greedy sheen of conquest in my eye, devouring the raw landscape. "And so it goes."

"Del Cano," I said. "He was a Basque, like me. Cortez came to a bad end."

"Never heard of him."

"Magellan was the captain, Del Cano the navigator. He circled the globe, and found his way home."

He had an odd face, as I remember, fallen on one side as if he had suffered a stroke. But he grinned with the living half, said, "You will end up far from where you started, I think."

Now I soaked my shoes, standing there alone in the marshy grass, feeling the wind stir through my hair, and was chilled to the bone by the time I returned to the house. In the privacy of my own rooms I shed my cold wet shoes and stood barefoot, toes curled into the carpet. I undid the metal snaps of the stiff white collar insert, pulled it out and set it carefully on the dresser in its place between crucifix and breviary, rubbed the places on either side of my trachea where the snaps chafed. I turned on the space heater. I lay down on the bed, curled, face pressed down to the pillow.

Permit me not to be separated from Thee.

Dear X,

What is soul, if not memory? And is a faulty memory a symptom of an incomplete soul? I don't know what it is, this thing you would call a soul. But I know there are pieces of my life I can't remember. When I look back on certain portions of my life, it is not a continuous stream I see so much as a series of compartmentalized images, and nothing in between them.

I remember a string of pearls coming undone and bouncing down the steps, but I don't remember gunfire, or how I got home that day. Just pearls, falling with that special chalky clack. And I remember your incredibly white, even teeth, how you tried to be gentle until you couldn't help yourself, juniper on your breath and the taste of you, or was it some renegade trace of blood, a faint metal that faded in an hour or so. I opened my lips for you. My throat was marked, a blue and yellow point; I remember thinking that you would not have bruised me if I had been more compliant. But the mark was small, probably unnoticeable to anyone but me. I would cover it with a scarf for a few days, wearing gloves too, as if that made me less conspicuous. I don't remember if you said anything else to me. Try as I might, I also can't remember the two weeks following that event, or how I got back to the dormitory without being noticed, tie undone, footsteps dazed in the halls. Those memories are gone; it is as if they were burned, like film beneath a glaring light, out of existence. They are dark windows to me now.

The soul is separate from the memory; surely I had a soul when I was a child, despite the fact that there are many things I don't remember. What, for instance, did I do with the first three years of my life? So I have a soul, but memory is different, its beginning is the beginning of others, of our perception of something outside ourselves.

We live in a blankness, alone, until something impinges on us, some shock or great pain (my earliest memories are mostly painful ones). Do we need pain to wake us from the blankness? Is it like that glass, darkly, through which we see before the perfect comes to strip us down, to make us who we are? If this is the case, and I am my own mind, then I was not myself before I could hurt.

Where are we this time? The Slaughterhouse, of course. On a bed of leaves you reach for me, oh, God, and I am arching back, falling backward into the earth where the stones lie and the living roots forever search for water. I arch backward, spilling out of your arms and into the waiting leaf bed. Again and again, you spill me. You kiss away the gooseflesh all down my torso, where my shirt and sweater have been unbuttoned and nudged aside. I become aware of the mystery of myself. The ache of stiffened nipples, damp with your saliva in the cold air, the muscles of my belly under your lips and abrasive chin, your hot tongue, your beautiful teeth, the green, pine scent of the fork of my legs, a fist still zippered, one fact you have demurely avoided, as if you would rather have me limp and shrinking, as if you don't know what to make of this telltale sign of my willingness. You linger over the curve between hip and ribcage, the killing spot were we at battle, perfectly sized to fit your hand.

You are incomprehensible to me; I know only myself, stranded in myself. I fall hard, with sickly, profound force, as only the young can. I open my mouth to sigh for you in the airless dark and you spill me, dirt between my teeth, dirt filling my ears, crawling things in my pockets and my hair. I reach for you in all the panic of life, with the singular passion, yes, of a teenager, and you draw me down into your arms, introductory thumb slipped beneath the waistband of my jeans, reaching finally for that guilty knot, unraveling me all over again. You lay your head against my chest so that you can hear my heart jump.

It's a sad truth: we lose the ability to want with so much force. Seen from the far side of adulthood, this may be the most disturbing fact of all: that I lay in your arms and loved you, in a way I no longer can.

"If you tell anyone," you say, knotting my tie for me. And I answer, "Tell them what?" It isn't to tease or admonish you. It's just that I don't see any of this as wrong, only perilous, and see no reason why I would ever tell anyone; why should I share my secret world? How instinctively cautious I am, how jealous of your wandering attention. "Tell them what?" I say, and duck to scrape my mouth, back and forth, along the blue inner-side of your wrist. This is another time, not the Slaughterhouse. This time, you pull away from me. I know I frighten you, in these moments when I overstep myself. And what a shaky line to walk, a boy in love with his teacher. Who do you want me to be, today? There's something about the light in the room, something that makes us both uneasy; when you move away, your shadow spreads. It covers the wall and bleeds across the ceiling. Where are we? A window lets in daylight and voices, the sounds of shoes on a gravel walk. Another bleak, institutional room with no scent and no memories.

I must have sensed it even then, your brutal hypocrisy. When all is said and done, you will reproach me for my corruption.

Dr. Orpel keeps telling me to reframe these events, to recognize my weakness and your exploitation of it. But I can't make myself believe that version; it just isn't what I recall. Near you, the pain was less. As if your attention was a kind of opiate. Which, I suppose, is what Dr. Orpel is trying to make me see, with her insistence on renaming the signposts of my past.

But I chose you; I can't believe otherwise. I can't let that shadow of you vanish. What will it mean to start doubting now, to lose that history? When you fade, what nightmare will replace you?

I collect stories. I tell myself that ours were days of grace. I tell myself that by your side, I was worthy.

Yours,

T

Down in the leaves, he said, "Bring her back." His face was hidden from me in the darkness cast by a rafter, blocking the moonlight. The night was cold, except where we touched. His skin lay taut under my mouth, my teeth teasing his chest. He was impossibly silken, almost painful for me to touch, cool and sharp. The space between his neck and collar gave off a whiff of cigarettes and nervous perspiration. Initially, I had been overwhelmed by this impossible windfall. My cold fingers fumbled with the innumerable buttons of the layers he wore, sweaters and shirts, while he lay there in the leaves, letting me undress him as if it were a matter of no importance, looking for all the world like I had killed him. But when I had laid bare his upper body and reached for the belt buckle, he panted, terrified, staring at the dark wall beyond my shoulder, white teeth bared and breath misting the night, and I beat a tactical retreat, hands off the buckle, kissing the hollow below his navel. I thought of a hurt fox I had seen once holed with a broken leg in the corner of Jack Savage's garage, turning fear-crazed yellow eyes to me, writhing a black lip. I lay myself out alongside him, trapping him with my knee. "You're cold," I said, and he said he wasn't. But he must have been, half-naked, the leaves under him edged in frost. I worked my way down slowly this time, until my hand rested on his abdomen, two fingers under his belt in the sparse, silky floss. It was loose enough to slip beneath without giving me too much trouble. He quaked, but didn't resist; no, he slapped his hand down over mine. And he may forever think me a monster for the consideration I failed to show in taking him at his word, or at his cue, rather, but at that moment, monster was precisely what I was. I wanted the chase to end. I wanted to earn the guilt I had been covered in. I grabbed him, listening to his shocked breath. There is no other way to say it. He was erect under my hand. He bucked against me frantically but without any sound, as if possessed. How I twist with shame now, not for the act but for the frank brutality of it. It was unforgivable.

We had slipped out separately after midnight, taken the forest path to the ruins the boys loved; tonight these woods were indeed haunted, by Adonis and Hades. He had brought a flashlight, and, for some reason, a backpack with provisions, as if we were about to make an escape, but it had all long since been lost somewhere, dropped and kicked away in our hasty scramble. The leaves were damp, my knees soaked through in the cold. In darkness, he panted against my ear, breath smelling of milk and leeks, catching noisily on an unswallowed mouthful of spit. Distant wood smoke tinged the air, and the sweet, blue smell of frost. Miles away, a coyote yipped and a dog answered. He came to the end of himself very quickly, and lay in my arms, gasping. And then he whispered, "Bring her back."

"Bring..?"

He sprang alive and lay hold of my coat with startling force, showing off the architecture of his arms and chest, plunging forward from the shadow of a rafter. He pulled me hard, and I had to yank my hand ungently from the damp waistband of his jeans, to catch myself with both hands against the ground to avoid falling on him. I saw the moon shining from his eyes, huge, delirious, rolling like those of a horse in pain. Spittle frothed the corners of his mouth. I heard the squeak of his teeth against each other.

Then he arched backward under me, his body an iron bow, taut and quivering. At first I thought he was having some kind of fit, but then I saw that it was his way of weeping, this horrible spectacle. He sobbed with full voice, like a child. I recoiled; I couldn't help it. I feared him in his alien suffering. I didn't understand the cause of it. He sank his fingernails into my wrist and squealed in a high register, "Murderer!" And I couldn't help it, my hand flashed out of its own instinct, and I slapped him.

It wasn't hard, just enough to make him gasp. I didn't want to hurt him, only to shake off whatever trance he had fallen into, to knock that unbearable word out of his mouth. But he folded under me into the leaves, hand to cheek, doubled over, sobbing, strings of spit stretching from his lip, jeans rifled and sticky, nude chest still damp from my kisses. Leaving him at that moment was unthinkable. But I did leave him.

As I pulled myself together and backed away, feeling for the door, he named me again. "Murderer," he croaked. From the ground, he pierced me with his flat, silver eyes. "Murderer." I ran. From an animal brain I pulled the runner's pace, the hunter's pace, my eyes well able to see in the dark. I followed the trail by looking at the stars, the night sky visible in a narrow swathe over the cleared path, the black river of heaven. Behind me, he screamed into the night, in English. "I'll own you, when this is over!"

TWENTY-ONE

It was at this time, Tony reflected later, November of '87, that he contracted the waking sickness. In the night, the ghost would come, the female ghost who said the dormitory was no longer safe (and Tony agreed, it did not feel safe at all). They would walk together through the sleeping school, always to Wolf Chapel, the only safe place. Always they would stay there together, hidden in the sacristy, the closet where the soft vestments hung empty, which was so small they had to hug each other, front to back or chest to chest, hearts beating together, sharing each other's breath. And always, when the light came, Tony would be alone, would climb to his feet, push aside the fabric and walk slowly back to the dormitory to begin the day. It was in reaching for the sacristy door one morning that Tony first noticed the shake in his hands, the shake like Ochoa's that would plague him, off and on, for the rest of his life. This, he supposed, must be a symptom of the waking sickness.

He would never know how Matt knew, but then, Matt was a perceptive soul. As Tony was traversing the halls from one class to another, a blond, hurtling shape forced its way through the throng of boys and crashed into him. It took him a moment to realize that it was Matt Kelly. They fell together against a trophy case and then to the floor, kicking and thrashing, Tony curving inward to protect his face from Matt's fists. When the other boys pulled Matt off him, Matt produced a howling sound, and Tony, looking up at him, saw the other boy's face flushed red and streaming with tears, saw how he leaned against the arms that held him back, clinging to them, and the other boys, instead of cheering and egging them on, were silent, shamed. The two would never speak of it afterwards; they would go on watching movies, telling jokes, breaking bottles against the walls of the Slaughterhouse, exchanging friendly cuffs and glances, pitching violent fastballs in the leaves. But Tony knew that he had broken Matt's heart, and that any friendship between them from that moment on was strictly superficial. Years later, he would look back on the sacrifice of a friend as one of his first actions as an adult. Now, he took in Matt's stricken face, leaking snot and tears, his thin hands hanging down, palms out, seeing him as entirely alien, no trace of the friend he knew.

Rough hands pulled Tony to his feet. It was a senior, a tan and golden Irish boy with a football player's physique and hyphenated name, Kennedy-Something. "Fighting in the halls," said Kennedy. Tony stared at Matt, who was now hanging, empty. The senior boy glanced from Matt to Tony; he looked like Matt, Tony thought, that same color scheme, blond and delicate blush. Turning his back on Matt, the senior barked into Tony's face.

"You think I don't know who started this? You think I'm stupid?"

Tony said nothing.

"You sneaky little shit. Pulling a thing like that."

Behind the senior's back, Tony watched as the other boys closed ranks around Matt.

"Have you looked at yourself lately?" said the senior boy. He was leaning in close now, his eyes, broken blue, illuminated from within by undisguised contempt. Tony tried to count the freckles on his nose. "Do you know what you look like?"

"No," said Tony.

"Guilty, that's what."

On the week before the boys went home for Christmas holidays, it was announced that there would be a new language teacher for the spring semester. Father Ochoa was leaving St. Ignatius. The reasons for his leaving were not made clear to the boys, and so joined the host of other unsolved mysteries surrounding him, ripe for speculation and outright invention.

"He's going to India, that's what I heard," said Billy Cato in the hall outside the music room. "Did you know he speaks Indian?"

"That's just gossip," said Andre, though it was all gossip. "He's been called back to Rome. He's done teaching, is all."

Tony passed by them all, shouldering his satchel, hurrying away.

PART III

DAKSHIN RAI

TWENTY-TWO

"I called my dad today," the girl said. "I told him where I am."

Tony, knowing the girl was lying, affected a tone of unconcern. "That's wonderful. Will he come pick you up, or will you hitchhike to Oregon?"

She was wearing her enigmatic face, and smiled at him with what could have been distracted sweetness or pure loathing. "You're a strange man. You're the strangest man I've ever known."

He knew that Schwartz was cunning, and so he should have known, when she appeared in his office in his favorite blue shirt, clutching a half-bottle of bourbon he had been given by his editor last Christmas, that she had planned something. But what obvious snare would he not fall into, for the feral girl? She sat on his desk, next to the typewriter, put one foot in his lap and the other on the back of his chair, took a swig from the bottle, swished it around her teeth, swallowed, and offered the bottle to him. "It combines well, if you're nervous. Just go easy."

"Combines with what?"

"I've got a present for you. It's to say I'm sorry," she said. There was something clutched in her other hand, she held it against her chest like a little trapped moth she was preparing to throw out the window.

"What is it?"

"Do you trust me?"

"No."

"Close your eyes and stick out your tongue."

"No," he said, "no way."

"Doesn't it get boring, being you?" She wriggled, settling into the desk, pressing with her toes against the pocket of his trousers, where the top of his leg joined the hip, just left of center. He grabbed her foot and placed it on the arm of his chair.

"If you think you're going to get me to drink that, you're wrong."

"Once burned, huh."

He made a soft "ha" sound. Schwartz. She was as honest, he thought, as any friend he had ever had, and far more interesting than most. The girl held her cupped hand toward his face, revealing two paper tabs in its pale little nest, saying, "I guess I'll just do these by myself, then."

"Chingada," he said, and opened his mouth for her, letting her place the paper on his tongue.

He did not have much history with LSD. The few forays he'd made in teenage years had produced nothing but a vague sense of disorientation, and finally a memorable episode in which he was trapped, gripping the toilet seat, as the appliance shot skyward like a huge porcelain obelisk, the floor dropping away with alarming speed, for several hours. It was so long ago now that he no longer knew what to expect, but decided that any distorted nightmare was better than being sober by himself. Then there was the distance, that awful fissure that had opened on the night of the Starr Hotel. He thought perhaps that it would go, in some similar dark element; he and Schwartz only truly understood each other, it seemed, with a certain special chaos.

This was not what happened. Tony made popcorn while they waited, and they sat on the couch watching TV, some show about beautiful people marooned on an island. After an hour, the girl started to laugh, and walked through the apartment, opening the windows, letting in the cold. "I'm exploding," she said, the wind lifting her hair, and he believed her, she looked ready to sing, and he was as far from her, and every human, as he had ever been in his life. When she spoke, it was to the room at large, as if he had made himself invisible. It was a failure on his part that seemed more epic, somehow, than any other.

In the safety of his office, with the girl in the living room and the door locked behind him, Tony sat on the windowsill and tried to finish what was left of the bottle. The steam pinged in the radiators, fighting with the outside air, reminding him in its suddenness of that long ago, distant gunfire in the pines beyond the compound. He watched the icy street, silent and empty of cars, and the stunted ginkgos, glassy and bent almost to breaking under pounds of solid ice. He trembled in reasonless fear to see the windows across the street go black one by one, leaving a heavy, blank curtain, dark windows in a sea of darkness, a hole in the night without stars, pinging and moving away from him with great and terrible purpose.

"J," he said, opening his office door and moving carefully into the living room, away from that fierce nothing, "tell me you see that."

There was no reply, no sign of her in the apartment, though he went from room to room to room, thinking she might be hiding. Her bag, too, had vanished, and the air from the open windows pushed the front door on its loose hinges, back and forth. The hall, too, was empty, and the stairs to the street.

Schwartz had gone.

TWENTY-THREE

On a Thursday afternoon, Tony hid from Father Carol, sneaked out of school and went alone to the Slaughterhouse, wearing three sweaters and a coat, and fell asleep on a pile of old sacking. It was late December, cold; the night before, snow had mounded up in the school grounds and the forest surrounding them, snow so thick and deep that there were no cars on the road, no wind in the trees, just padded silence, like the inside of a gun. When Tony arrived at the old building, he removed the loose brick and lit up a cigarette, the last one, and then held the lighter to the empty pack until it burned and shriveled at his feet. When he had finished, he ground out the stub with his heel and lay down on the sacking with the soggy *Dialogues on Natural Religion*, but the silence was so exquisite and his weariness so great that the book made no sense to him, and maybe it would not have made sense anyway.

"Somebody should burn this, too," he said to no one. He nodded, blinked his heavy eyes. Sleep descended so quickly that he could not even put down the book, which slipped from his gloved hands and flopped onto the ground among the leaves and bottles.

He woke suddenly, chilled to the bone, and for a moment could not remember where he was; it was dark, and the moon shone down between the cold brick walls. He scrambled up, blinking his eyes, and headed for the door, looking for his bicycle before he remembered that he had walked because of the snow. In the doorway, he saw the white forest illuminated by the moon, stretching out before him, curving gently away where the black trees ran down to the empty, silent road. Someone was there. A dark shape moved through the trees, a man walking with his head down.

Tony thought of Lupe María, heard her sly voice, "Tonight, I saw *El Morro*." A chill went through him that had nothing to do with the cold, and he watched as the tall shade passed him by, continued into the forest, a black stain against the brilliant snow, a measured step that Tony would have known anywhere. And then, as he had that first time when he followed Ochoa through the slumbering halls, he followed him into the trees.

His tracks were easy to discern, straight and unwavering, through the trees just to the side of the snow-covered road. His long, even stride had spaced the footprints far apart, and Tony had to stretch to place his own feet inside them. The tracks went on until they broke through the edge of the forest, where the trees gave way to the hills and white fields that bordered the school buildings. But then, instead of climbing the brow of the hill and continuing down toward the school, Ochoa's tracks stopped, hesitated and doubled back into the bare trees, still visible in the moonlight.

Tony found him in a clearing. The priest had heard his soft tread in the snow, and had turned to face him, waiting for him there. For a moment, neither spoke. They were both flushed from their brisk walk in the cold, their breath carried away in the still night air. There was a small glint of silver from Ochoa's hand, and Tony saw a black rosary, wrapped tightly many times around his palm. He wondered if Ochoa had been saying a rosary as he walked, and found it hard to imagine.

"They're looking for you," said Ochoa. "Didn't you hear them calling?"

"I fell asleep."

"You would have gone here to be alone, I thought." He looked vaguely off into the dark trees. He must have been walking, Tony thought, for a long time, and could have found Tony easily enough if he had wanted to. He knew where to look. And what, Tony wondered, if they had both disappeared in the woods, not just the troubled kid but the prefect as well? He imagined the frantic calls, dogs leaping at the ends of their leashes, the roving beams of flashlights in the night. He wondered how long it would be before they were found.

"Father Carol came to see me today," Ochoa said carefully.

"Yeah?"

"It was a strange conversation. He seems to think you threatened him. I told him he must have been mistaken. That you have been out of sorts."

"Out of sorts."

"I'm not going to say I'm sorry, just to please you."

"As you like. In three days I'll be gone." He hooked a finger under the scarf he wore around his throat, gazing off into the snowy woods.

"Carol's been making me write compositions. He's been saying…" Tony trailed off, gagged with indignation. "I'm going to kill him."

"You have no need to punish anyone else."

"You really think I'm sticking around this hellhole when you're gone?"

"That's a mark for language."

"Fuck you."

"You're past curfew," Ochoa said crisply. "And you've been smoking," he added. "Keep going, and we can make it an even dozen." He was speaking English. Tony saw this denial for what it was, and hated him suddenly with a sick, aching rage.

"But, you…" He faltered. "You actually think this is all about you." His voice climbed, out of his control, that trembling recklessness taking hold of all his muscles. Dampness from the snow had seeped into his shoes, and he shivered. "If I have enemies here, it's your fault. And now, you pray."

"I've done everything in my power to protect you."

"What are you saying to God?"

"Go back now, and I won't tell anyone I found you here. You can make up some story, no doubt, to satisfy them."

"No!" his voice came out uneven, hysterical and full of rage, and he stopped in consternation, his eyes prickling, the tears in them making the moonlight break and shatter. He wiped his nose on the back of his sleeve, humiliated. "How can you be like this? What did I do wrong?"

"You'll do as I say."

"Not anymore."

"Aizu! You'll do as you're told!"

Tony jumped at the brutal snap in his voice, something he had never heard before. "You should just do it," he said. "I'm tired of these stupid games."

"Stay back."

"What are you waiting for? I couldn't be any weaker."
He stepped forward and placed his hand on Ochoa's chest.
"What's wrong? Scared, mariquita?"

The shock to his jaw caused the night to explode in a
cascade of silver sparks, his head jerked to the side and he
heard, felt, something inside him snap. He staggered back
three steps, stood with his head down and his feet splayed
apart, and as the blindness faded he saw Ochoa's face full
of shock and anger, the back of his hand pulled back. And
then Tony lunged forward and everything else was gone,
just the solidity of the man's body, which gave to his
charge with a winded grunt, toppled and rolled, and he felt
the snow under his knees and the body under his hands
and then the ground under his back, and Ochoa was
stronger than he was. Tony grabbed a handful of black
robes and held on, felt the heavy cloth tear in the struggle,
struck out blindly, found a chin, a neck, a collarbone.

"I'll tell them!" he cried out, hearing his voice break with
fury, not caring. "My father will have you put down like a
dog!"

He felt fingers on his jaw and a thumb digging into his
throat, and he was overwhelmed with coughing, choking
for air, unable to speak, but still fighting. His hand flew
wildly, snagged on something and then came away, just
before Ochoa flipped him over, forcing his face down into
the snow with a hand on the back of his head, pinning him
down with his arm behind his back like Farriday had done
(did they teach that in the seminary, Tony wondered?), a
hand pinioning his lower back, all the weight of the man
pressing him breathless into the ground.

"Yes?" Ochoa's voice came again as that terrible growl
through his teeth, hot and close to Tony's ear, English
thicker in his rage. His grip was agony, he was shaking

Tony, his shoulder wrenched almost past endurance. "What will you tell your father, exactly?"

"You're a monster," Tony could barely force the words out. "I hate you!"

"You're lying. I know it. Do you know why?"

Tony pulled an arm free and thrashed under him, fingers scrabbling in the snow, reaching for anything, a weapon, a stone, a handful of hair. Ochoa grabbed him again, twisting his arm back so that he cried out involuntarily and stopped moving. "Hush," said Ochoa. "Stop it." In the stillness, Tony could feel him breathing, felt a rough chin glance against his temple. "I'll tell you why," Ochoa said, close to his ear. "You can't hate a man after you've brought him down."

He gritted his teeth, felt Ochoa's warm breath on the back of his neck, wrenched his pinned arm, struggled mightily with real terror, and then suddenly gave in. Facedown in the snow, he wept, crying hot tears without sound. Ochoa paused, and the boy listened to the air whistling in his teeth, his harsh, uneven panting. But his grip loosened and relaxed, and he hung there uncertainly, holding himself up on his elbows, sunk in the snow. "Idiot," Ochoa said, a soft growl, "why are you so impossible?"

Tony wanted to burn, to disappear, to howl and scream his anguish in some far, secret place where even the stars were black. Finding the crook of Ochoa's arm, he hid his face there. Again he clenched his fists, shaking Ochoa with ineffectual struggling, the scream, when it finally came, scarcely a whimper, muffled by silence in the cloth. He fell still, resting with his ear in the snow, face hidden in Ochoa's sleeve. His hand hurt; he was worrying round beads between his fingers. He was clutching a broken rosary, gripping it so tightly that the little crucifix cut into his palm. How had it come to be there? He pushed his face deeper into the dark cloth, the sweet scent of old paper, of cedar, dampened by his tears and saliva, said in a broken whisper hardly audible to himself, "Tell me I mean more to you than the others."

"Never cry in front of a man. Understand? Not the other boys, not your teachers, not your enemies, and not your father. Weakness makes men cruel. Cry when you are alone." Tony felt the warmth of a sigh across his scalp, the hard weight of a chin resting for an instant there. The white collar, pulled loose in the struggle, folded its papery wing across Tony's vision, its starched edge brushed by his lashes. Ochoa spoke into the hair behind his ear. His face ached. "Listen," Ochoa said. "Let there be some mystery left. You will hate me less." For years, Tony would revisit that moment, turning over in his own mind exactly what Ochoa meant to say.

It was then that they both became aware of the rushing sound, the crackling, eating sound, like bees, like the mandibles of chewing insects. They saw that there was a curious light, not from the moon but from the earth, illuminating hill and snow and the night around them, a light that moved and was quick, red. And they heard the sound of distant voices, coming, with the light, from the direction of their twin tracks.

Ochoa recovered first. He stumbled to his feet, started running with long strides back toward the school, Tony close at his heels. As they neared the school, and the flames illuminating the windows of Wolf Chapel became visible, Loyola and the beasts and Christ ascending, Tony quickly outstripped the priest. The chapel had clearly been burning for a while, building up slowly, now gutted with fire, sagging as its timbers warped in the flames. Dimly, Tony saw other running shapes silhouetted against the fire, frantic boys and the priests shepherding them, flashing lights and the wail of sirens, the late stages of a surprisingly organized evacuation born of fire drills, but Tony did not stop. He was close now, lungs searing, sprinting toward the chapel. He could feel the heat of the fire, overpowering, could smell it, could hear, over the fire's rushing, the creaking, tearing sound of the collapsing ruin. And then the great window broke, exploding outward in a shower of colored glass and fire, and there were shapes twisting in it, burning snakes carried high up in the air, burning and writhing in agony. And out of the blaze, something else was moving, a blind, struggling something, running in fits and starts on black spindly legs, hairless, its body made of fire, arms stretched out toward Tony, who, as if in a dream, raised his own arms and stretched them out. But he was stunned, swept off his feet, bowled over by a charging weight like a bull, he was fighting, struggling, being dragged away from the fire and that ragged, running thing that lived within it, his lungs full of smoke, blood in his nose, Ochoa's broken rosary still clutched somehow in his hand, and someone stronger than he was pushing him down again.

"Stop it, you crazy ass!" It was Nunzio's voice screaming over the roar and snapping, Nunzio's big, flat hands slapping at his smoldering sweater. "Goddamn it, there's nobody in there!"

They told him later that he woke up when they were loading him into the ambulance, that he was in shock, that he fought them so hard the paramedics had to stick a needle in his arm and lie across his chest till he stopped moving. Tony had no memory of this, though it sounded true. He was still drugged when the hospital room swam into focus, and he saw a face leaning over his, a blond, white face haloed by fluorescent lights. "Tony," said Matt Kelly, "I'm supposed to tell you that everybody made it out okay, so you won't be worried. They put us up in the Ivy Lodge, but nobody's sleeping, of course. They're sending us all home tomorrow."

Tony tried to move, but managed only a tremor, not sure if it was only drugs or a physical weight holding him down. He turned his eyes to the side, saw a black blur against the white, a priest, not Ochoa, waiting for Matt in the doorway. Something was beating in his temples, a panic steadily building. Matt glanced over his shoulder and leaned in closer, whispered into Tony's ear. "He won't come back. I want you to know that, while you're lying here. It was me that told them. That's all." He straightened up, smiled at Tony with his beautiful, angelic teeth, and said, loud enough for the priest to hear, "Feel better soon." He turned away and disappeared, and Tony blinked his eyes, and let the room fade away. They told him that while he slept, his eyes streamed with tears from the soot and smoke of the fire. They gave him a plastic bag with his personal belongings inside it, a wallet, a lighter and a broken rosary. The next day, he boarded a plane and went home.

TWENTY-FOUR

It was with an unearthly focus that he moved through the crowds, like a clever drunk, moving too carefully, concentrating on the distance from foot to floor and hand to metal rail. On the subway platform, a cold wind slicked off the flanks of the arriving train, faster than usual, lifting his damp hair. A man in a vest patched with tape stood on the platform near him, vomiting into a garbage can with a look of empty resignation, and Tony watched the people passing by or waiting, like him, as he concentrated on the numbers of trains, watching them carefully avoid both him and the sick man, knowing he must look equally sweaty and lost. On the train to Grand Central, he found a pole and hugged it, pressing his forehead to the oily metal till it ached between his eyes, fighting the sudden nausea, and the car shrieked and shuddered in its black canal, and when the doors opened at last he was exhaled onto the platform in the moist and bilious air of underground, people streaming in wakes from his shoulders, their faces swimming in his vision like wet paper plastered to a telephone pole, not one among them recognizable, not one eye meeting his.

He stopped at a payphone, and, though he had a cell in his pocket, dropped in the money and punched in Matt Kelly's number. At this point, Matt would be more likely to answer an unlisted number than any call from Tony Luna. Though it must have been quite late, Matt did not sound as if he had been sleeping. "Oh," he said frostily. "It's you."

"Matt," said Tony, "what am I not getting about all this?" He struggled to hear, over the clatter of the station, that soft, grown-up choirboy voice. "Matt?"

"You don't remember, do you? Not accurately?"

"What?" He could make out a soft, rhythmic tapping over the line, Matt's index finger, he thought, against the receiver. "Matt," he said, "I need you."

"Are you impaired?"

"Yes. I mean, no. I may have taken some things."

There was a long pause, in which Tony strained, over the noise of the station, to hear Matt breathing on the other end of the line, or even the panting of the white, spectral dog. "I think I'm about to make a scene." He stared at the wads of chewing gum, stuck to the side of the phone box, the moldy Yellow Pages dangling from its chain. "Matt?"

"About to make a scene, huh?"

"Yes."

"God forbid I should miss that."

"I'm at Grand Central. Please come."

"Tony, wait..."

He hung up.

Up the gray stairs, into the passages and finally into the granite hall, those ticket counters, those women sitting on the floor beside their suitcases, those vaulted ceilings, those lights, those stars, those angels and animals revolving gently round the verdigris dome of heaven. She would come back here, he thought, where the watchmen paced and an old man changed the light bulbs in the stars. Here, at the edge of Purgatory (what was Purgatory, if not a train station?) he was sure he would find Schwartz. He understood now why she had chosen this place, because she was a liminal figure, here and gone. The copper vault of the night sky was large enough for anyone to vanish into, even J.

He couldn't find her, though he looked everywhere, tracing the walls with one hand, just endless strangers hurrying with their children and luggage. He accosted a security guard, asked after a black-haired girl with a green army bag, and the man placed his hand on his radio, wanting to know if the missing person was a relative of Tony's.

"Yes," said Tony, "she's my cousin."

Tony found himself in an open space just off the main hall, an intersection of two hallways leading to a street exit, cold with the draft from the street. It was the whispering wall, a place where, because of the curve of the stone, you could magically hear a friend's quiet words from the other side of the room. As Tony leaned against this wall, he saw a woman carrying a red milk crate, walking slowly away, and something tugged at his mind, some small thing J had said the first day they met, that beggar woman with her cup and plastic crate. Tony approached her, caught up with her by the glass doors.

"Please," he said, and the woman flicked her veiled eyes up to his face, her jaws chewing over the knot of her scarf. The woman's eyes were silvery with cataracts; he wondered if she could actually see at all. Her jaws trembled, as if with a palsy. But Tony saw a spark of recognition in her face when he described Schwartz, and he knew the woman had seen her; he was momentarily stunned by this, for this sighting by another person was the first evidence he had that the girl actually existed. When she had gone, even though he was surrounded by physical traces of her, some part of him had been unable to believe that she had ever been real. Tony extended his hand to the old woman. "I have to find her." He struggled for an explanation, some dire reason that would be undeniable. "She's run away." Somehow, his hand had found the old woman's, and she did not pull back, gazing at him as if in a trance; he held her cold hand with both of his, gently, as he would a bird. "She's run away," he said again, and searched for the woman in the pale depths of her eyes. The voice that issued from her was lower than he expected, burnt by the lingering traces of a cigarette cough.

"Guards turned them all out a few minutes ago." With her free hand, she pointed down 42nd Street. She pulled her other hand away from him, then held it out palm up, glaring from the folds of her milky eyes. Tony gave her a twenty, and she muttered some word of gratitude, tucking the money into one of the many pockets of her coat.

On the sidewalk, crowds seemed to converge in front of him, giving Tony the feeling of running in a dream, all his movements delayed. His eyes scanned the crush of bodies (a plunging herd of tall women in heeled boots), searching for the spaces between strangers. Schwartz was fairly short, there was no way he would be able to see her hidden among these taller people unless he searched, like a trail guide swinging a machete. He realized the futility of the whole exercise, but was unable to stop, knowing that she might be there, just ahead of him. It was dark, the street crowded, cars throwing up sprays of steam and rock salt from the street. In a patch of brightness, where the lights of a bar threw a green puddle on the sidewalk, Tony caught a glimpse of a slender figure, a thin wrist with black bracelets, and an army surplus backpack with faded, block letters, the name Dubois. He pulled himself from the crowd, swimming blindly toward the spot. It was not Schwartz, but another young girl, holding a cigarette and Schwartz's backpack, standing among a group of other girls, staring through the window of the bar. They looked to be about the same age as Schwartz, maybe a little older, and they had that same hard look about them that had so disarmed him in Schwartz's presence, that bitter mixture of coquette and flight animal, stained with the salty rime of the street. He stood there, catching his breath, until one of the girls noticed him and pulled at the sleeve of another, and they all turned around, surveying him with addled, pink eyes.

"Take me to your leader," he felt he could have said to those alien, carnivorous stares. But he was unable to speak. The girl in the center stepped forward. She was the one he had first seen with the backpack, dirty blond hair and eyes smeared with greying kohl to hide the dark stains beneath them, a metal ring through her lower lip, skin translucent in the green light; Tony felt that, if the light had been better, he would have been able to see all her veins beneath that thin, stretched dermis, down to her skeleton, frail and clear as glass.

"What?" said the girl. "You lost?" She sounded foreign, and wore a thin, papery anorak over a shirt that said *Tavi is a Faker*, her mouth blue with cold she didn't seem to feel.

"Yes," said Tony.

The girl lifted her cigarette to her lips and inhaled with her head turned to one side, eyes narrowed. She held the glowing stub between two fingers in the shape of a narrow V with the back of her hand turned outward, and he saw that her fingernails were painted black, like Schwartz's had been that first day; he remembered them so vividly, clutched around a coffee cup, tamping up spilled sugar from the table, the faint, crunching sound. The blonde exhaled through her nose, and the smoke hung around them, a green, clovey haze in the lights of the bar. Tony felt sick. It was too surreal, too much like madness, this girl who was not Schwartz with Schwartz's backpack and nail polish and one-time scent of subway tunnel, taunting him with her cigarette. His cell chirped, and he held it to his ear, still watching the girls. Matt's voice sounded irritated. "Where the hell are you? Did you actually stand me up, after all that? And did you call me from a payphone?"

"I'm Saskia," said the girl.

"Ruby," said another girl, at Saskia's elbow, reaching past her toward Tony's hand. Saskia elbowed her in the ribs and she backed off with a little grunt of pain.

"Whose voice is that?" said Matt, in his ear. "What have you done?"

"Cunt," said Saskia. The girl muttered under her breath but did not protest. Saskia was obviously the leader.

"Matt," said Tony, "I'm on 42nd. Go out the door and take a left. I'll wait for you."

"If you want me to chase you, just say so."

"So, mister. You a cop or something?" Saskia smiled at him with open hatred. Her gums were dark.

"No," said Tony. "No, I'm not a cop." People pressed past him on the sidewalk, making it difficult to remain standing still. "I need to ask you some questions, that's all."

"You sound like a cop," said Saskia, that awful smile still in place. "I'm not holding, if that's what you're after." The girl called Ruby was crying softly, wiping her nose on her sleeve, the other girls were shifting, restless. Tony was afraid they would all evaporate like smoke before his eyes.

"Do you know J Schwartz? I have to find her. Please help me," he said, all in a rush.

There was a long silence, in which someone bumped into Tony's shoulder and cursed him, and the girls all looked at each other, even more guarded than before. Ruby stared off into space as if she had forgotten why they were there, cheeks stained with mascara, her eyes washed-out blue rimmed with pink. They were all so young, clustered together in the cold night; it made him ache. "Have to?" said Saskia finally. "That sounds pretty urgent."

"You know her," said Tony. "She was just here, wasn't she? You're carrying her backpack."

"Tony," Matt said in his ear, "are you still there? Don't move."

"Yes," Tony said.

"Jessica Schwartz, huh."

"Yes. Jessica. Jessica Schwartz." After all the mystery, he couldn't help but feel slightly let down. Jessica?

Saskia looked sidelong at him, down her emaciated cheeks. "You're the one she talked about, the rich trick." Fair enough, he thought. She looked him up and down, drew her lip ring into her mouth and clicked it between her teeth. "She said you looked like that actor, what's his name. Said you were some kind of pervert artist."

"Please, it's very important that I find her. She's in danger."

"We're all in danger. You've got this whole big city full of girls, you know."

He dug for his wallet, dropping his phone on the sidewalk in the process, picked it up and put it in his pocket, extracted a few fifties, and shoved them in Saskia's face. She snatched them, examining them while the other girls pressed closer, regarding first the money and then him with their soulless, hungry eyes. He spun around, searching the crowd for Matt Kelly. Saskia fanned the money between her fingers like a royal flush, displaying again Schwartz's black nail lacquer, then crumpled the bills and crushed them down in the pocket of her anorak, shrugged, and said, "What do you want me to do with that, Mr. Sugar?"

He held out more bills to her, his hand shaking, thrusting them into her face. "Schwartz," he said. "Now."

"She got into a car. Wish I could remember." She tongued her lip ring pointedly, staring at him.

"Listen," he said, "You're right about me, I'm very rich, and very stupid. So tell me where she is."

Saskia dropped her cigarette, ground it out with her heel without looking down at it. "Get a cab," she said. "You won't find it unless I take you there."

Matt appeared then as if by magic, looming out from between two women in furs. Flush with wind and hurry but perfectly tailored, the poster boy of wealthy all-American fun; it seemed impossible to Tony that anyone so glamorous could be looking for him. Matt raised a blond eyebrow at the girls. "I should have known. What have you done?"

"Matt," said Tony, "Matt," reaching out to clutch at Matt's cashmere scarf, slipping through his fingers like the tail of a squirrel. He scraped a kiss across the corner of Matt's cool, startled mouth, laughed, and then burst into tears. Matt put an arm around him. He smelled bafflingly of ozone, of summer, as if he had been strolling in the rain. The large solidness of him was comforting, his shoulder high enough for Tony to rest his forehead on without effort. Tony leaned, gripping the back of Matt's beautiful coat.

"I assume there's a plan of some kind," Matt said to Saskia.

"I'm taking you to Jess," said the girl.

"Jessica," said Tony. "Schwartz's name is Jessica."

Saskia stepped up to Tony and linked her arm through his, and he found himself walking between Matt and Saskia, Matt's hand on the small of his back, steered forcefully toward the street. The other girls watched them go in silence, clustered together in the green light.

Saskia did not know the names of streets, navigated by telling the cab driver what to do, turn left, turn right, keep going. He realized that she was older than she appeared to be, or maybe it was her voice that made her seem so. Matt kept shooting her glances, seemingly torn between irritation and amusement. Tony sat between them, wedged in by the sharp bones of the girl and Matt's more familiar solid shape. "Where's your dog?" Tony asked him. "The ghost dog?" Matt said nothing.

"Why didn't she sleep with you, that stupid bitch?" Saskia said, in what Tony thought, confusingly, was a show of sympathy for him. "She's crazy." She had a tattoo on the back of her wrist, a horrible, crooked outline of a star that looked homemade, still scabbing, pricked with a sharp instrument too deeply into her skin, looking fuzzed and out of focus. Saskia could not seem to stop scratching it. "She must be fucking crazy. Left, left," she told the driver. "It's far," she said, turning back to Tony. She patted his knee. "Relax." He sat in the middle of the cab's narrow backseat, Matt on one side and Saskia on the other. "I wouldn't treat you bad, you know," Saskia said. "You wouldn't have to go chasing me through the city. Hell, you'd never have to leave your apartment again, I promise you."

Matt stared pointedly at the girl's hand on Tony's knee, and said, "I confess this was not what I had in mind when you said, 'I need you, come find me.' " Tony leaned against him, pressing his face into the cashmere scarf and the green scent of his cologne, nudged up between Matt's chin and the collar of his coat. "God," Matt complained gently. "You smell like you've brushed your teeth with Jim Beam.

Can't we just go home? You need a bath, among other things."

Saskia gave him a withering look. "Who are you, anyway?"

Matt said, "Virgil."

Tony did not recognize the place where she eventually guided them, some lost neighborhood of darkened streetlights. The cab moved slowly, sliding in places on the still-icy street. It seemed that the power was not yet back on in this neighborhood, dark, empty windows giving the place the look of disaster. A few scattered sparks drew his eye, flashlight beams and fire barrels, the flicker of hurricane lamps, an occasional movement. A man walked by with a dog tugging forward against a leash. The animal was low to the ground, straining forward, making a dry sound with its claws against the pavement.

"This is it," said Saskia. Matt paid the driver, and climbed out onto the street, pulling Tony after him, sliding on the icy curb. Saskia took his arm again, leading them toward the door of one of the dark buildings, shapes of moving figures dimly seen behind its upper windows. "A blackout party," said Matt. "How avant-garde."

"What is this place?" Tony said.

"Wolfy's," Saskia told him. "He gives us a place to sleep sometimes, when it's cold."

"Wolfy's," said Matt. "Tony, this really must be your month."

"Is it a halfway house for girls, or a brothel?"

"No one cares what goes on in this neighborhood. Wolfy's is a place people go," she said vaguely.

Tony had never attended a party without electricity, and wondered, yet again, if he was still in a dream. At the last second he held back, afraid to go through the door, and Matt had to push him, the warmth of him pressed against his back in the doorway, a hand steering his hip. "Gotcha," he said in Tony's ear. "Come on, you're killing me." Saskia looked back at them, curling her hand. "Come on." The so-called Wolfy's apartment was slightly warmer than the night, filled as it was with bodies, but there seemed to be a dresscode requiring fur coats. Shrouded in ermine, fox and leopard, guests milled about in the light of the candles that dripped from every surface, tracking a gory rainbow of wax across the floor. The absence of music left an eerie dead space into which a few people whispered, as if self-consciously waiting for the music to return. Most of the guests, Tony observed, were supine, littering every surface like dead mannequins; there were three women on the couch – at least Tony thought they were women, one in a coat that looked to be made of horse fur and two in men's tuxedos, breath steaming, one with her head hanging backward over the armrest, pale throat lifted in grotesque offering. A doleful screech in the window alcove caused them all to turn their heads, fixing on a lone violinist, a young man with white hair and pinkish, mealy eyes, wearing collie fur, playing the melody of Chopin's Nocturne in C Sharp Minor. So there was music, after all; the guests revived slightly, sipping, glancing, chatting with a blurry urgency. Tony glanced at Matt, but Matt appeared to be at a loss for words. The party was in the final stages of decline, a debauched exploding star, which meant it must have started before sunset, unless it was much later than he thought (Tony had no idea what time it was). The air in the apartment was thick with opium and liquor. Saskia, surprisingly fastidious, wrinkled her nose as she took in the place. She continued on through the apartment, and Tony and Matt followed her, stepping over bodies and overturned lamps, feet crunching through broken glass.

In the kitchen, a crowd of people were clustered around something, and as Tony approached he saw that it was a bald man in a bathrobe, holding a fishbowl in his hands. A single fish was swimming in the bowl, upside down, its eyes glued to the bottom of the bowl. "Eddie," the man said to Tony, who thought for a moment he had been mistaken for another person, but the man raised the fishbowl toward him. "Eddie," he said again, "swims upside down. It is because he sees his own face in the glass. Eddie is an original narcissist."

A woman in the crowd gave a wavering laugh, then fell silent. Matt was whispering urgently in Tony's ear, "I was prepared to comfort you in a cemetery, but this is going to turn into a bad Kubrick orgy." Saskia, having nudged her way through the crowd, laid a hand on the man's bathrobe sleeve. "Mr. Simon," she said, "Mr. Wolf, he's looking for you know who." She and Simon both smirked at Tony, who struggled with his desire to tear the place apart, disrupting what seemed to be their shared joke on him. When Simon smiled, his teeth were stained with wine. "Of course," he said, winking a pink, protuberant eye. He handed the fishbowl to someone, pulling the slipping bathrobe back over the white dome of his belly. He had a coy, mincing walk, like a geisha; Tony observed his tiny feet, covered in velvet slippers, and felt a fresh wave of nausea. Matt pinched his arm, and Tony nudged him away.

"You must be the surly Adonis we've all heard so much about," said Simon appraisingly, his little finger crooked backward in a kind of miniature salute. He ignored Matt completely. "That lucky girl. Saskia, where ever did you find him?" A man in the crowd turned at his words and gazed at Tony, his slick, pale hair and hollow cheeks reminding Tony for an instant of Matt Kelly, though Matt was still standing behind him, and there was a moment of disconcerting terror as Tony wondered if he had managed to double himself.

Saskia bounced on her heels, looking pleased with all the confusion, scratching her wrist.

"Jessica Schwartz," said Tony clearly. "Where is she?"

"We all want what's best for the little..." Simon stumbled sideways, catching himself against the wall, and took a moment to straighten a framed picture, obscured by the darkness of the apartment. When he turned again to Tony, his eyes glowed knowingly, with a muted, predator intelligence. "Wolf Simon. Forgive me," he said sadly, "I wish we had met under happier circumstances, Mr...?"

Tony pulled his hand from Wolf Simon's fleshy grip, wondering when he had ever met anyone less wolf-like. But there was a hint of the lycanthrope in the man's pouched chops, and something gave Tony a creeping but implacable suspicion that they had met before. Simon sighed, patting the palms of his hands down the front of his robe, as if looking for glasses, and shuffled off into the destroyed living room, Tony, Matt and Saskia following, on into a completely dark hallway, aiming for a strip of weak light that came from beneath a door at the end. Tony stumbled in the darkness over something warm and living, someone's leg, he thought. Matt grumbled in the hall. Ahead of him, Simon paused at the door, as if for dramatic effect, then opened it, spilling the light from the room across his face.

"There you are, Mr. Adonis. L'enfant sauvage."

Schwartz lay on a bare mattress illuminated by candles, those red glass votives Tony associated with Mexican cemeteries, asleep, her hair covering her face. She was wearing clothes Tony did not recognize, a white slip and one black boot, a man's silk tie wrapped around her wrist. In the corner, Tony faintly registered the presence of her other boot, lying on its side among the tangle of street

342

clothes and the sheets from the bed. Her bare foot was bandaged, the gauze coming unwrapped and trailing across the mattress.

"That's it?" Matt said.

"It's not what it looks like," Wolf muttered, still patting for his missing glasses.

"What is it, then?" said Tony. He was surprised by the calmness of his voice, coming from a place of emptiness, a great void that had opened suddenly in him, so that instead of killing Simon, he only wished for the man to disappear. Even in the safety of that emptiness, his bubble of shock, he could feel his hands itching for the other man's throat. He looked at Simon, who smiled at him and shrugged in an embarrassed way, spread his hands, saying, "Came in, and keeled over, poor little thing. She was ever so tired." His eyes were shrewd, even through their drunken glaze; he knew what Tony had been thinking. "That's right," he said quietly. "She's quite unspoiled. At least, no more than when she arrived."

"Please leave," said Tony, his eyes on Schwartz's crumpled form. "If you come near her again, I'll kill you."

"Of course," said Simon. A burst of laughter came from the kitchen, heard faintly through the walls. "Good night, Mr. Adonis." He shuffled off, closing the door behind him.

Tony listened to the sound of Simon's retreating steps, that geisha shuffle. Saskia was still in the room, squeezed into a corner behind Matt, clutching Schwartz's backpack; he had forgotten her presence.

"You can leave, too," Tony said, and Matt stepped aside, looking pointedly at Saskia, saying, "You heard him," but Saskia hesitated, plainly reluctant to leave Schwartz alone with them, which he found baffling since she had led them here in the first place. Hating himself, he drew out his wallet, lay down three hundred dollars on the bare mattress near Schwartz's leg. "For you," he said. "You should go back home."

"Oh, Jesus," Matt said. "She's just going to shoot it up her arm."

Saskia stared at him, the side of her face twitching. "You stupid or something?"

"Just take it. Do whatever you like."

Saskia snatched up the money, not looking at Schwartz or him. As she left, she dropped the backpack, saying, "She'll be needing this." Tony closed the door behind her. Somewhere in the apartment, someone was crying softly, pounding against a wall.

Tony sat down on the bed, immobilized, and watched a cockroach scurry across the wall above the headboard. Matt glanced at the one chair in the room, piled with the girl's clothes, and remained standing. "Is this where your plan runs out?" he said quietly, and Tony could only nod.

Matt sighed. "Talk about a case of the fifth wheel," he said. "Twenty years pass, and when you call me, it's to go see about a girl."

"Matt," said Tony, "doesn't she remind you of someone?"

"An underage hooker?"

"I was going to say she reminds me of you. She reminds me of both of us, really."

"Tony," Matt said. "It's not working."

"She needs us."

"There is no 'us'. There is no 'we'. It's just you and you. Like it's always been." He turned for the door. "I think this is where I climb off."

"No," said Tony. "Please. If you leave…"

Matt gave a tired laugh, rested his forehead briefly on the doorframe.

"Matt, please don't leave."

"What reason do I have to stay?"

"Why didn't you tell me?"

"I've said everything I need to say about that." He fixed Tony with a pale blue eye, and Tony could see that the whites had gone slightly pink. "Besides, if you really wanted to find him, it would have been you looking, wouldn't it? Not me?"

"It's not him. Not really. It's the whole...why don't I feel..?" He wished that Matt would toss his head just once, in that old way he had, leaning on the doorframe with his body skewed to the right. It seemed painfully unfair, suddenly, that they were no longer boys. They shared nothing, were bound by nothing.

Matt straightened his scarf. "You'll be okay. I mean...right?"

"Where will you go?"

"Oh..." he gestured vaguely. "To bed. That's what people do. It's getting late, you know."

"Please don't. I didn't mean...I'm sorry, Matt."

"Oh, stop. It's hardly a tragedy. I'll just crawl in next to the dog."

"Ha."

"I'm happy, most of the time. See?" He smiled, and Tony knew that in a city this size, they could avoid each other for the rest of their lives. "I mean, I want you to know that. And I wish I knew that you were alright. But I'm not helping. I'm just part of the problem."

"That's too abstract for me right now."

"I don't have to worry about you, do I?"

"No," said Tony.

"If you find yourself on the verge of making another scene..."

"I'm sorry," Tony said. "About all of it. Everything."

"For God's sakes, don't cry again. Who needs it?"

Tony blinked. "I'm not. I'm just sorry."

"Oh, fuck it." Matt sighed, and thumped his forehead down against the doorframe. "Alright. But can we please get out of here?"

Tony tugged at the girl's arm. "We can't leave her here, Matt. Hey, Schwartz. Hey, kid." He patted her cheeks, the girl's head rolling from side to side. "Schwartz, get up."

She stirred slightly, and he lay the back of his hand against her neck, finding her warm despite the coldness of the room, far warmer than he was. Her sleeping face was one of tension, stress around the eyes, her brows drawn toward each other. He wondered how close to consciousness she really was, and if she was aware of him, in some buried part of her mind. The crying continued, the pounding, lost in the cold and dark walls. In the city, a lone siren piped up briefly and fell silent.

"J," said Tony, "Come on, kid." He reached under her head, turning it, cradling the fragile bones of her skull. "Matt, what do I do?"

"Turn her on her stomach so she doesn't choke? How should I know?"

The girl stirred again, made a small sound in the back of her throat. He stood, removed his coat, and draped it over her, wanting, if nothing else, some gentleman's credit. He stood by the bed, watching Schwartz slowly climb toward wakefulness. It was a painful process. Her head would be agony, he thought, and then decided she deserved it.

When she finally sat up and caught sight of him, she did not seem surprised or frightened; it was more, thought Tony, as if she could not remember who he was. He watched her try to smile at him. "Give me a minute," she said. "Did I...how?"

"It's okay."

"Jesus," she said, "I feel like an ashtray." When he didn't reply, she looked around the room, her forehead crinkling, catching sight of Matt. "Are you the dinner friend?"

"Time to go," Tony said.

"Where?"

"Shut up. Put your clothes on."

She shrugged, obeyed slowly, moving as if her limbs weighed her down. She picked up her boot, fumbled it and dropped it, laughing at her own clumsiness, protesting indignantly when Tony grabbed it from her, throwing her jeans down on the bed. "Those first," he said. "Pay attention."

"This is a bad idea," Matt offered.

"You shut up. I'm not leaving her here."

It was rage, he realized, catching up with him so slowly that he no longer knew the cause of it. The girl glared at him, still too disoriented to do anything but follow his directions. The fight had not returned to her yet. This was good; he would use the time he had.

When she had finally managed to dress herself (he had to help her with the boots, the buckles turning out to be too much for her), he shouldered her backpack, took her by the arm, his hand completely circling her narrow biceps, and marched her down the hall and through the apartment, Matt following. Schwartz looked startled by the presence of the people. "I heard Saskia," she said, stumbling over a woman's discarded shoe, "Wait, I want to say goodbye." Tony ignored her. He pulled her along, and she stumbled and clutched her headache and made no effort to free herself.

"Hey," Matt said, "Take it easy, you're hurting her." He took the girl from Tony, steadying her gently. "Come on, kid," he said. "You okay? Here, just lean, that's better. Tony, where are we going?"

On the sidewalk, the outer cold hit them like a wet sheet, and Tony hailed a cab. J (Jessica, he reminded himself) nodded off in the back seat between Matt and Tony, her head falling before they even left the dark, lost neighborhood, and Matt clucked softly, pillowing her head against his shoulder. "Poor kid," he said. "Look at these clothes. She's going to freeze to death before we get to Bushwick." Tony watched the driver's eyes in the rearview mirror, rimmed with weariness, glancing and quickly looking away. You can't judge, Tony thought, when you make a living transporting drugged runaways and soulless men through the early hours of the morning to home or crime scene two or wherever it is they go. Then he realized he had not told the driver a destination, which was why the man kept glancing at him.

"We need a rental car," he said quietly.

"We do?" said Matt.

"I used to be a pilot, you know," said the driver, which, in the framework of that evening, seemed completely reasonable to Tony. "Had a family. That was before everything went to shit."

"I'm sorry," said Tony. "That's really sad."

"What you guys got? Treasure it." His red eyes moved back and forth in the mirror, glancing over the road. "I have two sons, and I haven't seen them in five years, not since the wife split. Don't be too hard on the kid. Family's everything, man."

It was not as difficult as Tony had feared to find a rental car at that hour. An old man took his money through a slot in a bulletproof window into which someone had used a pen to scratch a message, now partially obscured, "Call 845 693 2819 for..." and a younger man, possibly the old man's grandson, pulled a car up from the bowels of a parking garage and handed him the keys. Tony woke Schwartz where she lay, still sleeping, across Matt's lap in the back of the idling cab, shaking her roughly until she got up, blinking in the lights.

"I'd offer to drive," Matt said, "but I don't drive." Matt was beginning to enjoy himself, Tony thought. "Dare I ask where we're going?"

"We're taking J to her parents."

"You know where they live?"

"Yes."

"I see." He smiled crookedly. "Well. This is the most ill-advised thing I've done in a while."

The old man's grandson watched the three of them as they climbed from one car to the other, and Tony felt that slow rage again, growing stronger now. Matt settled Schwartz in the backseat, and climbed into the front, strapping himself in place. Tony dropped into the driver's seat, took the wheel, and wrenched the car into gear.

TWENTY-FIVE

It took him three years to find me. Another year passed before I answered his letters.

In a Cyprus hotel, light came in to embrace the wreck of the night, sheets glowing bright and pure as flame. I had not slept, and sat now, taking him in. He had pulled the bedclothes round himself and flung them off again, his back bared to the morning sun, slim hips and shoulders, the nape of his neck where the shadows clung and ran between the shoulder blades, dark head tousled on a hotel pillow. His face lay in the crook of his arm, hiding from the light. And time had changed him; he was a man. He was nineteen, on holiday with friends from university, a bohemian with a backpack who laughed with gleaming teeth and quoted Proust, and I had just turned fifty the week before. I watched him, as I had half the night, from a chair in the corner, listening to the night sounds fade to the steady thrum of day. Now the shadows of the room gathered close to me, the only place the sun could not reach, and I gazed at him still from the other side of darkness.

"I've enraged my father by becoming an artist," he had told me the night before, wine glass held with his palm cupped beneath it, fingers split by the stem. "It was between studio art and urban planning, and I thought art would upset him more. But what can he do?" He laughed, and tapped the ash from the end of his cigarette, invincible. We faced each other over the flame of a small candle, just outside the circle of briny light spilled from a street café, girls in shorts and sandals walking by, the old town. At the next table, a group of French students on holiday lounged in their chairs, sunburned and smoking, and Greek teenagers shouted in the street, laughing and revving a motorcycle. And he was the only thing in the world I cared about. I devoured him with my eyes, every piece of him, struggling to comprehend the reality of him. I imagined the people around us must be staring too, as lovingly as I, because this boy, this young man, was the center of life itself. He did not hide in the shadows like me but wore them carelessly, glamorous as the spirit of the age, gaze dark-flamed with youth and wine and summer, peering at me from under the sweep of his hair. I saw that he had learned at last how to use his fringed eyes, in the time we had been apart. He had adopted the mocking self-awareness of all affluent youth, the charm once natural to him now brandished and cast idly like a token. But it didn't matter; he wore conceit gracefully. His white linen shirt hung open at the collar, cuffs rolled up to the elbows in the heat of the Mediterranean. I said, "It suits you," and could think of nothing else to say. Voices washed around us, waves lapping and sighing in and out of a fragrant, somnolent sea, loud and rich, a Cyprus street of bars and awnings and narrow cobblestones in the old quarter of a city whose name I have now forgotten, Larnaca, maybe, crowded with its summer throng. The youths in the street dispersed with more shouting, a girl and boy on the motorcycle wobbling off down the lane. In the laughter of the young, brown people and the clatter of forks and knives we sat, drinking but eating nothing, grasping after the words to say to one another. He looked down at the glass held in his hand, and said, "My father has a sort of bourgeois morality," and I said, "Shall I go?" and he said, "No. Stay. I do everything I can to upset the old bastard." He looked up at me again, all trace of mocking smile gone, so that I could see the uncertainty in his gaze, and his throat moved in a dry swallow, giving him a pained look, pulling down for a moment the corners of his lips. Laughter floated over us from the surrounding tables, shouting, singing, and I gathered myself but could not summon even the barest ghost of the smile I intended, saying, this is crazy, you are reckless, or some other foolish thing. An insect flew into the candle between the glasses and was gone in a white instant. He stubbed his cigarette, said, "I know it is. And I don't care."

"I don't know what to say to you."

"Then be quiet." His mouth twitched into a fleeting smile, eyes tracing and re-tracing my face, searching for me in the darkness. He leaned in close, said, "The thing is, if I don't now, I never will." And in the middle of the crowded café, he lay his empty hand across the table next to mine, palm pressed flat and steady, so close I could feel the heat of him and the knocking of his pulse. It was a moment I remember years later with pain, the moment when I realized I was unable to do as he asked, could only stare at him, mute and powerless, in the middle of the crowd. We sat on opposite sides of the table, peering at each other from across three decades and their revolutions; it was another world, another age that had made me what I was, no marches, no flags, no slogans. It was six thousand

Spanish clergy pulled from their homes and burned, horses brought to slaughter, father's rage and mother's silence, the unmarked graves of rebels in the hills. It was a soldier's fingers, counting the vertebrae of my neck, the violation that would not dare speak its name. It was India, darkness and faith-swallowing malarial jungles, where I had fought for the eternal light and lost. And when I had left St. Ignatius, used up and broken in spirit, it was to be informed by a Provincial younger than myself that I had come highly recommended, an outstanding teacher. He had smiled at me in a friendly way, announced that I could now look forward to a professorship in a small Pennsylvania college. A promotion from my old post at St. Ignatius. It would offer me more time for my own scholarly pursuits, he had said. Owing to the trauma I had no doubt experienced because of the fire, I should take some time to rest, reflect and consult my faith. "A retreat," the Provincial had called it. He had shaken my hand with rare effusion, clasping my elbow, as if I had come home from a war. No mention, of course, of any other record I might have come with. A promotion, then, close on the heels of rebuke, to remove Old Stripes from the scene of his iniquities. I was to forget them. I was to understand that if I could forget, the Order would do the same.

And now I sat across from this young person, the opposite of everything to which I had I had resigned, this one who had come to me, an ephemeral in a world obsessed with eternity. And I thought, when all was said and done, that he might be the only thing I could be sure of. I sat there, and did not take his hand, and after a while he withdrew it.

"I don't care," he repeated. He leaned back in his chair but his gaze remained, now touched by a smile as bright and full as the time that held us, promising and forgiving all, night in a city where no one knew our names, a place where we could have been anyone.

"Who are you?" I asked him. He smiled at me, shaking his head. "No," he said, "it's you who's changed. What are these clothes?" He mocked me gently, raising his eyebrows at my white button-down shirt, the costume of a civilian without a trace of clerical black. He was speaking English now like an American, had been all evening, and I found it cheap and crude and strangely sad. He said, "God. You have no idea how weird this is." He thumbed another cigarette from the pack, then tapped it back in, leaving the damp, crumpled packet on the table between us; amber wrapper, Sweet Aftons. Even his cigarettes had been curated with an ironic swagger, invoking the ghosts of bohemia.

"I have some idea."

"But seriously," he said. "Where do they keep you, these days?"

"I don't think I should tell you. Should I?"

He smiled, hugging himself. I couldn't help but oblige him with a smile of my own. He had always had that power. He said, "I won't lie; you don't look any older. You seem...it seems to have agreed with you." Perhaps it was a lie, but I let him have it.

"Past is past."

"Is it? Have you come to your senses, too?"

"I'm still what I was. If that's what you mean."

"You must have made quite a Ulysses bargain, coming here."

"Ulysses bargain. How regional of you."

"They keep you well tied?"

"We'll see."

"Colin says religious faith is linked to epilepsy."

"Colin?"

"Just somebody. A Cambridge friend." His almost smile; wouldn't I like to know.

"Cambridge Colin. I see. He's not endearing himself to me, so far."

"I guess not."

"It breaks my heart to see you smoking."

"Says the alcoholic."

"Does Colin mind?"

To my amazement, he blushed under his tan. But he gave me his enigmatic face, a secret for a secret, and I thought that for all his teasing, he didn't really want to know where I had been, and would just as soon the years between now and St. Ignatius hadn't happened. So would I. But it was more than that; he wanted me to be the person I had been. And how could I blame him, looking as I was past that rich young man sprezzatura for some trace of the boy that he had been, that magical teenage lothario? Hadn't I been wrong then, as perhaps I was wrong now, attempting to see what I wanted to see? This was not the person I had come to find. I searched him for recognizable traces, as if by doing so I could erase the past years. He threw money on the table without looking at it, and we left, walking the cobblestones through neon lights and the beat of dangerous music. We walked the old town's narrow streets, knuckles grazing, away from the noise and lights of summer crowds. He smoked another cigarette, and I had one too, and we didn't say anything, passing a Greek Orthodox Church, skirting docks, listening to the ping of lines against the swaying masts. I picked a bit of stray tobacco from my tongue, trying to remember if I had ever in my life smoked an unfiltered cigarette, and questioning its charms. He turned to look at me, walking backward, bouncing on his feet and then turning again. He drummed his fingers on the leg of his jeans. "I couldn't find you," he said, after a while. "I wasn't sure I wanted to."

"Well, that's..."

"I was terrified all day thinking about it." He laughed, some of the terror escaping. "This is strange, isn't it?"

"Yes."

"There's no law against walking together in Larnaca, is there?"

"Is that what we're doing?"

There was a faint scar just above his left eyebrow I did not remember, a dark seam running parallel to the crest of it; I saw it when he turned toward me, the salty wind lifting his hair, and I found myself reaching to him, tracing his brow with a finger, one light brush stroke. He pulled away from me a little too quickly, shoulders skittish. "That's from two summers ago," he said. "There was some trouble with a motorcycle. And Colin, actually." That was just the way he said it: some trouble with a motorcycle. Some trouble with Colin.

"You are mortal," I said.

"But I've always been lucky."

"You take risks."

"I thought of you, actually. Lying there with him, waiting for the ambulance. Who knows why. But I wished you'd been there." He gave me a hard, steady look. "I wanted you there. And I thought that if you were, I would have been alright. Is that too much for you?"

"Say it again."

"I wouldn't have been afraid."

"Say you wanted me."

"I don't traffic in redemption."

I heard myself make a little involuntary sound. Was it a laugh? "You're still trying to destroy yourself. I see that. It's why you invited me."

356

"And here you are."

"You know why I came."

And there it was. We glanced around us, fearful of the eyes of others. He took my sleeve between two fingers, leading me away from the piers. "I have no idea where we are," he said. "Do you?"

Was there anyone, anyone he could not seduce? His loss of innocence hurt me more deeply than I had expected, because it made me want him more. It was as simple as that: I wanted him so desperately it made my stomach clench, made me feel faint. What was more, I longed for him. Had I been more experienced, or faced with anyone other than him, I would have grasped this distinction and seen through to the heart of the matter. Longing requires nostalgia, and nostalgia is a product of that which has long since died. I followed him, suspecting I had lost my mind. The complex world I had inhabited, built over decades and maintained, was falling apart before my eyes. The streets of the old town were a maze, no grid pattern that I could see, endless turns of dark doorways, lighted windows, the occasional pedestrian, bicycles, mopeds, dogs. I was suffocated by the heaviness of air between us, the weight of my clothes and the dirt of the city, repelled by the young man's charm. Not like this; it wasn't supposed to be like this. Cheap and easy, a seaside tourist town. I wanted space to reflect, to think. I longed to be alone with him, and knew that I should leave, taking the first taxi to the airport. But here he was, and here we were, and I wanted to be the smoke in his lungs and the shirt damp with his sweat. We moved briskly, not speaking, ever more lost in the streets. Every doorway mocked and beckoned me. Simple, sinful. I wanted to crush him with the frustrated violence of all my empty worship. I wanted to force him against a wall in some alley under cover of darkness, to press my longing into him, hard and brutal and insistent. To take what I desired. His weakening protests, his breath against my face, the wings of a trapped bird in a house. He would let me do anything and everything that was in my mind. He dared me to do it, exhaling plumes of blue smoke, rushing headlong into this crisis, my darkest fantasies made flesh, the dross of human weakness thrust into what Aquinas would have thought the sacred matter of the world, that pure existence of Being. And he was that Being, this young man at my side. He was holy. My thoughts were the aberration. There was the warmth of him, so close beside me. I had conjured him and his willingness many times over, in places darker than this Cyprus street. I had memorized the secret language of his body and yearned to speak it now, to hear it spoken to me, in me. With my lips on his body I wanted to speak the name of God and to hear him speak mine, to hear him call me, why did he never call me, why was it forever up to me to be the one who worshipped, the one who ached, who called out in some desert place, hearing nothing? Was it my destiny to wait forever for a call that would not come?

And there it was, my vocation, my wasted life. No one to save me, no one to punish me, no one to rejoice of me. It was I, calling to myself. It was the disgraced priest and the dirty angel, alone on a street in Larnaca. And he was holy, he was my blasphemy, he was grace made flesh: I worshipped him. There was a sheen of clean sweat above his collarbone. We passed by the neon lights of an apothecary, its red cross flashing, coloring the night. His heart-shaped face, turned to me in those red flashes, then plunged into darkness, a green cross burned into my vision, the sound of his breathing near me. Sacred and profane.

I wanted to kill him.

Something in the way he watched me that night, as we walked those interminable streets, a softness in his eyes. It was yearning of a kind I had seen many times before, that transfixed, supplicating gaze of the faithful. Not a sexual dilettante, not a rich and spoiled student on holiday, but an otherworldly pilgrim, lost in the world of matter. I had found him there at last, and he had found me. Might he still adore me in that way after all these years, with sacred love?

Perhaps that was calling enough.

This was the narrow door left for me; we were together now, in this world, and the light I threw still dazzled him. He was still the one who had been dear to me, that boy with green eyes who had inclined his head on my breast. Midnight in the Americas; I had carried it with me. The world of matter, white cold, of northern lights and distance. He was still that same boy. And he was really more innocent, I thought, than he wanted to be.

In an alley of the old town closed in by white stucco walls, we passed a chained-up moped and a door with red flower boxes, beneath iron window bars and stripes of yellow light, and when I tried to speak he put his hands through my hair and kissed me, veiled in the long shadows cast by a line of someone's washing, held me steady long after I would have pulled away. He gave me all of him. The fingers of his right hand curled into the hair at the base of my skull, the other rested, warm and alert, on the narrow of my back. His tongue tasted of salt and cigarettes. He drew my lip between his teeth, and when we broke apart the night was cool against my mouth, and his hand fell from my hip, swinging empty.

Voices came in at the end of the alley, two women in the adjoining street, walking home. We stood slightly apart, between a flower box and a metal rubbish can. The beat of a distant radio drifted in and then faded, lights swinging down our alley before turning to some other route. If we were seen. But it seemed not to matter just then. Somewhere, a dog barked.

"You're so thin, under my hands," he said. He was still in shadow, the light from the end of the street reflected in watery points on the surface of his eyes, intent, glossy orbs that seemed, like those of a night creature, to have lost the art of blinking. And he said, strangely, "You'll come back with me?"

"Yes."

He nodded gravely, then laughed. "I'm completely lost."

And we were hurrying breathless through the hot night, one narrow street whirling into another, laughing like children, losing our way. On the main thoroughfare, we had to stop for a parade, an endless stream of decked-out cars, horns blaring, and in the dancing light, as the crowds pressed us in, I leaned in and inhaled the scent of his hair and he turned and said something that was lost to me in the horns and shouting. They had mounted a huge picture on one of the trucks, a stern face framed in flowers, a martyr or a politician, scowling into the lights. Police whistles shrilled. Young men leaned out the windows, throwing bright wrapped candy and fake money at the crowd, cheering and howling and scrambling together in the gutter. But he pulled at my sleeve and I followed his slim, dark shape, squeezing and weaving through the spaces between, aiming for a street where we could move more easily. I followed him, white shirt flashing to me, head thrown back with his loose stride, everything about him breathing freedom, a young man hurrying into his life. And what I wanted to say to him was, Stop. Wait. Don't ever lose this. But the world he lived in moved at a hotter pace than my own. I said nothing, tumbling through a dream of cobbled streets, a plaza of fig trees emptied by the parade, flowers and trampled ribbons, a clock tower with four shining faces, each a different time, their iron hands counting off the night.

He kissed me again on the dark landing of the hotel, breath wild, kissed me till I was desperate and bending at the knees, while he twisted with one arm behind his back, fumbling with the lock. "Come on," he said against my lips, "before I lose my nerve," whether to the lock or me I didn't know, his whisper an answer to my silent prayer, for no matter how I begged of him to wait, he would hurry, plunging blind. In a panic of desire I clung to him, my tongue tracing the edge of his jaw, the alarming sharpness of facial stubble, him pulling me forward into empty air, fingers tangled in my belt loops, a numbered door swinging open into darkness, a voice, his or mine, "Ah, please, please."

He closed the door behind us with a backward kick, soft light from the street extinguished, and in the darkness of an alien room he took me to the floor, simply and without ceremony. He was slight, but had become as strong as I, strong and savage, the body of a lightweight boxer, all wire and hard muscle, unyielding skin, damp streak of fur below the navel, a man's chest. At such close range, I didn't recognize anything about him, not even the sharp, feral cedar of his sweat. Against my body, in the dark, he might have been a stranger. Alone together, together alone. He gave a little shocked out-breath when I grasped him. Now that we were locked in the room, his handling of me was so hasty and inelegant it resembled the blunt swings of a fight, and I wondered for a minute if he wanted to hurt me. I yielded, taken aback. I didn't want to fight him. He wasn't going to let me win. And hadn't he earned the right, I thought, his left hand on the flat of my stomach, pinning me down, the other in my hair. He had torn my shirt, landed a blow on my cheek, a smart slap I made no effort to resist. His face, flushed in shadow, was panicked about the eyes. A snarl of lip was caught between his teeth. I remembered the winged bird in his hand; "I wanted it to be mine."

But then he crumbled, and it was all too much. He hung over me, eyes suddenly tensed, filmed with water. I caught his face between my hands. The prints of my fingers rushed pale to the surface of his skin, sunburnt, hot to the touch, visible even in that dim room. "Dear boy," I said, the words slipping out, moved and rather guilty, as if that was what he still was, as if we were still in school, and he had come to me for solace. "Hush."

But he shrugged off my gentleness, love's reared, ugly head. "Don't be a fucking Don Juan. I can't stand it." He grabbed a fistful of my shirt and pulled it to him, said, "Right here." My hands slid to the points of his hips, taking him down in one large motion, too quickly, the rug burning my elbow. It startled both of us. And I pressed him down in the pile of the carpet, one hand behind his head.

"I don't want to hurt you. Do you have any…?"

"In my backpack. The small pocket. Hurry."

A light in the square outside flickered and went out, plunging us into greater darkness. There was a lamp on the bedside table, within easy reach, but it seemed that neither of us wanted light. I pulled the pack down from a chair, rifling the pocket while he rolled onto his stomach, face turned away from me, staring off under the hotel bed. Some agency seemed to have deserted him; I could hear his quick panting. That awkward moment of fumbling, as if our stride was broken. It made me wonder suddenly why he was there, if not for this. I found the little bottle, the fluid strange and cold to the touch. I returned to him, chest pressed down to the hollow of his back, feeling for him in the dark. He seemed both nihilistic and terrified, lying with a disconcerting, slave-like limpness, and I tried to coax him. I lay suspended on my arms over him, arching down to kiss the nape of his neck.

And even then, he would not allow me gentleness. My hand was pressed flat next to his face, and he covered it with his own, squeezing, digging in the nails. "Come on," he said.

"Are you sure?"

"Christ," he said between his teeth, "I swear..." He let me. The rhythm of our shared breathing fell apart, then raced together, then broke again, hard fingers reaching back to bite into my shoulder, our soft, agonized sounds. He started to sob again. He didn't ask for me to wait, but I faltered, suddenly wondering if I had misread. With my mouth in his hair, I comforted, promised wild things. "No. Come on," he said, and some raw, inchoate cry I smothered with a hand, hugging his head into the curve of my shoulder, stifling his parted lips and the sounds he made. The salt at his temple, the bruising point of some hard vertebrae, the storm and flex and small flinch of pain, the hiss of breath in and out over my hand. His tears, cool on the back of my wrist. His tears. And I couldn't stop, and couldn't stop staring at him, half-obscured and out of focus, at his clenched, determined eyes and the line of his cheek, turned away from me into darkness, leaning and bracing into the rise and fall of it, the narrow slope of his back. He begged me eventually, pulling at me, crying out for God, but not for me. Undone, brought to the end of myself, killed at the last with silent crisis. Some final shred of something. Maybe it was the boy with the mark of sin, that white sugar halo, counting off the minutes. A hand flung back, braced on my shoulder, fingernails digging.

However he turned, my eyes followed. They were used to the dark by now.

He came with me, cried out as if it were some fatal part that left. It was not my name on his mouth as he unraveled. But he had seen me. He knew me with rage and with compassion. What I held for him was an orison of gratitude, a transubstantiation of the solitary self. It was an ache far deeper than love. It was the act of being seen.

Nearly every love eludes us, in the end. What remains, if not that other mysterious bond?

TWENTY-SIX

Two hours outside the city, Tony stopped at the Big Chief Diner, "Open All Night," a place shaped like a trolley car overshadowed by a giant neon war bonnet.

"Thank God," Matt said. "I'm seeing double."

Tony woke Schwartz again, more gently this time, reaching into the backseat, squeezing her knee and speaking her name. She moaned and twitched away from him, squinting in the orange, neon light.

"Where are we?" the girl said.

"Upstate. Come have some coffee."

Her eyes grew wider, taking in the two faces looking back at her, struggling to make sense of Tony's words. "Where?"

"It's okay," said Matt. "We're taking you home, kid."

"Who the hell are you?"

"It's okay," Tony echoed. "Let's just stop for a while, it's the middle of the night. Come on."

She shrank back from him against the door of the rented car, as if seeing him clearly for the first time. She glanced from Matt to Tony. "No," she said, her voice scarcely audible, "this is crazy. Please. You guys don't have to do this."

"It's okay," Matt said. "Everybody settle down."

For a moment Tony saw himself as J must see him, a hulking apparition of strange desires, and he felt suddenly doubtful about the wisdom of his plan. He thought of the years he had spent waiting for the darkness of his own experience to break to the surface. Waiting for the wolf to spring out of him.

Matt said, "You're scaring everybody, Tony. Stop it."

Tony wavered, hovering halfway out the door of the car, and maybe he would have called the whole thing off and given up, driven back to the city in shame, maybe none of it would have happened, if the girl had not overplayed her hand.

She saw his hesitation, and mistook it for weakness. She laughed, glancing again from one to the other, a nervous laugh, yes, but feigning scorn, said, "Jesus, what freaks."

Her fear had disarmed him, but now her derision hardened his heart against her, and he pulled the keys from the ignition and pocketed them. "We'll go back," he said, smiling at Matt and the girl. "After we have some coffee." He could see J's mind working away behind her frightened eyes as she tried to decide what to do. It seemed that she was still having trouble thinking clearly, because she climbed slowly from the car and walked ahead of them into the diner with no further protest.

They sat in a vinyl booth against the window, Matt and Tony on one side, feral girl on the other. Over coffee, J's spirits seemed to return, and she gave Matt a smile, brave with sweetness, saying, "Did he tell you how we met?"

"No. But I'm dying of curiosity."

"He took nudie pictures of me."

Matt turned to Tony. "Oh?"

"I'm sorry about what happened before," the girl said. "I ran away. It wasn't nice."

"Don't worry," Tony said. "It's going to be alright, Jessica."

Her shock was apparent, but she recovered quickly. She said, "Friends?"

"Of course."

She smiled again, slumping in the folds of his large coat, whose collar pushed up her hair at the back, shielding her up to the ears. He wondered why she had not removed the coat, even in the warmth of the diner.

"And how about you?" she said, pointing her chin in Matt's direction. "You a friend, or what?"

"A very special friend."

"The kind that does whatever he says?"

"If only."

"I need to go make a phone call," she said.

"No you don't," said Tony.

She pouted, as if it was a game they were playing. "Why can't I use the phone if I want to? I mean, who the hell are you?"

"Why can't the girl use the phone, Tony?" Matt said.

"Who are you calling?"

"None of your business."

"Then you can't use the phone."

"I thought you weren't mad."

"I'm not."

The waitress hovered again briefly, then made another pass without landing. Tony knew that he was probably underestimating J's ability to scheme, but he was tired and confused. "I have to pee," she said, exactly as a child would.

"Go do it, then," said Matt. "Take your time. I'll have a word with my friend."

Her eyes sidled awkwardly away from Tony's face, and she slid from the booth with an embarrassed laugh. He watched her cross the diner and enter the restroom door by the kitchen.

"Okay," Matt sighed, pushing away his menu. "This is wrong. Okay? Why is the kid scared? I thought you were friends, or something. I'm not going to just sit here..."

A movement in the parking lot beyond the window caught Tony's eye, and there was J, standing in the blinking neon lights of the giant war bonnet, standing against a fender and negotiating with a brutish man who, Tony assumed, had just offered her a ride.

"...catharsis, so I'm calling a cab, if you won't," Matt said. "Are you even listening?"

Tony watched for a moment, witnessed Schwartz's slumped posture and downcast eyes, both wary and defeated, how she flinched away only a little under the brute's hand, his thick fingers grasping at the lapel of her coat, Tony's coat, pushing her into the car.

Tony was out of the booth, Matt's protests passing through his ears, bell on the door clanging. He was crossing the parking lot with furious strides, pushing back the brute with a violent thrust that sent the man reeling, killing rage unspeakable, seeking for a deadly weapon but finding only J's elbow. He grabbed her so tightly that she cried out in pain, dragged her, kicking and sliding in the snow, toward the rented car, threw her in the front seat, climbed in himself and sped away, kicking up flurries and fishtailing out of the snowy lot. The brute in his rearview mirror stood still in the receding neons, watching them go.

For a moment there was only stunned silence in the car, and then she started pawing wildly at him and screaming, how could he, what was he doing, freak, pervert, rapist, kidnapper, in a high, hysterical voice that seemed to belong to somebody else, until he grabbed her flailing wrist, said, "Stop acting like a little girl." She fell silent, sucking in huge, panicked breaths. Five miles later she started to cry, and leaned against the car door, spine collapsed and hands over her face. He was moved by her crying, but didn't touch her again, kept his hands on the wheel and his face to the hard road, though his insides wrenched with pity and an odd, indefinite shame.

After a while she stopped crying, and he felt safe to palm her knee, said as gently as possible, "Are you alright?" It was a stupid question, and he didn't blame her for shrugging off his hand, saying, "Just keep driving."

"I'm sorry about all this, J."

"You left your friend," she said. "He was nice."

He kept to the back roads, hanging close but not too close to the little towns and villages scattered through the mountains and the pines. His route was unclear to him, the main objective to keep moving. From the passenger seat, Schwartz taunted him with her silence, for which he felt a building, steady rage; she would prefer, he knew, the company of any brute to him. She would hitchhike recklessly, staring into the face of every trucker and insurance salesman, daring them to do their worst, if they could, fearlessness her only weapon against crimes unspeakable, all this, rather than accept his help. Her back was stiff, knees clamped together; she was ready to fight for her life.

In the rented car, Tony scanned the slick back roads, another predator absconding with a fearless girl. He didn't know where he was, but it buzzed in his ears, an invisible direction in his movements, a thread lightly held between two fingers in the dark. And every time the road divided, his hands gripped the wheel a little harder, foot pressed farther into the floor, commanding some unnamable power to guide him to his destination.

He saw a tall, lone figure looming out of the darkness on the roadside near Maddox, and threw on the brakes only to be greeted by a surly face, bearded, a hunter with snow pants and a shotgun. Tony continued on, ignoring the girl's scornful glances. Farther on, the carcass of a deer, legs twisted and face appealing to the sky, made him pause for a moment with the portent of its blood, black tire tracks churned into the snow. Schwartz turned her face away. The stars began to fade, and they drove on.

Five miles outside Birnam, he made the mistake of pulling into a service station to refuel, and as soon as he slowed under the bright lights Schwartz was out the door and bolting away, not into the safety of the lighted station but into the trees along the side of the road. It took him several minutes to chase her down, cursing, his face whipped by invisible branches in the dark, and far longer to drag her back to the car. In the end he had to carry her, for she made him fight for every step, her feet dragging furrows in the snow. He wondered later why she did not scream; with the service station attendant so close by, she could easily have called for help. It was as if her objective was not to be rescued, but more to make a point.

"I'm warning you," she said, back in the car. They sat for a moment, both staring straight ahead at the dashboard and the lights of the instrument panel. The old service station attendant drowsed behind his bright window.

"You'll be safe, where we're going," he said. "J, I'm sorry about all this, I really am. But it has to be you. I need you to understand."

"Yeah?" she said, "Understand what?" She kicked her boot against the dash and left it there, where Tony watched it drip snow into the heater vent. Then she said, "How did you find me?"

"I'm lucky." Tony dragged on the wheel and swung the car back onto the road. "Not much further now." He always found what he wanted, sooner or later.

TWENTY-SEVEN

We lay side-by-side after, spent and too hot to touch. There was a fan with a metal chain suspended from the ceiling, and I stood up briefly, pulled it once, and lay back down in the cool stir of air. After a while he reached over and rested his hand on my chest, the touch startling me. I must have flinched, because he seemed to know; "Hey," he said, "it's okay. This is okay."

He crowded me gently, nudging his way into the curve of my arm and nesting there, a casual way about it, somehow more intimate than what we had just done. I found myself staring at the ceiling fan, damp fur at my crotch ruffled by the breeze, holding him. The fan was loose, whirling blades rocking as they turned. I wondered if it would fall on us. He pulled me closer, all his physical anxiety of a few minutes ago transformed. In the hollow of my arm, he seemed at home. Despite the show he had put on for me of being so modern and libertine, he believed in the importance of all this. It frightened me. Somehow, it made me keenly aware of how young he still was. And I knew there was a ticket in my trouser pocket, crumpled somewhere on the floor, a plane to Barcelona, and I was running again.

Worship was what I knew. Worship was limitless, and obscured its object. I buried my face in his hair and breathed in. Soon he needed me again. Gentler this time, but overturning something in me, a passion I have never since allowed. I now find it impossible to tell. And my lover said, "Don't leave." That caress, so idle, almost thoughtless, as if he were falling asleep, palm drifting down, voice thick with exhaustion. Casual as his confidence in me. Tied to his mast, Ulysses foamed, raged, and pleaded.

He turned his face to my shoulder. "I don't want to wake up alone."

In the end, I put him to bed. He would fall asleep quickly, my ruin would, lying curved toward me, face brave and quiet in sleep, his head on my arm. Leaving me alone with his sleep, as with a guilty ghost. The moon hung low in our window, giving me enough light to see him by. And it would be some hours that I lay there while the whole thing fell apart, hand tingling like slow death, still staring at him, unable to believe, brushing back the damp wedge of hair that kept falling across his face. When the sound of the night changed, I propped a pillow under his cheek and got up, because my arm was in agony and I was afraid to let him wake beside me. I was afraid of what it would mean. God may forgive me, for that moment of cowardice and other crimes. God can forgive things a lover never will.

In the square beyond the hotel window, the clock tower loomed with its four faces. Voices drifted up with the warm breeze and the murmur of traffic, the scent of auto exhaust and oranges, stone cobbles in the sun. I looked at him, and thought, it will kill me to leave him here. And then I admitted that it wouldn't. I would go on as before, as I had always done. And so would he. One could see it in the way he leaned into the night, parting a crowd, trusting I would follow without ever looking back; we would not weather the storm of the world, not together. I knew it, though in the heat of the moment I had told myself I didn't care. A time would come, and soon, when he would grow weary of my idolatry. I would make my exit, and he would be free. Morally, it seemed the right choice. It seemed the best gift that I could give him.

With that, the resolution came, to pass the years and never speak his name aloud. In a quiet place I would learn, through simple acts of devotion, to live within the faith that I had lost. He stood in bold contrast to all of that, everything that had claimed me; standing above it all in the quiet hours of the night, I thought that he had always reminded me of a younger, freer version of myself. A brave boy, rage in his heart and the world with him. And what had driven me was a desire for that other life; I wanted him because, for a while, I had wanted to be someone else.

The clock tower sounded its cracked chime, and I watched him tumble slowly out of sleep, reaching across the mattress and then scanning the room for me, toes treading the sheets, rumpled hair fallen into his eyes. When he spied me in the corner he stared for a long time, as if trying to remember where we were, and why I was sitting there, alone in the shadows, fully dressed. "Hi," he said at last, turning over and propping himself up on his elbows, his chest with its wisp of dark hair, sleepy eyes blinking in the sun.

"Hi, yourself."

"This is weird," he said, sounding American, chuckling, voice cracked with sleep. Then he sobered, looking at my face. "You're leaving now," he said, and I answered, "Yes."

He nodded. "I thought you might." He fell into a tight silence, still struggling against sleep, looking away from me, out the open window.

"I'm sorry."

"Why?" he said, roughly. "Why should you be? You got what you came for. We're taking a sailboat out of the port tomorrow. You're going to miss that. It would have been hard to explain, anyway."

Oh, cruel boy. "You and your American friends?"

He nodded, avoiding my eyes.

"And Cambridge Colin, I suppose?"

No answer.

"Do they make you happy, these friends? Are they good to you?" I could scarcely speak around the sudden tightness in my throat. I would hold onto my resolve, knowing it was for the best, though even now it wasn't too late; I could rush to him, and all would be forgiven. Just a little longer. "What do you want?"

"I don't know. Not this." He looked down at the sheet covering his lower body, the white mountain of his bent knee. "You."

"A dog you can kick to your heart's content."

"Why don't you believe me?"

I thought of the books, journals, binoculars and running shoes, odd handful of photographs, a few clothes, the sum total of my possessions held in a steamer trunk. A lifetime, held in a trunk. A lifetime of routine too powerful to put aside. What I said was, "I'm sorry for what I've done to you."

"You keep saying that, but it doesn't mean anything. It's all about you, isn't it? You and your...whatever this is."

"What can I say? That we'll run off together? Live on your father's money? You deserve better than a worn-out..."

"Fuck you." His eyes shone at me, jaw set. He was perfect.

We could walk the streets of the old city, now in daylight, and I could play the part of the doting older lover, buying him little things to please him, ices and saltwater taffy, basking in the smile of cold lips and the heat of his sunburn. I could fall down at his feet and adore him. But he would not want me for long, and he had always hated me a little. I knew this. I knew that I, too, had my limits. The close reality of this adoration was too heavy to be borne by time. I saw this truth, and claimed it.

No one has a wider frame of reference than a priest. We look into the world of matter with a farsighted eye; always, there is something brighter and more unattainable. Distance had become the measure of all my passions. With such distance, one had no choice but to love the world; one could see in every face the image of God.

I said, "I want so much for you to be happy."

"Why did you come here?" He stared at me, all his attention balanced on my face, waiting for me speak, and the silence hummed, the silence went on, filling the space between us, getting away from me. And that little thing he wanted me to say was not in my power, just as I would never take his hand. There was nothing I could say. I watched him give up on me.

I thought about telling him that I was facing ruin, that I had lost almost everything, the vocation I now stood in was everything. That sacrifice had to mean something; could he not see it? He had never wanted to know these things about me.

But they were part of me. After a lifetime of practice, it was all there to be summoned, and I pulled that sacred weight down onto myself, bearing up under what had to be done. Both of us knew the power of signs and wonders. It was my special gift; I could make myself as visible or enigmatic as I desired, because in the end the symbol obscured the man. I retreated into it now. And as if I had actually become invisible, his eyes wandered from me, focusing on some imagined point held in the air in front of him.

I said, "Tell me you'll be alright. You'll not do anything stupid."

"Don't flatter yourself." He put a hand up, rubbed his eyes viciously. "You're making a mistake. I don't forgive, you know."

"Yes. I know. You don't traffic in redemption."

"People like you only know how to punish." He rested his head back against the wall. "Go on, then. I'm tired."

I started forward, thinking to sit beside him, to press my face to the warmth between his shoulder blades, but then thought better of it, knowing that if I lay down I would never get up again, and stood with my heels rooted in the middle of the room. He stared away from me, green eyes bunched up in the light, glistening behind their dark lashes. "You're making a mistake," he whispered. "That's what I think. You'll see that later. And I hope it hurts like hell." He reached for the bedside table as if to dismiss me, took up a packet of cigarettes, drew one out and set it between his lips, hand trembling with contained fury. He looked for the lighter, couldn't find one, pulled at a drawer, couldn't open it. He gave up and sat back, slightly curved in on himself, the unlit cigarette clinging to his lip. The hair came forward over his eye, and he let it stay there, partially hiding him. The shadow, the green left eye, shining at me.

"Listen," I said, and he looked up sharply, to let me see that stubborn chin, raised one last time in defiance. "You will never know..."

I saw it for an instant, the way his face tightened, before he turned it to the wall. But when he spoke, there was a careless ease to his voice that could not have been completely feigned. "If you're leaving, you should do it now, while I'm still half asleep."

In the streets of the new city, people pressed in close to me. I walked among them, drifting with the crowd as with a tide, step by step, trusting them to draw me where they would. Every one of them holy, the face of God turned to me, that flame of a billion aspects, brushing my shoulder in passing. "Take this," he had told me, standing in the doorway with the bed sheets pulled around his waist, "It's yours." He placed it in my hand, a black rosary, broken in the middle. And there was no goodbye, no scene, no slamming, just a nod and a door slowly closing, leaving me alone on a hotel landing now flooded with harsh light, to find my own way home. I walked the city with the rosary at my fingers, finding my way back along that broken strand, one bead after another, eyes filled with sun and salt and blinding sky.

Dear X,

Have you forgotten me?

If you should happen to be in Cyprus on July 29th, and you find a café called Neptune in the old quarter of Larnaca, and walk into it at 10:00 in the evening, you might be pleasantly surprised. That is, of course, assuming I haven't simply imagined everything.

Yours,

Tony

P.S. I hope it wasn't too bad for you.

TWENTY-EIGHT

When he was twenty-three, Antonio Luna saw Miguel Xavier Ochoa in a spice market in Mohammedia, wearing civilian clothes, a white cotton shirt and tan slacks, the strap of a leather bag across his chest. Ochoa spoke briefly to a tea seller, sidled past a man carrying sacks of yellow turmeric, slipped between two taxicabs, and vanished among a crowd of women with plastic market bags doing their shopping. Tony ran across the street where he had gone, pushed frantically through the women, nearly causing an uproar, but Ochoa had disappeared. It might be, Tony reflected later, that it had not even been Ochoa at all, just some stranger wandering Mohammedia, someone like Tony Luna with a camera and a summer to kill. But he could have sworn he had seen, just for an instant, that lupine backward glance, the flash of a white stripe in the man's dark hair. And he pushed his way through the crowds, looking in every shop on the street, heard overwrought Sephardic music cranked from a car's radio, a song something like "At one o'clock I was born, at two o'clock I grew up, at three o'clock I took a lover," something like tossing paper into the wind.

The next time he saw Ochoa, Tony was twenty-eight and in Michoacán for his father's funeral. The wake was held in the house where Tony had spent his childhood, all carved wood, terra cotta tiling and lace curtains, dozens of bedrooms never slept in, a stable empty of horses, a fleet of cars, a Botero, a pet monkey, flowers on every surface. The things Juan Caspar had done, trying to win Françoise's empty heart; Tony could feel the dead man's frustration, and knew that he, too, would always be doomed by this place, would always be mon loup, Françoise's motherless child. But it had less power to hurt him now. He was standing on a balcony with an iron railing that overlooked the Sierra Madre del Sur, and saw a man walking at a great distance down the rocky beach, who turned his face to Tony for an instant as he walked away, and then was gone from sight.

After the death of his father, Tony embarked on a search, inquiring through every channel he could think of for a Jesuit priest named Miguel Xavier Ochoa. He found nothing, and was too proud to seek professional assistance. Ochoa had receded into a mythology, a poetical creation, just as Tony had first imagined him to be: the man was his own invention.

When Tony met the wild girl, he was thirty-six years old, cursed with Ochoa's waking sickness, the beginnings of grey in his hair, and he had not seen the priest for years. It was as if Ochoa had become so close that Tony no longer looked for him. Which was, in Tony's estimation, just as well. What would he have said? What could one say, to such a person? When Tony met the feral girl, he had long given up finding Ochoa, and had not thought of him at length in several months.

They sat in the parked car with the engine idling, the headlights throwing their pale beams across the expanse of snow and onto the edifice of St. Ignatius Academy. The building was long abandoned, roofless, its walls half collapsed with a few windows improbably intact, standing in their frames with the night on both sides. The Chapel of St. Frances of the Wolves was little more than a blackened crater at the corner of the empty complex. At the end of the long drive, Tony felt uncertain why he was there at all. He gripped the wheel and stared at the pools of light gathered in the snow, letting his eyes drift out of focus, feral girl alert but silent in the seat next to him, and wondered distantly if he should simply go back to the road and find a motel. But then the lights in the cabin of the car ignited as Schwartz pushed the door open, and she climbed out into the snow, tugged Tony's jacket closed around her and started walking toward the building. He watched the backs of her legs in the headlights, then, mute, withdrew the keys and placed them in his pocket, cut the lights, got out of the car himself and followed her.

They walked around the massive ruin, following the wall until they came to the spot where the damage was most severe, the heart of the great fire. Tony and Schwartz climbed over piles of tumbled stone, all that remained of the ancient chapel, until they were standing in the middle among birch saplings, ghostly white in the light of the low moon, where the pews would once have been. The lost girl stood, hands in her pockets with her back to him, the overlarge jacket giving her an indefinite look, small, somehow neither male nor female, a wraith of indeterminate sex standing in the ruins under a sky strafed with soft lights, her eyes on the snow-covered fields, wandering on. Then she turned toward him, and, feeling through the darkness, he reached for her cold hand.

But Schwartz's hand, withdrawn from her pocket, was clutched around the dark handle of a box cutter. For an instant, he saw the steel gleam in her eyes, and then she slashed, with bared teeth, at his outstretched palm. It was over; Tony staggered, clutching his bleeding hand, and the girl backed away, her face collapsing on itself, turned and fled toward the trees at the brow of the hill. He saw the gleam of her face one time as she looked back, white as paper, dissolving into darkness. She did not look back again, and he let her go, muffled footsteps giving way to emptiness, leaving him alone. Tony clutched his hand to his breast and stood in the perfect dark, bleeding, but finally still. He looked up, raised his eyes to the place where the chapel ceiling once had loomed, and found only sky. He gazed into a mighty company of lights, November's lion stars, cold, close and startlingly clear.

acknowledgments

Thanks to Robert Kelly, Edie Meidav, and Mary Caponegro for believing in this story and supporting it through its infancy. To Carey Harrison and John M. Keller, for keeping the faith, keeping calm, and providing me with constant support and inspiration. To Chris Regan, the love of my life. To the many people who have offered encouragement and hours of reading, especially Andrew Calhoun, Woody Williams, Charlotte Hendrickson, Ben Mayne, Pat Mayne, Florence and Charlie Mayne, Peter Barrett, Alex Davis, Terry Moore, Cat Greenstreet, Rakesh Lowe, David Anderson, and Ann Arensberg. To the real Tiger Prince, Phani Gayen, whose story of survival was recorded and immortalized by Caroline Alexander. To the girl on the train who told me about the tiger living in Lincoln Tunnel. To the man with the camera.

Chris Regan

about the author

Ashley Mayne is working on her latest novel.

To the memory of my beloved mentor, the distinguished Brazilian educator, Dr. Emanuel Cicero, born in 1907 in Ubatuba, São Paulo. Rector of the College of Rio Grande do Sul from 1943 to 1978, he died in 1988 in Lisbon.

–Maximiliano Reyes, publisher

-**FIM**-

DR. CICERO BOOKS